FOR SALE
MURDER

L.C. BLACKWELL

FRONT DOOR
PRODUCTIONS LLC
CHICAGO

Edition 1, September 2017
Copyright © 2017 L.C. Blackwell
Publication Date: 2018

Cover Design: Dan Ryder, Creative Director, Los Angeles
Interior Design: Erika Blackwell

Version 1
ISBN: 978-0-990711520

DEDICATED TO THE REALTORS®
WHO PRACTICE SAFE REAL ESTATE
AND WHO HELP AND ENCOURAGE
OTHERS TO DO THE SAME.

For Sale Murder is pure fiction, but the concept is based on reality: Realtor® murders across the country. An empty townhome or condo, a foreclosed property, a single-family dwelling, they've all been scenes of brutal murders. At open houses. At scheduled or call-in showings.

What's more, male as well as female Realtors® have been victims. They've been shot, raped, bludgeoned, kidnapped, stabbed, and more. Their killers—remorseful buyers, unhappy sellers, and those people posing as sincere in their search for a home.

Who knew that a profession built on helping people to find the home of their dreams could be a conduit to murder.

The National Association of Realtors (NAR) as well as local Associations urge Realtors to be wary and take precautions, particularly one month each year designated as Realtor Safety Month. And NAR continually stresses safety with How-To features and articles. Some Associations even promote self-protection classes.

And yet, there are no cumulative registers or even periodic announcements that identify or list the victims, crimes or locations on a national scale. This book's epilogue puts a name and cause of death to each of the murdered Realtors I've discovered. Local papers run stories when a murder occurs, but it's rare when a national publication or media source follows up.

Perhaps this fictional story of what could be will bring a greater wariness to an agent's thoughts and practices, saving them from being brutalized or becoming an addition to this book's death register.

And to mystery readers, I hope you'll enjoy reading For Sale MURDER, as well as learning a bit more about the business of Real Estate.

Chicago
Friday, December 16th, 2005

1

Peter Dumas sat quietly, eyes closed, head bowed. The fax he received resting at his feet; the message it delivered, short and to the point, "Peter, it's murder, my man. Need your special talent. Two real estate brokers murdered. Brutally. Call with flight info. We'll meet you at the gate. Mac."

It had been a few years, Peter thought to himself. The Lewis kidnapping, that's when he and Mac met, and their friendship began. Mac, ever grateful for Peter's involvement, boasted to any LAPD cop who would listen: "The boy would surely have died without Peter's intuitive skills."

Those unique talents were telegraphing vivid thoughts to Peter's mind in response to Mac's request. Bloody thoughts. Savage thoughts. Murder most vindictive, but mostly murder in plurality.

After making reservations, he wrote a note to Mac telling him he'd be on the first flight out on Saturday and would cab it to the station. He gave the note to the doorman at the Drake residences and asked him to fax it to the phone number he had written.

Of course, he would help Mac. He only wished it was not too late for the others.

NORTH CREEK MICHIGAN
LATER THAT SAME FRIDAY MORNING

2

The 40-mile an hour wind pummeled the yellow police tape as it danced violently across the snow-covered road, thick with deep ruts from a parade of vehicles led by a single police car, followed by an ambulance and a coroner's van.

The Charleston Crossing Sales office was officially closed for the day, and possibly much longer.

One lonely car waited close to the main road, wearing a blanket of snow. The driver, a reporter from the North Creek Courier, was snapping pictures of the sign that welcomed visitors to the newest Goody Home Development. He prayed he would get a decent shot using the camera on his phone, but considering how relentlessly the snow was falling, he wasn't too hopeful.

He hadn't been able to round up a photographer when he heard the alert on his online scanner. *What do you expect,* he thought, *small paper, four reporters, one photographer, snow storm.*

Billie Barkette was looking for a big story to get out of what he considered a one-horse town, and he didn't care what he had to do to get it.

He returned to his car and bundled up, happy that he kept a kitbag with every kind of emergency clothing and equipment in the backseat of his Range Rover. Sorel boots. Check. Oakley glasses. Check. Orsden slope jacket. Check. Sealskinz gloves. Check. He was ready.

It was early afternoon, but low-hanging clouds and the unyielding snow made it difficult to see exactly where the activity was centralized. Flashing police car lights, barely visible, offered the only reliable guide. It was apparent that the best route to take was a dirt track by a copse of trees just below the north ridge. It was also, the one route safest from detection.

Mobile phone in his pocket, Billie inched along, hidden by the trees. Hearing distinct voices, he crouched low under tree branches, and when he did, he was able to look straight up into the eyes of an older woman in the front loader of a bobcat. A dead older woman, sitting awkwardly with her head bowed and eyes wide open.

He almost dropped the mobile phone he'd pulled from his pocket, but Billie Barkette knew a story when he saw one and exactly what to do. Snap. Snap. Snap. The woman would be immortalized, that is if his phone's camera was as high def as purported to be.

The snow-weighted tree branches arched protectively over Billie and his unfortunate model. He winced as he took a series of shots, one of them a close-up of her dead eye with a single snowflake resting on an eyelash.

Billie couldn't see the detective as he began to back away, but he heard him and stopped to listen: "The coroner says a couple of hours, max. That's it. The mailman saw a dark stain on the snow and walked over to check it out. Poor guy. He lost his lunch."

A second voice asked, "Any ID?"

"Purse in the office has business cards and a license for Marsha Marshall. She's a VP with PK Goody Real Estate—they're building the development."

"How'd she die?"

"Stabbed in the back and then it looks like an ax finished the job. We found a bloody ax near the bobcat. Haven't found any knife. We'll know more after the autopsy."

"Did the mailman see anything at all?"

"He said a white Range Rover was pulling out to the main road as he waited to turn in. The driver's side window was down, so he got a good look at the driver. The guy had shaggy blond hair and blue-tinted glasses, the size of almonds. We got a BOLO out for the Rover. Other than that, we got nothin'. "

Billie started to move toward his car once again, and within a few minutes, he was able to pull out. A short time later, the coroner's van drove away with what was left of Marsha Marshall.

◆◆◆

Barely an hour after arriving at the newspaper office, Billy Barkette was finished with his online search for more information about Marsha Marshall. He didn't learn much. Marshall was divorced with no children. Her ex-husband had been a trader but evidently not too successful. When she divorced him, he was a bank teller at a local bank.

Billie's next stop was the PK Goody Real Estate office where several of Marshall's colleagues were in shock, genuinely saddened by the news of her death. According to them, Marsha joined the Goody group shortly after getting her real estate license and built many friendships at the office.

One of the agents said Marsha was a natural in new construction sales. "She loved creating an environment from a simple floor plan, as much as she loved taking a prospect to a development site. She could turn a foundation and studded shell into an ideal dream home. They couldn't resist. That's why she was the top agent in our office."

Letitia Goody, the managing partner of The Goody Group, confirmed Marshall's sales record, "She sold 2 out every 4 homes sold! She was fantastic."

One agent in the office questioned Marshall's business sense, "She could have had a partnership, but she was a short-term thinker: company car, bonus, free repairs and decorating for her home. Letitia knew how to control her."

Another agent disagreed. "Marsha was getting ready to demand a partnership. She even talked to an attorney about it, but I doubt she told Letitia. Our managing broker has been in and out of the office frequently in the last several months."

Billie next probed the internet for the scoop on the Goody Group. According to the advertising, Goody homes were the kind of homes that evoked a memory of those turn-of-century lithographs, embodying the charm and sentiment of the proper, traditional, family home.

Billie was not impressed; he was a fan of glass and steel, particularly a Mies Van der Rhoe building. And Herman Miller and Knoll were Billie's favorites to fill it. But what did he know? A lot of people bought Goody homes and had been for a couple of decades.

An article profiling Parker Goody identified his first wife, Jane, as an agent who died twenty years earlier. While inspecting a home in the final stages of construction, she had a fatal fall from a second-floor landing, leaving her husband to raise their only child.

Goody married Letitia Fairfax, the office manager/secretary a short time later. Together they established several offices and completed over 50 developments before Goody suffered a heart attack that led to his death in mid 2005. Charleston Crossing was the last development with his influence and control.

Billie had more than enough material to write his article, but seriously doubted it would be picked up by any national paper. *Who really cares about a Real Estate Agent with two claims to fame: she made a lot of money, and she was murdered.*

There was no evidence, according to Billie's pal at the police department. "No prints. No nothing. Just an entry in the guest register for her killer, Nathanial Cutter."

CHICAGO
EARLY THAT FRIDAY EVENING

3

Susanna Ryerson arrived home early to get ready, but not early enough to accomplish anything of significance, except of course, the frittata she put in the oven. Susanna rewarded Peter Dumas every time he read the Tarot for her; she welcomed him as family and always celebrated his visit with a home-cooked meal.

After pouring Jack Daniels Black Label into the delicate crystal glass she held in her hand, she took a few moments to sit back and enjoy the strains of Beethoven pervading the dimly lit apartment.

Outside the winter waves crashed into the shoreline under a slightly less than full moon. To the west, the Hancock Building and all the hi-rises surrounding it glowed with life. At the Bloomingdale building's twin towers, green and red lights heralded the season. All the while snow fell gently on the almost deserted Lake Shore Drive some 30 stories below; the shoppers were back in the suburbs.

She put down her drink to complete setting the table: soft gray, hand-pleated placemats and ornate silver flatware much older than her own 45 years. They joined pewter goblets resting alongside cream-colored china, rimmed in a gray embossed design, so delicate you could see the outline of her fingers holding each plate.

Perched in the center of the table was a pewter, long-necked swan holding a blaze of daisies. Not a shabby achievement in the dead of winter, but Susanna loved daisies and had them delivered fresh every few days.

The six chairs around the carved Queen Anne table overlooked the city and its lights through a wall of 10-foot plate glass windows. One could see people a half-block away settling in for the evening with silent TV screens flashing, window shades and draperies opened to drink in the city, the lake, and all its combined splendor, much the same as Susanna did.

When she finished the table, Susanna went to check on the frittata. The opened oven door unleashed a heavenly scent. It was one of Peter's favorites: an egg pie with chopped spinach, cottage cheese, chopped shallots, freshly grated Romano, and sourdough breadcrumbs, seasoned with fresh thyme and white pepper and topped with a generous sprinkling of Gruyère.

The phone rang as she whisked the oil and vinegar for the salad; it was the doorman announcing Peter's arrival. She collected her Jack Daniels and went to the door to await her old friend.

Peter Dumas was indeed a friend, but he just happened to be a clairvoyant and not a run-of-the-mill clairvoyant. Nothing about him was ordinary. Absolutely nothing about the diminutive man exiting the elevator was ordinary. Neither his demeanor nor his clothes. He wore jeans, almost threadbare at the knees, yet the crisp white shirt under the chamois-colored suede shearling jacket announced his membership in the Lauren ranks. His gold Rolex and the purple snakeskin cowboy boots provided just the right punctuation for one comfortable with himself.

His presence was a study in contrasts: 5 feet 2 inches of pure maleness with skin as smooth as a baby's bottom and a brilliant mane of magnificent white hair. He may have been as petite as a ballet prima donna, but an animalism seemed to permeate his being, suggesting a man capable of incredible extremes.

As he closed the distance between himself and Susanna his smile awakened lazily while his blue eyes exploded with light. "Long time no see, chickadee!"

Susanna laughed and hugged him with abandon.

"I have so missed you, Susanna. It's good to be back."

"Oh Peter, you visit way too infrequently. I hope you'll be here for the holidays."

"And then some. But there are more important things, like what's for dinner?"

She chuckled, turned and led him into the apartment. Peter hesitated for just a moment, a cold chill engulfing him: evil was nearby.

CHICAGO
THE VOYEUR

4

The voyeur adjusted the telescope's focus until it could reveal Susanna's diamond pendant. The voyeur was in the room with her, perhaps not physically, but still there.

"It's almost time to meet," the voyeur whispered to the empty room. After watching her for three weeks, her habits were becoming the voyeur's habits, her life, the voyeur's life.

Watching from several stories above Susanna, the voyeur was not quite a block away in an atmosphere very much in contrast to her traditionally furnished aerie; the voyeur's home was a contemporary study in black and white, leather and wood, steel and glass. There was nothing within the surroundings to indicate personal interests, or passions: no paintings, no art of any kind, no magazines, not even a book prop for the coffee table. It had been the same in California, Michigan, New Mexico and Indiana. No surprises. The voyeur could depend on sameness, the comfort of expectations always met.

A creature of habit, a lover of life without complications, the voyeur studied his prey to learn every detail, and to eliminate as many obstacles as humanly possible.

Susanna was the first one like Amanda Brewster. Same light brown streaked hair, about the same height, 5'5 to 5'6, athletic build, good legs, attractive but not beautiful, and most probably about the same age, middle to late forties. Even their clothes were similar; Amanda had dressed in classical Donna Karan and Calvin Klein with a little of Eileen Fisher thrown into the mix.

Tonight, Susanna looked casual in light gray slacks with a stark white sweater that accentuated the highlights in her hair. She wore it loose, just grazing the bottom of her ear allowing a glint of gold from the large hoop earrings she always wore.

Ever so slowly, the voyeur moved the scope to the face of the man sitting beside Susanna. *This one's unfamiliar,* the voyeur thought; *a strange little man, not anything like most of the men who visited Susanna.*

When Peter Dumas turned, the suddenness of his turn and the startling blue of his eyes, rattled the voyeur who released the scope as though it were burning hot. It appeared, for the briefest of moments, that the watcher was being watched.

The voyeur inhaled and exhaled slowly, several times until calm spiraled from head to fingertips. In icy control, the voyeur resumed the evening's entertainment in the darkened apartment.

CHICAGO
DINNER WITH SUSANNA

5

Peter didn't know what caused him to turn, but he recognized the feeling that came over him when he did. It was a sense of foreboding, a fleeting moment, but genuine nonetheless, yet he gave Susanna no indication that he experienced anything out of the ordinary.

"Well, what is your wish, my lady? Will it be Tarot? Runes? I Ching? Shall I retrieve a turban or crystal ball, or shall I merely hold your hand and expound?"

"Turban! Crystal ball! Are you going storefront on me, Peter?"

"I jest." He suddenly became somber and reached for her hand. Something was amiss. The hair on the back of his neck bristled.

"Ah, but before I read, we dine." Peter wrapped his arm around Susanna's waist and led the way to the table. "Spinach with arugula! Cranberries, walnuts, sweet balsamic dressing! You have done it again, my Susanna. An interesting assignment of tastes for my incredible palette."

"Peter, if I didn't know better, I'd christen you a pompous ass."

"All the world is a stage, Susanna. Never ever, forget that. I am in constant performance." And with exaggerated relish, he watched as she poured his favorite balsamic dressing on the salad.

"Honestly Susanna, you should give up real estate and become a chef. Everything smells incredible."

She bowed, he applauded.

They ate leisurely, reminiscing and recalling names from their pasts.

"How about my ex-client, Sunny?" Susanna asked.

"Sunny? I don't remember a Sunny."

"Don't remember, or don't want to remember. You certainly made an impression when you told her that she was an overweight stripper in another life."

"Not an overweight stripper, an overweight streetwalker. If you are going to make a point, be accurate Susanna. Besides, she roamed Rush Street and took anyone home who bought her a drink."

"You do remember! Well, she married several times, since you saw her. Husband number two was a three-week romance who waltzed out of her life on Day Two of their honeymoon. Told her he was going to get a Starbucks. After a while, Sunny called looking for him." Susanna put her hand to her lips to stop laughing before continuing. "When he answered, he said he was on his way to the airport and wanted a divorce. Claimed she was too high maintenance."

"My goodness, she must have been crushed."

"Crushed? Not Sunny. She kept her cool and made him wait for the divorce, so she would get the benefit of filing a joint income tax return."

"A shrewd lady of the night!"

"You can say that again. And when hubby #3 asked for a divorce after one year, she suddenly remembered me. She wanted a suggested listing price for her old one-bedroom and his Gold Coast condo!"

"Well, at least Sunny thought enough of you to sell them."

"Oh, I never got the listings. She just wanted a list price and comparables so she could sell the one-bedroom herself, and negotiate a settlement with her husband for the other one."

"Susanna, you must learn to cut the cord earlier when clients aren't serious."

"I know, it's smart business to do that, but I've made so many good friends, it's hard to change."

Suddenly Peter's eyes turned slate blue, and his smile disappeared.

"What's wrong, Peter?"

"She's going to die."

"Sunny?"

"No, not Sunny. She looks like Sunny. She's alone ...waiting."

"Where Peter?"

"A deserted place. That's all I can see."

"Are you trying to frighten me?"

"No, no. It was just a flash, one of my Kodak moments. It's gone now, forget it. Probably nothing."

"Oh Peter, do you want to focus on it?"

"No!" he said almost fiercely, then softly added, "You know I don't like to force an image, Susanna."

"I certainly hope it has nothing to do with me. Ordinarily, you pick up vibes from people around you, at least that's what you've always told me."

"Look around you, Susanna. We are in a fishbowl; the world is watching us. I could be getting a signal from across the street or from the suburbs for all that matter.

"Now are you going to sit still long enough for me to read you, or not? There's a sword hanging over your head, and we have to address it."

"Oh Peter, you have such a wonderful way with words. Let's cut to the chase, just read my aura. I don't want Tarot because I don't want to see any bad cards from the Major Arcana and I don't want I-Ching with all that philosophical mumbo-jumbo. I just want you to tell me everything will be better."

"My precious Susanna. I cannot kiss it and make it go away. I can only help you look at things from another perspective. I can tell you what the future looks like, but only you can make it a reality, and only you can change it."

He took her hand in his and closed his eyes. Breathing deeply, he began to see a multitude of images flowing into each other, colors deep and bright, soundless. Slowly the images began losing their momentum, the amorphous shapes taking form. Peter's eyes opened, small slits growing in size, and color changing from sky blue to almost black.

"There is a presence around you," he said. "There's emotion with it... love and hate. Complex. There's a man...no, two men. Mature men. And two women who could possibly be twins. Interchangeable."

"Maybe they're Geminis," she laughed.

"I'm going to ignore that, Susanna."

"Sorry," she smiled.

"Unfortunately, there's more than one issue facing you. Someone will introduce you to a dark-eyed woman who will not favor you. She's not from here...a warm place...Florida, California. She may attempt to destroy a past connection between you and a man. Possibly a colleague or perhaps your ex-husband. She is not what she appears."

"How about my son, Peter. Will I ever have a healthy relationship with Chris? Will it always be manipulated by him, or someone he knows?"

"Susanna, you let him manipulate you. Quit feeling so guilty about your divorce. It is done. Over. Your son knows it, and now it is time you realized you did the best you could. Give your love but don't provide it at the expense of your happiness."

"If it were only so easy."

"It is. Focus on changing yourself. Don't be so available to Chris. Treat him as an adult, and engage him to help you. Be receptive to opportunity. Business looks very promising. You'll have a spectacular year coming up...but there is a difficult client. He'll be very demanding, expecting you to be at his beck and call."

"Peter, every client expects you to be waiting for their call, their text, their email!"

"That's real estate, Susanna. Leave, if you don't like it. As to this client, I can't quite get a fix on him...he's not clear. Ah, but there is someone else, and the images are strong. A forthright individual, tall...you'll like him, and he will want to know you better. It may even be a romance if you allow it, Susanna. And it's about time, too. You've been alone too long."

"Peter, I can't think about romance. My family is unsettled, my work has become all-consuming. I barely have time to read, and I absolutely have no time to paint."

"Prioritize, Susanna, prioritize. Life is waiting for you. Embrace it. I sense tremendous activity around you, powerful emotions. You must be thoughtful, and most importantly, be cautious...extremely cautious."

"Is that a warning or a firm nudge, Peter?"

"Strong emotions create an aura of uncertainty whereby a split-second decision can have a life-threatening impact."

She smiled, "Does that mean if I decide to have Chinese instead of

Italian for dinner, my life could be in jeopardy?"

"You jest, yet strangely enough, it could happen," he said, the smile in his voice returning.

"Consider for example an Italian restaurant on Taylor Street. Ordinarily you would drive there, but for some reason, you decide to revisit your favorite Thai place on Hubbard."

His voice resonant with the vibrato of a tenor and the drama of a Shakespearian actor, plus the suspense of an experienced storyteller, he continued, "Instead of driving, you take a cab. The driver is talking on a cell phone. You ask him to refrain from using it. He turns to tell you something and does not see the car running the red light. The very last thing you see is the car hitting you broadside."

"Well, I guess I'm never going to have Thai food again. Or get in a cab with a driver using a cell phone."

Peter sighed and laughed a deep throaty laugh.

"I know, I know, Peter. I know the drill. A sudden decision could set off a chain of events that I cannot control. It may be meant to protect me, or bring me to a life-altering place."

"Just question your reasons, Susanna. And, if that voice inside insists, don't argue with it. Do what it tells you. I have never felt this sense of urgency around you when reading you in the past. Take heed."

"Wow. I wanted answers, and you give me questions."

"Questions are the answers, Susanna. Remember that."

"If I didn't know better, I'd say you were talking in circles, but I know you too well, Peter, and I trust you. I'll listen to my instincts, and I will ask questions, I promise."

"Good. Now I've got to get home and take care of a few things before I leave tomorrow morning. The Los Angeles Police Department has requested my help with a murder investigation, and I agreed."

"I have no appointments tomorrow, I'll be happy to drive you to O'Hare."

"I'd rather you didn't Susanna. I do not want to take your aura with me; it could affect my read on their case . I'll just grab a cab."

Peter was often called in when police officials had nowhere to go with homicides, or an abduction when families were pleading for action while condemning the investigative abilities of the police.

He gathered his case, coat, and phone, kissed Susanna, told her he would call and left, leaving her to contemplate the warning in his reading.

She poured another glass of wine, put a Renee Flemming CD into the stereo, retrieved a notebook from her desk and began to think about Peter's thoughts.

SATURDAY
DECEMBER 17TH

Chicago
Prelude To Death

6

"Susanna, how about the Bistro for lunch? I could do with some. mussels. Both varieties!"

Susanna looked up, startled. "Huh...oh, I'm sorry Terry, I was in another world. Did you say lunch?"

The striking redhead shook her head, "Lunch. The Bistro. Mussels. Come. Now!"

"Got it," laughed Susanna. "I would love to if you'll wait till I return a few calls."

"I'll go ahead and get a table. Just look for the redhead holding a glass of a '96 Pinot Noir. Just don't be too long. You know how much I like a '96 Pinot Noir." She flashed a smile and disappeared in a cloud of Boucheron.

Susanna, still grinning softly began returning her voice messages, tucking into her subconscious that something was different about Terry.

It was rarely busy the few days before the holidays. Most people were looking for a pair of gloves, a silk scarf, or another toy to round out a gift list. The last thing on their minds was searching for a new home. January would be the big month for real estate. According to most real estate gurus, post-holiday blues, transfers, and big bonuses made everyone want to sell their home and buy a bigger and better one to start off a new year.

Just as she was about to leave, her phone rang. She hesitated for just a moment then took the call before it went into voice mail, even though she had no intention of showing any of her properties that afternoon.

"Susanna Ryerson," she answered.

"I'm interested in seeing a condo you have listed on Lake Shore Drive," a deep, resonant voice commanded.

"To whom am I speaking?"

"Matthew Stark."

"And your phone?"

"Is that necessary?"

"The owners require a 24-hour notice, so I'll have to contact them and get back to you. What is your availability tomorrow?"

"I'm free at lunch and after 4."

"And the number where I can reach you?"

"Call my cell," he said rattling off the number.

"I will..." she started to say but was interrupted by a dial tone. Her caller had hung up before she could ask if he had an agent.

"Rude bastard," she said aloud. *Why do people treat Realtors so poorly,* she thought to herself? *We are not all ex-hairdressers or manicurists; some of us actually have college degrees. Besides, some of those ex-hairdressers make a killing in this business.*

Susanna left a message for Patti & Keith Polk, the owners of her listing at 1313 Lake Shore Drive. She recalled they were returning from a week in New York and most likely would not return her call until late that night or tomorrow morning. She asked for a 4 o'clock appointment for Sunday.

Ordinarily, Susanna did not make appointments for someone she had not met, but this listing was more than 60 days old, and there had been no worthwhile showings for the past few weeks. *It only takes one,* she thought to herself and tore off to meet Terry.

The Bistro was just east of Michigan Ave, a little bit of Paris surrounded by towers of glass, concrete, and marble, ideally situated for people-watching as shoppers made their way to the heart of Chicago's Magnificent Mile.

In the summer, the windowpane doors opened to an outdoor garden created by tall potted palms and flower-filled window boxes atop mock fencing surrounding small umbrella tables. However, when Susanna arrived, the windowed doors framed a modern Currier and Ives scene with heavily falling snow, bundled shoppers, laughing children, twinkling lights and glistening trees.

Terry was at the bar on her second glass of wine, deep in conversation with a balding, slightly overweight, grey-haired man with an enormous beard.

The late lunch crowd had thinned to a manageable number. They were guaranteed service with a smile from the French-speaking waiters, but not assured that all daily specials would be available.

"Susanna, Susanna, we're over here, honey!" Terry was in rare form judging by the sudden recurrence of her Texas drawl.

Susanna walked toward the pair, a knowing smile starting on her lips: *Terry must have smelled money.* "Sorry I'm late."

"Oh sugar, you're not late. Little ol' Jim and me were just getting acquainted. He is stayin' at the Hyatt and looking for a city home, and I am going to find him the perfect pied-a-terre. Jimbo, say hello to Susanna and show her those eyes. He has the bluest eyes."

Jim nodded bashfully, and Susanna responded with an engaging smile and a note of reassurance.

"You are in wonderful hands. Terry knows every part of this city, and of course which buildings are the best buys."

He smiled and lowered his head.

They chatted a few moments, Jim barely turning his face from Terry's giant green eyes. She, on the other hand, managed to appear glued to his attention with a perfectly directed smile, while scanning the room for additional prospects. Susanna decided the threesome was a crowd, and with a work-related excuse left to finish her holiday shopping at Bloomie's.

"Honey, call me tomorrow morning...late. I'll take Jimbo to your listing at 1313 if the keys are still with the doorman and you call Patti. Tell her I'm coming with a prospect."

Terry was truly in form; her drawl was thicker than ever.

"Patti's not coming back into town until late tonight, so you can show it...if Jim promises to buy the apartment! It is one heck of a deal, Jim. There aren't many re-done two bedrooms that you can buy here, on the lake with a balcony, parking, and all the amenities for under $800,000," she said with a straight face.

He nodded and smiled, his head still lowered bashfully.

"Don't you worry Susanna; I'll show Jimbo all the pluses of living at 1313 Lake Shore. Trust me, honey."

CHICAGO
MURDER IN THE GOLD COAST

7

It was long after dinnertime when Terry was found. She was sitting in the wingback chair facing the lake, opposite two silk striped traditional sofas.

The sliding doors were open wide, and the lake breezes left a decided chill in the room, despite a roaring fire in the ventless fireplace.

Two lamps on tables behind each sofa created a soft glow that turned the blood spatters on her green cashmere sweater into even darker shadows.

Patti did not see her when she first walked into the room. The high-backed chair concealed Terry until Patti went to close out the cold at the sliding doors, angry that they had been left open. When she turned, Terry was watching with cold eyes, her bloodied head resting on her lap.

Patricia Anne Borden Polk did not stop screaming until they broke the door down.

CHICAGO
ARNSTEIN AND DAVIS ARRIVE AT THE SCENE

8

The paramedics gave Patti a shot, wrapped her in a blanket, helped her to a gurney, and then headed to the elevator.

The newest arrival, David Arnstein, a homicide detective from the Near North Station played Moses, parting a path through the growing army of police officers and techs in the hall outside the Polk apartment.

Two women, one rather tall in workout clothes and the other, short and wrapped in mink, watched from the opposite end of the hall.

Inside the apartment, the Medical Examiner completed his examination of Terry's lifeless form while the photographer gave her the attention that one would expect if she were a celebrity in flagrante delicto.

Arnstein watched, taking in every detail of the elegant living room. Nothing was out of place, not a chair, not a book, not even the Handel lamp on the contemporary glass library table at the room's entrance. Everything was business as usual, except of course, for the wingback chair and its headless occupant.

His on-again, off-again partner, Jefferson Davis, had arrived a few minutes earlier. "Looks like he took some time posing her in the chair before putting her head on her lap," he said to Arnstein who nodded in agreement.

The two men were not at all alike. While Arnstein opted for designer suits, Davis was strictly a warehouse shopper who occasionally hit Carson, Pirie, Scott's basement. One worked out, the other didn't, and on down the list. They were two puzzle pieces that somehow seemed to fit; the other men at Area 6 swore it was odd that they worked so well together.

"Never saw a beheading before," Arnstein said letting out a soft low whistle as he pulled latex gloves onto his long elegant fingers.

He had been at a hundred crime scenes, bloody, crude, but never quite so gruesome. While he contemplated Terry Playmore's beheading, he watched the techs from the Mobile Crime Unit looking for that single hair, that print, that wisp of anything that would nail the coffin shut for Terry's executioner.

"Not much of a blood trail," Sully, one of the techs said in Davis' direction. "This perp was a clean freak; he did her in the bathroom, and then cleaned her up,"

"How'd he get her to chair?" Davis questioned.

"My guess, he dragged her. Probably wrapped her in the shower curtain. Blood's too concentrated. Besides most of the blood is on her chest and behind what's left of her neck. Most likely he pulled the plastic from the top of the chair, out from under her."

"Then he plopped her head on her lap." Davis finished.

Arnstein nodded agreement as he watched the ME pack up.

"Bag her," the ME said as he walked to the pair of detectives. Terry waited politely for the ME's men, her head leaning against her stomach, her glazed eyes staring upward, and a bloody scarf wound around what was left of her neck. One of her hands rested on the top of her head, the other, on the arm of the chair, while her feet were delicately crossed at the ankles.

"Weapons?" Arnstein asked.

"Clean throat cut, possibly a razor. But the beheading... cannot say. Might be a hacksaw. I'll have more for you after I get her on the table."

Arnstein nodded and turned toward the hall bath. The white ceramic tile on the floor had a faint pink cast to it. *He must have swabbed it, but the towels are still on the rods. No,..the face cloth...it's a slightly different color."*

He made a note in the small red spiral book he always carried—a new one for each case he ever worked.

When he opened the medicine cabinet, he saw the splayed bristles on the toothbrush.

"Hey Davis, looks like he used the toothbrush for some of his cleanup." He dropped the toothbrush into an evidence bag then checked the commode, first raising the seat then the cover of the water reservoir, being careful not to disturb any prints that *the killer* might have missed. The water was pink.

LOS ANGELES
PETER MEETS HARRY AND MAC

9

When Peter arrived at the West Hollywood station, Harry Krachewsky was deep in conversation with the desk sergeant, animatedly discussing the Rose Bowl combatants, and obviously on different sides of the coin. Harry was Michigan all the way.

Peter walked up to the two men and introduced himself and his destination, the office of William "Mac" McHenry. Harry stretched to his full 6-foot 5 stance and looked down at a little man wearing a shocking blue shirt, a black leather jacket, jeans and burgundy lizard boots. He glanced at the sergeant with a quick roll of his eyes, and then said to Peter, "Follow me. I'm Krachewsky. Harry, Mac's partner. So, you're the crystal ball guy he always talks about."

Peter just nodded with a hint of a smile and followed the green-suited detective, known affectionately at the station as 'the-not-so-jolly-green-giant'.

"Just to set the record straight, Peter, I don't believe in this psychic mumbo jumbo, but my partner, well he's into this stuff. His wife probably got him hooked on it. Me? I'm strictly into evidence. DNA, prints, fibers...I'm into science."

Peter nodded and followed the not-so-jolly-green-giant. "What I do is a science, Harry. I don't just use physical phenomena."

Harry, rolling his eyes once again motioned for the diminutive intuitive to follow him down a deserted corridor. Peter smiled to himself, then said in the most serious voice he could muster, "When did you begin playing the trombone, Harry?"

The 300-pound, former NFL linebacker turned suddenly. "Who told you I played trombone?"

"I saw it in the stars," Peter said, a broad smile in his voice recalling

Mac's description of his partner when they last spoke.

Krachewsky grunted and led Peter to a small office at the end of the hall gesturing for Dumas to enter. Mac was just finishing a phone call.

"Peter Dumas, you haven't changed at all." William "Mac" McHenry rose from behind his desk to reach for Peter's hand.

"The Lewis kidnapping in '99. You saved my ass."

"No... I helped save a child."

McHenry looked at Peter thoughtfully, remembering and slowly nodding his head. "You're right. When it ends well, it's easy to forget the what ifs...." He suddenly smiled, his old thoughts retreating.

"First things first. Where are you staying?"

"Haven't decided. Will worry about that later. I'm ready to help all I can," Peter answered, a sudden heaviness in his voice.

"I'm glad Peter. I'm hoping you can impart some valuable insight into a new case we have on the books and one older one. They're not nice. How would you like to begin? Crime scene or with the Murder Book?"

"Crime scene. You can brief me on the way."

The three of them left the building for Krachewsky's car as McHenry began his recap for Peter.

"Two weeks ago today, a female real estate broker had an appointment to show a home in Laurel Canyon—vacant house, deserted road. Her clients arrived, a young couple, married a few years. Walked through the house and said they were interested in making an offer. Valli told them she had to meet an agent for another showing and asked them to meet at her office later that afternoon. She never showed. The office secretary called her home number, her voice mail, and her mobile. Nada. They called us to check. One of the patrols found the house unlocked."

"Where did they find her," Peter asked from the back seat of Krachewsky's car.

"In a tub, one of three second floor bathrooms."

"Rub a dub, Realtor in a tub, isn't why you called me, is it, Mac?"

"Naw Peter. This is number two; at least we hope it's only the second one. We've got an unsolved from the middle of November. Another Realtor, another showing, roughly the same M.O. The perp..."

Peter interrupted, "No. do not tell me about the killer; tell me about the victims. What did they look like? What kind of women were they? Where did they come from?"

Krachewsky watched in the rearview mirror as Peter's demeanor changed. The brilliant blue eyes darkened, the finely chiseled jaw tightened, and an almost animal scent pervaded the whole of the unmarked Ford as it sped to the place where Janna Valli exhaled her last breath.

"This one wasn't a looker. Valli bleached her gray hair, strawberry blonde. According to the women she worked with—by the way, I haven't met a cattier bunch—Janna Valli was short, a little overweight and always carried a Shih Tzu. An animal, I'm told, notorious for peeing around the office. Krachewsky will fill in details about the pooch, and the Realtors she worked with; he interviewed quite a few of them.

"Our November victim had her own office. She promoted herself as Amanda Brewster, Real Estate Broker to the Stars. Only handled high-ticket properties for people in the movie industry. Had an appointment to show a vacant house on the ocean to some Italian director. It turned out he was shooting a film in Italy while someone borrowed his name and reputation to lure Brewster in for a slice and dice."

"We're here," Krachewsky announced as he made a hard right onto a small roadway barely visible from the highway. He drove a few minutes then stopped before an incredible glass house wrapped in flowering bushes and towering palms.

Yellow police tape crossed the front door as well as the path to the back of the house.

"I'd like to walk around a little before I go inside," Peter said deep in concentration. He moved away from the car, pacing slowly in a zigzag pattern, tensed in anticipation of reacting to the scent of his prey. His body movement was imperceptible, yet his eyes blinked with the speed of an S.O.S. in Morse Code signaling data to an unseen receiver deep in his psyche. You could almost hear him whirring.

He closed his eyes, his breathing becoming slower and deeper, giving him an almost trance-like appearance.

"He could be a machine," McHenry whispered to Krachewsky. "I've never seen anything like him. You can almost feel the energy he sucks up. It's like he collects fragments, too minute to measure, and rates 'em on some internal scale. Then he keeps or tosses 'em. And he does it in a heartbeat. He has a gift, no doubt about it, and when he's focused, man, it is raw power. It's got to take a lot out of him."

"I'm sorry, Mac, I just don't buy into it. Maybe he's got a super good eye, and he just spots things we overlook."

"After we find the nutcase who did this, remind me to tell you what Dumas did for us on the Lewis kidnapping in detail. Then decide if he just spots things we overlook."

Bits of conversation drifted through Peter's mind. Words were filed, thoughts categorized, smells defined. For Peter, the essences lingered, even after months. Boucheron wafted from the leaves to his left. He turned and called out to McHenry, "What kind of perfume did she wear, Mac?"

"Our victim, or her client?"

"Determine if either one wore Boucheron."

Krachewsky sighed and wrote himself a note, knowing full well he would be on perfume detail, seeing that McHenry was senior man on this one. *Boucheron! Where does this little man get this stuff,* he thought to himself.

Confident he could learn no more outside the house, Peter motioned he was ready to enter.

McHenry removed the tape and opened the door for Dumas. Though neither of the LA detectives sensed anything other than the stale smells of a closed house, Peter staggered at the onslaught of the color, sound, and scent that pierced his senses.

He paused, shaking his head as if to shake free an ill thought caught mid-air in his mind. Then he heard her scream, a bloodcurdling scream that telegraphed incredible pain. Again, and again, the screams echoed, softening with each cry until they became whispered whimpers suddenly silenced by an eerie quiet. The horrific sounds escaped the hearing of the two men with him.

As he climbed the stairs between McHenry and Krachewsky, the sweet smell of blood became overpowering, masking another hint of Boucheron. And yet, he could sense no real smell of fear.

Krachewsky pointed out the tub where Valli was discovered, but Peter walked past, something urging him on to the bath at the far end of the hall. At the doorway, Peter paused. Flashes of red, sharp red daggers attacked him while the screams hammered his eardrums. He stepped back into the hall and steadied himself.

McHenry came up to him. "You OK, Peter?"

"Yes," he answered with little emotion. "She died here."

"No, the other tub was a bloodbath."

"She was killed here."

"Nothing was touched back here. We just assumed... Krachewsky," he yelled, "get some techs back in here."

"Are you nuts?"

"No, we might have missed something."

McHenry followed Peter to Janna Valli's final resting place.

"How did you find her? Describe everything."

McHenry closed his eyes and replayed the scene in his mind once again. "If it wasn't for the blood and wounds she could have been asleep. The tub was half filled with water. Her head was resting against the back, eyes closed, some 20-stab wounds to her chest and back.

"She was wearing a long dress with slits on the side and a big flowered jacket, short black hose to her knees and all her jewelry...a bracelet, watch, gold earrings, big diamond ring. A thin gold chain with a gold pendant that said "mother" was on the floor next to the tub.

"The floor and walls were wiped down with the towels, then he rinsed and folded them real neat on the stool. Oh, and she was wearing some kind of eye mask."

"He didn't kill her here," Peter whispered. "Not here. She was stabbed at the back in the other bath. She never knew what hit her, but she knew the pain. Did she have long hair?'"

"Yes, she did," Mac said, surprised at Peter's question.

"Most likely her killer yanked her hair back to slit her throat after pushing her over the tub edge. The cut was right to left, wasn't it?

Krachewsky just watched. Mac had never said her throat was slit. Mac answered Peter, "Yeah. Did a real job on her neck. Sliced through the carotid almost down to the vertebrae."

"He closed the drain to save her blood and bring it in here." Peter stared at the towel rack, "There were no towels in the other bath. No shower curtains. No water glass, either. I would have your men check for a cup or glass somewhere in the area, towels and shower curtain, too. I do not see him walking away with anything he did not bring. He wrapped her in the shower curtain and dragged her here. He took his time, Mac."

"Did the couple who met her see anyone before or after the showing?"

Mac nodded, "A UPS man was driving away when the couple pulled up, and they saw a young woman riding a bike when they were leaving.

"UPS guy is clear. Oh, and a mailman delivered some mail about 2 hours after the couple left. Said he saw a car parked in the side drive when he arrived, and a jogger about half mile down the road as he was leaving.

"Mailman's clear, but we haven't gotten anything on the jogger or the biker."

Peter walked slowly to the top of the stairs, "I'm finished Mac, I need to go and check into a hotel. I'm tired." He walked away from McHenry down the stairs away from the sound, the smell, and the pain.

Krachewsky watched, his mouth slack, eyes blank. If he hadn't heard it himself, he never would have believed that Peter Dumas knew what he did.

✿ ✿ ✿

Peter was an intuitive long before he recognized his gifts. His mother experienced premonitions, and her mother before her. In fact, generations of daughters passed on their growing intuitive natures to Peter, the first male descendant of Marie Dauphine Sophia Fillibran DeMent.

In 1789, Jacques Pierre Phillipe St Denis DeMent, a distinguished aristocrat took his wife's premonition to heart. With her and his two baby daughters, he braved an ocean crossing to flee his beloved France, fortunately, mere days before the fall of the Bastille. The family eventually settled in what is today St. Martinsville, Louisiana.

DeMent, a keen diplomat, advised and counseled by his wife Marie, used her jewelry to become a landholder—one who made a choice to dramatically increase his holdings after Napoleon sold the territory west of the Mississippi River to President Jefferson and the United States. The Louisiana Purchase delivered almost 900,000 square miles for an average of 4 cents an acre.

DeMent became a powerful and wealthy man, but little by little the lands that he owned were divided among the families spawned from the daughters' DeMent. In the late 1800's, Peter's great, great grandfather created a trust that managed the remaining families' properties for future generations, thereby giving Peter the freedom to eventually nurture his gifts and follow his heart.

Initially, had he been given a choice to accept or decline his inherent power, his decision most assuredly would have been to refuse it, thus relieving himself of future ridicule, disbelief, and mockery.

Exceptionally keen perceptions and visualizations were first visited upon Peter at the age of four when he awakened to his nanny's screams. Peter ran to his mother's room, frantic with urgings to help Anie whom he said was hurt at the bottom of the stairs.

Emmilliene Sophia DeMent Dumas was awake. Aware that nothing had happened, she assumed Peter had a bad dream. She hugged him tenderly and explained there had been no accident, but Peter was adamant. So, Emmilliene slipped on her robe and opened the hall door to the sudden screams of Anie as she fell down the stairs. Peter had inherited his mother's predictive powers. For the first time in seven generations, the matriarchal gift was bestowed on the firstborn son.

The premonitions and visions became more frequent, more intense; Emmilliene taught Peter how to focus his thoughts and more importantly how to prioritize his life so that his gifts would not devour him.

Peter learned well; he protected his clairvoyance, sharing it with just a select few. He fully adopted his matriarchal gifts, and more importantly, he chose to stay in the background avoiding controversy, and above all, the media.

SUNDAY
DECEMBER 18TH

CHICAGO
ARNSTEIN DELIVERS A DEATH NOTICE

10

Susanna was reading the paper when the doorman called to say she had a visitor from the police department. Somewhat startled, she told Wallace to send him up, only then beginning to wonder why on earth the police wanted to see her.

By the time she refilled her cup with coffee, Arnstein was knocking at the door. When she opened it, she looked up into the darkest eyes she had ever seen; eyes that assessed her, head to toe as their owner introduced himself with a flash of badge.

Susanna stared back defiantly, her arms crossed protectively, over her breast, "You must have the wrong Ryerson...I haven't called..."

"I'm sorry to disturb you Ms. Ryerson, but your office suggested you might have some information about Terry Playmore."

"Terry? Has something happened?"

"When was the last time you saw her?"

"Yesterday at lunch...at the Bistro, the one off Michigan Avenue. Is something wrong?"

"Was she alone?"

"No... she was with a client...look, I'm not answering another question until you tell me what this is all about."

"Terry Playmore has been murdered." He said it without skipping a beat: no voice change, no expression of concern, no preliminaries, just a sudden stab of five deadly words.

Susanna gasped, her eyes wide in disbelief, her mouth moving wordlessly as her arms reached out to support jello legs collapsing beneath her. Arnstein caught her just she fell in a dead faint.

When she came to, she was stretched out on the black-green leather sofa, a wet cloth upon her face and Arnstein beside her in one of the high-backed dining chairs, watching with expressionless black eyes.

Susanna sat up, remembering his words. "You must be mistaken. Terry can't be dead. No one would hurt Terry. Everyone loved her."

"Apparently someone didn't."

"When, where?'

"A few hours after you saw her," he said, looking for something on the pages in his notebook. He stopped, "It happened at 1313 Lake Shore...a Mrs. Polk's apartment."

"Oh my God. My listing. Terry was taking someone there to see it. Jim...Jim something," she cried excitedly. "He was with her...at the Bistro. From out of town. He wanted an in-town place."

Arnstein poured a brandy from the silver tray on the side table and handed it to Susanna. "What did he look like?" he asked, his voice, soft and gentle.

"He was short, no, no... I think he was tall, but he hunched over, so he appeared much shorter." She clutched the brandy glass, her voice rising then falling, her breathing shallow than deep. "Light brown hair, as I recall, and not much of it. Very pedestrian, not a city looking guy. He wore a medium brown suit, a cheap sweater vest," her voice rising in pitch. "Light shirt...terrible tie. Black shoes, I remember those. Very expensive. Italian," she cried, tears streaming down her face.

"He looked pasty. He didn't look dangerous. He looked harmless, very shy. He never looked me in the eye...oh my God. He didn't want me to see his face."

She gulped the brandy attempting to swallow between her cries, but it ran down the corners of her mouth.

Arnstein watched her cry. He hated this part, watching them realize that their friends, or family were gone never to return, eventually regretting things they said, or never said. You could see the emptiness in their eyes. No history, no future. The memories would come later along with the anger. He was jealous of their grief. He no longer had anyone to grieve for and more importantly, no one who would grieve for him

CHICAGO
THE INVESTIGATION BEGINS

11

Murder Visits The Gold Coast

An unidentified woman was found
dead late Saturday by a resident in a high
rise on Lake Shore Drive just north of
Chicago's Mag Mile. According to wit-
nesses, the woman was visiting the ...

"Hey Arnstein, did you see the ME's preliminary report?" Davis
asked.

"Yeah, she almost bled out before he cut off her head. Maybe we've got
some kind of vampire on our hands," he joked.

"He's no vampire, but he sure is 'Mr. Clean'. I swear the guy vacuumed
the place before he left. The techs found a couple of hairs, but they could be
anyone's. According to the doormen, there have been a couple dozen people
in and out of the place to paint and clean since the condo went on the market,
and the owners have been in and out of town."

"Leaves nothing...and no one sees him." Arnstein shook his head.

"Let's get some help on this one. We've got to make some progress
quick...every real estate office in the city will be on our ass, not to mention the
mayor and the aldermen now that the media is on it."

"Give me a few minutes. I'll see if they found any prints in the
bathroom, but don't hold your breath."

"How about the toothbrush? Anything?"

"Uh uh, forensics says it was dipped in ammonia. And there's no
friggin' ammonia in the apartment, either."

After Davis had left, Arnstein leaned back in his chair and swiveled
slowly recalling the setting where Terry's body was found. He questioned what

the killer was saying. *Why did he orchestrate such a grizzly scene with such delicacy? And how did he get out of the building?*

Deep in thought, he once again reviewed the ME's notes.

Anyone watching David Arnstein would not tag him as part of any police department; they would, though, credit his persona to that of a Wall Street power broker: the Armani suit, the tasseled alligator loafers, the Hermes tie. He had all the trappings. He could even have passed for a movie idol if it were not for the scar from the inside corner of his eye to well below his earlobe. It traveled across his cheek as if chiseled by a drunken sculptor,

Plastic surgery could have softened the keloid scarring that formed, but Arnstein said no, opting to wear the scar, perhaps as a badge of defiance against anyone or anything that attempted to reach into his heart. It was his warning to others: stay away, blood does not flow thru these veins. To Arnstein, it would always be a reminder of the accident that erased his reasons for living: the death of Joanna, the woman he loved with his very soul and their baby boy, his son. As if he needed a reminder.

Arnstein had never expected much in life, particularly after his own parents were stolen from him during a home invasion that turned deadly.

However, that was way before Joanna, before she taught him to trust, to feel, to be. And when she bore his first child, his transformation was almost complete. But a turn of his head, an instant in time, and Joanna was gone.

She never saw the police car's flashing blue lights approaching before it struck her door; Joanna only saw the scream at Arnstein's mouth that caused her to turn and face her executioner.

The police car had blown a tire during a chase. If only Arnstein had turned his head sooner. If only he had stopped. If only she hadn't unbuckled her seat belt to put the baby in the harness. If only...if only, he always thought.

Some nights in his dreams, he unwillingly played the scene again and again in slow motion. He watched in horror as Joanna was thrust toward him, then pulled away, out the opened window; the metal of the Mustang crunching and spinning in a soundless dance as she kissed the windshield of the black and white in a growing cloud of red, their son tight against her in the harness. He reached for them, but the scene always froze.

They never caught the men the cops were chasing; they never caught the pair who killed his parents, either. Therefore, Arnstein left a successful law practice and joined the force. His goal: punish the guilty; his advantage: he knew exactly how far he could go.

When Davis returned, Arnstein was already briefing Bugs Kramer and Terry Calahan, 2 detectives from the 3rd district, assigned to his team.

Davis interrupted, "We got a print, back of the commode. He must have lifted the top to clean it. Lucky for us, he touched the rim."

"Hear that guys. Finally, something," Arnstein said showing a thumbs-up. He made a quick notation on the ME's report, then continued, "According to Charlie, the first wounds killed her. Deep stab wounds between the fifth and sixth thoracic vertebrae, right between her ribs, up to her heart. The knife was double-edged with about a 6-7-inch blade."

"He sure knew what he was doing. She didn't have a chance with him coming at her from behind like he did," Davis added.

"Maybe he's had lots of practice," Kramer suggested.

"I'll run a computer check with the Crime Lab for similar MOs in the past couple of years, and I'll see what VICAP has on file."

"Great," Arnstein nodded, then directed his gaze to the other detectives. "Terry, you and Kramer comb every apartment in a 2-block radius. We'll have a composite drawing of Playmore's client in a couple of hours; the real estate agent who saw him with Playmore is meeting with our sketch artist this morning. Someone had to see this John leave that building."

Bugs Kramer, the taller of the two men wrote a note in a small black leather notebook while his partner shifted his eyes toward Arnstein asking, "What's the time of death look like?"

"Roughly 4 PM, but we have a four-to-six-hour window, so we need to get a timeline going."

Davis listened, nodding his head, "I'll hit the Bistro and check all the credit card receipts. The maitre d' should be able to get me the names of the regulars; maybe one of them will remember Playmore and her client."

Arnstein nodded, as he struggled with his jacket. "Let's all meet back here tomorrow, 8 AM." Turning to Kramer and his partner, the mid-morning sun caught the face of his gold watch giving additional punctuation to his gesturing hand. "Get that composite sketch and run with it. I'll be at the ME's office if anyone needs me."

The telephone rang as the men began to file from the office.

Los Angeles
Peter Checks The Valli Crime Scene

12

After two unsuccessful attempts, Peter tried Susanna one more time; after three rings, she answered. Relieved to hear his voice, she began sobbing, releasing all the pain, fear and anger welling from her heart. He listened attentively, stroking her with words to soothe as he devoured news of Terry's murder. Before saying goodbye, he promised to call as soon as he returned to the city. He said nothing about the two Realtors in Los Angeles who had been murdered.

Krachewsky was waiting when Peter came down from his room. "McHenry's gonna meet us in Malibu," he explained.

"Good morning to you, too, Harry."

"Oh, yeah, morning. Here, I stopped at Dunkin Donuts and got us some coffee and somethin' to chew on," he said handing Peter a steaming cup and a sugared donut wrapped in translucent paper.

"I'll pass on the donut, Harry, but I welcome the coffee."

The trip to the Palermo home where Amanda Brewster showed her last listing was uneventful except for the constant sound of Krachewsky chomping on donuts and the mountain of powdered sugar that collected on the front of his dark suit.

According to Harry, Palermo chose not to sell the house. Industry gossips claimed he was holding back for big bucks, waiting to film a movie about Brewster's death, so the house stood quietly gaining history as a testament to mystery and murder.

Peter drank his coffee, his mind churning with unconnected thoughts he desperately tried to merge. *Could Terry's death be tied to the LA crimes? How did she die? Did the two women in LA know each other? Would the Malibu crime scene offer any answers?*

McHenry was waiting when they pulled into the driveway. Peter greeted him, and then the two men began to walk the perimeter of the Palermo property.

"How did her client get here?" Peter asked.

"A limo," Krachewsky explained. "According to the driver, this Scalparelli clone was waiting at the Hilton. We checked; he wasn't registered. Probably called for the service at a courtesy phone and waited."

Peter nodded his agreement, treading quietly on the overgrown lawn, listening attentively for the sounds of a killer. But there was only calm; no violent images or sounds interrupted Peter's thoughts in the serene setting.

"Where was her car?"

"It was here when the limo pulled in. The driver got a 100-buck tip, and Scalparelli told him to wait 10 minutes, then leave. He just assumed the real estate agent would be taking his ride back to the hotel. By the way, Scalparelli wore gloves, and carried a leather briefcase."

"Was her car here when you found the body?"

"Yeah," McHenry continued, "her assistant came looking for her, found the car and an open door. We think the fake Scalparelli just walked away after he killed Brewster. Cabs and limo services were contacted to report any pickups in the vicinity. Nothing came up matching our guy."

"May we go inside, now?" Peter asked.

McHenry nodded and motioned to Krachewsky. He had been waiting at the front door, fingering a ring of keys identified with small discs, appropriately labeled for each door at a crime scene under investigation.

Krachewsky opened the door, and Peter walked into the house. Unlike the scene at the Valli murder, here he was greeted with deafening silence, frozen in place by the whiteness of each room, lifeless and yet brilliant in the late morning sun.

This one was quick, he thought to himself. His mind heard a quiet moan, barely a whimper, as he turned to a room at the end of the hall. He opened the door, and the smell of death attacked him, the whimper, now a fading guttural cry.

Part of the sheer drape was ripped from its mooring, an onyx pole with small brass globe finials at either end, a stark contrast to the contemporary lightness of the room. Spurts of rusty red marked an irregular path on the plush white carpeting to the French doors where dried blood stains covered most of the torn drapery sheer.

Peter stood quietly. He could feel her presence and even now, smell the sweet scent, once again, of Boucheron.

"How was she found?" he asked aloud sensing McHenry behind him.

"Looks like she was stabbed walking toward the French doors, and finally collapsed, bent over, grabbing at the drape to hold her up. If her throat wasn't wide open, she coulda been an actor on her knees, bowing to an audience, one hand clutching the drape. A silk scarf that matched the suit she wore was wrapped around her head covering her eyes like a blindfold, and she had a crown on her head."

"A crown?"

"Not a real one, just a stage prop."

"Interesting. Hairs or fibers?"

"Plenty, the house was a friggin' revolving door for 2 days. Workmen were all over the place. We even found hairs from a wig. Coulda been one of the guys' rugs. Everything else in the place was clean. No prints. "

"I'd like to see the Valli and Brewster cars if it's possible."

"Peter, no problem on Valli's, it's at the pound, but Brewster...nada, it was sold at auction. I don't know what you expect to find though, she was a real estate broker, a friggin tour guide. Hell, people were in and out of that car."

"I know. But it still may help me," Peter said, and then added softly;

"There's been another Realtor murder, Mac."

"What do you mean another murder?"

"Chicago. I don't know any details, or even if there's a connection, but it's extraordinarily coincidental."

"Let's get back to the station. You check out the car and Murder Book with Krachewsky. I'll call Chicago."

CHICAGO
SUSANNA STILL IN SHOCK

13

Describing the man she saw with Terry was difficult; vivid images of her friend's smiling face continued to interrupt Susanna's memory recall of his image. But after several hours, she announced to the artist, "That's him," confident that an accurate sketch was completed.

As she prepared to leave the police station, Susanna decided to make a quick trip to the office before heading home, hoping to fill her mind with anything that would keep her from thinking of Terry's murder. She did not see Arnstein until they collided at the end of the hall.

Her apology came a second after impact. "I'm so sorry...I guess I wasn't paying attention; I just can't get Terry out of my mind."

"No apology necessary. I understand." His emotions in lockdown, Arnstein looked right through her, mouthing thoughts from a past time and place, "It's difficult enough losing someone you care about...but knowing you met their murderer...that's rough. Just don't keep any anger inside. You'll be giving the killer your life in addition to your friend's." He gave the same advice given him by a friend after the tragic death of his wife and son.

Susanna began to thank him, but he nodded and was gone before she could speak. She turned and watched him, unnerved yet experiencing an incredible wave of warmth and understanding. Two uniformed police followed him down the hall. She watched a moment longer, then turned and continued out the building to hail a cab for the office.

Her mobile rang as she searched her bag for enough money to pay the driver. "Susanna Ryerson," she answered breathlessly.

"This is Matthew Stark."

"Matthew Stark?"

"You evidently don't keep track of appointment calls, do you? 1313 Lake Shore. Sunday."

"Oh. Oh..." Susanna cried remembering her phone conversation and the showing she set up just before meeting Terry at the Bistro. "I'm so terribly sorry. There's been...."

"A lapse in your capabilities," he admonished.

"Mr. Stark..." She searched for control of the anger waiting to impact her words. "There's been a tragedy at the apartment. A police report will most likely be on the news tonight."

"What happened?" he asked, somewhat subdued.

"The police have asked that I not repeat details. Suffice it to say that the apartment is off the market indefinitely," her voice telegraphing brevity of patience.

He offered an apology, his voice softening just enough to say 'truce' to Susanna, and then he asked if they could meet. "Perhaps I could come in and discuss my requirements. Of course, we could meet at your convenience. You may have other properties that could be of interest."

"Yes, that would be best. Let me check my schedule and get back to you tomorrow morning; shall I call the mobile number you gave me before?"

"That number's fine. I'll expect to hear from you."

She was about to respond when she realized she was disconnected. *Is it me,* she thought, *or is it becoming a natural phenomenon to be cut off in mid-sentence?*

Upstairs, the atmosphere at the office was deceptively ordinary, lending a shallow verisimilitude to what was, for the most part, a phony family of caring independents. There was Chuwana in her black tights and artist's smock, perched on the swivel chair, her chubby feet barely touching the floor, bending everyone's ear at the reception desk with her countless stories of a life unfulfilled.

A newer agent at the floor desk was circling the For-Sale-By-Owner ads in the classified section of the Sunday paper, waiting for that one floor-call that could develop into an eventual sale with enough commission to cover expenses.

Susanna nodded to Chuwana and quickly stepped toward her desk in the center of the office. Over 100 agents were members of Storey & Beckman

Realty, a family owned operation that had grown to well over $200 million in sales in a matter of 5 years. Terry had been an agent there from day one; Susanna, relatively new to real estate, was about to celebrate a three-year anniversary with the company.

Most of the agents in the office had finished the Sunday Open Houses; some had not heard the news about Terry, but the whispers soon began and one by one, their eyes focused on Susanna.

Quickly checking her voice mail, she noted the appointment requests, grabbed a few papers and headed home to make her calls, avoiding any discussion regarding Terry.

Susanna's office was in the Water Tower Mall, so throngs of shoppers greeted her when she stepped from the commercial elevators at the back of the building, near the newsstand that catered to a sweet tooth, nicotine habits, and avid readership of any gossip magazine ever published. The shoppers who were not satisfying their addictions at the newsstand were queued at the Chocolate Shoppe checking out the mind-boggling chocolate display: hand-dipped strawberries, luscious chocolate turtles, truffles, an assortment of milk and bittersweet chocolate delights, and more.

She both loved and hated this time of year when her corner of the city was overrun with suburban mothers and squealing children who should be home and tucked in bed. Instead, the cranky, chocolate-faced little angels in their extra-wide SUV-style strollers invaded Susanna's privacy, monopolized her walkways, and filled her air with shrieks and offensive diaper perfumery. She resented mothers who made a mockery of being a parent, dragging a child to inappropriate places at inappropriate times with an attitude that claimed an inalienable right to disturb the world merely because they had given birth.

Susanna relegated these character flaws to those parents who could afford a stroller as costly as a small automobile yet somehow could not find a babysitter within their economic means.

She walked from the mall into the cold, early evening air. It was just 6:30 but the sky was glowing, a black canvas interrupted with silver stars. The street was covered with a delicate blanket of snow, tire-tracked into abstract pieces of art. The wind, rushing like a riptide, almost upended her as she walked toward the lake pulling her coat tightly around herself, hoping to ward off the weather; but the wind and the cold were brutal and attacked without pity.

Just two more blocks, she thought to herself, wiping away tears of cold and visualizing her softly lit condo, warm and inviting.

CHICAGO
THE MEDICAL EXAMINER'S OFFICE

14

It was after 6 PM when Arnstein arrived at the morgue. Charlie was in his office finishing his notes on a gang shooting victim when Arnstein entered. The room was stacked with folders and books along with various skeletonized body parts serving both as paperweights and as reference guides.

In the cabinet behind Charlie, a collection of skulls fought for space on crowded shelves; it reminded Arnstein of the infamous Capuchin Brothers Cemetery where the pieces and parts of departed monks were woven into a mosaic work of art, for a burial scene unmatched in its awesome splendor of horror.

Arnstein recalled that place of death each time he entered Charlie's office, but a shake of his head and the image erased from his mind. "I don't know how you find anything in here, Charlie. I'd go nuts."

"The trick is having a great assistant. So, what brings you to our hallowed halls, David? And on a Sunday, no less." Charles Kenton Peel was one of few people who called Arnstein by his given name.

"I need help. Give me something, anything. The Playmore body."

"Ah, the beheading. My first one." He pulled a file labeled Playmore with dark red letters from a metal shelf on his desk. "She was dead before he removed her head, of course. She died of massive stab wounds, 9 of them."

He pushed three of the photos across the desk to Arnstein. The first image was a woman, neck to mid back, skin icy white except for 9 dark slivers, left and right of her spine.

"One of the first 2 stabs punctured her heart," he said, circling two of the wounds with the tip of a pencil. "These two were thrust upward. Hard. The hilt of the knife left an impression."

"Anything distinctive?"

I'm still working on it. The impressions almost look like very small flowers, but I can't be certain at this point.

"What about her head?"

"Nothing special. Her killer sawed it, pretty much the way a bad chef might hack a leg off a chicken. The cutting weapons were different, though, both very sharp, but the stabbing knife was more of a dagger type. The other was serrated—nothing distinctive about the blade, except that it went through the vertebrae like cutting butter."

"How about blood?"

"She almost bled out. There was some bruising on her chin, so she probably fell over the side of the tub, before he beheaded her. Then he let her hang there. He had to be covered in blood. We pulled the drain. Nothing. Everything was clean. This man was a neat freak. He used ammonia to clean the tub, and he even shampooed her hair."

"Shampooed her hair?"

"Yep. Well, not the way you would expect someone to shampoo hair. Our boy just rinsed out the blood and towel dried it."

"Any sign of a sexual attack?"

"No. She was clean. Funny thing about her hands, though, they were dipped in ammonia."

"We've got ourselves one sick puppy."

"I hate to say this David, but I don't think this is the last we hear from this puppy. I'll get you a full written report by tomorrow."

HARRINGTON, WISCONSIN
ANOTHER MURDER

15

Ruann Beidermeister rarely read a newspaper at her Sunday Open Houses, but it was almost 4 PM, and she was bored; only three brokers had driven up the long winding driveway of her new listing for a peek at the sprawling ranch.

Ranch, she thought to herself. *These Midwesterners wouldn't know a ranch if it bit 'em on the ass.*

Ruann was originally from Dallas, home of the real ranch. She would have preferred to live and die in Dallas, but she met a traveling salesman who promised the world and unfortunately delivered a tract home on the outskirts of the city.

When he left her with a mountain of bills, 500 dollars in a money market, 2 kids, a 2-bedroom house at Lake Pine Villas with a mortgage on the verge of collapse, she went to work for a development company as a broker's assistant until she could get a license to sell.

She worked hard, receptionist during the day, hair stylist on the weekends. And it paid off. All those women to whom she listened eventually sold their homes, and within a few years, Ruann became a very successful real estate agent. Of course, being one of the pets of the development company owner did not hurt.

Eventually, she chose to leave Texas and move her family to the Midwest. She chose Wisconsin joining J.S. Kennicott Real Estate, a Midwest selling arm for Goody Homes and soon became their listing queen.

She was a natural listener; her mind could be a million miles away, but she was able to swallow every word a client uttered. They loved her. They did whatever she said, and she laughed all the way to the bank.

She was not particularly attractive; in fact, she was born to be a matron. What's more, her pear shape, her pendulous breasts resting on a pregnant-like belly, and her short, thick legs were an advantage; she did not threaten wives, and roving husbands were perfectly mothered by her. In fact, she was a mother to everyone, except of course, to her children.

She was beginning to gather up her newspaper and listing sheets when she heard a car door slam shut. She managed to reach the foyer just as a tall, dark man wearing a Levi jacket and jeans entered. Of course, everyone was tall to 5 foot 1-inch Ruann.

He nodded with a broad, friendly smile, and said, "I can see you're leaving, but kin I still see the house and the barn. I really do need a place to keep ma' horses."

"Are you a broker?"

"No, ma'am. I just saw your sign. My name's Colin Axman."

"Well, Mr. Axman, are you working with an agent?"

"No ma'am, but kin you still show me the house and barn?"

"Absolutely. My name is Ruann Beidermeister; I am the listing agent, Mr. Axman. If you would please sign my Open House sheet, then we may begin. Sellers love to know who comes to see their home."

He took the pen she handed him and signed the guest register on the hall table.

"Now, would you prefer to start with the barn or the house?"

"The barn, ma'am."

Ruann smiled and directed him back outside, then locked the door as she left.

"It's a bit of a way back on the property. We can walk it or, take the car."

"Why don't I drive ma'am. I don't want to keep you from your family any longer than need be."

"Thank you, Mr. Axman," she said as they walked to his car, a new Jaguar Xj8l.

"I know this ain't the most comfortable car for passengers, ma'am, but my daddy gives each member of the family a new Jaguar when they turn 30."

"What a charming tradition," she gushed aloud as she struggled to get comfortable. To herself, she promised *this boy is going to buy before we leave name's not Ruann Beidermeister.*

"Let me tell you a little about the property," she went on in her warm, motherly way, her Texas drawl growing with each word. "I do have a full-color brochure at the house with all the details, so if I miss anything, you'll have the information at your fingertips.

"Originally this property was 60 acres, but it was subdivided. The owner sold the balance of his horses and retired to Florida, so he is very negotiable on the price. The Goody Builders—they're a pretty well-known developer in the Midwest—they built the original house, but it was redone about 5 years ago, top to bottom. New electrical, new heating, new plumbing, new roof, you name it. No expense was spared! The barn was renovated as well...just pull over there by the fence," she directed, her finger jabbing the air.

Colin was the personification of the good ol' boy: Southern mannered, handsome and shy; so, he did exactly what Ruann told him to do.

"I sure do like the privacy here," he volunteered.

"Oh, that is one of this property's most outstanding features," she gasped, a little out of breath as she struggled to get free of the Jaguar. "Your next-door neighbor is over 2 miles away. The properties are separated by the tip of the forest preserves."

"I like that. Now, may I see the inside of the barn, ma'am?"

"Of course, let me unlock the doors."

Ruann turned a key in the padlock and slipped it free of the chain links it joined together. She pulled one of the doors open and walked inside followed by the slim, young man.

"Whew, sure is big," Colin Axman whistled.

The cavernous barn was dark except for the last vestige of late after-noon light creeping thru some of the rafters. Bales of hay were stacked in two of ten empty stalls. A baler, parked at the far end of the barn created alien shadows at rest, waiting quietly in the semi-darkness.

After a few moments of struggling to find the light switches on the wall, Ruann finally connected with three of them; light exploded in the barn from track lighting, anchored on chains attached to a roof some 30+ feet above.

"Now we can see everything this barn has to offer for all of your wonderful horses."

"We certainly can," Colin said. The change in his voice startled Ruann and she began to turn, but a sharp pain low in her back forced her to fall forward slightly. A second sharpness made her cry out and reach for some support to help her stand. When the third stabbing pain came, she lost consciousness.

The Levi-clad killer took the dagger with its intricately carved jeweled hilt and wiped it clean on Ruann's jacket then stepped past her to the stall with the bales of hay. He struggled to pull two small bales to the center of the barn, spacing them about two feet apart.

Gathering one more bale, he pulled, tugged and pushed until it linked the others at the back, creating an oversized armchair. Then he went to his car, opened the trunk and removed a Prada satchel. After unzipping it, he removed a red suede bag that held his tools: a surgical knife, a kitchen boning knife, a small ax with a sharply chiseled edge, gloves, and clothing.

The sun was setting, and the sky was a wondrous burnt orange haloed in lavender, purple and blue. He admired it for a moment, then sighed and returned to the barn to finish his work.

After replacing his leather driving gloves with a latex variety, he removed his jacket and slipped on a type of white hazard coverall retrieved from the red suede bag. He then commenced his immortalization of Ruann Beidermeister.

When he completed his body sculpture of Ruann, she sat on the ground between the two bales of hay, her body resting against the third bale that linked them. Her legs were crossed elegantly at her ankles. Her arms, detached from her torso, rested atop the bales of hay at her sides.

MONDAY
DECEMBER 19TH

CHICAGO
DAVIS AND KRAMER REPORT

16

Arnstein's hands were swatting the air, but the buzzing around his head would not stop. He finally woke enough to realize that the masked man's voice in his dream was nothing more than the bedside clock announcing 6:30 AM. He shook himself fully awake and headed for the shower.

The hot water revived him. He stood there slowly turning his head, unlocking muscles tight in his shoulders and neck. He knew it would be a long day.

He dressed quickly then started the coffee and grabbed the Tribune at the front door, scanning headlines while cooking a quick bowl of oatmeal. He was not always the breakfast type. In fact, black coffee had been his usual morning meal. However, Joanna had changed all that. She insisted he start his day with a hearty breakfast, and now, making breakfast for himself seemed to bring her close again.

By the time he left his townhome, it was 7:45. He would be a few minutes late for his meeting.

Davis was already waiting in the squad room, sipping his Carmel Macchiato and skimming the Sun-Times that he bought on his way to the Station.

"Boy, none of our guys make the Starbucks run," Terry Calahan said with a smile as he entered the room.

"Dunkin Donuts coffee beats Starbucks by a mile," added Bugs Kramer, walking behind him.

"Dunkin Donuts! Where have you guys been?" answered Davis. "Starbucks is like a fine wine."

"Yeah, with a champagne price tag, besides, I don't like wine this early in the morning," Kramer chimed.

"Who's drinking wine in the squad room?" asked Arnstein as he joined the group. "Let's have a little decorum here. Although I must admit, the more I look at our case, the more I think I need a drink. Who has some news to change that?"

"Let's begin with the bad news," Davis started. "Credit card receipts. Checked everything one hour before and one hour after Playmore walked into the Bistro. About 20 charges. All cards were legit. Met with all but three of the chargers. Left messages for the others. No one remembered the Jimbo guy, but five guys remembered Playmore, as soon as I said *redhead*. Evidently, she was a looker when she was all in one piece. Sorry, bad joke.

"According to the bartender, Playmore was a frequent diner and drinker, and a lot of guys asked about her. He had a deal with Playmore so he would check out if the guys were from out of town or the Gold Coast and Streeterville; if they were planning to buy or sell he'd give her a sign. She would mosey up and bingo, a connection. He got twenty-five bucks for every connect, and if they bought or sold, he'd put a Benjamin in his pocket. She connected a lot.

"He doesn't remember the exact time this Jim guy came in, but he had one drink before Playmore got there: white wine. Kind of a pansy drink for an older guy, ain't it? Anyway, he told the keep he was looking for a place to buy.

"When Playmore walked in, the barkeep winked and nodded toward the guy. And, she did her thing. About 10 or 15 minutes later, her friend came in when he was serving Playmore another drink. Things got busy, so he didn't pay any attention until the guy asked for the tab. He paid cash, left a big tip and walked out with Playmore. It was about 2:30."

"How about you guys?" asked Arnstein.

Bugs Kramer pulled out his notebook, "I don't know who is worse, city condo people or suburban types. They're all wise-ass monkeys: Nobody sees anything, hears anything and has nothing to say. You know they know something, but getting them to talk is like getting a sticker off your windshield. I finally got one woman to admit to seeing Playmore in the elevator. Asked her if she remembered seeing a woman wearing a fur coat with an older guy. And she said, 'oh you must mean the redhead'."

"I'm beginning to think redhead is the new blonde," interrupted Davis.

'This woman remembered that the guy was carrying a garment bag and a soft duffel bag. No one else remembers the guy, let alone the bags he had. But she remembers them, and better yet, said they were Louis Vuitton. Verrry expensive."

"Why a garment bag?" asked Davis.

"Maybe a change of clothes in case of blood splatters," offered Terry. "I checked with coat check at the Bistro. Our Mr. Jim checked a garment bag and a duffel. He was prepared for something, or for getting out of town quick. Coat check tossed the tickets, so no chance to check for prints."

"Anyone leave 1313 with a duffel and garment bag?" asked Arnstein.

"Not till 7 o'clock or around there. Bout the time we were at the scene. Some woman wearing a fur coat had a duffel type but on a carrier and she didn't have a garment bag. Doorman did not recognize her; he was occupied by another visitor. She could have been a guest or a resident, but she didn't ask for a cab, she walked toward the garage entrance," Calahan offered.

"Is there an attendant or just deeded parking spaces?"

"Deeded only."

"How about camera surveillance?"

"Just in the elevators and the garage entrance, but the doorman was busy, so he didn't see which floor she entered the elevator."

"You and Calahan, check the tapes. See how long they're saved and get a copy. Let's find out where she came from and where this guy went."

"This guy is somethin'. He pulls a roach motel—checks in but never checks out. At least, no one remembers him leaving at the main door. And the guy in the receiving room said no one left at the back exit all afternoon. Last person was a delivery guy with a pizza for 21N. The owner was called and said send him up. He left about 10 to 15 minutes later. About 6:30."

"Humph, we've got a clean-freak killer who slices off a woman's head, disappears into thin air with a bottle of ammonia past door people, and doesn't leave anything behind," Davis said shaking his head in disbelief.

Calahan tapped Davis on the shoulder. "He's not a magician, Davis.

We just haven't figured out how he left the building."

"Check any tapes for both entrances to the building and the garage. He is no a magician, but he may well be a serial killer," Arnstein announced. "It looks like there are two more murders that could be connected to ours. An LAPD detective called and left a message. Victims were real estate brokers, and both were stabbed and posed."

All three men stared at Arnstein in silence.

"I'll call him for more intel. But I'm planning to take the Red Eye to LA tonight to see if we do indeed have a serial killer who is targeting Realtors. I'll be back tomorrow night."

LOS ANGELES
PETER SEARCHES JANNA VALLI'S LEXUS

17

Krachewsky and Peter left Mac at the station and headed to the auto pound.

"What do you know about Amanda Brewster, Harry."

"A slick operator. She definitely had an in with the Hollywood bigwigs. I bet she had one hell of a client list. Her card said she was the 'Realtor for the Stars'."

"Successful and independent."

"You think she has anything to do with the Chicago Realtor who was killed, or if the Chicago victim has anything to do with our perp?" Harry asked.

"I don't know, Harry. My friend did not have all the specifics, but two LA Realtors brutally slain, one of them murdered just weeks apart from another one killed in Chicago, I can't buy that it's just coincidence."

"Hey, maybe our guy bought a lemon and is taking it out on the real estate community."

"If he is targeting Realtors, Harry, he's only just begun. There is a quiet yet violent rage around our killer, and it is a growing rage. It's not from buying a lemon, as you call it."

They pulled up to a chained lot, and parked alongside several police vans and cars, next to an enormous garage. Inside, a black Cadillac was at the head of a reverse assembly line. The black leather seats, already dismantled, were carelessly lined up behind two police mechanics who were methodically ripping out the carpeting in the late model car.

Krachewsky walked to a glass-enclosed area and spoke to one of the police officers behind the desk while Peter watched as the police denuded the Cadillac of its posh interior.

"It's the silver Lexus all the way in back," Krachewsky called out, signaling Peter to follow. Unlike the Cadillac, the car in stall 22 looked as though it waited for assembly, its parts carefully organized, a king-sized Revell model, ready for a gloved enthusiast to glue together.

Peter walked slowly toward the Lexus, the sweet smell of Boucheron gaining in strength with each step. He paused. He sensed heavy breathing, deep almost meditative. The garage sounds around him disappeared. All he heard was the steady hypnotic breathing.

Krachewsky watched. It was a little like spying on a cat in the zoo, a big cat, eyeing people outside the bars, ready in its wait to attack. *It's creepy,* Harry thought. *Next time, Mac gets the privilege of chauffeuring the little guy around. That is if there is a next time.*

Peter closed his eyes. Bright colors spun before him, first yellow, then red, converging on some far away horizon, while soft, steady footfalls sounded, repeatedly. He focused on pulling the sound and color together until he could see the yellow and red disappearing once again into some horizon, but this time accompanied by fading footfalls. Suddenly, he opened his eyes to the sounds of hammering and the sawing of metal from another part of the cavernous garage.

Janna Valli's automobile had said all it had to say. He turned to Krachewsky and softly whispered, "Let us go."

Krachewsky nodded and wondered what the little man had discovered that a highly trained forensic team and four mechanics had missed. He followed Peter Dumas out of the garage to the unmarked sedan.

Peter did not offer any insight or information. Krachewsky took his lead and drove back to the station in silence, glad that this mumbo jumbo stuff was over so he could get back to real police work.

When they walked past the squad room to the back office, Mac was on the phone. "Yeah. I see," Mac motioned to Peter and Krachewsky to sit down. "Sure. Anytime. I know. Oh, I know. I'll do that. Yeah, I look forward to meeting you, too," he said turning to Peter and Harry.

"That was Chicago. You were right, Peter. They've got one, too."

"Same MO?" Krachewsky asked.

"Pretty much. This real estate agent took a client to see a condo; it was the last one she showed. The owner found her stabbed with her head in her hands."

"Was she staged with as much care as the two here, Mac?" Peter asked thoughtfully.

"According to the lead, a Detective Arnstein, the killer did a real case on her. Propped her in a chair, crossed her legs and put her head in her lap. We'll get more tonight; Arnstein's coming in on the Red Eye."

"Want me to get him?"

"That'd be great, Harry."

"I've got some reports to catch up on, so I'll let Peter give you his reaction to the Lexus. Let me have Arnstein's number. I'll get the flight info and call when I pick him up."

Mac tore a page off his yellow pad and handed it to Krachewsky who left with a goodbye salute to the two men.

Peter smiled, "I think Harry has reservations about my contributions."

"Harry's not a believer in anything he can't see or touch, Peter, but he surfs the net now, so there's hope!" Then more , he added, "See anything with the Lexus?"

"A runner, in a yellow or red jacket or pants."

Northwest Indiana
Monday, Late Afternoon

18

Number 3 was golden for Millie Frobisher: her third attempt to pass the state real estate exam was her winning ticket. It's not that she was stupid, tests were always difficult for her. Always suspicious of multiple choices, she found right and wrong with every choice, so she clutched.

Millie joined Carey Real Estate 2 days after she passed her exam, fully intent on making *more money than God.* She was through working for nothing; she had groomed dogs for the past 5 years, not a particularly rewarding life for Millie. She dreamed of money, lots of money. She fed on the litanies of good life heard from pet owners whose dogs led a better existence than she had for the past 30 years.

She took to real estate like a duck to water. Buyers and sellers were a means to an end, and she did not intend to hold their hands. She was good at what she did because she never wasted time with shoppers. If someone were not ready to buy, she would pull the plug and never call him or her again. To Millie, it meant only 3 days with a buyer, showing perhaps a total of 10-15 properties.

If any buyer could not make up their mind in 3 days, "next" was Millie's response. Moreover, buyers concerned with the cost of utilities got the hook as well. Millie believed if someone liked a property, little things like utilities or taxes were not important in the grand scheme of things.

Sellers, on the other hand, got the big sell before signing on the dotted line; afterward, they never saw Millie again. She rarely showed their properties personally; keys, lock boxes and newbie agents were in her arsenal of weaponry. She only appeared at the transaction's closing to pick up her check.

Real Estate, according to Millie, was quick, painless, and profitable. Anything else was fine for another agent, but not her. When she arrived for her floor time that cold December afternoon, she found a gaily wrapped package on her desk; she tore off the colorful "thank you" paper wrapping wondering who would have left a gift, and why. Inside the box was a spray bottle of perfume: Boucheron.

"Hmm. Nice!" she said aloud to no one in particular, as she gave herself a double dose of the heady scent. "It's about time someone appreciated me, but I'd rather have a new listing or a referral."

When she found the unsigned Thank You card, she hesitated for a moment considering the possibility that the gift might not be for her—but being low on perfume, she tossed the card in the trash along with the box and wrapping paper, and deposited the Boucheron in her handbag.

Millie activated her computer to begin a search for FSBOs and expired listings, planning to hit them on the phone and drum up some activity. Business was slow, it was always slow before Christmas; she didn't have a listing, and she didn't have any active buyers.

She was saying a silent prayer for some walk-in business so she would not have to face the dreaded phone when a tall, dark-complected man walked into the almost empty office. Her heart skipped a beat. His blue-black hair fell in curls framing high cheekbones; he was slim and looked as though he stepped from the pages of GQ, perfect in his straight leg jeans with a crisp white shirt opened at the neck, and a jean jacket with sleeves rolled up slightly above brown leather driving gloves. She was out of her chair like a Derby horse out of the gate, all 5 feet 2 of her.

"Good morning," she chirped, best smile forward, eyelashes fluttering in the wind. "I'm Millie Frobisher, may I help you?"

"I want to buy a house," he stuttered in almost a whisper.

"Well, you certainly came to the right place. Come into the conference room, and we'll get started." She led the way to a small room a few steps from the floor desk where she had been searching the computer for 'For Sale by Owner' leads. "Have you been working with a Realtor," she asked over her shoulder.

"No."

"Good, then we can get right to work." She directed him to a chair and poised her pen atop a lined yellow pad. "Let's start with your name and phone number."

"Eric Daggert. I'm staying at the Clausen Hotel."

Millie could smell money a mile away, and she was convinced she had a live one in her lair; the Clausen was the most expensive hotel in town and anyone who stayed there expected tradition and the ultimate in service.

"Eric, why don't you tell me what you want in a home and, more importantly, what's the most you want to spend."

"5 acres plus. Money's no object."

Be still my heart, she said to herself. Those were the words Millie loved best. She knew only two properties that fit the bill, both of which were listings from her office.

"You're in luck. There are 2 homes on 6 and 8-acre sites just outside of town, and both are vacant and listed by our office, so I can get you right in this afternoon."

"Excellent."

"Oh, are you pre-approved for a mortgage?" she asked.

"It'll be cash. I have a letter of credit at the hotel."

"That's even better! Let me make the arrangements." She left the conference room and headed toward the reception desk, her fisted hand pumping downward and a 'yes' formed on her lips.

All appointments for office listings were scheduled with the receptionist at Carey Real Estate, much like they were at other real estate agencies in the quiet university town. The scheduler would contact the owners with showing times and then place a call with a confirmation to the agent who requested the appointment.

The listing agent rarely showed a home after putting it on the market. Lockboxes were used to hold keys for the property; showing agents punched in their Real Estate Board ID number, and if they were active Realtors the lockbox opened and spit out the keys. It was a convenient way to show homes, particularly for the listing agent.

The two listings Millie scheduled were a slam-dunk; no owner calls were needed as both properties were vacant. "If I get any more floor calls while I'm gone, stick 'em in my voicemail. I should be back with Mr. Daggert in an hour," she told the gum-chewing receptionist who nodded while continuing to file incredibly long, red nails while she read the latest People magazine.

It took a matter of minutes for Millie Frobisher to line up what would be the very last showing appointment of her life.

LOS ANGELES
LATE MONDAY NIGHT

19

When Arnstein's plane landed, the temperature in Los Angeles was a mild 55, a full 50 degrees warmer than the city he left behind. It felt good, almost too good. He was disappointed that someone was coming to get him because it would most likely be in an unmarked sedan. Resigned, he stood outside the American Airlines arrival gates and waited, coat in hand.

Arnstein would never drive a sedan when the temperature hit the 50s back home—to him that was convertible weather, and his Porsche became the vehicle of preference. So, when Krachewsky pulled up with the top down on a black Chrysler convertible, Arnstein paid little attention until Krachewsky tapped the horn a few times. When he identified himself, Arnstein's opinion of the LAPD warmed considerably.

"How'd you know it was me?"

"I just looked for a guy with a big scar and no tan, holding his coat... lookin' for an unmarked sedan. Piece a cake. Harry Krachewsky," he announced, thankful to be chauffeuring a real cop, and not a mini-man who went to crime scenes, sniffing the air for perfume and listening for cries.

"You're right; I was looking for a sedan. Didn't think you tough guys drove ragtops."

"Normally, no, but tonight, I figured anyone from Chicago deserves as much of our weather as they can get. I grew up in the windy city, and I'd still be there if it weren't so friggin' cold."

Arnstein laughed and then asked, "Yours?" as the car's eight-cylinders revved up to pass a silver Corvette.

"Hell no, I borrowed this mother from the pound. A dealer beefed up the engine to wipe out anyone in a chase. Of course, the perp had to know how to handle it. Our boy didn't. We borrow it until someone comes asking for it."

"I think I'm in love with the LAPD."

"Hey, is that Mr. Beef still there near the expressway ramp?"

"You are from Chicago. That's one of our treasures."

"Yeah, we got tamales. Not that they're terrible, but gimme a great Italian Beef with hot peppers. Or wait, I've got one for you. The Busy Bee under the tracks at Damon. Greatest pierogi in the city."

"I was a fan of their chicken soup, but unfortunately, the Busy Bee has buzzed away, Harry. You know, you are making me very hungry."

"Got just the place. In fact, I'll call Mac and have him meet us there. We can talk while you and I have a midnight snack."

ARNSTEIN MEETS PETER
AT JERRY'S DELI

20

When Arnstein and Krachewsky pulled into the parking lot of Jerry's Deli in Studio City, Peter and Mac were already drinking coffee at a back table.

It was well after midnight, but it could have been lunchtime considering how many people crowded into the oversized deli-restaurant. Actors and would-be actors filled tables alongside a host of industry production people, gaffers to cameramen; the walls behind them, papered with photos of LA celebrities autographed with scrawls that passed for signatures.

After introductions, Krachewsky ordered a cholesterol-laden special as the group of men began a serious discussion about the possibility of a serial killer.

Mac started the ball rolling, just as the waiter dropped a plate before the new arrivals. "So Arnstein, what have you got in Chicago?"

Prepared to bite into the cream cheese topped raisin bagel he ordered on the way in, Arnstein smiled and responded, "You show me yours, and I'll show you mine." Then one-quarter of the bagel disappeared behind his lips.

"OK, I'm not eating, I'll start. We have two unsolved homicides—both victims were real estate agents. One of them was killed in mid-November, the other, a couple of weeks ago. Each of them was showing a home to a prospect.

"Based on what we've learned, victim #1 was an elaborately planned kill by a man assuming someone else's identity. Vic #2 was either surprised by the killer, or scheduled an appointment that piggybacked an earlier one, and just failed to put it in her planner."

"Anything else connect them besides the posing and the fact they were real estate agents?" Arnstein asked.

"Uh uh! Both women were stabbed from behind; this guy was a

savage. Then he posed them the way a photographer might who was planning a publicity shot for a film. And, aside from a few hairs, we didn't get jack from either scene."

Arnstein let his napkin wipe away any trace of cream cheese from his lips, motioned for the waiter to bring more coffee then addressed the other men.

"You pretty much described our kill. Our vic was a real estate broker as well, throat slit, stabbed and posed with her head in her lap."

"Whew," Krachewsky whistled, "we got a real sick puppy on our hands."

"That's exactly what our M.E. said."

"What about the scene, any worthwhile forensics?" Mac asked.

"We did find a print. Nothing concrete yet, and we do have a witness who saw the agent with the man we believe is the killer. You should have a drawing at the station right now, I asked my partner to fax it to you."

Peter, who had silently been observing the three men suddenly spoke, "The drawing is worthless; it's a face your killer wanted you to see. This killer is a chameleon."

Although Arnstein was not aware of Peter's background, he sensed something unusual about him and politely waited for Peter to elaborate.

Krachewsky, on the other hand, rolled his eyes and looked to his partner to explain Peter's proclivity to startling statements without benefit of solid proof.

Peter preempted Mac's attempt to define him.

"David, may I call you David?" Arnstein did not recall anyone identifying him as David during the introductions, in fact, he didn't recall anyone ever using his given name other than Charlie Peel, but he hesitantly nodded yes.

"I am known to a few people as an intuitive, others consider me a clairvoyant, and still others address me as a psychic. And, there are those who have called me a charlatan," he smiled. "I answer to all the above, except charlatan. I have been called upon by the FBI and numerous police departments who require a fresh mind to look at an old crime, or one where the investigation has reached an impasse."

"Peter is an old friend of the LAPD," Mac chimed. "We called him to give us his read on our murders."

"So, what do you bring to the table, Peter?" Arnstein asked.

For the next 2 hours, Peter mesmerized David and his LA associates, answering the question with snatches of sound bites, auras of scent, visions, connected thoughts, unconnected thoughts—an incredible mental list of each crime scene, and his description of what had transpired there. Never once did he preface his statements with 'I believe' or 'maybe' or even 'perhaps'; his thoughts were the observations of a witness with a finite sensitivity and incredible recall, but of crimes he had never witnessed.

Mac, although listening intently, could barely keep his eyes open; he was not a night person, and if he did not get to sleep soon, he would not be the early riser he prided himself to be. "I'm sorry guys, can we pick this up after a little shut-eye?" he yawned as he rubbed his sleep-deprived eyes.

Peter and Arnstein, both night people, smiled understandingly, and offered to meet with Mac later that morning. Meanwhile, Krachewsky, eager to hear and file any pertinent information, said he would stay and chauffeur the two men to the hotel.

Mac yawned once again and left.

"The way I see it," Arnstein started, "the tie has to be more than the victims being real estate agents."

"What if it's just opportunity, vacant or unoccupied homes, the thrill of picking out a crime scene?" Krachewsky interjected.

"You introduce an important factor, Harry. The scene." Peter offered. "If our killer is purely focusing on real estate agents, he could kill them anywhere, in their car, or in places other than where they work. But our killer makes a point of being very selective about his killing stage. To him, the agent victim and the crime scene are joined inexorably. The scene gives him permission to kill, in his time frame and in his manner. What's more, our killer has studied his victims. He knows their habits, their schedules, their personal agendas."

"Peter, the killer could just as easily go after an owner selling on his own without the benefit of an agent," Krachewsky began.

"But he hasn't, has he?" Arnstein interrupted.

"No, but we don't know if he's killed anyone else," Harry answered.

Peter, listening attentively, added, "There are others. Begin a search, and you will uncover several others. What's more, our killer is not sated yet. But to warn his specific targets, I strongly urge you to put out a warning to all real estate agents. His past and future victims are part of the whole—by occupation, vulnerability and their accessibility to a perfect stage for murder."

"Perfect, it is," Arnstein added. "All that agent/buyer traffic is a forensic nightmare, and that doesn't include painters, cleaners, and God knows who else."

"Yeah, we collected dozens of hairs and prints," Harry confided. "No matches yet, from any of our scenes. It's like looking in a vacuum cleaner bag. If we only had a common print, we could check it against yours."

"If only...a match could rubber stamp that we've got a repeater," Arnstein added.

"But, we ain't gonna solve anything tonight, so how's about I drop you both off at a hotel. Crashing for a few hours isn't gonna hurt any of us."

"I agree. Don't forget, though, I'm still on Chicago time."

Krachewsky left a couple of twenties on the table and followed the men out of the still packed restaurant.

CHICAGO
3 A.M. MONDAY, THE KILLER CALLS

21

The phone's sudden ring woke Susana just as the clock's digital display clicked 4 A.M. She grabbed the receiver prepared to read the riot act to the caller, but her "do you have any idea what time it is?" prompted no verbal response. She listened intently waiting for some sound, but only silence rewarded her.

"Who is this?" she pleaded but silence was all she heard, until an ever so slight intake of breath, at least that's what she thought it was. She stared angrily at the receiver before slamming it down.

"It was probably a wrong number, probably nothing," she said aloud. But images of Patti finding Terry, suddenly flooded her mind.

She turned on the bedside lamp, threw back the covers, slipped on a robe, and went to the bookshelf to get something to read, hoping the images would disappear.

The voyeur watched as she searched for a book.

"Susanna, Susanna. Poor baby. What's the matter? Can't sleep? Soon you will…a deep, deep sleep, Susanna."

The wind whipped up crisp, white waves on the lake, iridescent in the moonlight. The temperature had dropped to below zero and the freezing snow, piled high on the shoreline, braved the icy shower of black water.

But the voyeur only saw Susanna whose bedside lamp was a beacon in the night.

TUESDAY
DECEMBER 20TH

LOS ANGELES
LATE MORNING

22

Arnstein was last to reach Mac's office much later that morning; it had been a late night, and he was still yawning. Krachewsky, who seemed to thrive on little or no sleep during high-profile investigations, had sent a black and white for Arnstein. He had other business to take care of—his usual morning donut run, but this time he included bagels in honor of Arnstein.

"You Chicago boys really need your beauty sleep," he chided Arnstein as he entered the room.

"That's why we look so good, Harry. Hell, if we lived here we would be movie material. You know, the good-looking, smart, charismatic leading man type," he responded.

"You've been going to the wrong movies, Arnstein. The good-looking leading men are not tall; they are two sandwiches short of a picnic and always kissing ass or looking for it. Now the real leading men, they got a lifetime on their face, and their bodies aren't that buff, either."

"Woo woo, our Harry knows his Hollywood heroes!"

"Harry is a man who studies people, David," Peter interjected. "He knows an original, and he definitely knows a copycat."

Mac entered the room at that moment and said "Original or copycat? You said it, Peter. Did our boy do 'em all, or do we have multiple killers out there?"

Peter looked thoughtfully at Mac and the others in the room then quietly uttered, "He's one and the same Mac, and I know he is not new at this."

"No, I don't think he is either, Peter. While you boys were catching extra z's this morning, I've been talking to a couple of Detectives who responded to an email I sent yesterday to all state crime labs.

"I think we've got ourselves a serial killer alright, and he's been quite a busy boy—at least I believe he is 'boy' singular."

Krachewsky stopped his powdered donut midway to his mouth. Arnstein put his coffee cup on the desk and took a deep breath. Peter slowly nodded.

"Where?" Arnstein asked.

"Albuquerque, early November. They found her in a pool, throat slit wide open. Another one, two days ago in Wisconsin, she was doing a Sunday Open House. They found her in a barn on a horse farm, dismembered. And yesterday an Indiana agent was stabbed 75 times and posed."

"Holy Spam!" Krachewsky whistled. "That makes six."

"Maybe a profiler might give us some insight," Mac stated flatly.

"What? White male, 25-40? We don't have enough to profile," Harry added. "We're guessing that he's done two in California, and one each in Illinois, New Mexico, Indiana, and Wisconsin. I say we pool our data, and see if there is anything that ties all these murders together. We can do it faster than the Feds. Besides, I'll bet dollars to donuts that Albuquerque never checked other departments outside the state. If we find a real connection, then we call the Feds."

"Peter, what do you think?" Mac asked.

"I tend to agree with Harry. You guess, to a degree, that you have one killer, but all you really have is a similarity of victim, not an established M.O.

"I know you have one murderer, but psychic thoughts are not what will put him away or prove to anyone that he is a serial killer. You need concrete evidence. My thoughts can help to direct your investigation if you wish, and I will do all I can to help."

"I'm in," Arnstein nodded.

"You've got my vote," Mac agreed.

"Augh, what happened to old-fashioned police work, Mac?" Harry whined. "What's the captain gonna say? No offense, Peter, but I gotta be honest— I like you even though you are a little guy, but I don't like the idea of looking for a killer, especially a serial killer, with a friggin' crystal ball."

"Oh Harry, I promise I will not bring a crystal ball, unless of course, you change your mind and request one."

Arnstein looked at Peter with an approving smile, suddenly realizing how much he respected this little man. He felt as if they had known each other for a lifetime; there was a connection between them, and David Arnstein knew they would be friends for life.

The men had talked for almost an hour before Peter and Arnstein called to reserve seats on the next plane to Albuquerque.

Together, the four of them outlined a plan of action. Peter and Arnstein would visit the crime scenes in New Mexico, Indiana, and Wisconsin and relate anything pertinent to Mac. Krachewsky would begin doing finite background checks on the victims, and Mac would assemble any trace evidence and profile descriptions of anyone at or near any of the scenes. They would assemble next, in Chicago.

CHICAGO
SUSANNA'S SON CALLS

23

When Susanna awoke, the sunlight was streaming into her room. She was glad she had not set the alarm; it was her first decent night's sleep since Arnstein's news about Terry.

She retrieved her slippers from under the bed and headed to the kitchen to make coffee, but first, she glanced out the window at the traffic below. Lake Shore Drive was still in the throes of the morning rush hour, and swirls of exhaust competed with the icy mist rising from the lake. It was another brutally cold and silent Chicago morning.

Susanna did not have any appointments; she had planned to catch up on phone calls and a few tasks she'd left undone. But first, coffee. She ground the beans and filled the pot with icy water, then unlocked the door to the hallway to gather her newspapers. The Journal was just outside the door, but the Trib was almost 10 feet away, tossed most likely from the elevator at the opposite end of the hall.

Terry's death made page two of the Trib, this time along with her picture. *One of her better ones,* Susanna thought. She poured a cup of steaming coffee from the pot burping its brewing cycle finish and began reading. The shrill ring of the phone interrupted her.

"Hello," she said in her husky morning voice.

"Hi Mom, what are you doing?"

"What do you think I'd be doing at 9:30 A.M.?"

"Why are you always so grouchy in the morning?"

"The same reason you are so grouchy at night."

"I am not grouchy at night. You just always call when I'm in the middle of something and ask stupid questions."

"Chris, what do want? I've had a very bad few days, and I'm really not in the mood to make small talk."

"I just called to find out if that Terry who was murdered was your Terry, the one you worked with."

"Yes, she was."

"I'm really sorry, Mom," Chris softly replied. "I really liked her. She was great, not like those other dingbats in your office."

"You don't know them, Chris."

"I hear you bellyache about them, all of the time," he emphasized.

"Mom, why don't you get out of that creepy business? You hate it. You're way too smart, and now there's some nutcase out there who just killed one of your best friends. You are way too vulnerable. You don't know who the hell you're taking into some condo. Hell, it could have happened at one of your listings."

"It was at one of my listings."

"Mom! It could have been you!"

"I know, I know, Chris. I do not need any more chastising or drama. For once, I agree with you. I may go back to the paper. Lately, I've been toying with the idea of doing a column again. It's not that I hate real estate, I just think it's time for a change"

"That's great! The sooner, the better, but until you do, get some mace or pepper spray."

"Fine, fine. What's happening at work?'

"What does that have to do with pepper spray?"

"Chris, I'm just trying to change the subject! Oh, never mind, I really must run. I slept in. Anything else?"

"Yep, I'm going to be in the city tonight, and I thought we could have a little din din together, Mom-a-reeno. How about it? I want to try that Firehouse place on South Wabash. Have you been there?"

"Hmmm. It's wonderful. I'll join you if you promise not to call me Mom-a-reeno in public."

"You're on. I'll make reservations for 7:30. Meet me there."

"All right, I'll see you tonight, sweetheart!"

No sooner had she ended the call than another ring announced a new one.

Boy, I'm really popular this morning, she thought.

"Good morning," she answered.

"Hope I'm not waking you."

She recognized the smile in the caller's voice. "Peter! Where are you?"

"Still in Los Angeles, but I'll be back late tonight. Free for lunch Friday?"

"For you? Anytime. Of course, *ahem,* you could join Chris and me at the Firehouse tonight when you get in."

"I don't think so, Susanna. It will be too late," he said, slowly emphasizing each word. "Besides, you and Chris need some quality time, free from worries that a resident mind reader might be listening to your thoughts."

"Frankly, I'd relish a resident mind reader translating Chris' thoughts for me."

"Tell you what; I'll give you a guideline for a pleasant dinner: Keep conversation on a positive path."

"From your lips to God's ears, OK, OK. How about Tucci for lunch. I have to watch my waistline so we can split a chopped salad, and that way I'll be able to have a glass of wine."

"Perfect. High noon at Tucci's, it is. Oh, and Susanna, I hate to close our call on a down note, but I have no choice. Two other Realtors have been murdered in LA. I want you to be very careful."

"Peter, that's terrible. Were they killed by the same person who killed Terry?"

"We can't say with real conviction, but that doesn't mean you should be lax about security. I must go. Be careful. Love you," he said warmly, ending his call. Peter's calls usually brought a smile to her lips, but for once, she was feeling uneasy.

After a quick scan of the papers and more coffee, Susanna headed for a long steamy shower, an indulgence she rarely gave up. It was the one place she avoided interruptions from her cellular phone. As she lingered under the hot water, two calls registered on her mobile, charging on the bedside table.

One hour later, elegantly dressed, casually coiffed, and gently scented in Panthere, Susanna started her laptop to check the hot sheet for any new properties that might be right for one of her clients. She was glad to find something to take her mind off murder.

December was always a slow time for real estate; not many new listings hit the Multiple Listing Service near the holidays.

Traditionally, buyers and sellers came out of seclusion after the first of the year. However, people who looked for properties in December were serious; they certainly were not buyers one should ignore. In fact, Susanna always did significant business at the end of the year. She seemed to have a knack collecting buyers who turned early bonuses into homes of distinction, as well as getting sellers who wanted to try to cash out before the crowd.

She printed several listings then addressed the messages on her mobile. "Oh God", she said aloud, "that pompous ass has called again. I will never be accommodating to another agent's client—ever, ever, ever again!" The phone screen identified Robert Gosling, a has been architect who believed Susanna was his personal assistant simply because she listed a condo that he purchased.

The property was yet to close, but he always had a need to bring in contractors, or relatives, or neighbors, two or three floor refinishers, or some third party that simply had to have access to the unit.

Not only was he pompous, but he was also condescending. And of course, his agent told him to call Susanna directly to 'avoid confusion and unnecessary calls'. Susanna vowed she would get even with that agent for giving away her mobile number. As his voice message began, she deleted it.

The second missed call was identified as coming from 'out of area'. A woman's voice requested a call back to set an appointment for a preview of 1313 Lake Shore. Susanna made a note of the phone number, and once again deleted the message.

She returned a few important calls, then decided she had just enough time to pick up a few gifts at the Water Tower. Ordinarily, she avoided Chicago's famous vertical mall during the day and especially in December when it was a Mecca for out-of-towners and suburban shoppers.

She regularly shopped in the early evening or an hour before the stores closed but she needed an infusion of holiday spirit; the music, the crowds, the scent of Christmas always gave her a warm and tingling sensation that made her glad to be alive.

The Water Tower shops filled the bill with beribboned trees, perfumed aisles, and jingling bells...holiday music echoing throughout the shops and restaurants...children pressing noses against glass-walled elevators, watching with wide-open eyes as magical holiday characters danced among crowds of shoppers. Happy female sales clerks, anticipating a long and busy day, set smiles in place on faces, artfully made-up with shadow and mascara eyes and pouty red lips.

Chicago
Playmore's Listings

24

Susanna walked into the office shortly before noon. Her manager, Ty Collins, interrupted his conversation with another agent at the reception desk and asked Susanna to stop by his office. She nodded she would, then headed to her desk.

Checking voice mail was a mistake— she now had another half-dozen calls to return. *But first things first*, she thought to herself. *I better call Matthew Stark.* Whether she left the business or not, she could not afford to let a live one get away, especially a prospect whose price cap was about a million dollars. She dialed his mobile number, but the 'voicemail lady' greeted her, so she left a short message and decided to catch Ty before she got started on her other calls.

Ty was on the phone when she walked into his office, so she sat down and thumbed through the Realtor magazine on his desk, checking the index for articles: 'Build your own website' – *sure*, she thought, *in all that spare time I have.* 'FSBOs! Are you getting your share?' "Who wants them," she laughed; 'Lawsuits? Could you be at the wrong end?' another headline screamed at her. "I'm sure there's some buyer or seller out there gunning for me,' she said aloud, softly.

Concluding his call, Ty softened his expression and said with manufactured concern, "Susanna, how are you?"

"I'm fine, Ty. How are you?" she replied with a hint of sarcasm.

Caught up in his "I'm more than your boss, I'm your friend" act, he missed Susanna's inflection and answered her, even more humbly, "I'm OK. I'm finally accepting that Terry will never return. Her smile will never make my day again."

Yes, and her listings will disappear if you don't pull off some scheme, you phony bastard, Susanna thought to herself, but aloud she smiled and said,

"We all have to go on."

"I'm so glad to hear you say that. That's what Terry would want, so I've taken the liberty of giving you all of Terry's listings—since you and Terry worked so closely together. Furthermore, I told corporate that we must help you. A young woman whom Terry interviewed for an assistant position has indicated that she would like to help you as well."

"Me?"

"Evidently Terry spoke of you, and Pippa offered her services because she felt you would be Terry's natural replacement, and I agreed."

"I don't need an assistant."

"You will, with Terry's listings as well as your own; I've convinced Corporate that you deserve them. Besides, the company will pay her salary."

"And take it out of my commissions?"

"Don't be silly Susanna. We'll take a 40% referral for Terry's share of any of her listings that you cover. Pippa won't cost you a dime, and she will be a big help. At least meet with her, Wednesday, at lunch. Let us meet at the Ritz. Noon. How about it?"

Do I really have a choice, she asked herself?

"Fine. Lunch, Wednesday." And she left. *Good ol' Bottom-Line Ty,* she thought. *What a piece of work.*

Ty Collins rocked in his chair proud as a peacock at his maneuvering. *These agents,* he thought, *hold their hands, ask about their days, congratulate them on any sale or listing, and smile, above all, smile; they eat it up. They actually think I care about them,* he laughed. *What a sick bunch of lonely old women.*

Ty Collins joined the company 8 months earlier and smiled his way from agent to Managing Broker in record time; he went from Marshall Fields' off-the-rack to Armani in the blink of an eye.

There was much speculation about his gender preference, prompted by his proclivity to gay-oriented social activities, but looks could be deceiving. It would have been difficult for him to ignore the gay community considering the number of gay agents both in the office and in the city.

Of course, his appearance did add fuel to the gossip fire. He was not exceptionally tall, just under six-foot, but certainly a man with a presence. In fact, he was beautiful: a chiseled face, long eyelashes framing piercing blue eyes, and a lean body that screamed religious devotion to a gym.

Both men and women, gay and straight, acknowledged his startling good looks, but his divorced status and teenage son weighed the gossip for his having a heterosexual orientation, at least in the minds of some of the gossip mongers. He was the ultimate schmoozer. A likable man, yet one could sense something unpleasant about him.

CHICAGO
STARK CALLS...THE VOYEUR STALKS

25

The phone was ringing as Susanna unlocked her apartment door. She ran frantically through her apartment searching for her mobile phone; at the beginning of the fourth ring, she found it and breathlessly answered, "Susanna Ryerson."

"Tomorrow afternoon will work fine for me," the voice on the other end offered.

She desperately searched her mind to identify the voice and message, but her mind search was fruitless. "Tomorrow afternoon?" she asked searching the display on her phone only to find 'CID BLOCKED.'

"Yes, I can do 4 o'clock at your office."

"Fine, I'll meet you there, and we can discuss some options."

"Four o'clock!" The caller disconnected.

She entered the appointment on her calendar then ran a check of previously dialed numbers in her phone's memory. After a few moments, she narrowed the caller down to Matthew Stark (buyer) or Phillip Bloom (seller), opting finally for Stark simply because of the caller's brusque telephone manner and presumptive behavior telegraphing his belief that everyone must know his name. Then she remembered his last call suggesting they meet.

What a prick, she thought to herself. *Does he think I have nothing to think about but Mr. Importance! Humph, he probably can't get it up.*

It was just past 3 o'clock when Susanna realized she had not worked out for a few days. She needed to get rid of her tension; it was time for a run. She threw on running gear and a baggy sweatshirt with cut off sleeves. It was her favorite with a faded "Cheers" logotype above an equally faded script which read 'where everybody knows your name' "How appropriate," she said aloud catching a quick look in the mirror.

Susanna had several fitness club memberships but decided to drive to the FitFlex Club on Dearborn simply because it offered valet parking. She thought it ironic that she would drive rather than walk to an exercise club even when it was just a few blocks away; but then, with the temperature a balmy 10 degrees and a wind chill of 10 below, it was a walk she would prefer to avoid after her workout.

Of course, when the weather was not so brutal, she ran along the lakefront; nothing gave her calm and serenity as much as the lake did. She watched the blue waters roll in excitedly in the spring, contemplated the grayed waves as they crashed the shore angrily in the fall, and in the early heat of a summer morning, she drank in the sensuality of a shimmering wet glassy skin masking an undulating breast of water.

The lake was Susanna's refuge, her confidant, and her living art. She loved watching the sun peek out slowly just at the horizon as it burst into golden flames over the water; in her mind, it was an expression of color that no Impressionist could match with oils, despite fame or talent.

She took the elevator to the garage and walked to a black Mustang convertible tucked away in the far corner. Her son always chided that every teenage stud in the city drooled for that leathered chariot with its eight cylinders and the sound system that wouldn't quit.

"I like convertibles. American convertibles.' she always answered. "And classical music needs a full sound system." Of course, in the summertime, she would put her life in her hands when she pumped up her Beethoven to drown out a rap song—should one be playing in a car alongside her at a light. It was rather funny. The rapper screaming "my bitch woman" among other equally memorable phrases becoming a foreign tongue drowning in a sea of Beethoven's 5th.

Sometimes Susanna drew applause for the background music she contributed to a rapper's musical expression.

It took only 5 minutes to get to FitFlex, a few of those minutes spent waiting for a light to turn green.

A surprisingly big crowd greeted her, unusual for 4 o'clock on a week day: serious weightlifters, attorneys struggling with an elliptical trainer after a long day at court, and assorted shapes and sizes from the Pilates class that was just concluding. Susanna weaved through them all to the indoor track, stopping only to stretch before starting her run. She had always been a distance runner; speed was not her thing, so she picked up her pace gradually until she felt a relaxing rhythm overtaking her body. The silence was golden.

She had run for almost 20 minutes before she acknowledged echoes of footfalls behind her. The same rhythm, the same speed. She tried to look back without disturbing her pace, but she could not see anyone. It was as though the runner behind was stepping into her footprints, the way someone close could follow your thought and finish your sentence. She forced her mind to think about other things and soon drifted into a conversation with herself.

Should I just leave the office? Or am I just depressed because of Terry? she asked herself. *No, I've been feeling a need to get out, long before Terry. But am I too old to begin again?"*

Despite some of the great people she had the opportunity to meet, there was a preponderance of mediocrity surrounding her. For every professional agent, there were slick ones, hucksters with only one motivation: money. Also, they were usually young and primarily associated with a new brokerage that used unorthodox training to teach them how to hustle for the listing. From acting classes to improv they learned how to answer questions with a rehearsed script.

The running footsteps again interrupted her train of thought. The runner was about 5 feet behind Susanna, just enough to keep from being seen when she turned slightly to look back.

As they approached the end of the track closest to the exit, the runner suddenly turned, leaving Susanna alone on her trek. When she upped her pace and rounded the curve, she kept looking left and right, but the runner was gone. She was alone, at least she thought so.

From a small window on the exit door, the voyeur smiled.

CHICAGO
SUSANNA MEETS HER SON FOR DINNER

26

When she returned home, Susanna decided to drive rather than cab it to meet Chris; she did not want to be late. However, it was after 7 o'clock when she drove her car from the lower level of the garage. A light snow was falling, so she opted to avoid Michigan Avenue, taking the Outer Drive to Roosevelt Road instead. However, the remnants of rush hour traffic and the road's slick pavement still reduced the winter's 40 mph speed limit to less than 20mph.

She drove south past Navy Pier jutting out into the cold, black lake water, its shape defined by thousands of lights; its famous Ferris wheel outlined defiantly in the sky with circles of colored lights.

It was amazing to her how much her city had changed. She remembered the shrimp shack that once sat on the lake's edge just south of the Pier. She would often go there for lunch with a group from the office, risking the walk past the darkened warehouses, some of them deserted, just for the pleasure of those heavenly shrimp. Back then two bucks would buy her a big bag of deep fried shrimp, oozing oil, hot & spicy.

Susanna loved to sit at tables outside the shanty and watch the sailboat and cruiser skiffs motor to the ladder, allowing passengers to pick up carry outs of string fries and onions and double bags of shrimp or scallops.

Today tony hi-rises and pricey townhomes are skimming the lakefront, and the family-friendly Pier packs in every vendor possible hawking t-shirts to stuffed animals and costume jewelry. It has become a tourist Mecca with a host of restaurants and food carts catering to dewy-eyed couples, with-it teens and encumbered parents with their strollers and kiddy-sacks.

Susanna rarely went to the Pier, she didn't enjoy crowds. She did enjoy Shakespeare, though, and the Pier housed what she considered an extraordinary theater with a production company that more than earned its stellar reputation.

When she finally turned off the Drive at Roosevelt, it was almost 7:30. Chris would be waiting, most probably tapping his foot. Just like his father, he was punctual to a fault.

After her divorce, Chris walked out of her life convinced by his dad that she was having a love affair that was ripping the family apart.

Conveniently, her husband was unable to tell him whom Susanna had taken as a lover or what proof he had. It took Chris almost two years to realize his father manufactured fact to suit his needs.

Chris looked nothing like his dad; he was all Susanna, lean, tall and blond and blessed with her streak of independence and penchant for solitude. Unlike Susanna however, Chris thrived when thrown into a large group; he masterfully worked them with a smile here, a word there, a hug, a pat. He could sell you the Brooklyn Bridge, ask for change, and get it!

Susanna believed that Chris had the role of manipulator, down pat. Unfortunately, she was always taken in. She just was not proficient at working a crowd and mesmerizing a target as he was. Her face always telegraphed what she was thinking.

She wanted only complete loyalty and honesty, even from mere acquaintances, but especially from her son. Yet Chris always played the game, and despite her attempt to be a player with him, she always seemed to express disapproval. To him, that was his green light to manipulate her.

When she stopped at the corner, it was exactly 7:35. *Not too bad, only a few minutes late*, she thought, handing her keys to the valet.

As she stepped from the car a black Porsche paused before turning the corner; she had the sensation that someone was staring at her from behind the tinted windows. Hesitating for just a moment, she turned and entered the revolving door, convinced that her nerves were simply getting the best of her.

Chris was waiting at the bar, a drink in hand, and a foot furiously tapping on the brass railing just above the wood plank floor. "Mom," he whined reaching over to kiss her, "are you ever on time?"

"Occasionally," she answered. "I believe one is allowed a 5 to 10 -minute window either way. How nice to see you too, Chris!" She hoped her voice reeked a little with just the right amount of sarcasm. It did.

"Touchy, touchy."

"Do they have a table for us, or do I have to make polite conversation atop a bar stool."

Chris signaled one of the waiters, OK, OK, I'm sorry, Mom." The waiter led them to a corner booth near the fireplace where Chris attempted to add a positive swing to their conversation as he helped Susanna with her coat.

"I have really wanted to come here," he said.

"You're forgiven. It's not you, it's me. I'm in a particularly bad mood and should have just canceled, but I really wanted to see you, sweetheart."

"So, what's the problem? Is it still Terry?"

"Terry, yes, and a few more."

"What do you mean a few more?"

"I heard from Peter. He is on assignment with the LAPD. It seems that other agents have been murdered same as Terry, and there's a chance it could be the same killer."

"Hey, I like Peter, mom, but a real estate 'ripper'? Give me a break. Duh…nobody gets that pissed about buying a house."

"I felt the same way at first, but now, I don't know, Chris. I can believe anything."

"If you recall, I did tell you to get out of the business, and if Peter's right, I wouldn't waste any time. Besides, your heart isn't exactly in it anyway."

"Well, to be honest, that's why I particularly was glad that you wanted to see me tonight. I want you to feel out Mossback for me."

"Mossback! He thinks I'm a twit."

"Don't be ridiculous. You have pulled in more corporate clients for the paper than any rep in the last 5 years. Mossbach is a numbers man; he does not think you are a twit. Besides, I just want you to bump into him, accidentally of course. Tell him you and I had dinner and that I sent my greetings. If he asks how I'm doing, say terrific and casually mention I have begun writing again. I just want to know his reaction, that's all."

"Mom, he told you to call him you when you were ready to come back."

"I don't know if I'm ready. I think I need to be convinced."

"OK I'm going to see him tomorrow. We have an internal workshop to develop promotions that could tie in with editorial. I'll be sure to *bump* into him."

"Don't be obvious!"

"Hey, I didn't get all those corporate clients by being obvious."

"You're right, I'm sorry, honey."

"You are forgiven," he smiled.

She smiled back at her first-and-only-born, happy they were having a normal conversation, if discussing a change in profession partially motivated by murder was normal.

"So, Mom, you really gonna pack it in?"

"I'm thinking about it. Suddenly I understand just how fragile life can be. I feel this need to accomplish something, to...to fill my life, to test and have faith in my gifts. What happened to Terry brought it all home. Of course, I must determine if I still can write. Then I'll take it one day at a time."

"Is this my mother talking? The consummate optimist. The manipulator of the written word. You need a pep talk, big time. Let's order the chops and see if they are sensational, I'll give you a motivational speech that'll get you rolling--until the chops come."

She laughed, "Let's do it."

CHICAGO
THE VOYEUR'S LAIR

27

The Porsche turned into the lower level of the dimly lit garage then quickly slid into an oversized space near the elevator. Grabbing a high-tech Prada duffel bag from behind the seat, the driver locked the car, set the alarm, walked to the elevator and pressed the call button for one of the high-speed elevators in the John Hancock Building.

When Skidmore, Owings, and Merrill designed the John Hancock Center in 1964, the plan included over 700 hundred apartments. That number diminished when the building went condo in 1973 as some new owners combined as many as four and five units, creating plush homes with views that spanned several states.

Despite the building's size, no one walked into the garage, and no one waited on the 44th floor where everyone changed elevators to get to their personal residence floor. The double elevator ride was a little like taking two empty buses to reach home, late at night.

When the elevator stopped on the 46th floor, silence greeted the lone occupant who quickly walked to the unit at the end of the red-carpeted hall. Once inside, the unit's occupant dropped the duffel bag, entered the dark blue Scavalini cabineted kitchen, and retrieved a 1985 Cabernet from the wine chiller. The only lighting was the soft glow of under cabinet floor lights that set the color afire in the bordering walnut plank flooring.

After pouring wine into paper-thin crystal stemware, the voyeur again walked to the telescope at the window and waited for Susanna to return.

PETER AND ARNSTEIN
LEAVE FOR NEW MEXICO

28

Krachewsky shook both men's hands after he helped them unload their luggage from the trunk of the Chrysler Sebring convertible.

"Hey Harry, I won't be able to reciprocate with a ragtop on wheels, but Chicago's arms will be wide open when you arrive," Arnstein promised, "regardless of the temperature."

Peter smiled, "Mr. Beef will be anticipating your return, too, Harry."

"Are you a fan of Mr. Beef's," Arnstein asked Peter, a surprised expression on his face.

"I don't know him, but he and Harry are evidently old friends. His name just came to mind when you mentioned Chicago," Peter responded.

"Mr. Beef is one of Harry's favorite eating holes," Arnstein laughed.

"Aw, hell Peter, why'd you go psychic on me again?" Harry pleaded.

"Harry, you keep sending me mental messages."

"I'm not sending you crap!"

"Oh Harry, can I help it that you are an open book? I don't look for your thoughts, they continually bombard me. I do believe, Harry, you are testing me, and I may make you a believer yet," he smiled and broke into a full, throaty laugh.

Harry, red and flustered, threw up his hands and squealed away from the departures area at American Airlines.

"You're too hard on him," Arnstein chuckled.

"I like Harry. He is the ultimate Professional....everything by the book. It's men like him who in the end bring credibility to me. I respect him, I wouldn't tease him if I didn't," Peter said seriously

After checking in, Arnstein and Peter walked to a gate at the far end of the terminal and settled into seats to await their flight. Both men were exhausted from a marathon of meetings, checking crime scenes and reading reports. The board identified Flight 220, on time for its scheduled LAX departure and 4 P.M. arrival at Albuquerque International Sunport.

"Peter, I'd like you to meet a witness we have in Chicago," Arnstein invited. "Well, at least a witness who was the last person to see our victim alive, as well as the man with her," Arnstein continued thoughtfully.

"I've met your witness."

"What? Now you're going psychic on me!"

"No, Susanna Ryerson is an old friend."

Arnstein looked at Peter, saw a flash of concern, and yes, even fear, in his eyes. It was as though the little man was suddenly miles away in a world unknown to Arnstein. His lips did not move, his breathing became quiet and shallow, and his eyes turned from a startling blue to steel gray. It was as though an ocean had gone from a blue-green calm to a dark-grey angry, in the path of a hurricane.

Peter was sensing Susanna. *She was sitting across from him next to a faceless figure that was shaking her hand, exchanging pleasantries. The figure was partly hidden by a red curtain. In one hand was a bloodied knife.* He violently shook away the image, acutely aware that Susanna would know the killer, and indeed could be the next victim.

Arnstein did not probe Peter with questions or demands, he just watched and recognized the power of his new friend's mind. He had never met a man like Peter, and never had he been so relieved to have a man like him in his corner. Something deep inside warned him that he was about to embark on an experience that would shape the rest of his life, and Peter Dumas would be at the heart of it.

With eyelids heavy, Arnstein took the opportunity to doze while Peter elected to read that day's LA Times.

ALBUQUERQUE
PALMIERI MURDER MEETING

29

Detective Frank Gonzales was waiting for Peter and Arnstein when they landed at Albuquerque International Sunport. After name exchanges, the men tossed their carry-ons in the trunk and climbed into the detective's car.

"I'm sorry to hear about the other Realtor murders, but I'm relieved to think we may have a chance to solve this one."

"We can't promise these are all tied together, Frank," Arnstein said, "but anything we can learn might give us the connection we're looking for."

"Why don't we get you guys, something to eat and we can go over my notes."

"Sounds great," Peter said, "I'm starved."

"What's your passion? Steaks, Seafood, Italian, Mexican?"

"Mexican, and a beautiful Margarita."

"Arnstein nodded, "I second that, Peter."

"Know just the place. And it's less than 5 minutes away."

Frank was not kidding. In just a few moments, he pulled up to a small restaurant with a bright yellow and red sign reading Arturo's.

"It may not look like much, but I promise you will love the food. And the margaritas, I guarantee you will never forget. I recommend the gorditas. They are thick corn tortillas stuffed with chicken or steak, guacamole, lettuce, cheese and an exceptional sauce."

Both Peter and Arnstein took his advice and added two Margaritas to the order. The waiter returned promptly with two heavy glasses shaped like two-thirds of an oversized grapefruit. One sip of the heady nectar and both men nodded their heads.

Peter smiled, "This is a Margarita worth remembering."

"Now enjoy boys, and I'll go over our murder. Maggie Palmieri was a successful agent. She moved from Santa Fe twenty plus years ago. According to her old managing broker, she made one mistake: slept with a former boss.

"Unfortunately, he was married to a woman with real estate connections. The wife promised revenge and was successful getting her fired, as well as making her persona non-grata at the big brokerages in Santa Fe. Palmieri saw the writing on the wall and moved here, and ultimately, built a helluva business.

"The day she died she was the agent on floor, something she didn't do very often. That day a woman comes in looking for a big showcase kind of home. According to the other agent on floor, Palmieri found three possible listings that she printed out. One was vacant, and two needed a 24-hour notice to show. The woman was eager to see the one property, so Palmieri got the code, and according to the receptionist, they left in separate cars. Palmieri said she'd be back in an hour."

Peter and Arnstein listened thoughtfully as they ate.

"We know Palmieri arrived at 12:18 according to the lockbox that clocked her agent ID when she entered the code," he continued.

"The listing agent called later that afternoon for feedback, but no one could find Palmieri. So, the agent went to the property to make sure the key was returned. The door was locked, and the key was in the lockbox. She went inside to make sure all the lights had been turned off. When she got to the pool area, she found a body in the water and made a b-line to her phone to call the cops."

"What was the cause of death," Peter asked.

"Several blows to the back of the head and a slit throat. Her skull was smashed. The ME said it was a blunt instrument, probably something like a hammer. Knife was double-edged. No weapons found at the scene. She was dead before being tossed into the water."

"What's your best guess? The buyer do it?" quizzed Arnstein.

"Unless some character just happened to be passing the property at just the right time and knew just how to return the key, the buyer's our best guess. Besides, Mrs. Hammer just disappeared."

"Mrs. Hammer?"

"Yeah," he laughed, "that's what she called herself. No record of her checking into any hotel. No one knows where she came from, or where she went after going to the property. For that matter, we don't even know if she actually met Palmieri at the house. But her name, along with the ME identifying a hammer as a possible weapon, sure is a strange coincidence."

"An interesting coincidence," added Peter. "Find anything out of the ordinary on Ms. Palmieri's person or on her desk, Frank."

"She had an engraved card in her pocket for Mrs. Salvatore Hammer. No address, no phone, and no prints. Figure that one out.

"Nothing out of the way on her desk, but we found a small gift box and wrapping paper with an unsigned Thank You card in the trash next to her desk. And the receptionist said there was no delivery that day, but it may have come in the mail. Only prints on the box were Palmieri's."

"Any identification on the box," Peter queried.

"Some perfume name. I don't remember, but I can get one of the guys to check it in the evidence locker for you."

"Any other agents in the office the day she was killed?"

"One. All she could remember is how Hammer was dressed and what kind of jewelry she wore."

"Do you have a description of the jewelry?" Arnstein asked.

"As I recall, the agent was pretty focused on Hammer's charm bracelet 'cause it had rubies in each charm. She makes costume pieces she sells and thought charms with fake stones would be great to sell online and to other agents."

"Peter, any other questions?"

"Is the house vacant where she was killed?"

"Nope," Frank answered. "It was rented for about 6 months till it finally sold. A married couple with three kids bought it. I guess the price was right".

"Do you think we've got the same killer?" he asked.

"The idea of a female killer doesn't jibe with the other kills, but a couple of things fit," Arnstein answered. "Honestly, I don't know. Maybe it's a pair of killers. We're checking if there's anything that ties the women together, other than being agents. We'll let you know what we come up with, Frank."

"What do you think, Peter?"

"Unfortunately, I believe they are connected," he said. "One more question, Frank. Was anything at the scene unusual? Anything?"

"Well, there was one funny thing. The water in the pool, it was over 90 degrees, and the owner said it was always kept at 80."

"Where was the temperature control located?"

"There's a small cabana-like cabin with a thatched roof next to the house. That's where all the power connections were along with the pool control and equipment."

"Do you recall if the area produced any prints?"

"Quite a few but no matches."

"Perhaps, David, you might send Frank the prints you discovered as well as Macs. One never knows what we could learn."

"Will do. Thanks, Frank, for all of your help."

"Thank you. I'd love to get this one off the books. The description of the LA and Chicago kills you gave when you called gave me some hope," Frank responded looking at his watch. "We better get a move on to catch that 8:30 flight."

They paid the tab and left with Gonzales for the airport.

CHICAGO
MIDWAY AIRPORT

30

The snow was falling steadily now, and air traffic was becoming as congested as the Kennedy Expressway was most of any day. One runway at Midway was closed, and snow plow crews were frantically working to keep the others open.

Arnstein watched out the window for any sign they would be landing, but all he saw was a swirl of white.

Peter, who dozed off when the pilot announced they would be arriving on time, awoke suddenly, moments before the pilot's voice resonated once again over the intercom,

"It appears we'll touch down in about 15 minutes, folks; we're number 3 in the queue. The temperature in Chicago is 22 degrees Fahrenheit; snow accumulation is 4 inches with an additional 4-6 inches predicted. And the current time is 11:17 PM. If you are connecting to St. Louis, Cleveland, or Detroit, please check at the concourse, several flights have been canceled because of heavy snow heading our way from Canada. We hope you had a pleasant flight, and thank you for flying Southwest Airlines. Flight personnel, please prepare for landing."

"Peter, your timing is incredible."

"Not really. For some reason, I rarely sleep longer than 45 minutes when I'm flying, and when the captain said earlier we would be on time, I knew we had about an hour, so I took advantage of the time."

Arnstein shook his head smiling. "Where will you be staying, Peter?"

"I have a pied-a-terre at the Drake Hotel. It's not large, but it suits me when I'm in town. Where do you live, David?"

"Old Town just north of North Avenue off Wells. Bought a townhome. I need space, trees; I've got to be able to see and feel the outside."

The sudden sound of the landing gear made him turn to the window where a sea of light greeted him through a flurry of flakes like those in a glass ball after being shaken. But unlike the peaceful winter wonderland under glass, the plane began its descent buffeted violently by the snow-laden winds.

Arnstein disliked landing at night, especially at O'Hare where planes banked over black water.

Seeing the city lights balanced on his right and left as they approached Midway, he eased up on his armrest grip.

Peter watched him quietly, understanding fears and black memories.

When the plane finally came to a stop at the gate, most of the passengers began to pull bags from under seats, and then proceed to remove belongings from the overhead compartments. Peter and Arnstein were traveling light, each with a small bag, so they waited patiently for the majority of passengers to deplane.

"I vote we take the Express bus into the city, Peter. We'll make better time, and their drivers have so many alternate routes. Traffic's going to be a bear with all this snow."

"I agree."

The men strode quickly from Gate G17, joining a mass of other Holiday travelers, intent on reaching their destination before being forced to spend any more time at Midway Airport than necessary.

On the ride to the city, Arnstein and Peter planned their investigation schedule for Wisconsin. "I'll stop at the station. I want to see if anything came up since this morning, and then I'll give the boys in Wisconsin a buzz. I can get back to you early with a timetable.

"If you don't mind, David, I'd rather we left Thursday morning. I need tomorrow to handle a few personal things."

"No problem, Peter. I guess I'm anxious to get this guy."

"We'll get the killer David. I promise."

Somehow, Arnstein knew that Peter was not just speaking empty words.

WEDNESDAY
DECEMBER 21ST

CHICAGO
PETER AT TERRY'S MURDER SCENE

31

When Arnstein arrived at the station shortly after 9 AM, Davis was waiting for him. "So, we may have ourselves a serial killer, huh?" Davis asked following his partner into the office.

"Looks that way. We can only be sure after we get a read on all the data from the other murders. How about ours, anything come up?"

"Nada. Kramer and Callahan interviewed everyone in a two-block radius. No one recognized the face in the comp drawing except the 1313 doorman who was leaving his shift at 3:00. He was the one who got the key for Playmore. Said the old guy came in with her just before he left for the day.

"And, according to the doorman on the night shift, our Jimbo could have left through the garage, but he doesn't remember. There was a cocktail party on the 18th floor, and the building manager hired a few off-duty door-men to jockey cars for guests between 4 and 8 PM, so there were a lot of faces going in and out that he and the other doormen didn't know. I guess some snowbirds in the building let other residents use their parking for guests.

"By the way, Calahan and Kramer got a hold of the elevator tapes. The fur coat woman got on the elevator on the 16th floor around 6. She kept her face muzzled in her fur coat, which by the way was a silver fox—very stylish. We may be able to match her by the coat. No one else went down for at least 30 minutes; everyone was heading up to the party. That's it, the tapes are re-recorded every 24 hours."

"Great, the woman with the rolling suitcase is a mystery, and the guy's like smoke."

"The woman was probably visiting someone, Arnstein. I'll do a check with the units on that floor. Maybe I can get something on her."

"OK, but for all we know, she may be an accomplice. The cops in Albuquerque had a female suspect who disappeared into thin air, like our

Jimbo."

"Come on, Arnstein. We know this guy didn't evaporate. I say we head back to the building, that's the only place we can learn about our perp."

"OK. Let's do it."

The two men left the station and headed north up Michigan Avenue. It was a virtual conga line of buses and cabs as the morning rush hour traffic reached its peak on the street that drew tourist shoppers from all over the world.

As Davis wove through the cars, he briefed Arnstein on his credit card receipt search at the Bistro. "The last three chargers didn't remember this dick, but all of 'em remembered her. 'Red-headed knockout' was the general consensus."

"Hell, anyone in Chicago or LA who does remember our boy, recalls an entirely different picture of him. He is tall, dark, with a full head of hair; he is not so tall, light complected, and balding. And yet, I know he's one and the same, I'll bet my Porsche on it."

"Not the Porsche, Arnstein. You've been wrong before."

"Not this time Davis. I put together a cross-reference of the similarities between the LA murders and ours; there are just too many common elements."

Arnstein's cellular phone began ringing just as Davis pulled up to the building entrance. He recognized Peter's voice, "I thought you were taking the day off." He listened attentively to his caller as Davis flashed his badge while giving the car keys to the doorman after he parked at a corner in the driveway.

"We're at the 1313 building right now. Why don't you meet us here," Arnstein invited, as he and his partner walked through to the main entrance.

"I'll tell the doorman to send you up," he finished, closing the compact phone and slipping it into his pocket.

"Who was that?" Davis asked.

"Someone I want you to meet," Arnstein replied as he identified himself to the doorman, instructing him to admit Peter Dumas when he arrived. The two men walked past the front desk into the impressive marble lobby to the South Tower elevators.

When they arrived on the 17th floor, nothing gave hint to the bloody drama that unfolded just a few nights earlier, except for the yellow tape draped across one of the three doorways on the floor.

Davis pulled the tape as he unlocked the door and they entered. It was as quiet as a tomb and despite a wall of windows; the apartment was dark in the gray morning light. Black powder, chalk markings and a myriad of smells, welcomed them, compliments of the crime unit's earlier investigation.

"OK, you be Playmore, I'll be the killer," Arnstein offered.

"You're on. Let's start at the door."

They walked back to the entrance. Davis played with the key and walked in ahead of Arnstein. "This condo, blah, blah, blah," he said turning his head back to keep eye contact with his buyer, directly behind. "She had to turn the lights on as she walked into each room to give him the pitch," he continued as he enacted what he believed Terry Playmore's final steps might have been.

Arnstein agreed, "You're right. Most times I've been with a real estate agent, they flip on room lights and then let you walk in after them. It makes sense, but I don't think it's very smart to walk ahead of someone you don't know when you're showing a condo."

"If I were the killer, I'd attack her in a small room. Less of a chance that she could get away from me, or try to fight."

He followed Davis first to the living room and dining area, then to the kitchen. When they came to the second bedroom, Davis turned on the lights and then walked to the guest bath. Just as he reached for the light switch, he was jerked backward; Arnstein had one arm around him in a chokehold, while digging his hand, dagger-like, into Davis's back.

"She was expecting him to be in the bedroom," Arnstein said releasing his grip. "He caught her off guard…a stab to her back… she reacted to the sudden pain arching backward, he grabbed her hair and sliced her throat, then he continued stabbing as she fell forward."

"She didn't have a chance to fight back."

A knock on the door interrupted them.

"That's got to be Peter," Arnstein said as he went to open the door for his new best friend, leaving Davis to continue the hunt for anything that could possibly have been missed or misinterpreted.

As Davis directed his flashlight to highlight the edge of the inlaid carpeting where it met the baseboard, he noticed a flash at the corner just left of the entrance to the bathroom. He was on his hands and knees when Arnstein returned with Peter.

"You find something?" Arnstein asked.

"I think so," he used a pair of tweezers to retrieve a small object deep in the corner. Seconds later, he rose to his knees holding something between the long metal tweezers, held gingerly between his finger and thumb. "Did Playmore wear contacts?" he asked rising to his full six-foot-four-inch frame, suddenly aware of an elfin creature with a shock of white hair standing nobly next to Arnstein.

"What did you find?" Arnstein asked.

"A hard lens. Tinted." He said placing it carefully into a small evidence bag. Not missing a beat, he turned toward Arnstein and his friend,

"You must be Peter Dumas." Davis shook Peter's extended hand, surprised at the firmness of his handshake.

"You must be Davis," Peter smiled.

"Now that's great detection!" he laughed.

Peter responded with his laugh, deep and throaty, one that would rarely be attributed to a man with a small, lithe frame, as Peter's.

Arnstein began reporting Peter's history with the LAPD bringing Davis up to speed on the agreed plan of action when his mobile started to ring. "It's Mac," Arnstein said to the men.

Peter, meanwhile, walked the condo pausing to focus on sights, sounds and smells from another time. He breathed deeply, the smell of death like a cloud, but one generously seasoned with a scent becoming particularly familiar to him.

Again, he thought, *Boucheron is here.*

Arnstein finished his call and walked up to Davis who was watching Peter as he moved silently on little cat feet, listening, pausing, anticipating. Then with a sudden movement, he turned sharply, as if in response to a cry or perhaps to someone shouting his name from afar.

As the two men spoke in whispers, Peter walked to the guest bathroom, his head hanging. He stood a few moments then walked back to the living room and held onto the top of the wingback chair where Terry had greeted Patti Polk, head in hand.

He began speaking, inaudibly at first, "She actually believed he was seriously interested in what she was saying." His voice rising indignantly, "She had no expectation of evil; her gullibility was her demise."

He turned to Arnstein, almost pleading, "It's as though she were with two people. I sense a dichotomy of feeling, uncontrollable anger, and melancholy knowledge of guilt. It's an unbroken succession of emotion, love to hate."

He stopped suddenly, then almost as an afterthought, whispered thoughtfully, "The killer could be a twin or have multiple personalities."

"Whatever he is, Peter, he's on a roll leaving very little behind to identify him."

Peter stared beyond the condo's terrace at the blue-grey rush of waves pounding the sand at the Oak Street beach. He hesitated, a few steps away from the French doors, his fear of heights overwhelming his need to secure a peaceful balance that nearness to water brought him.

Arnstein watched with understanding, recognizing the depth of feeling that death and violence could unleash when it walked in and out of one's mind. Peter's face told the story of surprise and unconscionable pain that Terry Playmore endured in the final moments of her life. Arnstein chose to break Peter's memory thread to the past.

"Peter, could this 'dichotomy of feeling' simply be the difference between Terry and her killer."

Peter turned, shaking away his uninvited memories, "No, no, there were three people here. Three distinct personalities. Two bodies, yet three diametrically separate egos. If not a twin, our killer is a tortured soul with two faces, one for evil and one for revenge."

CHICAGO
SUSANNA MEETS HER NEW ASSISTANT

32

The temperature had dropped, and the wind was bitter cold as Susanna crossed Chestnut Street toward the Water Tower. She pulled the full collar of her fur coat tight around her neck, shrouding her ears up to the brim of a matching fur hat. She resembled most of the shoppers on the street who bared only sunglassed eyes and a peak of nose.

Her decision to finish shopping before meeting Ty and Pippa for lunch became an excellent diversion. It put Susanna in a real holiday mood, and what's more, she managed to buy a final three gifts before heading next door to the Ritz Hotel. She hoped Chris would like the cashmere pullover; it was chocolate brown, his favorite color, at least she thought it was, considering it was the color of his car, his living room walls and most of the suits in his closet.

Relieved to be leaving the building, she inched her way through the crowds, past the cosmetic counters to the back entrance of the building. *And they keep insisting the economy is going to the dogs,* she thought to herself. *They ought to visit the Water Tower Mall.*

When Susanna arrived at the Ritz lobby, several floors above the hotel entrance, she found Ty and Pippa seated near the bar. She began walking toward them just as Ty began to wave.

He greeted her with a kiss on the cheek and then introduced Pippa Kaye-Goody, a tall, willowy blonde with brown eyes, almost as dark as night. Susanna nodded and sat in the chair between her two lunch companions.

"I'll have a Cabernet," she said to the waiter who appeared with drinks for Ty and Pippa just as she settled in her chair.

"Good shopping, Susanna?" Ty asked as he helped her stack her packages on the empty seat.

"Just a few things for Chris."

"Well then, why don't we get our lunch order out of the way, and we can get down to business," Ty responded, confident that enough pleasantries had passed.

"I'll just have a Cobb salad," Susanna offered.

"Pippa?"

"I think I'll have the Cobb, too," she purred, in a smoky-throated voice.

Susanna, considered by friends a confident, take-charge kind of woman, seemed a trifle intimidated by Pippa's body language. There was no I-am-an-assistant-here-for-your-approval stance; approval was the last thing Pippa Kaye-Goody was seeking. The 20-something young woman telegraphed intelligence, power and an unyielding sense of self.

Susanna did not have a good feeling about her new assistant. "Tell me, Pippa, how did you and Terry get together?" she asked.

"She knew my stepmother in Texas," she drawled.

"I'm surprised, Terry never mentioned she was even considering an assistant."

"We actually just began discussing the option," she answered staring directly at Susanna, almost daring her to disagree.

"Do you have a license?"

"Yes."

Oh, this is going to be fun, Susanna thought to herself turning suddenly to Ty. "Well Ty, since this is your party, let's have your game plan."

Without a pause, Ty announced the company proposal. "I certainly don't want to see you overburdened Susanna, so I've suggested that you and I personally call upon all of Terry's sellers to reassure them that Terry's accident will not affect the sale of their property. We'll explain that two people will take on Terry's responsibilities—you and an agent assistant who will manage the day to day paperwork, ad placement, and appointment scheduling."

"Terry's *accident,*" she repeated, ignoring the other content of his freight train delivery.

"Susanna, we don't want to remind our clients that a murder took place in one of your listings now, do we?"

"Fine," she answered.

"Now for compensation. Terry's listings are written at a 6% commission giving us, as the listing office, 3.5%, and the cooperating office, 2.5%. If we sell the property in-house, you will receive your regular split of the 3½ percent amount less a 25% referral fee. If the selling agent is from another office, we will take 20% off the top of our listing side, and you will get your regular split on the balance.

'It's a great deal, Susanna. $8.6 mil in listings and Pippa will do most of the work for you, showings, ads, the works. All you do is give her the OK on paperwork and negotiate the deals.

"What do you say?"

Susanna picked up the wine goblet the waiter had placed before her and said, "I get my regular split on the full 3 ½ if we sell in-house. And you get 10% off the top if it's not in-house. Take it or leave it." She took a sip of wine not sure if she was drinking to calm her shaking hands, or only because the ruby red liquid was inviting her to taste.

Pippa, not having expected any hint of negotiation on Susanna's part curled her lips upward ever so slightly and watched with newfound interest.

"I don't know, Susanna. I'll have to speak with corporate," Ty responded, nervously picking at his nail.

Susanna smiled and took an even longer second sip of her Cabernet.

To keep the conversation amicable, Ty launched a series of inane utterings that focused on anything other than real estate. He was surprised and angry that Susanna questioned the compensation package on the table for handling Terry's business. *Who does she think she is, bargaining for pennies from someone who's dropping over $8 million worth of business into her lap.*

Ty knew though that Terry's clients were familiar with Susanna, and would feel comfortable with the change; an unknown agent could jeopardize the listings and his bottom line.

Pippa watched Susanna and Ty throughout lunch. She rarely spoke, responding only to direct questions and always with answers as brief as possible. There was an awareness about her that spoke a maturity far beyond her years. She was like a cat, sensual in her movement, commanding with her eyes, and very comfortable in her surroundings. She dressed expensively: her suit, an Escada pinstripe with short skirt revealing chorus girl legs; her black leather boots, Manolo Blahniks; her jewelry, real.

When the waiter came with coffee, Susanna took a pass, offering the excuse of a new client meeting. She stood to say her goodbyes and offered her hand to Pippa, "It was a pleasure. I look forward to working with you if Ty and I can come to an agreement."

Pippa shook Susanna's hand and smiled her Cheshire kind of smile. Ty nodded and helped Susanna with her coat and packages, then he and Pippa watched her leave.

CHICAGO
A NEW CLIENT

33

The receptionist at the front desk announced Matthew Stark's arrival just minutes after Susanna arrived at the office. She answered her phone with a request that Chuwana offer him coffee and direct him to the front conference room as she gathered a folder and a few pens. Susanna did not want to appear unprepared, professionally or personally, before meeting this man for whom she already felt an intense dislike.

She checked her lipstick in the mirror on her desk and then hurried to the conference room, confident that Matthew Stark was not a man who appreciated waiting...for anyone.

When Susanna entered, a tall man with a shock of white hair was studying the framed Brueghel print on the wall. *This cannot be Stark*, she thought to herself. She was prepared for a short, balding, portly man, pompous and above all, impatient. However, there was nothing short, balding and portly about the man slowly turning to her. He didn't have a pompous air either, and he certainly did not look impatient. What's more, he was good-looking, incredibly so.

He smiled a languid smile as he extended his hand. She returned the smile, "I'm Susanna Ryerson, Mr. Stark."

His handshake was firm and confident and seemed to linger a second or two longer than necessary, at least that is what the warmth rising in her face led her to believe. What's more, her discomfort increased under the unceasing directness of his gaze.

She placed her folder on the conference table and began assembling papers to regain control. When she looked up, Stark was still staring at her. Ignoring the stare, and with businesslike aplomb, she began her standard delivery, "I usually begin this process with a few questions, if you don't mind."

He nodded and settled himself in the chair next to her, close enough for Susanna to inhale a crisp scent about him that reminded her of a cold, crisp New England morning.

His answers were brief, yet complete; what he lacked in verbiage he more than compensated with long, steady stares. Susanna managed short glimpses of him with each question, conscious of his penetrating eyes.

"Well, based on your needs and time frame, I'd say there are only a few buildings with condos that might work for you. One Mag Mile has a few units in your price range, and they don't require major overhauling. And of course, 1313 Lake Shore."

"That building has balconies, isn't that correct?"

"Yes, and there are 2 units available right now, other than mine which is off the market indefinitely. One of the units is vacant and would work with your time constraints. If you liked it, we could push a closing to under 30 days."

"OK, when can I see them?"

"How's tomorrow?"

"Fine. I'm free all day."

"Great, I'll call you as soon as I firm up appointments." She rose and extended her hand, "It's been a pleasure."

He took her hand in both of his and looked at her again with his slow smile, "The pleasure's been mine. Till tomorrow." He released her hand, turned, and left Susanna standing quietly, slowly inhaling then exhaling an inaudible *WOW*.

She packed up her papers suddenly aware that she knew little about Matthew Stark, in fact, hardly more than she surmised after their phone conversations. She knew he was returning to Chicago from Manhattan's Upper East Side, and one of New York's most prestigious financial institutions gave him the green light for any property he elected to purchase, *in writing*.

Without question, he was a man of few words, and certainly one of the most interesting men she had met in the last 5 years—as well as one of the better-looking ones. *This is one buyer I can't wait to see again*, she thought. Ironically, it was the first buyer she had not looked forward to meeting, at all.

CHICAGO
THE END OF THE DAY

34

It was snowing when Susanna left her office at the Water Tower, and she was happy to see the beginning of a promised accumulation. She loved the blanket of white that erased the dirt and dinginess of the city, and she loved the lights sparkling through the lacy cape of snow atop the trees on Michigan Avenue.

Winter was her favorite time in the city, especially late in the evening when the streets were hushed, and the stores closed; there was something magical about it. Even as a little girl she imagined a world of dolls and mannequins awakening inside the stores, alive and excited, ready to begin their day. And like Cinderella at the ball, they were bound by the clock that would announce a new shopping day when they would again freeze with smiled poses to await the shoppers.

She stopped at the deli for a take-out salad, opting not to cook that night. A small loaf of French bread and some fruit for breakfast completed her purchase. Then, she slowly walked the two blocks home, recalling the two new people who had entered her life that day: Matthew Stark, a man whom she would like to know better, and Pippa Kaye-Goody, a woman whom she would prefer not to know at all.

Stark...she was instantly attracted to him, and not just his height or his good looks. He had a face with a history, good and bad, and oh, the secrets she could sense that he kept. Besides, he was a Midwesterner; she could hear it in his voice. He was not from out east; he belonged here, yet she wondered why he lived there and more importantly, why he was coming back.

For the first time in a long time, Susanna felt an instinctive connection that just might possibly be worth allowing to blossom. *Well, Mr. Stark, I think you and I are about to have an adventure,* she thought, suddenly recalling Peter's reading about a man with hair like his own who would be fond of her. *A romantic relationship, if she allowed it, isn't that what Peter said,* she mused.

Of course, when it came to Pippa Kaye-Goody no one had given Susanna any warnings, yet she was certain that something was not right and planned to do some checking about the young woman. She simply could not believe that Terry seriously considered Pippa as an assistant, especially since Terry had never mentioned it.

When she walked into her Lake Shore Drive co-op, Garry, the night door person greeted her with his smile and a 'Welcome home, Ms. Ryerson.' It was a simple statement, but one that made her smile each time Garry made his welcoming pronouncement.

A giant holiday tree, complete with hundreds of mini lights held court in the soaring lobby of the building's entry, shielded from the falling snow by two walls of 25-foot high glass panels. It was an incredible sight: the lake's blackness, the city lights, the star-filled sky, the snow, all framing a tree of light.

Oh, what we need is Handel's Messiah...here...now, she thought, as the elevator door quietly closed and took her upstairs.

CHICAGO

35

Susanna tossed her mail on the hall table and checked for messages on her home phone. There were three.

Corporate, according to Ty, agreed to Susanna's demands regarding Terry's listings; *I knew they would,* she thought.

Pippa would like to meet with her on Thursday.

Matthew Stark asked that she push the 1313 Lake Shore Drive showings to as late as possible on Thursday as he had an unexpected meeting scheduled and wouldn't be available until after 3 PM. *Darn it, now I 've got reschedule 3 appointments!*

She pulled up her call list and in a surprising 15 minutes was able to move two of the showings without a problem, but if she included the condo on Michigan Avenue, there would be a 45-minute gap. The listing agent said if Susanna's client didn't care to wait, a last-minute cancellation would be no problem. Susanna confirmed the time slot and finished with an "I owe you!"

She had barely replaced the phone in its cradle when the sound of its shrill ring startled her. She picked it up once again, and a rushed "hello" escaped from her lips.

"That was quick! Were you sitting on the phone, Susanna?"

"I just hung up with an agent, Peter," she said, immediately recognizing his voice. "When did you get in?"

"Last night. I'm leaving town again, so I just wanted to confirm lunch on Friday?"

"Of course! Tucci?"

"I'll meet you there at one. I have quite a bit to tell you," Peter said, a serious tone in his voice.

"Me too. See you at one!"

Eager to get business out of the way, Susanna left a message for Pippa confirming a Thursday morning meeting, and another message for Ty requesting that he leave Terry's listing files on her desk. Then she hit the computer to work up a Comparative Market Analysis for Matthew Stark. The breakdown of condos that were active, under contract and recently sold would give him an idea of values in the buildings she was showing. It was an incredible range of prices considering that every unit had spectacular lake views.

Of course, she knew there were so many other factors that influenced the price. A few of the units at 1313 Lake Shore had been totally rehabbed with hardwood floors, gourmet kitchens, and marble baths, while others were in original condition, including those with avocado-green shag carpeting.

More and more it was becoming her experience that many buyers in the million plus range were bottom feeders, looking for the 'deal of the century' so they ignored value and just took the lowest sold price to use as an excuse for an insulting initial offer.

She felt much differently when she first got her broker's license. Her early buyers were young and trusting, looking to her for advice. They actually considered all the features, the location, condition. They didn't pass on a home because it was minus a Sub-Zero refrigerator or a Dacor range.

Susanna lost her real estate idealism, somewhere in the late 90's; now, she was losing her enthusiasm. The longer her tenure in the business, and the heavier the hitter with whom she worked, the more she was treated like a tour guide, a chauffeur, an administrative assistant, and even a maid.

Of course, Susanna had much to be grateful for—some of her best friends were once her clients, but they had grown with her, and the business relationship had matured into beautiful friendships that she cherished. However, she often thought her son was right; it was time to leave the business, time to regroup and explore other options once again. It was something she was thinking about, more and more.

LOS ANGELES
HARRY MEETS BREWSTER'S ASSISTANT

36

Krachewsky finally tracked Candace Morley, Amanda Brewster's assistant; she was due at the station at noon. He had planned on flashing his badge for quick answers to his questions, but he was hungry, so he decided to ask if she would join him for lunch. Much to his surprise, she accepted.

It was a pleasant day in the low 60s, the sun was shining, and traffic was the way Harry liked it, fast and light. Lunch would be a nice break. He indicated the diner just up the street from the station, and they walked toward it chatting small talk.

"You live in Studio City, Miss Morley?"

"Yes, but not for long. My lease is up in 3 months, and my roommate is leaving. I really cannot afford the rent by myself. Studio City is the best place to live, but not on the salary I'm making today."

"Ms. Brewster paid good, huh?"

"I made more than twice what I'm earning, now."

"Whew! you have to be making, what, at least 30K right now?"

"Thirty-five! She was paying me almost 100k."

"Wow. I knew real estate agents could make a lot of money, but if she could pay you 100 grand, she had to be pulling in a fortune." Harry opened the door for Candace, and they chose a booth at the back near a window.

"I don't know what Amanda earned, but she never hurt for anything, and I mean, anything. She developed a very unique system for getting clients."

Candace was interrupted by a tall, bleached blonde holding two menus and wearing a name tag identifying her as Sally. She dropped the menus on the table and waited for an immediate order. Telegraphing her impatience with rapid gum chewing, Sally proceeded to dart glances rapidly from Harry to Candace.

Ignoring the menu, Harry responded first. "I know what I want. A big juicy hamburger with extra blue cheese, a thick slice of onion and some Jalapenos on the side."

"I'll just have a bowl of the minestrone, thank you."

"Two coffees?" Sally asked.

"Just water for me," Candace replied.

Harry nodded 'yes' then turned his attention to Candace.

"What kind of system did she have?"

"Amanda hired full-time researchers who scouted areas for homes with construction trucks in the driveway. They made nice with the contractors and entered the home improvements into a master database."

"So, she knew the homes inside and out?"

"Definitely. The city tax records gave her all the ownership details, and the researchers provided the inside blanks. They even checked out interiors of homes with moving vans out front. And when Amanda had a want from a client, she scanned her database of house histories until she found a match."

"What if it wasn't for sale?"

"That was the easy part. Amanda would personally introduce herself to the owners, and explain that she had a client who wanted their home. She'd name a price well over market value that also included her commission and 7 out of 10 times she had a deal. Of course, it was dependent upon buyer approval. Then she'd contact her client and tell them the price, adding a buyer commission.

"She never advertised, and she always got a double bubble."

"Double bubble?" asked Harry.

"Commission from both sides, the buyer and the seller."

"Sharp cookie! How long did you work for Brewster?"

"About 4 years. I met her when I was a receptionist for a real estate firm; they carried her license. About a year after she took her broker's exam, she left to start her own agency and called me. Offered me ten-thousand more than I was earning. That wasn't chicken feed, so I joined her."

"Was she good to work for?"

"The best! I had so much freedom, and that just made me work harder, and the harder I worked, the more money she paid me. But it wasn't just the money, she was so smart. I learned a lot from her. I haven't had a boss like that since."

"How did she get her clients?"

"Referrals. Amanda said the best thing she ever did was finding the perfect house for a big Hollywood producer, and introducing him to the perfect casting agent. He became her one man, word-of-mouth, public relations agent. And it just grew, client by client because she knew her market, and I am not just talking houses.

"Amanda knew the film culture. When anyone got a picture deal, she knew about it. She sent congratulations, then a gift. She was an incredible promoter. And her contact file, now that was something else. It was a Who's Who, What, Where, When and Why. Producers would call her, actors would call her. She really was the "Realtor for the Stars.""

Without notice, Sally unceremoniously dropped a bowl of minestrone and one plated hamburger, piled high with fries, before Candace and Harry. He immediately popped a Jalapeño pepper into his mouth, rolled his eyes and asked, "How did she pull her data?"

"She was smart; she hired beautiful and struggling actresses who were college-educated. Some scouted the party circuit, others researched houses, and she paid them all very well. Of course, anyone who needed cash, or a favor was quick to sell her information, too."

"Who didn't like her?"

"I don't think anyone really liked her. Most people were afraid of her because she knew so much, but I don't think anyone hated her enough to kill her."

"Well, did anyone feel as though she got 'em a bad deal?"

"No way. She was probably the most successful Realtor in LA If you wanted a quick sale and the best price, she was the one to call."

"How about any people who worked for her, anyone leave on a bad note?"

"Not really. Even when Amanda was unhappy with an employee, she always gave 'em a bonus when they were let them go. No one kills a money tree in Hollywood. Although, she said thoughtfully, there was one person who had a beef with her. Amanda hired her for the party circuit. I believe her name was Patsy or Hetta, or something like that; I never met her. She called Amanda once, screaming about some producer who hit on her.

"When I gave Amanda the message, she told me to forget about it, that she'd spoken to her and let her go."

"Ms. Morley, did you talk to the fake director who met her at the house."

"Several times. Whoever he was, he was very good. His speech, his knowledge of Hollywood, and the names he dropped. I did not doubt him.

"I checked his financial situation for Amanda, but I was checking on the real Scalparelli, so he checked AOK."

"What happened to all of her files?"

"We went through her computer, and nothing showed up that wasn't archived in the system at the office, so her attorney erased her hard drive. He has all the records and archives from the office."

"Who gets her assets?"

"Everything she owned went to charity, most of it to a women's shelter. She didn't have any family."

Sally appeared, offering more coffee, but Harry passed and asked for the check.

"Was she from LA, Candace?"

"Amanda? No! She was Midwestern all the way, but you would never know it. There was an East Coast air about her, very formal, even spoiled."

"Do you know where in the Midwest?"

"It might have been Michigan. I don't remember. Her mom was a doctor, and her dad died when Amanda was ten or twelve. That's all I know. She just never talked about her life before coming to LA I brought it up several times; she just changed the subject."

Harry left the tab plus a 5 dollar tip on the table, then he and Candace walked out to the street.

"You know, it's been several weeks, but I still can't believe she's gone. I never was afraid of her; I felt sorry for her. No family...no real friends. I think she had a lot of sadness inside; she had secrets, but didn't share them with anyone and, frankly, I don't believe she had any desire to."

"Just thought of one other question, Candace. What kind of perfume did Brewster wear?"

"Bellogia. It's by Caron. Amanda loved it. In fact, when they stopped making it, Amanda had Saks pull up every bottle in the U.S., and she bought them all."

"Did she ever try a different perfume?"

"Well, just before she died someone mailed her a gift with a 'Thank You' card, unsigned. It was a bottle of Boucheron. Either she tried it the day before or the day she died. She didn't like it and asked me if I did; I loved it, so she gave it to me."

"Do you still have the box or the bottle?"

"The box I tossed, but I still have the bottle."

"Thanks, Candace. If we have any other questions, I'll be in touch."

THURSDAY
DECEMBER 22ND

WISCONSIN
PETER AND ARNSTEIN BEGIN THEIR TRIP

37

Peter had been up for more than an hour waiting for Arnstein to arrive. He had been unable to sleep, unable to erase the non-stop images and sounds bombarding his subconscious.

When sleep failed him, he positioned himself cross-legged in a corner of the room and began to breathe deeply until finally able to transcend the bloody clutter in his brain. He sat there until Arnstein called with the alert that he would be out front in 15 minutes.

It was a dull, cold and gray day, not particularly conducive to a long drive to Wisconsin, and Peter knew that the worst would be realized when they arrived at their destination. He would need all of his concentration.

He poured the last cup of coffee from the silver server so graciously presented and delivered to his apartment by the Drake Hotel's room service staff. Like his mother before him, Peter maintained a home at the Drake Tower. It suited him— the old-world elegance of the co-op with all of its bonuses: mail delivered directly to one's door, the staffed elevators, the services available from the Drake Hotel and of course, the Palm Court.

Peter was an advocate of the almost obsolete, yet wonderfully delicious tradition: afternoon tea. How civilized, he believed, to nibble on bite-sized portions of cucumber sandwiches, egg salad, and salmon triangles, plus an array of beautiful chocolate, and sweet cheese delicacies, all treats for the tongue.

He could survive on the chocolate morsels, stuffed with crème and fruit fillings. He always had a sweet tooth, one he satisfied with gusto, particularly at the Palm Court in New York.

When the phone rang announcing Arnstein's arrival, Peter had already left his suite. He waited at the elevator area, gleaming in brass and beeswax-polished wood paneling.

Except for the uniformed operator, the elevator was empty when the doors opened, but a few floors later he was joined by a large man, most assuredly in his middle to late 60s, accompanied by a tall woman, wrapped in sable, and at least, 30 years his junior. They did not speak, and yet they spoke volumes. She had the look of expectation unrealized, while her companion glowed with the knowledge that he received so much more than he could ever hope to repay.

"I'd like to stop after breakfast, at Bulgari," she said flatly. "I saw something quite lovely in the window."

"Of course," he answered, obediently as the elevator doors opened. Peter smiled, ever so slightly, as the couple turned toward the Tower's interior entrance to the hotel, while he turned right to East Lake Shore Drive where the doorman greeted him with particular fondness, knowing Peter's penchant for big tips. When asked if he would like a cab, Peter smiled and nodded 'no' then crossed the street to the Porsche idling at the northeast corner.

A light snow had begun falling, but it did not halt the early morning walkers and runners passing before the Porsche, on route to their path along the lakefront. Only the serious athlete braved the early morning cold, and Chicago bred an unusually high number of them, resplendent in their Patagonia and North Face outerwear. Gloved and capped, some with face masks and Oakley glasses, they moved with a rush of breath visible in the cold air.

Peter opened the passenger door and slid into Arnstein's car. "Good morning, David. I see you are prepared for a long drive," he offered, noting several cups of coffee in a convenient holder.

"Good morning!" he replied, more cheerfully than one would expect at 7:00 in the morning. "One of those cups is for you, Peter. Cream and sugar are in the bag."

"How thoughtful," Peter commented. "One can never have enough coffee on a cold, gray morning."

"Is that an *I wish we weren't going* tone in your voice, Peter?" Arnstein probed.

"Not wholly. I react with disdain to the long car trip. As to our murder, I look forward to turn assumptions into fact, and discover other pieces for our murder puzzle."

"I'm not as confident as you are, at least about any puzzle pieces that fit together, but we'll soon find out. Look, why don't you just lay back and catch a few zzz's. I've got a great collection of cd's if you want music, Blues to Beethoven."

"I would enjoy a little music," Peter answered and began searching through the CD holder that Arnstein tossed him. Peter was impressed with the eclectic choice of music: Vivaldi, Tchaikovsky, Pachelbel, Sinatra, Enya, Streisand, Santana, but he stopped at Flemming, and opted for the incredible Renee's Bel Canto.

He took a sip of coffee, closed his eyes, and waited for her magnificent voice to blanket him in the low-slung Porsche.

WISCONSIN
THE BEIDERMEISTER SCENE

38

Peter woke as Arnstein pulled into the Police Station just off Route 41. "Did I actually sleep the entire trip?", Peter asked with a yawn.

"You certainly did. Thank God Renee Flemming doesn't have that effect on me," he laughed as he slid the Porsche into a visitor's spot.

"Let me assure you David, Renee Flemming does not put me to sleep. I had a difficult night; I have a feeling that I've forgotten something."

"Well, let's hope you remember it before we head home. I would love to have some company on the trip back," David said as they left the car and headed to the station.

Inside, Arnstein flashed his badge and asked to see Detective Wallins, the lead on the Beidermeister murder. In a matter of minutes, a tall, distinguished African American walked toward them holding an expandable file.

"Arnstein?" he asked to neither of the men directly, "I'm Wallins."

After introductions, the trio headed to one of the interrogation rooms where Wallins pulled a stack of reports and photos from his file.

"After you called I pulled everything we had. Don't know if there is anything here that will help you, but you're welcome to look through it. I've never seen a murder like it," he said handing Arnstein a stack of 8 x 10s. "It was brutal."

Arnstein skimmed through the photos of Ruann Beidermeister's murder sculpture. Like Wallins, he too had not seen anything as hateful or vicious perpetrated on another human being. He passed the photos to Peter.

"Did you have any suspects?" Arnstein asked.

"Not one. She didn't have too many friends, and as for enemies, they were the garden variety. We even went back to her hometown in Dallas; she married a salesman there and then moved to Wisconsin. He walked out on her eventually, leaving her with two kids. Hard working woman...she was a hairdresser during her lean years as an agent."

"The kids any help?"

"Nope. They hadn't seen her for two years before she died. Both are married and live on the West Coast."

"Could I have their names?"

"No problem," he said, opening a three-ring binder and removing a single sheet of paper, "I'll make a copy."

For the first time since they entered the room, Peter looked up and directed a question to Wallins, "Who reported her missing?"

"No one. One of the neighbors went to the barn to get a few bales of hay. They called us."

"Where was her car?"

"Parked right in front of the main house. The Carters, they're the owners, were out of the country. Left several cars parked in the driveway, so Beidermeister car didn't arouse any suspicion."

"When did the neighbors find her?" Arnstein interjected.

"Second day after the Open House, late in the afternoon."

"And no one reported her missing before that?" Arnstein shook his head in disbelief speculating if her children would at least grieve for her. He was reminded of his own solitary existence. Would fate be beneficent and give him someone who would remember him.

"The victim lived alone," Wallins answered. "And according to her receptionist, she never worked in the office the Monday after an Open House; she kept tabs through her Voice and email. And Tuesday is the day brokers set aside for broker open houses, so they just thought she would be in later that day.

"We figure she was killed at the tail end of the Sunday Open House. There's a sign-in sheet among those papers," he pointed to the folder he had given Arnstein.

"We checked everyone who signed. The last name on the sheet was Colin Axman, but he does not exist, and neither does his phone number. According to the couple who signed in ahead of him, he was not there when they left about 10 minutes to four. He had to be waiting for them to leave. Oh, and they don't recall the Open House sign being on the road pointing to the driveway when they left, but remember it being there when they drove into the property. That's how they knew where to turn."

"Any prints on the sheet," Arnstein asked.

"Plenty, but we accounted for each of them. Frankly, we don't have squat. The drive was gravel, no tire tracks. It hadn't snowed for over a week, no reliable footprints. And as for the barn, the owners sponsored a winter hunt before they left. There must have been 100 people walking in and out of that barn, not to mention the horses and everyone who comes with them. We had a forensic nightmare.

"I'll be happy to call the owners if you'd like to see the barn. They padlocked it and haven't been inside since."

"Yes, we would," Arnstein said looking at Peter who nodded in agreement.

Peter, who had been listening intently, quietly asked, "Did she die quickly?"

"As far as our ME determined, yes. Her killer stabbed her in the back then slit her throat. She was definitely dead when he started carving her like a turkey."

"One other question, did she get any gifts at the office just before her death?"

"There's nothing in the follow-up reports, but I can check for you."

Both men stood and followed Wallins to an area at the back of the station where he photocopied several pages and photographs that he had removed from the file for Arnstein.

After calling and confirming that the owners of the Carter farm were indeed available, Wallins made his goodbyes and gave Arnstein and Peter directions to Ruann Beidermeister's final real estate showing.

CHICAGO
PIPPA KAYE-GOODY

39

Since she scheduled Stark's first appointment for 4 PM, Susanna had more than enough time to meet with Pippa and make a noon Pilates class.

Pippa, fresh from having her nails done, was waiting in the conference room for Susanna. It had been a particularly relaxing day for her, beginning with a workout at her club followed by a late breakfast at the Ritz. Afterward, she opted not to do any shopping on the Avenue as the temperature outside had dropped to the twenties with a wind chill of two below zero. Instead, she chose to pamper her body with a facial, massage, pedicure and manicure at Elizabeth Arden's.

She was very much a California girl at heart, preferring light winds and convertible temperatures to Chicago's sometimes unbearable winter weather, but still, she was a Chicagoan in her soul, and even the warm winds of the Pacific weren't enough to keep her in that sunny state.

Pippa's love affair with the city began during her years at Northwestern University. A double major in drama and literature saw her haunt Chicago stages, from start-up theatricals to touring companies of Broadway hits.

No longer the ingénue, her pleated skirts, designer jeans and skinny sweaters took a maturity turn. Now silk blouses and sweaters, expensive suits, and designer shoes and bags were de rigueur, not to say she completely gave up her jeans.

Sitting in the conference room, skimming through the Wall Street Journal, she could have been mistaken for an upscale professional in search of a city home, as there was nothing, absolutely nothing about her that telegraphed 'I am a real estate agent.'

Yet, real estate was in her genes, perhaps more so than her lust for the theater. Her father was a major developer when he died, and his company was thriving; but his partner took Goody Homes far beyond the expectations her father had before his death. And now Pippa owned almost half of the company.

Parker Goody died at 57 years of age after meeting with his partner at the newest design in the Goody Home lineup. Shortly after speeding away for another meeting, his brakes failed, causing him to break through a guardrail and plunge into a lake. Unfortunately, his heart gave out as the car smashed into the water. He died instantly.

Pippa's loss was not a deeply personal one; Parker Goody was not the ideal father. He deposited Pippa in the arms of a nanny at the age of seven, when a fall down a flight of stairs took her mother's life. Daddy Dearest comforted himself in the arms of Letitia, his mistress, along with other women he bedded.

Boarding schools became Pippa's family after she turned 10 years old, but occasionally there would be a holiday spent with her father when he and Letitia were in town.

He had not planned to marry Letitia, but Parker Goody had formed more than a sexual partnership with his girlfriend; marriage was inevitable. They were partners in business as well, and Letitia more than earned the company's majority interest left to her in his will. He knew that his daughter was not focused on his dream to turn Goody Homes into a nationally recognized brand, so she did not get control. Nevertheless, he also acknowledged that she was a brilliant young woman who could be an asset to Letitia.

Pippa hated the woman who took the place of a mother she could not remember, yet missed. Moreover, she blamed her for her mother's death when she learned that Letitia had been her father's mistress while her mother was alive. As a result, she kept clear of the corporate office in Michigan, only visiting upon command from the woman who sat in her father's chair.

When Pippa closed the paper, Susanna was standing at the door.

"I didn't want to interrupt."

"I was just killing time," she exhaled with her deep, smoky voice as she tossed the paper in the corner wastebasket with a flash of red-hot color from her nails.

Susanna sat down and began pulling files, ignoring Pippa's flair for the dramatic. "I've pulled all of Terry's listings. Are you familiar with any of them?"

"As a matter of fact, I am."

"Oh," Susanna responded with surprise. "Did Terry go over them with you?"

"Literally, just before she died."

It was evident that Pippa was attempting to unnerve her, so she kept her voice calm and pressed on, "I still can't recall Terry mentioning you. Were you ever in the office?"

"No."

"Where did you meet to discuss real estate?"

"At a restaurant."

"I believe you said Terry went to school with one of your aunts?"

"No, my stepmother." she hissed.

Convinced that she would not learn much more than yes or no, Susanna decided to skip the interrogation and get down to business. "I'd like you to manage Terry's listings since you have a license."

Pippa nodded, and Susanna continued, "My name and number will be in the MLS, so appointment requests will come to me, but I'll forward them to your extension. You can schedule and show the properties. If anyone asks a question and you cannot find the answer in Terry's notes, tell the agent that you are my new assistant and you will get back to her. If anyone submits a contract, I will negotiate it. Of course, you certainly can be part of the negotiation if you like."

"Not particularly."

"Alright. I've drafted a note to all of Terry's sellers explaining that I am taking over her listing and that you will be assisting me. Chuwana will send the notes out today, and I'll call the sellers as well.

"All the information you need is in the listing folder—phone numbers, times not to show, etc. Please list all showing calls and give the agent a buzz the next business day for their client's feedback on the property. I give clients a weekly report of showings and comments.

"If you'd like we can go to the properties, and I will help you put together a crib sheet on the buildings and neighborhoods. Actually, it might be smart to schedule a Broker's Open and get there a little early."

"I'd like that," she drawled in that smoky voice.

"Fine, enter 3 of the properties for next Thursday, one at 9:30-11:30, one at 12-2 and the third from 2:30-4:30. Start with the listing that's the furthest north. I'll get you sheets with building specifics on the condos. Since Terry only had one single-family home, why don't you schedule it for an Open House the Sunday after New Year's, from 1-3."

"Where do I enter them?"

"Oh, I'm sorry. There is a scheduling book in the Resource Room. Chuwana will show it to you. If there is a request for a showing before we have an opportunity to go through the property, I'll do the showing with you. If you have any questions, give me a buzz. I have appointments this afternoon, but you can reach me by phone if you have any questions. Enjoy the rest of your day," she said lightly.

Pippa just gave her a long, cold stare and a slight nod. Susanna turned and hurried to her desk. She did not like Pippa; there was something unnatural about her.

CHICAGO
STARK SHOWINGS

40

Susanna hurried home, changed clothes, grabbed her gym bag and began her standard search for her gym shoes. There were several incongruities in Susanna's organized lifestyle: Never putting her gym shoes in the same location twice, was one of them. A ten-minute search resulted in a single shoe sighting under the bed; shoe number two surfaced in the hall closet.

With keys in hand, shoes on feet, she grabbed a jacket and headed to Fitflex, again opting to drive rather than walk the few blocks to her club, the light falling snow from the overcast sky contributing to her choice of transportation.

The class was just beginning when Susanna walked into the small studio where a handful of women were seated on rubber mats scattered around the room. She plopped down on a mat and pulled her knees to her chest, to stretch her back muscles.

To anyone watching, it would appear Pilates was natural and very gentle, but that was not the case. Improving deep-seated muscles took strength, concentration, proper breathing, and great control.

Susanna was introduced to the exercise program by a dancer friend, who explained that the concept was named after its developer, Joseph Pilates. She described his methods as the perfect balance of mind, body, and spirit. According to Jane, Pilates was a pioneer in the field of human physiology and was highly regarded among dancers, gymnasts, and athletes because his program had helped to heal many of their injuries.

One Pilates class and Susanna was hooked; after several, she saw dramatic results in her posture and flexibility—in a very short time period. As a result, she kept a mat at home, in the event she was unable to get to class.

After a 45-minute workout, she ended her session with the same stretch with which she began. Perspiration dripping from her face, she turned her clipped back hair into a mass of damp ringlets at her cheeks and neck. Perspired, yes, but she was invigorated and ready to conquer the world—well, after a hot shower of course, and a cup of green tea.

By 2:30 she was drinking her second cup and reading the business section of the Tribune. *If my mutual stocks continue to drop,* she thought, *I will be a pauper when I finally do retire. Stark had better buy something, and hopefully it will be expensive. Or better yet, Mossbach will offer me my old column at a substantial raise in pay.*

Earlier, she had left Stark a message that she would meet him in the 1313 lobby at 4 PM. Two units, other than her listing, were available, and she was quite certain he would like either one of them. She was saddened that her listing was unable to be seen; it would have been a perfect choice.

Lingering over her cup of tea, she considered the possibility that Stark could actually be the real estate ripper, as Chris so creatively tagged Terry's killer. *Impossible,* she thought, *he's too rude and too good looking to be a monster. But look at Bundy. He was good-looking, suave, friendly, and he butchered women. Not every killer looks like Manson.*

She was really frustrated. For once, an attractive man had aroused something in her that she hadn't felt in a long, long time; an interesting man who seemed relatively normal. "But is he," she said aloud. "And how can I be sure?" The only thing she was certain of was that she would learn everything she could about Matthew Stark, or die trying.

A cab was delivering his fare just as she left her building. "1313 Lake Shore, please," she told him as she scrambled inside for the 5-minute trip. The cabbie flipped the meter, made a hard right and followed the inner drive past Oak Street.

She loved this stretch of the drive, but would not trade her Streeterville location for it. There was an element of the Big Apple just east of Michigan Avenue between Chicago and Oak Streets, and she reveled in it; her proximity to Mag Mile shopping, her favorite restaurants, and the Lake. She would not give them up lightly.

For others, it could only be the Gold Coast. With its lovely row houses and Greystones, the ten-block expanse of Lake Shore Drive held court at the edge of Chicago's incredible lakefront.

When the cab deposited her at 1313, she saw that Matthew Stark was waiting at the doorman's desk. *Prompt, aren't you,* she thought as she paid the cabbie and turned to enter the building. He looked even better than their first meeting, but her thoughts kept returning to Bundy and she held back as much of her excitement as possible.

"Hi," she smiled. "You beat me, and I'm early!"

"My meeting ended earlier than expected, so I had time to read the paper, and then decided to walk over."

"Where are you staying?"

"At the Hancock in a friend's apartment," he answered.

"Convenient," she responded turning to the doorman.

"I'm Susanna Ryerson. Peg Willis is expecting me. She's the agent for 14M."

She motioned Stark to follow, and they walked to the North Tower entrance just as the doors swooped open. "Peg is the listing agent, and she'll be showing us the unit,"

Susanna explained. "We'll pick up a key from the doorman for the vacant unit on twenty-two; it's in the South Tower."

He nodded and followed her into the elevator. A little uncomfortable under his steady gaze, Susanna began her usual pitch for the building, "No other building on the drive has balconies the size of 1313's, Matthew, but I must admit the unit's square footage does include the balcony area. By the way, are you a swimmer?"

He nodded yes.

"This building has the most beautiful lap pool; the only pool that can beat it is in the Hancock, and the views are sensational." The elevator doors opened on the 14th floor, where Peggy Willis waited in the smartly appointed hall, interrupting her pitch.

Peggy took one look at Stark, ignored Susanna and opened her eyes brightly as she smiled an open mouth smile that left little to disguise her interest in Susanna's client. She inhaled deeply, and then exhaled a whispered *hello* in the sexiest southern voice she could muster. "My my, you certainly are a big ol' man. My name's Peggy, and you are?"

"My client, Mr. Stark," Susanna answered flatly.

"Oh Susanna, I didn't even see you, *darlin'*," she said dismissing her while directing Stark to the door ajar at the end of the hall.

Susanna shook her head in disbelief and followed the pair into the unit.

Peggy Willis was a legend on the Gold Coast. She looked to be fifty years old, but some of the old timers swore she was well past seventy. If they were right, Peggy had an astonishing plastic surgeon. As to her libido, that was legendary as well. It accounted, according to some, for sales records envied by every Realtor in the city. She was a little bit of a thing, barely 5 feet tall when not towering in her Manolo Blahniks. Plucked and perfumed, with a figure that defied gravity and hair masterfully styled, she always made an entrance, and with her southern drawl, it was usually an unforgettable one.

Stark followed Peggy as she described everything in the unit, remotely considered an upgrade; it was simply the value-added concept that all Realtors carried in their bag of tricks. When they came out of the second bedroom after a tour of the unit, they were bosom buddies, joking and laughing.

"Susanna, you didn't tell me that your client was a good ol' boy from Alabama!"

"I wasn't aware of that."

"It will be so nice havin' a fellow Southerner here in Chicago," she said turning to Stark, "Now you come on back, Matthew. This unit could be a sensational buy; my seller is very motivated! And it is so easy to show...I live in the building." The heat of her goodbye was palpable.

Susanna semi-smiled a thank you, then walked out of the unit for some fresh air, and to call for the elevator while Stark gave his farewell, "Susanna will call you with my decision, Peggy. It has been an experience."

Another owner on the floor exited her unit just as Stark left 14M. Recognizing Susanna, she exchanged pleasantries as they waited for the elevator. When learning that Stark was a prospective buyer, she extolled the benefits of living at 1313 for the entire trip to the first floor. She, too, was bedazzled by the likes of Mr. Stark.

Amazing, Susanna thought, how a man in his late 50s with a tan and weathered face could turn any woman into a flirting machine, while a tan and weathered 50-plus-year-old woman would simply be helped into the elevator.

Of course, she was no different; he bedazzled her as well. *Slim chance I have,* she thought, *I'm in my late forties; he probably hits on women my son's age.*

After retrieving the key from the doorman, the pair took the South-Tower elevators to 22C. Susanna suddenly realized that she had been chattering non-stop, so she paused and asked Stark what he thought of the building.

"I've always liked it. It is contemporary, yet it has the elegance of a traditional style. It's the way the columns engage the balconies. They're not just fixtures hanging on the building."

"You're right. It's probably the only building on the drive that incorporates the balconies so well in the design. Do I detect a lover of architecture?"

"Most assuredly," he answered, his eyes even bluer than Peter's, staring at her intently.

She turned quickly, and unlocked the door of the unit, convinced that her heart was beating loud enough to be heard. Stark walked ahead of her saying, "May I just roam?"

"Of course." She followed him in, leaving the door to the unit wide open. *My exit,* she thought, *just in case he is not what he seems.*

She pulled her mobile phone from her bag and surreptitiously pressed 911, making it ready for a quick dial; her pepper spray, tucked into her left-hand pocket, was ready to assault. *If he is the real estate ripper,* she thought, *at least I'll give him a fight.*

Stark walked through the unit quickly and then opened the doors to the balcony admitting a rush of cold air. "The woman who died, she was murdered in this tower, wasn't she?" he asked suddenly.

Susanna stopped, one hand clutching the pepper spray, the other feeling for the 'Send' button on her phone.

"Yes," she answered quickly.

"Did you know her?" he asked bringing an eerie silence to the room.

"Yes, ah yes. She was a friend," she said, her mouth bone dry.

"I'm sorry to hear that. She died in your listing, the one that's off the market, didn't she?" He walked deliberately toward her, his eyes zeroing in on hers. She took a step back.

A knock on the door rocketed through the room and left Susanna feeling as though a bullet had shattered her into a million sharp pieces. "Ms. Ryerson, it's the engineer," a voice with an Irish brogue called out, before entering the room. "The doorman said I'd find you here. He wasn't sure if you'd be going to another unit, so I came up to get the key. The owners just came in for the day, and they left their key at their home in the suburbs. Could I wait for it?" he finished.

Any other time, she would have joked with him, but not now. "Oh, I...I think we're finished, so we'll go down with you. Unless Matthew, you would like to go through once again," she offered nervously.

"No, I'm fine."

They walked out together.

LOS ANGELES

41

When Harry checked in with Mac and shared his Wednesday interview with Brewster's former assistant, he learned that absolutely none of the hair samples or prints from the Valli kill matched anything from the Brewster crime scene.

"Anything more on the jogger and the kid?" Harry asked.

"We ID'd the kid, he lives about 4 houses up the road. No fix on the jogger, yet. By the way, the trash detail found the towels and the shower curtain."

"You're kidding?"

"Nope, it looks like Peter hit a home run. A private scavenger whose regular route covers about six houses in that stretch picked them up. The driver directed us to the dumpsite and to the section where he dropped his load. Talk about timing! One more day and the curtain and towels would have been landfill."

"Anything on 'em?"

"Don't know yet."

"I'm heading back to Valli's office this morning to catch a few of the agents I missed...and get a little perfume info," he added begrudgingly.

"I'm sure Peter will appreciate that information," Mac laughed.

"You and that little twerp; he oughta be your partner."

"Come on Harry, Peter wouldn't begin to know how to work a case the way you do."

"OK, OK, you can quit the butter act. I'll meet you back at the office around lunch. And, you're buying!"

Mac laughed, as he picked up the phone to call Peter to let him and Arnstein know that they found the towels and the shower curtain from the Valli kill.

WISCONSIN
THE BARN

42

Wallins' directions took Arnstein down several two-laners into a secluded driveway that led to an impressive farmhouse. Giant pots waited in one area of the veranda encircling the house, ready for soil planting when and if spring ever arrived.

He walked up the path to the front entrance. A white-haired woman greeted him, holding a little boy with dark curls who stared at Arnstein intently through saucer-sized brown eyes.

"You must be the policeman Mr. Wallins called about," she stated.

"Yes, ma'am," he said showing her his badge.

"Hello mister," the little boy said clinging to his grandmother.

"What's your name, little guy?" Arnstein asked.

"Dabid," he answered with a big grin.

"I had a little 'Dabid' once," Arnstein said.

"Can he play with me?" the little boy asked.

"No, he went far away."

"Can I go and see him?"

"David, the policeman is very busy. He can't take you to see his little boy." Turning to Arnstein, the older woman continued, "I'm sorry. He is a little bored; his mom is shopping. This is the key to the barn padlock. Go around the house and follow the road all the way back past the cluster of trees, you can't miss it."

Arnstein took the keys, thanked her, then took little David's hand in his and shook it, "It was a pleasure meeting you, David. I wish I could take you to see my little David. I know he would have liked you."

"Bye, bye," the little boy said with a flash of a smile.

Arnstein walked away quickly overcome by the memory of his own baby, and all the smiles he would never see.

When he jumped into the car, Peter sensed a change in his demeanor but did not pursue an explanation for the source of the mood change. They drove to the barn in silence.

It was picture perfect, almost idyllic: snow covered the roof and the trees, now bereft of their bright green leaves; a small stream flowed nearby, the sound of the moving water, crisp and clear in the cold air. *It was not at all a place for murder*, Peter thought.

Arnstein pulled up next to the barn, exited the car, and then began navigating his Cole-Hahn's through the snowdrifts. Peter followed, pausing after a few steps, suddenly aware of the sound of tires turning on a gravel bed. It was a small car, he thought, judging by the sound of the tire turn. The wind was blowing; it was a warm December day, the day Ruann Beidermeister met her murderer.

Arnstein unlocked the padlock and opened the door to the cavernous barn, then waited for Peter who had walked into the clearing beside the copse. He marveled as Peter took small steps, pausing to listen to sounds from the past that only played in Peter's mind.

Peter heard the footsteps: two people walking away from the car, then one returning and away again; and finally, one returning. Alone. He filled his lungs with the cold air until it hurt, and again, the scent of Boucheron wafted through the morning cold. He turned suddenly and joined Arnstein at the barn door.

"Well, Peter, ready to go in?" Arnstein asked.

"Ready," Peter answered.

They walked inside, Arnstein fumbling for the light switch just as Ruann had, before him.

Peter maneuvered around Arnstein into the silence of the barn. There were no screams for him to hear. No struggles, no pleas.

"It was a total surprise to her," he said aloud. "She trusted him." Arnstein walked the perimeter of the barn and stopped at the pedestal where Ruann was immortalized. "I can understand why Wallins said this was a forensic nightmare, but then what crime scene hasn't been, at least so far."

Peter paid no heed to Arnstein's comments but continued to smell and listen to his world of scents and sounds. *There was another perfume*, he thought; "light, floral, another woman was here just before the victim," he said aloud.

"What did you say?"

"Someone may have seen our killer," Peter said with more confidence. "I'd check out who kept a horse in this barn...and who rode that horse the day our victim died."

"Don't forget there was a hunt, Peter. There were a lot of women in this barn."

"No. It was on the day she died!"

"OK, I'll ask Wallins to do some checking. Anything else?"

Peter failed to answer; he was once again in another realm. He heard excited breathing, short gasps, almost an asthmatic gasping for air. Was it the victim's response, he asked himself, or the killer's reaction? Or... suddenly his eyes widened in realization.

"Do you have those photocopies; I'd like to see them again, David."

"They're in the car."

"Good. I'll go through them on our way back to the city."

CHICAGO
A PAUSE BETWEEN APPOINTMENTS

43

Susanna was silent in the elevator as Stark questioned the engineer about the state of the building. "Have there been any recent capital improvements?" he inquired.

"We just replaced two of the risers. It was a pretty big job."

"There was a special assessment last year that covered several issues," Susanna interjected, "but the reserve is healthy, roughly 800,000 dollars."

"How much was the special," Stark asked Susanna.

"Between three and seven thousand per unit. The association elected to use money from the reserves to pay half the cost of the special assessment. The owners would pay the balance, as well as any specific personal window issues. Those would be addressed separately according to the size of the unit, so that's why there's a dollar range."

When they reached the lobby, the engineer shook hands with Stark saying, "It's a good building. We keep it in beautiful condition. If you decide to buy here, you won't regret it." He smiled at Susanna and then walked away toward the management office.

"The lobby was part of the improvements that were accomplished last year," Susanna noted as she directed Stark past the doorman. She felt a mix of emotions as she rattled on about the location, the appreciation of the property and the architectural significance of the building.

Stark watched her, aware she was offering a canned speech to hide a sudden uneasiness.

"Will we see the condo at One Mag Mile?", he asked.

"We do have an appointment, but we have to kill about 45 minutes."

"Perhaps you'd allow me to buy you a coffee?"

She hesitated a moment, then smiled, "That would be pleasant," telling herself she was foolish to plant a 'real estate ripper' label on him without concrete evidence.

Besides, she thought, *he is just too perfect to be a murderer. Oh, let it be true!* "There's a convenient coffee place in the Bloomingdale's building."

"Do you mind if we walk there?" he asked noting the snow that was gently falling.

"I'd love it. And, I'll be able to point out some of the highlights along the way."

Susanna explained the tunnel walkways under Lake Shore Drive—how they made the lake and all features and activities accessible. "Chicago really utilizes its lakefront," she explained. "The miles of paths are perfect if you are a runner. And for those of us not privileged to have our own private outdoor space, the beaches and park areas are our haven."

"Hence the desirability of a balcony or terrace."

"Oh yes, and of course, that extra bit of real estate affects the price of the property!"

When they arrived at the coffee shop, Stark suggested Susanna grab a table while he gets the coffee.

"Just a regular for me, no cream, please."

"Oh come on, no skim latte with a cinnamon something or other?"

"Afraid not," she laughed and turned to find a table.

She checked her office for messages while she waited for Stark: two appointment requests for Friday, plus a call from Peter saying he would call again in the evening. Stark set the coffee cups down just as she finished noting the phone numbers for the appointment confirmations.

"Are you one of those 24/7 Realtors?"

"Not if I can help it, but the job is a little like being on call 24/7, and for more than real estate. I get the most incredible requests."

"Yes, but do you enjoy it?"

"Yes and no, but then doesn't everyone have mixed emotions about their work. Are you 100% happy doing what you do? By the way, what do you do?"

"I'm a consultant, Susanna." It was the first time he addressed her by her first name, and her heart skipped a beat when she heard it.

"Now that is one word that allows for a multitude of interpretations, Matthew." Tit for tat, she thought to herself. "A sales consultant? A financial consultant? A real estate consultant, a marketing consultant, shall I go on?"

"The lady challenges me. Interesting. Let me say three of the above and more."

"I know! It depends on who needs the consulting and the reason they need it."

"I think she's got it!" he laughed.

She returned the laughter, and a lightness enveloped her, a feeling she wanted to hold onto. "And how long do you anticipate being in Chicago to consult?"

"That all depends on my acceptance here," he said much more intimately. She almost shivered feeling the depth of his stare.

No, she thought, *he cannot be flirting with me. I'm misreading him.*

"Susanna, have you always lived in the city," he asked, sensing her ambivalence.

"Chicago, yes...city proper, no. I raised my son on the North Shore."

"Your husband?"

"Divorced. How about you? When is your wife arriving?"

"I'm afraid she won't be joining me; she died several years ago, when we lived in Los Angeles."

"Oh, I'm terribly sorry."

"Thank you, but it was a long time ago." He paused a moment then took note of his watch and once again, changed the subject. "What time is the appointment?"

Susanna looked at her watch and said, "Oh my goodness, we should be walking in the door right this minute. Ready to run?"

Grabbing coats and briefcases, the attractive couple hurried toward the Michigan Avenue exit.

LOS ANGELES
HARRY MEETS VALLI'S ASSISTANT

44

When Harry arrived at the U.S. Real Estate Properties office, only a few agents were at their desks. He introduced himself to Stella, the receptionist, a woman in her late 40s with a voice that betrayed her penchant for wine, whiskey, and unfiltered cigarettes. The lines above her lips, offering vertical pathways for the dark red color at her mouth, confirmed one of her habits, while her bronzed and weathered skin verified her love of sand and sea.

"Well...Mr. Krachewsky," she emphasized, rolling his name over her tongue as though it were a chocolate truffle. "Whatever can I do for you?"

Harry, turning a bright red, pulled at his collar and stuttered, "I...I just have a few questions."

"Well now, I will definitely try to answer any of your little old questions."

Harry was no looker. Years of pro ball had seen to that, but his sheer size left many people in awe of him, and for some unknown reason, a good many of them were mature women. Unprepared for the attention, the king-sized teddy bear often reddened when a woman of a certain age went on the offensive while fluttering her eyelashes. He could not understand why, but he was becoming far more desirable than he had ever been, even as the ravages of age collected on his face and body.

He gave a half smile, concerned that the fragments of the chocolate nut bar he had inhaled before he arrived were in evidence between his teeth. He sucked and probed earlier, but his tongue was a poor excuse for a toothpick.

"I appreciate your help. I know this sounds like a dumb question, but do you know what kind of perfume Janna Valli wore?"

"Oh, I don't think that's a dumb question. I think it says you're sensitive." Stella laughed raising her hand to pause conversation and answer the ringing phone.

Harry rolled his eyes, *this is all Peter's fault,* he thought. *Perfume! Like I give a rat's ass.*

"Good morning, U.S. Real Estate Properties. May I help you?" She listened for a moment, wrote down an address, and then said, "I'll give you to the agent on floor. She will be more than happy to help you."

Without missing a beat, she looked at Harry and recalled, "Janna loved Jessica McClintock. She wore it all the time, but about one week before she died; she started wearing a new scent. I can't remember the name, but I'll think of it," Stella said thoughtfully. Then suddenly remembering, she added, "Oh, wait a minute, Donna may know, she was Janna's assistant. I'll call her."

Harry watched the receptionist's long red nails punch out a telephone extension then continue to drum lightly on the desk as she spoke to Valli's former assistant. He wondered how she could get any work done with such long nails; he liked to clip his as short as possible. Of course, he thought if anything happened to her, the investigation would be a breeze — there would be a forensic mother lode under those nails.

The phones continued ringing, but Stella kept directing them into voice mail. "Oh, thank you, Donna, you are a doll!" she said looking directly at Harry.

"Donna said the perfume brand was Boucheron. It was a gift."

"Does she remember who gave it to Ms. Valli?"

"Donna, do you know who gave it to Janna?" She looked up at Harry once again, "She said it came without a card, but she still has the box it came in."

"I'd like to talk with her."

"Go right back, her desk is the second one from the window," she whispered, then aloud, "Mr. Krachewsky will be right there, Donna."

Harry, happy to leave Stella to her phones, walked away briskly before she could engage him in any more conversation.

Donna was going thru the back of a file cabinet drawer when Harry came up to her desk. He handed her his card and asked to see the box. She gave it to him; a bright blue gift box, a blue silk ribbon inside. "I kept it because the color was such a beautiful shade of blue, and it smelled so good. You could still smell that Boucheron after Janna opened it, even though the perfume was in a box, inside this one."

"Do you know where the bottle is, Donna?"

"She took it home, I'm sure. I never saw it after that first day."

"Do you remember how it was delivered?"

"It had to come with a messenger. I just found it on her desk with a 'Thank You' card, unsigned."

"Did you save the card?"

"No, uh, Janna tossed it."

"I'm afraid I'm gonna have to take the box with me, Donna. Do you have a large envelope?" he asked. She handed one to Harry, and he dropped the box inside.

"I'm glad you're taking the box; it sorta creeps me out anyway; I stuffed it in the file cabinet, so it smells nice every time I open the drawer. I didn't think it was right to throw something of hers away, and yet I didn't want to look at it."

"I understand, Donna."

"A lot of people didn't like Janna, but she was OK to me."

"What didn't they like about her?" he asked making himself a bit more comfortable on the edge of the desk.

"For one, they were jealous that she made so much money, but she knew how to butter up the right people. The old managing broker sent her a lot of business when she first got started, and it grew. Of course, Janna was all over her with compliments, dinner invitations, theater tickets, Louis Vuitton for Christmas.

"They even went on vacations together, but when the old broker left, she was smoke. Janna never ever returned her phone calls.

"No matter what anyone thought of her, though, no one could fault her success; she really was smart. Nevertheless, they all laughed behind her back at the way she dressed, sorta like a homeless person, but in expensive rags and jewelry.

"You know, it's funny how things happen. Janna had two appointments the day she died; one was with a young couple who were first-time buyers, the other was with an agent from another office. But that agent called twenty minutes after Janna left to say she was canceling the appointment.

"Unfortunately, Janna left her mobile phone on her desk, so I wasn't able to call her. If she had taken her phone, she wouldn't have gone to meet that agent, and probably, would still be alive."

"Can you give me that agent's name?"

"Sure, I keep a log of every call and appointment." She opened a three-ring binder and went back to the day of Valli's murder, then copied a name and number on to a card and handed it to Harry.

"I hope you find him. Janna was a little strange, but she didn't deserve to die so terribly."

Strange, Harry thought, *it probably means that no one liked her*. "By the way, did Ms. Valli have any family?"

"Two daughters. They both live in LA"

Harry nodded, and then asked for their addresses. With a thank you accompanied by a handshake, he walked away, the box packed into a manila envelope, and the slip of paper with the agent's name tucked into his pocket along with Donna's card.

As he passed Stella's desk, she looked up, smiled and said, "Now you come back and see me, Mister Krachewsky. Don't you forget!"

This time, she was wearing a pair of bifocals that she had not been wearing before; Harry smiled back a big smile no longer worried about nut pieces in his teeth. She winked at him, and he returned a military salute, promising himself that he just might visit Stella one more time.

CHICAGO
LUNCH EN ROUTE TO THE CITY

45

When Peter finally made himself comfortable in the Porsche, he attacked the copies of the crime scene photos, studying them intently. They reminded him a little of Guernica, Picasso's visualization of atrocities visited upon the people of that small Basque hamlet in northern Spain. Although there were no bulls or horses' heads in evidence, an equine presence surrounded Ruann's arms and torso, separated in chaos, a still life ready for creative interpretation.

On one corner of the hay bale, Peter noticed something near her fingertips. "Hmmm, that looks like something shiny. Yes," he mumbled aloud. "Jewelry? Wallins did not say anything about jewelry."

Thinking perhaps he had missed something from the LA murder scenes he closed his eyes, recalling those photos: Janna Valli's lifeless form sprawled in the tub as if asleep, hand casually tossed over the side, a neck chain with a pendant spelling 'mother' alongside the tub on the floor tile. *The Death of Marat?* he asked himself. *Murders replicating art. No, Brewster was different. Why the blindfold? What is our killer trying to say?*

Opening his eyes, he put aside the photos and let his thoughts slide deep in his subconscious. Like all creative people, he filled his mind with possibilities and then forced himself to close the door on his thoughts, letting his mind seek solutions to his dilemma.

He turned to Arnstein suddenly, "Where are we?"

"About 30 miles outside the city limits. I've been driving over an hour."

"I'm sorry, David. I have not been much company, but the photos have become a conundrum. They are telling me something I cannot quite hear, but I will. By the way, when you speak with Wallins, ask him if that was a piece of jewelry under the victim's fingertips."

"I didn't see anything."

"It's just the corner of something shiny. It could be jewelry."

"He's calling me again, tomorrow, with more info on anyone who boarded horses there, per your request, so I'll ask him. By the way, he said there was a Boucheron box on Beidermeister's desk with an unsigned Thank You card. No prints."

Peter sighed then asked, "Renee Fleming?" reaching for the CD control.

'How about Enya instead?"

"A satisfactory alternative, David," he laughed substituting the Enya CD for the Fleming one.

For the next 45 minutes, under Enya's haunting sounds, Peter probed into Arnstein's past, peeling away layers of hurt from loss, and guilt from survival. Arnstein was amazed he was confiding so much to Peter; it was as though Peter uncovered a nerve in him he didn't know he had, one that unleashed a torrent of memories, both happy and sad.

It felt right to share his feelings. After Joanna died, he avoided all discussion--no intimate conversations, no expression of grief; he locked up his feelings and discarded the key. Nevertheless, Peter had picked the lock, and the relief Arnstein felt was almost a celebration honoring the love and happiness he had buried in the brutal memory of that night.

Even the snow that was falling as he approached the Eden's Expressway reminded him of Joanna: the way snowflakes nestled in her dark curls, the way she licked the air catching the fragile wisps of white, always laughing. He missed her so very much, but Arnstein would so much rather remember the snowflakes and the laughter than that scream of red. He shook the thought away before the scene manifested itself once again in his mind.

"Peter," he said, almost startled. "We have to make a decision. Either it's a straight shot to Indiana now, or we hit the road again in the morning. It's your call."

"Can we reach Indiana before 5?"

"Depends on the weather. Usually, I'd say two hours, but the snow could create problems. Of course, it's all expressway travel, and the salt crews are pretty dependable."

"Personally, I'd rather get it over with, David, but I must have some lunch. And, a glass of wine, preferably a good French one."

Arnstein laughed. "I know just the place. It's in Winnetka, not too far off the Edens, and the wine list is phenomenal."

"I knew I could count on you. Onward, Sir David," he exclaimed, his cellular phone ringing, almost a punctuation to his directive.

"Peter Dumas," he answered. "Mac! I am assuming you are not calling to inform me that the temperature in Los Angeles is a balmy 80 degrees, am I right?"

Arnstein tensed, listening to hear Peter's side of the conversation.

"Interesting. I am certain Harry will find a connection. He was a bloodhound in another life, and I say that with ultimate assurances." He paused, then "Yes, we have questions though, and hopefully we'll get some answers before we return from Indiana." Nodding his head, he continued, "Yes, we'll be there later this afternoon. David and I will call you as soon as we have some concrete information. And you let us know what Harry uncovers." Listening for a moment, he finished, "I will. David also sends his regards. Until we speak."

"Well, let's see, Harry got a lead, Mac has nothing else to report, and he wants to know what we learned in Wisconsin and New Mexico and if we are going to Indiana. That about it?"

"Excellent, David, except Harry, has two leads: one resulting from the perfume search which I suggested, plus a call from an agent for an appointment that she later canceled: the murder appointment.

"A gift box of Boucheron was delivered the week before the murder and Valli's assistant kept the inner box to use as a sachet. They are checking for prints. And according to Harry, Valli's second appointment with an agent was a ruse. The agent claims she never called or canceled.

"So, we have someone who knows the appointment system, or is a part of it."

"That suggests another motive, Peter. Another killer, but then there is the Boucheron. I need a break, same as you. Let's pass on the murder talk. It's time for lunch and that wine list," he commanded turning the Porsche into the parking lot of a quaint bistro off Winnetka Avenue and Green Bay Road.

CHICAGO
ONE MAG MILE

46

Ana Marie Fazio, the listing agent, was sitting in the elegant reception area when Stark and Susanna arrived at the residential entrance to the One Mag Mile building.

She greeted Susanna and her client and then asked if Stark was familiar with the building. When he said 'no' she explained that the structure was actually 4 bundled tubes, each a hexagon with a sloping roof marking the height of the individual tubes at the 5th, 21st, 49th and 57th floors.

As they entered the elevator, Ana made note of the wall and ceiling lamps in the lobby that mimicked the structure's hexagonal tube design, as well as the marble and wood choices existing throughout the building.

The tour continued as they followed her to the unit a few floors beneath the building's crown. "There is a fantastic pool and fitness room on the 22nd floor. And, we even have an outdoor area," she added in an excited whisper, no doubt prompted by the quiet atmosphere in the wide hallway.

Greeting the trio at the unit was an impressive wood door with side panels that opened into an equally impressive entry with a dome ceiling, soft blue and cloud-flecked and anchored by four Doric columns.

Stark walked through the gallery then headed straight to the windows facing Oak Street beach, and the architectural sites east of the Drake Hotel. The proximity to the Old Mayfair, the Palmolive and Chicago's grand monarch structures on East Lake Shore Drive gave a new meaning to having lovely plantings in one's front yard. Indeed, it was a sight to behold.

The dark gray waters of Lake Michigan rolled along the beach as if propelled by some timed mechanism while building exhausts exploded in the cold, dark air creating high-rise dinosaurs snorting steamed comments to each other.

Both agents gave Stark free reign to discover the space and

comforts of the two-bedroom, two-bath unit. The contemporary kitchen was open to capture views and to establish a more casual living environment in the sky high-home. The deep cove moldings, the hardwood floors, punctuated with silk Orientals in a bounty of color managed to hold onto traditional warmth while sharing the stage with Herman Miller, Knoll, Miro, Klimt and Pollack.

It never ceased to amaze Susanna that original art collected throughout the Gold Coast, in some instances, even rivaled collections in public institutions. She watched as Stark acknowledged the Jackson Pollack painting as he moved through the unit, nodding approval occasionally at a feature or piece of furniture.

Fazio is a good agent, Susanna thought to herself. She didn't fill the air with mindless chatter. Fazio permitted the unit to sell itself.

The agents followed Stark into both bedrooms. Upon entering the main one, Fazio broke the silence, "All the built-ins here will stay, of course. However, if a buyer did not want them, the owner would be happy to remove them and repair any subsequent damage resulting from the removal."

Stark nodded and then motioned to Susanna indicating he was finished with his inspection.

Catching his signal, Fazio handed Susanna a packet, "Here are disclosures and a breakdown of recent improvements, both in the unit and in the building. If you have any other questions, please call me."

Turning to Susanna's client, she extended her hand and smiled, "Good luck with your search, Mr. Stark."

They left Fazio to turn off lights and draw the shades.

In the hallway, Stark informed Susanna that he was prepared to make an offer but wanted to see both units once again, the vacant unit at 1313 and the Fazio listing, but in the daytime.

"When?" she asked.

"Tomorrow, if possible. Around 10 A.M.?

As they entered the elevator, she said, "I don't think it will be a problem. Let's meet here at 10 AM and follow up with the 1313 unit. I'll call the agents to confirm and let you know if there are any changes."

LOS ANGELES
MAC AND HARRY RECAP

47

Los Angeles was under a rain cloud when Harry drove into the almost empty parking lot. It was just past one; the real rush would not begin for a few hours. Harry hated this time of year when rain invaded his world. He was a guy who loved the sun; it was the primary reason he left Chicago. If he had his way, the sun would reign throughout the day, and raindrops only allowed between 3 and 5 A.M., sufficient to keep grass green, flowers blooming, and drinking water in more than adequate amounts.

The greeter at the entrance gave Harry a high five and asked, "The usual, Krachewsky?"

"Yep," he answered and made his way to the back of the restaurant where Mac was already drinking coffee, while diligently making notes.

The back table at the deli had become an office-away-from-the-office for Harry and Mac. Bad coffee from the squad room was a poor substitute for a steaming cup at Jeri's. And pastrami on rye even delivered to the station, could not compare to the sandwich the waiter placed before Harry, moments after he sat down. Mounds of hot, pink pastrami surrounded by thick, sliced fries, crisp and golden made the not-so-jolly-green-giant's mouth water.

"Mac, what you need is a sandwich like this, not that rabbit food you order. I mean, give me a break, egg white omelet with roasted red peppers and feta cheese. No wonder you're losing so much friggin weight. Have you given up on meat, entirely?"

"Nope. I'm just trying to eat healthier, that's all. Harry, you should really think twice about all the fat and carbs you put away. When's the last time you had your cholesterol checked?"

"Ah cripes, you been watching the Discovery Channel again?"

"Well, I did see an informative program about plaque."

"Plaque, schmak, let's talk murder. It's a helluva lot more interesting.

Did you talk to your voodoo man?"

Mac laughed, "You know you love the guy, Harry. You just don't want to admit it."

"OK, OK, we make a great couple. Are you happy now?"

"Peter did ask about you. I think he cares a great deal," Mac said, trying to suppress his laughter.

"You really know how to push my buttons. Truce. What did Peter say about New Mexico and Wisconsin?"

"Not much, but knowing Peter he saw or heard plenty. We'll get the full scoop when they get back from Indiana. What did you get?"

"Well Mac, like I told you, both Valli and Brewster received Boucheron perfume gifts, just like your voodoo man said, but Valli's assistant kept the original box."

He took a man-sized bite of the pastrami sandwich and in between his chews, garbled on, "I bagged the box and dropped it off for prints. I'm hoping there's something on the inside flap, that is if our ripper actually packed the perfume." Taking a big gulp of coffee, he continued, "The receptionist always posts an entry in a daily ledger for all incoming deliveries by mail, fed ex or messenger. I got the name of the service and checked it out."

"Anyone remember who brought it in?"

"Yeah, one of the guys thinks a good-looking redhead brought it in for her boss."

"Why's he so sure it was the same package?" Mac asked.

"Cause this chickee made a joke about her boss's name being Hill sending a package to Valli. Get it, she says, hill and Valli. Stupid! But it made him remember her. Your turn."

"We traced the towels, and the shower curtain to a purchase Valli made when she put the house on the market," Mac explained. "Evidently, she staged bathrooms and kitchens with towels, flower pots and decorator chochkes. Would you believe the receipt was still in her purse, bunched up with an assortment of singles and twenties?"

"Yeah, from what I've learned about real estate agents, they save every scrap of paper, but they're not too big on organizing any of it. How about the blood match?" Harry asked, once again his mouth full of pastrami on rye.

"It's her type... we'll get the DNA results in a couple of days. The best news is a partial thumbprint on the shower curtain. It's not Valli's! The techs are checking to see if it matches any prints from the Brewster kill."

"I'd send that baby to the Wisconsin and New Mexico cops, pronto."

"Did that already, as soon as I alerted Chicago," Mac responded just as Harry's phone began ringing.

"Krachewsky," he answered. "Boy, that was quick. Yeah, I guess it does. Thanks, Joe." He looked at Mac and nodded affirmatively, a grin pasted on his face from ear to ear. "We got a match. Full thumbprint on the inside flap of the box and it matches the partial from the shower curtain."

"Now do you see why I put so much faith in Peter?"

"Yeah, I don't want to think how he does it, but I understand why you believe in him."

"By the way, Chicago is sending us another print as well. They found a contact lens at the Playmore scene, missed it first time around."

Harry raised his arm and jerked it with a "Yes, now we're talking. This is the way you find a killer, not with crystal balls, smoke, and mirrors, and nose sniffing."

"Come on Harry. You wouldn't have found that Boucheron box if Peter hadn't given us that lead. And print #2 on the shower curtain would have been smoke if Peter hadn't sent us searching for it."

Harry stared intently at Mac for a moment, then swallowed the last of his pastrami and gulped the rest of his coffee. "Humph, that tasted good," he said licking his lips. "Let's discuss Peter later after we catch this creep."

"Sure," Mac said as he sat back and laughed.

Chicago
Peter And Arnstein Head To Indiana

48

Peter agreed that L'oeil Affamé was as phenomenal a restaurant as Arnstein described. When the waiter came to inquire if either of the men would like dessert, both of them passed, but Peter added, "My compliments to the chef. The salmon was most délicieux, and the spinach and cucumber sauce, parfait."

The young man smiled and placed on the table a black bill holder, which Peter immediately picked up. Arnstein objected, but Peter insisted.

"You introduced me to this delightful place; you touted the wine list, and it was outstanding; you said the food was superb and it was 5-star. Consider this a thank you!"

"Well, I'm going to have to introduce you to many more restaurants, Peter!" he laughed.

Peter smiled, left a hundred-dollar bill in the holder and the two men left.

The snow had stopped but not before depositing a white veil over the Porsche's windshield. Arnstein started the car, removed a brush from behind the driver's seat and began dusting while his companion settled inside.

Peter pulled up his muffler, shielding his face from the frigid air; it was even colder than earlier that morning, but in a matter of minutes, warm air began to circulate in the small space.

"I think I'll make better time on the Drive," Arnstein said. "Besides, it'll give you an opportunity to see some of the great homes on the North Shore."

"Oh, I am very familiar with the North Shore, David. My friend Susanna lived in Kenilworth, and I was a frequent guest."

"She's the real estate broker, right? Terry Playmore's friend?"

"Yes."

"Where did she live?" Arnstein asked.

"Her home was right on Sheridan Road, just before the end of the village. It had a Consulate look to it if you know what I mean," he continued, his voice filled with approval. "It was impressive: a gray stone building shrouded in flowering trees with a circular drive that seemed to invite limousines with liveried drivers."

"She didn't strike me as the type to live in a Kenilworth mansion," Arnstein interjected.

"Oh, I don't think there is a type that lives in a Kenilworth mansion, David. I believe it is only our perception of what and who should live in a Kenilworth mansion that we envision. Of course, some people try to live up to those perceptions. Susanna could live anywhere; she creates a home wherever she is. I remember when she bought the place. There was a basket-ball net at one end of the living room; the rest of the place was in tatters. She saw the potential and pounced on it."

"How is she taking Playmore's death?"

"Not well. I've told Susanna that we believe Realtors are the focus of our killer, for the express reason of wanting her to be cautious. I did not say this to you, but I had a sense of death around Susanna before I left for LA It could have been thoughts of Terry I sensed, but then, my feelings were too strong. Nothing seemed to explain the aura of danger around her."

"I'm not surprised. Think about it, most Realtors go on showings with clients they don't really know. Or they sit at an open house like the Beidermeister woman where anyone can walk in. We may have a serial killer on our hands, but these women weren't the first to die while selling real estate."

"Have you called the Realtor's association?" Peter asked.

"Yes, not a panic call, but I certainly urged them to send out a warning and a reminder about safety measures. But let's be realistic Peter, most of these women will read warnings and toss them aside, convinced they're too smart to be a victim. You can lead a horse to water, but you can't make it drink."

"So true, David, so true," Peter said closing his eyes and settling back against the headrest. "You'll have to excuse me, David, I'm exceptionally fatigued; my subconscious must be working in overdrive. I'm going to rest for a bit."

Reading the exhaustion in Peter's face, Arnstein turned off the radio and focused on the road. If they were lucky, they could reach their destination between 4 and 4:30 that afternoon.

When he hit the outskirts of the city, Arnstein drove east to Lake Shore Drive along the city's majestic lakefront. *New York might be the big apple,* he thought to himself, *but Chicago is the real jewel.* In his eyes, like those of many others, Chicago was multifaceted with colors and cultures no city could match.

He loved every part of it, from the ethnic neighborhoods to the Gold Coast, from the architecture styles to the green of the parks, and the magic of the Lincoln Park Zoo. He soaked up the energy, and it gave him a life that never bored him.

Traffic was relatively light, so in no time at all he passed the new stadium. To him, it was an abortion, a flying saucer plopped atop the beautiful old columns of Soldier Field. He personally felt that it wasn't a compromise; it was a political maneuver that scarred the lakefront.

Just a bit farther south he approached McCormick Place, holder of the title 'largest convention and exposition center in North America, according to multiple press references.

Arnstein was born the year the Center officially opened, but a fire destroyed the building seven years later, just at the start of that year's National Housewares Show. The fire had a citywide impact responsible for initiating a raft of revisions to the Chicago Municipal Code, and in January of 1971, the new McCormick Place opened incorporating those changes.

But like the city it embodied, the center continually perfected itself, expanding with McCormick Place North in 1989, and McCormick Place South in 1996, thus maintaining its North American title.

Arnstein was always amazed at the logistics of bringing hundreds of exhibitors and their elaborate displays to the buildings. There would always be complaints about Union influences, booth set-ups, and payoffs, but no one could deny the sheer beauty of the orchestration, much like producing an epic film in a matter of days.

At the turn to Indiana, Arnstein glanced at his watch; he was pushing the limit, and it was paying off. They definitely would make it between 4:15 and 4:30.

He started, momentarily surprised at the full ring of his mobile phone. "Arnstein," he answered.

"Where the hell are you?" Davis shrieked at the other end.

"We're on our way to Indiana," he said softly.

"Why the whisper?"

"Peter's taking a cat nap."

"Well, I've got some news."

"Me too. Peter caught something in the photos I didn't. The corner of a piece of jewelry, at least it seems to be. Wallins, the lead detective, should have an answer. Would you call him and check; I left him a message at lunch."

"He called about 10 minutes ago. First, no one was there about a horse on the day Beidermeister was killed, whatever that means. And yes, there was a piece of jewelry. Not hers. It was a charm, a heart with a single ruby. And most important, she did get a perfume gift of Boucheron. We definitely got us a serial killer."

"It's the same guy, no question about it. Same M.O. By the way, did you get my message about her kids?"

"Yep, and I put a call into Mac to see if LAPD could get any info on 'em. By the way, they got a print on a shower curtain, and they're sending it over. And more great news! The contact lens? We've got a partial on it. Who knows when it was dropped, but it'll be checked against the LA prints as soon as we get em. I'm betting the beads they'll match. You back tonight?"

"I sure hope so. I'll call you after we finish. But one more thing, there was a situation with Palmieri in Santa Fe. She slept with a client and the wife threatened her. Forced her to leave the area and head to Albuquerque. Have Kramer see if the Santa Fe Association of Realtors will give him names."

"Will do." Not one for long goodbyes, Davis ended his call with "Later."

Indiana
Frobisher Murder Meeting

49

Arnstein pulled into the station parking lot at 4:25 and gently poked Peter who had slept the entire trip. "I'm beginning to think you either don't like my company, Peter, or you've got to quit watching those late movies."

"It's neither, David. I'm getting an inordinate number of visual messages, but they're all unconnected, and I can't find the thread. When that happens, I seem to go into sleep mode; my subconscious demands it."

"Well, buddy, I hate to tear you away from your dreams, but we are here. And right on schedule, to boot."

The men left the car and proceeded to the station where they were introduced to the lead detective, Sam Politis. He welcomed them, anxious to share information that in turn might help him with the unsolved killing of Millie Frobisher.

"Never had a murder like hers," he said, his face telegraphing the shock of the brutality Frobisher suffered. "She coulda been a piece of Swiss cheese, there were so many stab wounds in her. The coroner said, more than seventy of 'em. Here are the photos," he offered.

When they saw Millie Frobisher's death pose, Arnstein winced while Peter momentarily closed his eyes with a sharp intake of breath.

She lounged on a sofa, feet crossed, wine glass propped in her hand at her stomach and her head tossed back revealing a second open mouth at her throat. A small lampshade was perched on her head, and twenty-dollar bills were stuffed in her lips, in her blouse and under a bracelet wrapped at her wrists. She could have been a scarecrow at rest, except for the blood that blackened her clothes and body in the photo.

"According to the receptionist, some guy walks in the office, and the floor agent is on him like butter on bread. It was Frobisher, our vic. Little while later she makes two appointments for two vacant houses and tells the receptionist to put any floor calls into her voicemail...says she'll be back with this guy Daggert in an hour. No one else came in the office all afternoon, so the chick at the desk locks up and splits."

"Who found her and when?" Arnstein asked the round-faced detective.

"The listing agent. Next day. Those lock boxes they use to hold the key, well they register an agent's ID when it's opened, so she calls Frobisher the next day to get some feedback on the showing. No response. So, she goes to the house to make sure it's locked up."

"Was it?" Peter interrupted.

"Yeah, and the key was back in the lockbox, but one of the lights in the front of the house was still on, so she goes inside. She must've gone bananas when she found Frobisher. Who wouldn't? So, she runs from the house and locks herself in her car, then calls us on the mobile."

"How about Frobisher's car?" Arnstein asked.

"It was at the back of the driveway," Politis said. "We figure she pulled all the way to the back of the house, so she could show the stream running through the property."

"Get a composite from the secretary?"

"All the receptionist volunteered was a white guy with curly hair. All those white guys look alike she told me," he said rolling his eyes.

"Any prints?" Arnstein asked.

"At her office, about 100. Scary. I don't think the conference table was ever cleaned. At the house, too many to count."

"How about her car?"

"We don't think he was in it. Frobisher had the car detailed the day before she died—was planning on selling it. Only prints we found were hers. A woman who was walking her dog noticed Frobisher leaving the parking lot and said a sports car followed her out. She narrowed it down to a Porsche, a Corvette, or a Jag. Jeez, can you believe that? The one thing she was sure about was that it was red."

"Anything else at the office, anything unusual?" Peter queried. "Well, Frobisher got a delivery that morning; a teenage girl brought it to the office shortly after it opened. The receptionist pointed out the agent's desk, and the kid left it there. We found a perfume box and wrapping paper in the waste-paper basket... the office manager said the cleaning service only came on Tuesdays, Thursdays, and Sundays," he explained. "We put a call out on all the news stations for the kid. No one ever came forward. Checked the box and wrapping for prints, but only Frobisher's showed up."

Peter looked at him thoughtfully then asked what Millie Frobisher had in her handbag.

Politis opened his notebook and rattled off items from a list: "Lipstick, miniature flashlight, one brown eyeliner pencil, a compact with blush, three receipts for gasoline, two quarters, one dime and sixteen pennies, a perfume dispenser, a library card, three credit cards, two sticks of gum, breath mints, half a dozen business cards and forty-two bucks."

"You don't happen to have the brand of perfume listed, do you?" Peter asked hopefully.

"No, but the evidence room will have a list. I'll get a copy for you," Sam volunteered as he left the office.

"Well Peter, if Boucheron is the scent, we definitely have a connection to the other murders. It just might lead us to our man."

Peter nodded slowly, deep in thought. *Who was she? Where did she meet her killer? Why Boucheron? Why?*

Politis returned with the answer: "Boo-chair-on," he stumbled phonetically.

"Thank you, Sam," Peter whispered as if all his strength had been drained.

Arnstein slid the composite he had from Chicago across the desk to Politis. "Here's what a witness described to our police artist. Doesn't sound like your man, but I'd appreciate your getting it to that receptionist and the dog walker."

"No problem. Now, what can you tell me about your Realtor murder?" Politis asked.

Arnstein proceeded to share with him the background on Terry's killing and the specifics of the LA crimes. Peter listened, but his mind was a million miles away pondering questions that continued to perplex him. *What was the something other than being agents that tied these women together? What constituted the selection process? Why Boucheron? Was Palmieri number 1 or were there still others before her? Were there two killers?*

"Peter, do you have any other questions?" Arnstein asked breaking the clairvoyant's train of thought.

"Oh, oh yes. Did Frobisher have any family?" he said directing his question to Politis.

"No, not here. She was originally from Michigan but stayed after graduating from Indiana U. One of the girls in the office who was kinda friendly with her said her mom died about a year ago and left her a little money."

Any brothers or sisters?" Peter continued.

"We found a brother, but he said he left home when he was 17 and hasn't seen Frobisher or his mother since then. He never claimed the body, but he did put a claim on her estate, what little there was of it."

"Where does he live?" Arnstein asked.

"Out east," Politis responded.

Peter thought for a moment then asked if the house where Frobisher was murdered was still vacant.

"Yeah, but there's nothing to see. It's cleaned out, ready to be razed. The owner knew it was worthless trying to sell it. Hell, everyone wants an appointment just to see the scene of the crime. A lot of ghouls out there. The owner's attorney got him an approved order to raze the property as soon as we leave. He moved real quick. We checked him out, too, but he's clear."

"Well Sam, I guess that's about it?"

"If you boys are planning to have dinner before you head on back, we got a mean café in town. Bessie, she's the owner, she makes the best rhubarb pie you'll ever taste," he said rolling his eyes and licking his lips.

"Maybe next time, Sam. I always love a good rhubarb pie," Arnstein smiled.

"I think I would like to take Sam up on his kind suggestion. Rhubarb pie in Bessie's cafe might be just the thing before we head back to Chicago,"

Peter said with enthusiasm.

"You sure about that Peter?" Arnstein asked, surprised at Peter's response.

"Positively. In fact, Sam, would you care to join us?"

"Oh, I would love to, but my wife would have a conniption if I were late coming home tonight. Our boy's playing in the basketball finals, and we're hoping to have a celebration dinner."

Peter, having absolutely no understanding of what basketball finals meant to a family, smiled at Politis with the most engaging smile, "Understand completely, Sam."

Politis took Peter's hand and clasped it, appreciation written over his face.

A hastily drawn map, sincere goodbyes, a promise to keep Politis abreast of any new developments, and the two men set out into a brisk wind and lightly falling snow for Bessie's café and a slice of her famous rhubarb pie.

LOS ANGELES
HARRY MEETS JANNA VALLI'S DAUGHTER

50

Krachewsky was also convinced that the victims had something more in common than the fact that they were Realtors. *Why did the perp seek them out? He had to be stalking them, but why the Boucheron? Questions, questions with no answers,* he thought, on his trek to see one of Janna Valli's daughters.

The Sherman Oaks address took him to one of the old apartment hotels converted to a rental complex. LA was loaded with them. They were much like motel units, but complete with kitchenettes featuring dollhouse versions of the basics with tiny rooms and closets. Now they serve as apartments for struggling actors, or anyone able to cough up 800 or 900 dollars for 600 S.F. of luxurious living space.

Peggy Valli was one of the residents.

The entry with a slew of mailboxes and a buzzer system offered minimum security for 3 levels of apartments encircling the interior courtyard with its rectangular pool, badly in need of cleaning. Krachewsky pushed the buzzer for P Valli and waited for the long steady buzz that allowed him to push open the flimsy glass door to the courtyard.

Number 29 had to be on the second level and looking up he saw an attractive blonde leaning over the railing. "Take the stairs just past the pool and turn right."

The pool area needed more than cleaning, he realized as he walked to the staircase. Several tiles were missing or cracked, and the whole place had the look of a 1940s black and white movie. All that was needed was a bleached blonde in a one-piece bathing suit and a skinny hood wearing pleated pants and sporting a pencil-thin mustache and fedora.

Krachewsky climbed the stairs a little out of breath, acknowledging to himself that he indeed was out of shape. Maybe, he thought, Mac was right. Maybe it was time to start thinking about a healthier lifestyle, but suddenly in his mind, he saw a big, juicy Italian beef covered in hot peppers soaked in oil, alongside a giant bag of thick, greasy, wonderful French fries. Ah, he thought, maybe next month I'll go on a diet.

The blonde was even more attractive, as the distance between them diminished. But then, good-looking women are a dime a dozen in LA; they come from all over the world, hopeful that they will be the next Julia or Nicole, or Cameron. The don't realize that looks and talent are oftentimes not enough. It takes chutzpah, a connection, or a willingness to do just about anything to get 15 minutes of fame. Therefore, while they spend thousands on photos and lessons, they live like paupers working as servers, dancers, strippers, anything that covers the bills, in order to fulfill their dream— making it in Hollywood.

Peggy Valli could have been in her 20s or her 30s; she had an ingénue look about her, a Midwestern cheerleader type—the type that came in droves to the film capital of the world.

"You Krachewsky?" she asked.

"You Valli?" he answered.

She laughed and walked into her apartment, waving him inside. "You look like a cop."

"That's funny, most people say I look like a football player."

"The fridge?" she chuckled.

Looking at her with a very solemn expression, one that telegraphed deep thought, he paused then offered, "I weigh a lot less than the Fridge did," recalling the feared yet beloved William Perry of the Chicago Bears.

"Betcha don't."

"I know for a fact that Perry has tipped the scales around 400 pounds. The most I've ever weighed was 325, and I'm taller than he was."

"Methinks the man doth protest too much!"

She was either a born flirt or a pretty good actress, Harry surmised. "OK, OK, let's say him and I are close in strength, and call it a day."

"If you insist," she smiled, holding back her laughter. "How can I help you?"

"I'm here about your mom."

"Why?" she asked with surprise. "She sorta disowned me when I was seventeen. I haven't seen her since then. Neither has my sister if you're hoping she's got the poop."

"Why did she disown you?"

She plopped down in an old, bright yellow, bean bag chair. Harry remembered them from the late 60s and early 70s, primarily because he could not get up after he made the mistake of sitting down in one of them.

"Because when we moved here, she didn't want anyone to know she had daughters as old as we were," she said flatly. There was no hint of anger or hurt in her voice. She was just stating a fact. Harry could not fathom a mother so self-absorbed that she would walk away from her children, or that it did not matter to the kids.

"It's not like she really disowned us; she sent each of us money until we were twenty-one. Three hundred dollars a month! We learned priorities rather quickly. My sister put herself through school, and now she's an attorney. I'm still hoping to be an actress, but I've begun a marketing company for people just like me."

"You said you moved here. From where?" Harry asked genuinely enchanted by the young woman's attitude and hold on reality.

"Oh, we started out in the Midwest, moved to Texas and then came here after graduating from high school."

"Where in the Midwest?"

"We grew up in Birmingham, just outside of Detroit."

"That's a pretty snazzy suburb. Was your mom in real estate there?"

"Only for a couple of years. My dad was with a big advertising company, so mom stayed home, but when he met someone that he liked a little better than my mother, he left. That's when my mom went to work. Real estate was perfect for her; she loved taking care of other people."

Harry saw the independence in her eyes; she was a survivor, no question about it. Sad, he thought, *she asked for nothing, and she expected nothing; it wasn't fair, she was too young.* "Do you remember who she worked for?"

"Not really, I was about 9 years old when my parents got divorced. My sister might remember, though, if you like, I'll call and ask

Harry nodded, and while Peggy called her sister, his eyes scanned the apartment and its contents.

Despite the shabby exterior of the complex, Peggy Valli had created a charming and homey nest for herself, filled with interesting art and furniture. Most of the pieces were vintage Salvation Army but what she created with them was priceless. Stripped chests and armoires painted and lacquered with stripes or delicate patterns were one of a kind art pieces that probably could fetch a handsome price should she elect to sell her creations. The walls were sponge painted with floral borders that suggested the outdoors came in for a visit and opted to stay.

She should be in movies, Harry thought as he watched Peggy's infectious smile as she spoke with her sister; the relationship had to be a positive one to evoke such warmth in her responses.

She ended the call with a promise to visit that weekend, then turned to Harry. "She doesn't remember the name of the company in the Midwest, but in Texas, she said mom worked for a developer in new construction sales, and the only name she recalls is something like The Goodson Group, but she's not positive."

He nodded then asked, "Did your mother leave a will?"

"Funny, you should ask," she said thoughtfully. "My sister and I got a call right after my mom died from an attorney who told us not to worry about anything because my mom gave strict instructions in her will. He said all distributions would be made in January. Frankly, I was surprised to hear the word distribution, but my sister wasn't."

With absolutely no difficulty, she rose from the beanbag chair and walked to the kitchen, "Would you like some bottled water?"

"Nope," Harry responded still in awe that she could rise so effortlessly from the chair that battled him in the past, and won.

"Do you think she left you anything?" he posed.

"Naw, if anything she left all she had to an animal shelter or to that dumb Shih Tzu she always carried. Carrie said may was too smart not to lock everything up tight, you know, so we don't make any claims against the estate. Both of us will probably get some small trinket with the sentimental value mom gave it."

"Does that make you angry?"

"Not anymore. I was sort of hoping mom would remember Carrie and me, you know, with some kind of financial expression to say she was sorry for not being a better mother. But I finally realized, she never thought she was a bad mother; that's our perception, so she doesn't owe us anything. She gave us the best she could, emotionally."

"Would you get me the name of her attorney, Peggy," he said handing her his card.

"No problem, it's somewhere on that desk. I'll look for it and call you."

They shook hands, and Harry left. He felt a deep sense of contentment, amazed at the generosity and maturity that Peggy Valli possessed. Her mom might have been lax emotionally as Peggy and her sister reached adulthood, but the strength of purpose and understanding the young woman exhibited was not self-taught. There had to be seeds of love and positive direction to create the blossom that became Peggy Valli.

CHICAGO

51

Pippa set up the Broker Opens for Susanna on the Thursday after Christmas, then left the office shortly after 5 o'clock. She flagged a cab for the short trip to Louis Vuitton at the old Palmolive Building to pick up a small gift for Chuwana. The receptionist had been particularly helpful arranging the necessary paperwork for the Open Houses. Pippa believed in rewarding those people who helped her, especially when they could be perfect for small, discreet jobs in the future.

When she left Louis Vuitton, the cold was even more bitter. She wrapped her long sable coat tightly around her shoulders as she waited for a taxi. Amazingly two cabs pulled up to the Walton corner at the same time, one with a right blinker flashing northbound, the other heading west. She chose the westbound cab and told him "The Hancock, please."

The driver turned left onto Michigan Avenue then edged his way into the left lane at Delaware watching Pippa in his rearview mirror. *Hardly worth the trip,* he thought to himself as the green light signaled him to turn. Thirty seconds later, he pulled to a stop at the residential entrance of the glass and steel building on Delaware.

Pippa tossed a five-dollar bill at the driver as she exited the cab. He watched her enter the building, the wind whipping her long hair into a Medusa-inspired creation. He hated women like her, women who treated everyone as their underlings, women with money to burn; women who could afford to take a cab for a distance less than a city block.

He appreciated the five-dollar bill, but that did not mean he had to like his benefactor.

Pippa walked past the doorman who buzzed her in, and waited for the elevator, the first of two that would take her to her condo. When she reached the 44th floor, she ignored the mailboxes and headed straight to the market for some yogurt before taking the second elevator.

Ty Collins was just leaving the deli area as she entered. "I didn't realize you lived here, Ty," she said, her voice full of surprise.

He looked up, startled, but quickly regained his composure, "Well, Pippa, I wasn't aware that you lived here either! Evidently, we both have excellent taste."

"Evidently." She reached for the yogurt and followed Ty to the checkout. "I haven't seen you at the office."

"I had some personal business to take care of out of town."

"Someplace exciting?" she asked.

"Nothing exotic. We had a corporate meeting in Detroit regarding a possible acquisition."

"A realty company?"

"I'm not at liberty to say quite yet, but I promise Pippa, you'll be one of the first to know."

They walked to the elevator banks, each selecting the one servicing their own floor; two beautiful people dressed quietly in a collection of outrageously expensive designer labels.

"How are things working out with Susanna?" Ty asked just as Pippa's elevator chimed, announcing the door opening. She looked down her nose at him as though he were a fly on her sleeve, then she walked into the elevator turned and smiled her Cheshire smile, "Fabulously," she drawled as the doors closed.

She was not a woman whom one patted on the head or flattered with useless compliments. She was definitely one to be reckoned with, despite her age.

Just like her father, he thought.

INDIANA
BESSIE'S CAFE

52

When Peter and Arnstein walked from the cold into Bessie's place, a pleasantly robust woman greeted them with a "Welcome to my café." She escorted them to a table for two in the middle of the thriving restaurant.

"Bessie, Sam Politis says you make the best rhubarb pie in the county," Peter complimented the smiling greeter whose cheeks suddenly turned a bright, bright pink.

"Aw, Sam just likes any rhubarb pie," she chortled.

"Not to hear Sam say it, but let us be the judge when we're ready for dessert."

"Well, now I'll accept that. You boys aren't from around here, that's for certain, so I'd be pleasured to get an outside opinion of my rhubarb pie." She smiled a big toothy smile, handed them the menu and told them the special of the day was spicy black bean soup and pork tenderloin with raspberry and apricot sauce.

Peter did not hesitate for a moment, "I'll have both of those specials, Bessie, and a piece of that rhubarb pie."

David passed on the specials and ordered from the menu, "I'll have the oven roasted pork chops with the homemade applesauce." Bessie made a note on their ticket and said it would be a bit, then poured them each a steaming cup of coffee.

"David, I think we have struck the mother lode once again today. Spicy black bean soup is on my favorite list, in fact, Susanna makes a mean version that I thoroughly enjoy."

David laughed and took a sip of the hot coffee while Peter studied the lineup of customers occupying every stool at the counter. Peter insisted that the grey-haired woman with the sensible shoes had to be the local librarian.

Arnstein agreed, and the two men proceeded to play 'What's my line' about the other customers at the counter, mentally postponing their murder discussion until after dinner.

"The man with the rolled-up sleeves, he's the editor of the paper; and the young woman with the horn-rimmed glasses, she's got to be a banker," Arnstein guessed.

"Two for two, David. How about the man in the blue button-down shirt and corduroy Dockers?" The man in Peter's sight was 40ish with a touch of gray at his temple, his body rounded in the way most women round after a certain age, with thickened waist, a soft chin, and a generously folded neck.

"School teacher?" he asked.

"Dentist! You missed the mirror in his breast pocket. He's had a hectic day and must have absentmindedly put that tool there instead of in the sterilizer after his last patient."

"OK, how about the guy in the navy shirt and navy pants?" Arnstein gestured toward a younger man with a buzz haircut.

"Easy. Fireman."

"Why not a mechanic or a building super?" Arnstein replied in surprise.

"His haircut's a dead giveaway. Besides, he has no grease on his shoes."

Bessie interrupted their game with a tray delivering the most glorious smells.

"Delectable, Bessie," Peter sighed, as she placed a steaming bowl of black bean soup before him. Arnstein was equally impressed as he filled his lungs with the cinnamon scent of hot, fresh applesauce and a hint of sage from the lightly seasoned pork chop before him.

"It's time to replenish the energy required for those 'little grey cells' as my favorite detective quotes," Peter said relishing the soup's velvety texture and spicy tang.

Both men were silent as they devoured the best of Bessie's kitchen. When she served the rhubarb pie, Arnstein was certain he had died and gone to heaven. Peter, on the other hand, was convinced that he had found Nirvana. They topped off Bessie's pie with a fresh cup of coffee and vowed they would visit again and again!

Comfortably sated, their thoughts once again focused on the work at hand.

Peter suggested they organize their combined information and impressions and create a blueprint of murder scene similarities. Additionally, he believed a profile of each victim would help determine if anything tied the women together. Harry was doing just that with the LA victims.

"I'm still convinced there is something else connecting these women," he repeated to Arnstein.

"I don't know if I agree with you, Peter, but let's head back, and we can compare notes in the car."

Peter picked up the ticket from the table and walked toward the cashier ignoring Arnstein's repeated requests to pay for their dinner. Noticing they were ready to leave, Bessie followed the two men to say goodbye, and to get a report on her rhubarb pie, "Well sir, was everything OK?" she said directly to Peter.

"Bessie, you not only have the best rhubarb pie in the county, but I also wager it is the best in the Midwest! Furthermore, your spicy black bean soup is unquestionably haute cuisine."

Her beaming face turned redder with each compliment, "Aww, you are awful kind."

"Nonsense, I'm terribly honest! Till we meet again, Bessie." He bowed deeply took her chubby hand in his and kissed it with a feather kiss. If Bessie were not quite so robust, she most assuredly would have swooned.

Peter was a kind man, thoughtful and deeply appreciative of life and the people who lived it.

CHICAGO
SUSANNA MEETS JULIA DEVEROUX

53

Susanna walked into her apartment, dropped her briefcase, entered the kitchen, and opened a bottle of wine. Not until she savored the smooth Australian Cabernet did she remove her coat and hat. It had been that kind of day.

She fell into the chair and took another long sip of wine just as the phone began to ring. Without thinking, she picked up the receiver and answered a smoky "hello".

"My, don't we sound melted."

"Julia?" Susanna quizzed.

"Yes, it's Julia and yes, I know, I only call when I'm desperate."

"Howard's asleep and you need a drinking buddy. Right?"

"You make it sound so tawdry. I simply miss your scintillating conversation, and it's only a coincidence that my husband is asleep and I'm dying for a Jack Daniels."

"OK, but you're buying. How about the Tavern?"

"Oh, not the Tavern," she said dramatically. "That's such a tourist place. Let's do Portals at the West Inn, maybe I can pick up an out-of-towner."

"Julia! I will not be your wingman. Either you want to talk to me, or you don't. Skip the shock and awe, I'll meet you at the West Inn in twenty minutes—after I finish my drink."

"Oh ducky, Susanna is being wild again."

"Goodbye, Julia. Twenty minutes, at the West Inn."

"Chow, sweetie.

Susanna stretched out in the wingback chair, took a deep breath and another sip of her Cabernet. She was glad Julia had called; she needed to talk as well, and surprisingly Julia was a patient ear. She was an old timer, a twenty-year veteran with real estate stories no one could match.

Susanna found herself chuckling, remembering a story Julia told about the man in the shower. Julia was showing her listing and knew her seller was out of town, but had given a guest staying in the unit ample warning. When she entered the master bedroom with the buyer and his agent, a man toweling his hair, walked out of the shower wearing a few drops of water. He looked up, smiled, continued to towel his hair and said, "Can I help you?"

Julia, not missing a beat, smiled back and said, "Perhaps if you were more generously endowed."

Not knowing what to say, the seller's guest, dropped his towel to a more appropriate position, turned and walked back into the bathroom closing the door behind him.

She was notorious for speaking her mind and often did, shocking everyone within hearing range. Susanna loved Julia's spontaneity, her quick wit, and even her tempestuous temper. Julia could be many things, but she certainly was honest to a fault. Not having to work, most assuredly contributed to her saying whatever she pleased. She was not a big producing agent, yet everyone knew her name.

Susanna finished her wine and did a quick makeup repair then slipped her coat back on and left to meet her old friend.

A collection of visitors to the city packed the West Inn, along with Streeterville neighbors anxious for an evening out, content that their destination would literally be a few steps from home on this brutally cold night.

Susanna walked into the noisy bar and searched for a tall, salt and pepper haired woman of a certain age, exceedingly thin and as finely wrinkled as any red-blooded, fair-skinned woman of Irish descent could be. Julia was sitting at the far end of the bar deep in conversation with a tall man, smoking an extraordinarily large cigar.

"Susanna, Susanna," she called, "over here, over here."

Aware that everyone within a twenty-foot radius now knew her name, Susanna's cheeks colored a red-rosy pink.

"Why does she do that?" she asked herself.

When she reached Julia, she whispered in her ear, "If you don't walk with me to the corner of the room, I will leave."

"Oh, of course, Susanna, I understand," she said turning to the tall, balding man. "Unfortunately, my friend has severe allergic reactions to cigar smoke. Alas, we must move. Ta Ta my new friend." And with a swish of her fur, she followed Susanna to a table for two at the far corner of the room, near the Michigan Avenue exit.

"Must you shout out my name in a bar?"

"Oh pish, there are thousands of Susannas in this city, and probably a few in this bar. Besides, I didn't use your last name."

"True. I don't like being singled out in public, especially in a bar."

"Ok, OK, I won't do it again."

"Forgiven."

"That's what Howard always tells me."

"Why am I not surprised." Susanna's chuckle paused when the waiter came to take their order.

"Some food?" Julia asked. "Let's get appetizers?"

Susanna nodded agreement, and Julia spilled out "mussels, focaccia, and a little pate. And do not forget a good glass of Cabernet for my friend. I'll have Jack, with a twist." The waiter wrote slowly and responded, "Signora", then left.

"Doesn't anyone speak English anymore?" she said with a dramatic wave of her hand.

"No, it's been preempted by Spanish and rap."

"Rap, the result of a bad report card. It once was a pleasure to listen to music. Now Cole Porter lyrics are ancient history and words on some bathroom wall are getting Grammys."

"Am I to assume that rap is illiteracy in your eyes?" Susanna asked.

"Come, come, any idiot can rhyme fuck, bitch and ho, but can they use 3 and 4 syllable words. Can you hear syncopation, cunnilingus, or chaperone rolling off the tongue of a rapper?"

Julia suddenly looked to either side of her and leaned over the table, eyes narrowed, lips closed. A story was coming: "Once upon a time ago, I was having dinner with an odd group. They needed livening up. So instead of placing an order for focaccia, I said I was dying for a taste of fellatio; do you think it might have been wishful thinking! Of course, half the group exploded. A few others sat there stunned."

Susanna laughed and visualized the stir Julia must have created, wondering if indeed it was a deliberate attempt to wake up the party or just Julia being Julia.

With Julia, one never knew what lay behind her comments. She was a woman with many faces: bright, inquisitive, and passionate; she was quick to anger, yet equally ready to feel remorse. Married for 10 years to her current husband, Julia remained an enigma. An obviously educated woman, she never spoke of her past, her family or any previous marital attachments. She befriended Susanna and few others at the office, did a moderate amount of business and entertained lavishly to a multitude that included celebrity and the common man. No one knew much more.

The waiter brought the wine for Susanna and the Jack for Julia who sighed with exaggerated appreciation. She looked at Susanna and said, "I never order just bourbon, it sounds too alcoholic. But Jack Daniels, that just sounds so, so sexy."

When Susanna nodded approval of her wine, the waiter responded with another "Si, si" then filled the rest of her wine glass.

"Well, what's the scoop? Was it one of Terry's ex-boyfriends, or do we have a sicko out there?" Julia's face was serious now, the earlier flirt, and recent drama queen turned inquisitor in a few short moments.

"Sicko," Susanna confided, "and he's out for real estate agents."

Julia drank some Jack, inhaled deeply on her cigarette and closed her eyes, "I think I knew it." She exhaled a stream of smoke into the air, then said with eyes open wide, "It happened to a friend of mine in California, not that long ago. I didn't think hers was an isolated murder then, and I still don't."

"That's strange. Peter just came back from LA He was consulting with the police on a new murder there. In fact, he told me the police believe several murders are connected. I wonder if it includes your friend."

"Are they positive it's the same man?"

"I don't know. What all Peter said was that the crimes were similar. Who was your friend?"

"Amanda Brewster. I was her mentor when we worked together in Michigan."

All around them, men and women laughed and drank, unaware that the two women were engaged in a conversation that focused on the death and mutilation of women who sold real estate.

◆◆◆

A couple of fat and happy out-of-towners approached Julia and Susanna at the Portals, anxious to buy drinks for the pair, but Julia waved them off. However, when a startlingly good-looking man approached, she fluffed her hair and burned holes in his eyes with hers. Unfortunately, he wasn't looking at her, his eyes were directed toward Susanna who looked up suddenly and recognized Matthew Stark.

Disappointed that she was not the object of his direction, Julia quietly sighed before Stark reached their table, "I sincerely hope that you know this man and will convince him to run away with me."

"Susanna! I didn't expect to see you here," Stark said, pleasantly surprised.

"Oh, this is one of our neighborhood's watering holes. A convenient place to meet. Julia Deveroux, meet Matthew Stark."

Stark gave Julia his full attention, and she drank it up. "Join us, Mr. Stark. We are two bored females, anxious for some scintillating conversation."

"You'll have to excuse Julia, she doesn't get out much."

"Why is that, Julia?" he asked with a tone of voice that put a rare touch of pink in her cheeks.

Not missing a beat, she quipped breathily, "Howard keeps me chained to the bedroom door."

This time it was Stark whose cheeks tinged with color.

Susanna rolled her eyes and offered a white flag, "You'll have to pardon Julia. She loves to shock, don't you Julia?"

"Oh Susanna, such a spoilsport. Mr. Stark looks as though he is well equipped to take care of himself." Then turning to Stark, she asked with full drama- queen essence and a whiskey voice, "May I call you Matthew?"

A bit more composed, he sat down at their table and said, "Ms. Deveroux, you may call me anything you like."

"Matthew it is, and you may call me Julia. Understand, I do not extend the option of such familiarity with just anyone. I love a man who is not afraid to blush, especially a tall one, and especially a tall one with hair. If I were twenty years younger, I'd ask you to run away with me."

"Twenty years isn't a significant difference, we can still run away," he said, his voice full of laughter.

"Alas, Howard would object. Besides, he's been keeping me for so long, I owe him some loyalty. Don't you agree, Susanna?"

"Fortunately, I do. What's more, if you ran away with Mr. Stark, I'd lose a client."

"Oh, is that what you are," she said, turning to Stark, "I was hoping you were Susanna's secret lover!"

Now it was Susanna who blushed as Stark watched. "Oh Julia, sometimes you absolutely astound me. I apologize, Mr. Stark," she said to gain control, hoping that her attraction to him wasn't pasted all over her face.

Julia was no fool; she knew something had to be afoot to elicit such a defensive response and sudden rise in Susanna's color, so she tried to help. "Oh Matthew, I do get carried away at times with some of Susanna's old clients, but you evidently aren't an old client, you're a new one. Forgive me. I've no doubt had a little too much of the Black Jack."

"There's nothing to forgive unless of course Susanna is insulted at my being labeled secret lover material."

Julia gave up a throaty laugh, "Oh, perhaps we should run away together. What do you think Susanna? Could he be proper secret lover material?"

Susanna's only escape was to laugh, and she did. Heartily. "For you Julia, every man alive can be proper secret lover material—as long as Howard gives his approval."

Julia sighed, "Oh dear. Sorry, Matthew, Howard would probably think you're too tall!"

"Is that what my problem is?" he laughed.

"I doubt seriously if you have any problems, Matthew. Of course, you're not my client so I can be generous."

"I see. The client relationship makes all the difference, does it?"

Not usually at a loss for words, Susanna quietly sipped her wine and waited for the verbal foreplay to end between her friend and this man whom she both feared and fancied.

Julia the Inquisitor returned, "Sometimes. But practice makes perfect. So, keep practicing. Now for some details, why are you searching for a home in Chicago?"

"Business," he answered.

"Ah, monkey business?"

"You don't quit, do you?"

"That is what keeps one living life, Matthew."

Anxious to get the conversation back to a neutral ground, Susanna ticked off Stark's final list of properties at 1313 Lake Shore and One Mag Mile to which Julia nodded approvingly, "Good choices. Much better than all that new riff raff they're building today."

"Julia's not a particular fan of some of the new construction in the city."

"Construction! Papier-Mache would be a more appropriate description."

Stark interrupted, "Julia, I have to disagree with you. Some of Chicago's new buildings are incredibly well designed, and well built."

"Matthew, tell that to some friends of mine in million dollar condos whose ceilings leak, interminably. Or to investors hoping to reap untold profits with cookie-cutter floor plans and mediocre finishes. We've become a city of high priced flash, trash, and brass, unless of course, one is willing and able, to spend millions on coffered ceilings, inlaid floors, and kitchens that bespeak tomorrow. And with that, the defense rests."

Stark applauded. "Passion such as yours ignites change, Julia. Don't lose that edge."

"Unfortunately, most buyers have no taste, so my architectural passion is wasted on brand-conscious brains. If it's trendy, it must be a good buy. And with that, I must say goodbye. I leave you in good hands, Matthew."

She stood, suddenly looking fatigued, kissed Susanna on the cheek and with a "ciao", "Howard is waiting", and a "till we meet again, Matthew", she left in a blaze of fur and a curtain of Boucheron.

"You have exceedingly entertaining friends, Susanna."

"Yes, I do," she said, a little ashamed. "I may not always agree with Julia, but I admire her courage to speak her mind. It's sometimes difficult to be forthright and not offend. And with that, I must take my leave. It's been a long day."

Stark signaled the waiter, then helped Susanna with her coat. "May I get you a cab?"

"No, I think I'll walk. It's just a few blocks."

"Then permit me to walk you home," he offered, his eyes staring down at her.

"That would be kind." For some reason, she felt a flood of trust. There was something quiet and secure about him, something she craved to know better.

Stark insisted on paying the bill, then he and Susanna stepped out into the cold and starry night. They walked quietly, the air pregnant with unspoken words. When they arrived at Susanna's building, he took her hand in his and smiled, "I'll see you at 10 AM at 1313."

"Yes, everything is set."

"I'd like to commit to something tomorrow. Perhaps we can write up a contract late afternoon. Would that be alright?"

"That would work out well. Till tomorrow then." She paused then entered the building. Before entering the elevator, she turned. He was still standing there, collar up, a light snow beginning to fall on his silvery mane.

She smiled then pressed the call button for her floor.

LOS ANGELES

54

When Krachewsky rolled into the office, Mac was just ending a phone conversation: "Yeah, I know. I really appreciate your help."

"Who was that?" Harry asked.

"The print guys. They got the print from Chicago. We'll get a report within the hour. By the way, Harry, what have you got planned for Christmas?"

Mac's sudden change of subject startled Krachewsky, but he didn't bat an eyelash. He just eased himself into the upholstered chair next to Mac's desk and adjusted his brown plaid tie searching his mind for a reasonable Christmas activity that could halt Mac's forthcoming invitation.

"Not much. A few of us are getting together to play cards."

Mac watched his friend of 10 years and knew full well that Harry Krachewsky would probably be at the station on Sunday praying that a card game would be in the offing. It was the same every year; Mac extended an invitation and Krachewsky would pass. The excuse would be cards or a 'date' with an invisible no-name woman, but Mac wasn't going to accept a no, this time.

"Harry, I promised Tim you'd come for Christmas dinner and give him tips on getting noticed by the NFL scouts. He's really counting on you being there."

"Mac, why do you do this to me," he whined.

"Do what? Ask you to join us for roast turkey, candied yams, whipped cauliflower, homemade candied cranberries and a helluva lot more? Ask you to reminisce about your days in the NFL with my 16-year-old son, who happens to be a football fanatic? What's so bad about having a great dinner with a real family, and being idolized by a teenager?" He took a deep breath, "Hell Harry, you know you want to come, so quit the act."

"OK, OK, I'll do it for Tim."

Mac leaned back in shock. It was the first time Harry admitted, albeit in his own way, that he wanted more than what his solitary cop's life was giving him.

The shrill ring of the phone jarred them both as Mac quickly grabbed the receiver. "McHenry, here," he answered. A smile crept across his face as he recognized the familiar voice. "I don't know. I'll have to ask Harry. Me? I could use a couple days." He mouthed the word 'Peter' to Harry as he continued to listen.

Krachewsky rolled his eyes, in jest, aware that without Peter's uncanny direction they would not have the few pieces of evidence they were able to uncover. He actually looked forward to seeing the little man once again, of course, he would never admit that to Mac, or anyone else.

While Mac spoke animatedly, Harry's mind wandered to thoughts of spending Christmas day with Mac, Mary, and the kids. He was close to the family but kept his visitations to regular days, not holidays. Harry didn't want pity; no matter who extended an invitation he always felt like a third wheel, intruding on a very personal time. So, he did the best he could and simply got through the day. Being a Midwesterner, it was easy to downplay the significance of the 25th of December when surrounded by palm trees and mild temperatures in the 60's.

His thoughts were interrupted by his partner's question. "How would you like to hit Chicago with me on Tuesday? Arnstein wants a pow wow."

Harry's smiling face beamed back an affirmative nod. Chicago, he thought, home. He missed the city and its neighborhoods, not the snow or the wind, but certainly the city lit up for the holidays. As a beat cop, he often would walk the streets after his shift just to soak in the twinkling lights and the music that poured from every home, and every 'ma and pa' bar and store.

He was never alone in Chicago; he was part of a big family, a family of strangers, yet one that welcomed him with open arms, no matter when or where he visited.

In LA he was alone. There were no neighborhoods, no real ones at least, with corner bars where people congregated for easy banter or deep philosophical discussions. Here they all drank coffee lattes and a host of other concoctions with names and price tags that left him spinning. And talk? It was valley speak, I.T. gibberish, or simply, speech sounded by clicking words created on a laptop keyboard.

To him, LA wasn't a city or a hometown, it was a place where people connected—for business, for pleasure and quite often, not with any real human contact. As far as Harry was concerned the dealmakers and the laptop robots were single-handedly erasing human caring, understanding, and connection. Harry believed you had to be married in LA, even if the marriage failed you got a live connection for a while.

When Mac finished his call, he gave Harry a quick rundown on his conversation with Peter. "Now, he's really convinced there's more than just a real estate connection between our kills."

Harry agreed, "I think so, too. I can understand a sick, pissed off bastard offing one agent. But a series of 'em. Uh huh. These kills weren't chance kills, Mac. Sure, the women were vulnerable, but they were killed in high profile areas—witness Heaven. Hell, a nanny, a cleaning service or a gardener coulda showed up in a heartbeat. These women were stalked for a reason. They had to be."

"I don't know. This sicko's mother could've been a Realtor; maybe he hated her and snapped, then took it out on all big-time Realtors who wore the Boucheron he gave them. Maybe his mother wore it."

"Boucheron aside, Mac, you gotta believe these kills were planned."

"I do, and I don't. The kill sites throw in a monkey wrench."

"For me, the kill sites say they have to be planned."

"Either way Harry, this killer is smart, but he'll make a mistake. Hell, we've got a thumbprint, and we'll get more."

CHICAGO
PETER AND ARNSTEIN RETURN TO THE CITY

55

The highways were clear as Arnstein and Peter headed back to Chicago; the snowfall had stopped shortly before they discovered the tastes and smells of Bessie's Café.

It was a little after 8 o'clock: traffic was relatively light and the sky, a sheet of black velvet showcasing pairs of 10 karat star-shaped gems.

"Mac will get his flight information to us," Peter announced after he folded his mobile phone.

"Is Harry coming with Mac?"

Peter looked at Arnstein and laughed, "I doubt seriously that Harry will ever pass up an opportunity to come home. This city is in his blood. I'm frankly amazed that he ever left."

"Well, he was pretty badly beaten up in the NFL. Broken bones, torn ligaments, he must be a major league arthritic. I'll bet he moved because of the weather."

"That was just one of the reasons," Peter said with a little hesitance.

"Something tells me you're reading a lot more into Harry's motives than you're telling. And you're not planning to tell me your thoughts either, are you?"

"No," Peter answered with a smile, as he proceeded to get comfortable, removing his sheepskin jacket, and finally opening his briefcase to remove a pad of yellow lined paper. "I suggest we get to work and collect our thoughts and data as we drive. Agreed?"

Arnstein said yes and began the timeline of the known killings, rattling off what he knew. "Number 1 has to be Amanda Brewster. She was killed at a showing. The COD, multiple stab wounds, plus a slit throat. She was blindfolded by her killer who assumed the identity of an Italian director and left no trace of himself. Aside from those facts, we have your impressions."

"Don't forget the crown she was wearing."

"Right."

"I think Maggie Palmieri is Number 1?"

"For me, she doesn't seem to fit, Peter. Killer was a woman. She fell or was pushed into a pool after being struck from behind. No posing."

"Don't forget the Boucheron gift, David. Besides, we could have a pair of killers, or this one may be different simply because it was in his early stages. The poses could have escalated as the killer, or killers became more confident."

"OK, let's put her at Number 1 on the timeline, but I'm still on the fence. Occupation: Old time Realtor. Other than that, we don't know much about her; she seems to have been a loner. No intel on birthplace or schools, or friends. Our only connection is that she was killed at a showing."

"What about the incident in Santa Fe?"

"That was twenty years ago, Peter."

"True, but it may suggest a connection."

"Davis and Kramer are on it. Had them check with the Santa Fe Realtor Association. Haven't heard anything yet."

"We'll move Brewster to Number 2, and that makes Janna Valli Number 3. An elaborate and fabricated tub murder scene; a gift of Boucheron; a print on a shower curtain, a 'mother' engraved necklace, and an eye mask."

"Our guy has quite an imagination, Peter, but he outdid himself on Number 4. Beidermeister was gruesome, those arms!"

"What about Millie Frobisher? She was by far the most outlandish. The money, the lampshade! More and more I choose to believe the killer is telling us something with the body posing," Peter added. "For example, each one suggests a title. Palmieri was found in *Hot Water*. Beidermeister with her *Hands Off*. Valli's scene looked like the *Death of Marat*. And Terry Playmore simply says: *I Lost My Head*. I have yet to put a title to the Brewster scene, but I will."

"I get what you mean. The pix of Brewster's scene looked like a Hollywood set; the sheer flowing draperies at the French doors, the ocean in the background, her body clutching the drape, surrounded by a sea of blood.

"But it was pretty much the way she naturally fell. The only thing our fake Scalparelli did was turn her head so that anyone coming into the room would see the blindfold and the crown. That title could be *Uneasy lies the head that wears the crown.*"

"Bravo, David. What title do you choose for Frobisher?"

"That's a toughie. Maybe, *Money is the root of all evil,* or it could be *Lights out.* Or how about, *No light at the end of the tunnel?*"

"Admirable. If the scenes do in fact suggest a title or meaning, only the killer's apprehension will unfold the real significance of the posings, if they are indeed meant to say something. And that includes the gifts of Boucheron."

"As to the perfume, Harry has confirmation that Brewster and Valli both received anonymous gifts of the scent shortly before they were killed. Politis confirmed that Frobisher also received Boucheron as a gift."

"I, of course, sensed the perfume at both the Beidermeister and Playmore scenes."

"Correction. Beidermeister's a confirmation. Davis called just before we got to Indiana. You were napping."

"That makes five confirmed and one that I sensed," said Peter.

"I bet we'll get a confirm on Playmore. I can feel it. Two more notes. Wallins said no woman was at the stable. And yes, that was jewelry you saw, a heart charm with a ruby. You could be on the right track about the posing telling a story, Peter; it's just reading it the right way."

"Oh, quite definitely. And now I remember...the heart charm...didn't Det. Gonzales say an agent described Valli's killer wearing a charm bracelet with rubies on each charm?"

David thought for a moment and added, "You're right. It could mean we have a team of killers, or the killer's playing with us big time."

"I'm inclined to think one killer is playing with us. He's too methodical, David. The crimes are planned; the victim is chosen, perhaps even stalked. The only passion that erupts is the unbridled passion he feels during his killing time."

"If you really believe his victims are pointedly chosen, then the poses and anything we find at the scene is revealing something about our victim and more importantly, our killer.

"Well, let us look at it from a different perspective. What do the victims have in common, David?"

"First, other than Palmieri's drowning, they all were stabbed with slit throats. Second, they all were posed, and I include your reference to Palmieri's hot water. Third, they were all successful Realtors. Fourth, all of the victims were unmarried. Fifth, all of the cities they worked were west of Chicago unless of course there are other victims we don't know about. And sixth, the victims receive Boucheron gifts."

"You are right, David. Nothing brings them together. We don't know enough about them."

"You know, Peter, your suggestion to check Palmieri's twenty-year run-in, makes me think we should be checking all of their working histories. They all had to be licensed, and they all belonged to a real estate association. Maybe that's how we discover if they ever interacted across state lines."

"Excellent, David. Look at Ruann Beidermeister. She lived and worked in Dallas before moving to Wisconsin. We'll find the thread. Harry and Mac are already checking on the victims in LA They may uncover some past connections."

Victim by victim, the men identified every possible fact they discovered, believed or learned from all the detectives investigating the crimes.

It was late when Arnstein dropped Peter at the Drake Hotel where holiday revelers lined the entrance, men in black tie, and elegantly coiffed women, in silks and satins under mink, fox, and sable.

The men set a dinner meeting for Friday and Arnstein drove away, a little envious that he was not joining a crowd already emotionally intoxicated with the spirit of the holiday.

Traffic was light, so the trip home was a short one. He parked his car in the underground garage then walked up a flight of stairs to the townhomes in the complex.

When he had moved there several years earlier, his life was just beginning with a wife and new baby, now it was just a place to go after work. He should have moved, but he still needed the connection to that part of his life, even though the psychiatrist had told him he needed to let go. However, to Arnstein, letting go was akin to diving into a pool without the ability to swim. He was too focused or perhaps too afraid of letting go, and letting fate determine his life.

Opening the mailbox, he found a collection of bills, circulars, and catalogs for products he would never buy from places he would never frequent. Eliminating all but a few pieces, he tossed them into a silver bowl on a Sheridan table, just outside the living room in the foyer.

The living room was a contradiction of style in contrast to Arnstein's public persona. Deep cove moldings, startlingly white against the glazed chocolate-brown walls and dark walnut floors were the backdrop for over-stuffed leather sofas and traditional wing-backed chairs. A small antique table at the window played host to a carved wood game board with ornate sterling silver chess pieces waiting to attack an equally impressive army of brass, ready with its defense waiting a few checkered rows away.

He loved the room, remembering how his wife curled up with her afghan and current thriller as he read the papers. And how their fierce chess battles always, always ended in raucous laughter. Often, he would sit where she had read, touching the now empty cushion, hopeful that like the genie in the lamp she would reappear.

She was gone forever, he knew that, but until a new force entered his life, he grasped the mist of her memory and held on for dear life.

He was sorry for the victims whose lives at present he was dissecting, but he was glad for the need to focus intently on something other than another holiday minus his family.

He poured himself a drink and sat on the sofa, touching the empty cushion.

Friday
December 23rd

CHICAGO
PETER AT THE DRAKE HOTEL

56

Peter decided to breakfast in the Drake Hotel's Oak Room satisfying his need to watch the city awaken. He loved to watch hotel guests early in the morning eager to begin their day, their energy, almost palpable. They were like an orchestra: the brass section, businessmen and women hastening to check out and head home; the percussionists, weary travelers intent on wringing out every last shopping or sightseeing moment available to them; and the strings, locals without families enjoying the festive and friendly atmosphere away from their solitary existence.

The hostess gave Peter a California smile and chatted as she took him to his favorite corner overlooking Oak Street Beach and west along Chicago's priciest avenue. His server, Jose, who knew Peter from frequent visits to the restaurant, began pouring coffee for the little man as he walked to the table. Peter thanked him, inquired about Jose's daughter at UCLA, then ordered his usual: double thick French toast, lots of butter and real maple syrup, sausage, and a double order of fresh strawberries.

It was another gray day with a sense of snow about it, the kind of day one curls up and revels in memories. Peter realized how much he longed to return to Louisiana for Christmas, but he knew he could not. Throughout the night, horrific visions awoke him, visions that convinced him the killer had not finished his deadly quest. Susanna also was in his dreams. Somehow, a connection existed between the two of them, and he paled at the thought, yet his mind offered no direction.

He welcomed Jose's breakfast delivery; the thick eggy slices of golden browned bread and melting butter pushed his dream thoughts back into his subconscious. He was famished.

Considering how much Peter loved to eat, his friends were amazed that his weight never fluctuated.

"It's the voracious appetite of my gray cells," he would say quoting Agatha Christie's famous Belgian detective, and his favorite, Hercule Poirot.

Putting his newspaper aside, he watched the traffic off the drive as it turned onto Michigan Ave. It seemed lighter this morning, he thought, no doubt the result of office closings in anticipation of the long holiday weekend and of course, the promise of more snow.

Just as he finished his breakfast, a wonderful little girl with blonde curls and blue saucer-sized eyes, interrupted him. "Hello," she said. And Peter responded with a big hello and smile to match and then asked if she was going to see Santa Claus. And with eyes wide in amazement, she shook her head with authority, "Real Santa isn't here. He comes only on Christmas when I am asleep. That's when he leaves presents for me. The Santa Clauses in the stores are just his elves. They're for last minute people."

"Last minute people?" Peter asked the precocious child.

"Hmmm, mmmm, people who forgot to write Santa before."

"Oh, I see. Promptness is important is it?"

"Mommy and I wrote Santa way before turkey day!"

"And you've been a good little girl."

"Oh yes. I even helped mommy with my brother. And sometimes I don't like him 'cause he's not very nice to me."

A tall blonde woman suddenly appeared and apologized to Peter. "I hope Christina hasn't bothered you."

"Not at all," he laughed.

"Well Christina, it's time to say goodbye to the nice gentleman. We must leave."

Christina walked up to Peter and extended her hand. "Merry Christmas," she said. "I hope you're not a last-minute people."

"No Christina, Santa will come to my house as soon as he visits you. Merry Christmas."

She gave him one more smile before taking her mother's hand. Children often approached Peter. Perhaps it was his elfin size and wild mane of white; whatever the reason, he loved to hear life described through a child's eyes: the honesty, the simplicity, and the hopefulness.

An elderly woman whom Peter had often seen at the restaurant caught his eye. He smiled and wished her a good morning as he passed her table on his way to the cashier. "Lovely little girl, isn't she?" the old woman offered.

"Absolutely charming," Peter agreed.

"I have a great-granddaughter a wee bit older."

"Will she be here for Christmas," he inquired.

"Not likely. The family of my grandson's wife usually gets first dibs. A single old woman cannot compete with the convenient festivity of an army of aunts, uncles, and cousins who live within blocks of each other. Moreover, for me to travel there has become just too difficult. So, the phone company and I have developed an intimate relationship."

"You must call her often then."

"Oh, yes, and the conversations are so wonderful. A child's interpretation of everyday life is a joy. One forgets how beautiful life is through new eyes."

"I agree! I would love to share with you some stories I have heard, but alas, I must leave. Perhaps, though, you'll join me for tea during the holiday?"

"I would love that Mr. Dumas."

"I'll check my schedule and call. Have a wonderful day, Mrs. Chaney," he said taking her hand affectionately in his.

Peter, not one to take coincidences lightly, recalled his thoughts about a child's honest view of life, and then Mrs. Chaney's reiteration, 'life through new eyes'. *I must look at my thoughts with a child's eyes,* he thought. *No pre-conceived impressions, no complications. The simple truth. A child's eyes*

CHICAGO
THE MICHIGAN CONNECTION

57

Susanna did not want to get out of bed. She did not want to shower or dress. She wanted to hide under covers all day, perhaps several days. But, there was no choice, unless of course, she called Stark and told him she had to cancel the appointments. There was so much to do before Saturday. Oh, why she asked herself, did she invite the world for Christmas Eve?

Before her divorce, the night before Christmas was a quiet family affair that culminated in midnight services at a beautiful Victorian church in an affluent North Shore suburb. It was a chapel that might have been tucked away in a small English village with a cast of characters from an old Agatha Christie flick. It was familiar, comfortable, and intimate, absolutely nothing like its counterpart in the city. There, the minister had a marionette's smile that clicked on and off as if controlled by a string being pulled and released.

Susanna believed a good many Christmas wishes at the trendy city parish were quite superficial unless of course, you were an integral part of the church's hierarchy, a gifted inner group that dictated the social strata of the congregation. She had given up offering to volunteer for various functions— not one of the organizers ever bothered to return her calls; and yet, they continually pleaded for volunteers at all the services. Therefore, at holiday times she kept an anonymous persona, returning equally plastic greetings when she was unable to avoid the reception line of ministers and old liners.

Last year, for the first time, she attended services on Christmas day with Chris. They joined thousands of Chicagoans at the Catholic diocesan church. She felt there was a genuine spirit of holiday love and sincerity during the ceremony and particularly during the peace offering.

Strangers genuinely offered peace and holiday greetings, so unlike the little church where she was a member. Unless you were known, *sharing the peace* during the ceremony was a polite weak handshake, and a *peace be with you* without depth, meaning, or a smile.

Perhaps she really did not want to be known. Anonymity was safe, especially in a large group. One could enter and leave without creating a stir, without leaving a vacant space. Yet, she longed for more than superficial relationships. Polite hellos, goodbyes, and how are you just didn't cut it anymore. Susanna wanted depth of feeling and caring, a comfort in quiet, and most importantly, a giving and receiving. She wondered if Matthew Stark could bring a new kind of feeling to her life.

Oh, who's kidding who, she thought to herself. *He is either the Realtor ripper or another flirt who wants a great apartment, at a great price. So, I make some money and call it a day.* What she wouldn't admit is that she desperately wanted him to be different; a man with convictions, honor and all that good stuff that a man should have who happens to be riding a white stallion. She was like a schoolgirl, daydreaming about a crush when the sudden ring of her phone caused her to jump and knock the coffee cup on the edge of her night table. Fortunately, the cup was almost empty.

It was Peter. "Did I wake you, Susanna?" '

"No, the ring just startled me. I was in another world, daydreaming."

"That is a profoundly good world in which to be. Are you quite busy today?"

"Yes, as a matter of fact. I will have to cancel lunch. I have two appointments this morning and tons of shopping this afternoon."

"Well then, I won't tempt you with an afternoon at the Art Institute. I need to saturate my mind with beauty that will subjugate the violence I've recently seen."

"Oh, Peter. I feel so badly for you. Come visit me tonight. You can help me cook for the party on Saturday," she asked even though she hoped and prayed that Stark would officially extend an invitation.

"No, I'm having dinner with Arnstein, whom, by the way, I would very much like to invite to your soiree Saturday evening, if that's alright with you."

"Of course it is, Peter."

"Good then, I'll come by tomorrow afternoon to help, well, at least to keep you company as you prepare one of your feasts!"

"I'd love it. I will see you tomorrow. Oh, by the way, I had drinks with Julia last night. Someone killed a Realtor friend of hers in LA, a short time ago. I believe her name was Brewster."

Peter swallowed slowly then asked, "However did they know each other?"

"According to Julia, she was a mentor to the woman when they worked together in Michigan. Julia said she was convinced her friend wasn't the only victim of a killer. You should check on it."

"I will."

"Talk to her too, she'll be here tomorrow night with Howard."

A quick good-bye and Susanna forced herself to get up.

CHICAGO
ANOTHER VICTIM

58

Before heading to the station, Arnstein drove to Sammy's just off the corner at North and Clark to drop off some shirts. He could not believe his luck, a parking space twice the size of his Porsche and not an SUV in sight. He slid the black beauty exactly between the two parking meters, then turned off the engine just as his phone rang.

"Where are you buddy boy?" Davis chirped.

"About 5 minutes away. What's up?"

"There's been another one?"

"Where?" Arnstein asked impatiently.

"Michigan. One of our guys is from a little town outside of Detroit; he got the scoop when he traded horror stories with his brother."

"How much do you know?"

"Vic's name was Marsha Marshall. She got the ax, literally, her upper back was split like a coconut. Happened at a new home construction site the day before Playmore lost her head.

"Is it worth a trip?" Arnstein ask

"I'm not sure. I say we try a conference call first, then take it from there."

"OK, I'll head in as soon as I finish at Sammy's place. Why don't you set it up for a couple of hours from now."

"Done. You gonna call Peter?"

"Yeah, I'll see if he wants to listen in."

Arnstein asked Davis to call LA and let Harry and Mac know as well. He did not like hearing about another murder, that would be five in December, at least five that they knew for sure. The escalation did not bode well.

He entered the cleaners, chatted briefly with Sammy, gave him the shirts and wished him a Merry Christmas.

When he walked out, an SUV was double-parked next to his Porsche; it looked as though it could swallow the black beauty and spit out the parts, one by one.

The driver, a 30-something blonde with the traditional Black Lab in the back seat began frantically to wave at him when he walked to his car. "Yes, I'm leaving," Arnstein mouthed in answer to her pleading waves.

"Why on earth does anyone need a king-sized, gas guzzling SUV in the city," he asked himself. "It's bad enough they eat up two parking spaces, but driving behind them is almost like driving blind."

So that Arnstein could vacate the spot, the blonde backed up a little too fast, and without checking her rear or side view mirrors. She slammed on the breaks at the sound of crunching metal underscored by a piercing scream. She had backed into the intersection just as a car was turning onto the street.

Arnstein walked to the back of the SUV to see the damage: almost none to the SUV but the entire side of a Mitsubishi convertible was caved in, and a little girl slumped over in the back seat. He turned to the blonde who was out of her care and screaming at the driver for hitting her and denting the SUV.

Arnstein grabbed the blonde's arm and dragged her back to the SUV as he dialed 911 on his mobile. "Another word out of your mouth, and I'm going to throw the book at you."

She was about to hurl an insult at him but stopped when she saw the gun in his belt clip and then the badge on his billfold, conveniently pulled out during his call.

Paramedics arrived within minutes and rushed to the girl's side. She was not moving. They checked her vitals, braced her neck and gently removed her through the driver's side as a Blue & White drove onto the scene. One of the officers strode up to Arnstein who identified himself, then recapped the accident.

The blonde stood quietly next to her car as the officer approached. She began to cry when he asked for her license. Shaking her head, she said she left her handbag at home with her ID and registration. No driver's license, no city sticker, no registration. *She is S.O.L.* Arnstein thought to himself, as he started his car and drove off. *She had better pray that little girl is OK.*

If I had come out of Sammy's a few seconds later, the convertible might not have sustained the damage it did. A matter of seconds, a glance he thought to himself remembering once again his wife and baby's date with destiny.

Shaking the thought from his memory, Arnstein dialed Peter's mobile phone surprised somewhat at hearing him answer so quickly. "You must have been waiting for the phone to ring."

"Not really," he said recognizing Arnstein's voice. "I was talking to Susanna. In fact, I was talking about you."

"About me!"

"Yes. You are invited to a Christmas Eve soirée at Susanna's. I know you have no plans, and all of Susanna's get-togethers are pleasant, warm, traditional and well catered. Extremely well catered. Susanna does all the cooking herself, and I must add, outstandingly so."

"Well catered, huh. Still, I couldn't intrude."

"Nonsense," Peter admonished. "Most of the people who'll be there are souls with out-of-town families, no families, or families they can't tolerate. You'll be a breath of fresh air."

"Thank you, I'm honored to be included, Peter."

"Wonderful. Susanna wants us there around seven. You can park in my building's garage, and we'll walk over together. That way, you will know at least two people in the room. Now, the reason for your call, it's bad news, isn't it?"

"I'm afraid so, Peter. Another Realtor. This time it's Michigan, just outside of Detroit. Her upper back was split with an ax at a new construction site. Davis is setting up a conference call with the lead detective for later this morning. Do you want to sit in?"

"Yes. I had plans, but I will move them to later this afternoon. Shall I meet you at the station around eleven?"

"Eleven it is. See you then."

Peter put the mobile phone on the desk and poured himself another cup of coffee from the carafe he had ordered up to his suite. *Another lost life,* he thought.

He stared out the window at the waves crashing onto the beach hoping that his dreams were simply a rehashing of the earlier murders. But he knew deep inside that death was not leaving. *It is imperative*, he thought to himself, *I define the connection to Susanna.*

"Evil is here, and it is within her reach," he whispered.

Los Angeles
Harry Meets The Beidermeister Girls

59

Little Richard was screaming 'wake up' when Harry turned over and threw his pillow at the clock radio; it slid off the bedside table, but Richard Wayne Penniman, the rock and roll Hall of Famer, did not stop screaming until Harry pressed the radio's off button.

It was 7 A.M., too early to start the day, according to Harry's internal clock, and especially too early for Little Richard.

Harry was a night owl, preferring the dark and quiet to the sound of chirping birds, humming lawn mowers, and happy music, but he dragged himself into the shower and let the hot steamy water assault all 300 plus pounds of him. Whether he liked it or not, he needed this early start for what promised to be a full day.

First on the agenda were the Wisconsin victim's kids. They agreed to meet Harry around 8 o'clock at the station; both of them were leaving the city for the holiday weekend, and Harry wanted to finish their interviews before his trip to Chicago with Mac.

A quick shave and a stop at Dunkin Donuts for his powdered sugar favorites plus a king size coffee, and Harry began his route to the office—a patchwork of streets that avoided the freeway. He hated the freeways; they reminded him of an old Kingston Trio song about the MTA and some guy named Charlie who got on but could never get off.

When Harry arrived at the station, two women were waiting at the benches across from the desk sergeant. He walked over and introduced himself, confident they were the Beidermeister kids.

The woman, who identified herself as Harriet Coulter, thanked him and explained that she and her family had a flight out of LAX at two that afternoon.

Ushering Coulter and her sister, Megan Seehawk, into one of the interrogation rooms, Harry promised to get them on their way as quickly as possible.

He was surprised at how different the two women looked. Coulter was tall and carried herself with almost a regal air. Her chestnut colored hair worn neatly arranged in a French twist, gave her a polished look, unlike her sister who appeared as though she had dressed in her car and applied makeup at stoplights. He made an offer of coffee, but Coulter, seemingly the sister in charge, politely refused, so Harry began his questioning.

"When's the last time you saw your mother?"

"At least two years ago, right Megan?" Coulter answered, looking at her sister for agreement. "But we spoke fairly often."

"When was the last time?"

"About a week before she died, but Megan talked to her the day before."

"Mom called for my birthday," Megan continued.

"Did she talk about anything special?"

"Not really, just general stuff and that she was sending a check for my gift."

"Anything else?"

"Well there was one other thing; she said it was a coincidence, being my birthday and all. Someone sent her a gift. I think it was perfume."

"Did she know who sent it?"

"No, in fact, she was puzzled because a card was enclosed, but it wasn't signed."

Krachewsky looked at both women thoughtfully, then changing direction asked, "How long was your mother in real estate?"

"As long as I can remember," Seehawk offered. "She had other jobs, too, both before and after Dad left."

"Mom said she got the bug in Dallas when she worked part-time for a developer," Coulter added.

"Do you remember the developer's name?"

"No, but he was pretty big, according to my mother. You might check with J.S. Kennicott. The developer gave them a letter of reference for mom."

Harry spent another ten minutes with the sisters learning about their father, their mother's divorce and a little more about Ruann Beidermeister. According to her younger daughter, Ms. Beidermeister was not the world's most warm and cuddly mom. "She never showed up at school functions, and she never once talked to our teachers. We kind of had to grow up by ourselves."

"And we had to pay her a portion of any money we earned," Coulter added. "She didn't want us to grow up thinking we had a free ride."

"So, you weren't too fond of her, were you?" Krachewsky asked.

"On the contrary," Megan replied, "she taught us responsibility without emotion. She was practical and real.

"Our mother died a very wealthy woman, and her biggest concern was that we wouldn't be overwhelmed by our inheritance."

"Since we aren't, she evidently was very successful as a parent, all the warm and cuddly stuff aside," her sister added.

I guess that's not such a bad legacy, Harry thought to himself. Although he would have liked to see a little more passion, a little more emotion to color all the practicality Beidermeister bestowed onto her children.

He rose indicating the interview was over, and Coulter and Seehawk thanked him for keeping his promise of brevity.

After they left, Harry called J.S. Kennicott Realtors

CHICAGO
PIPPA'S INVITATION

<hr>

60

Pippa was in the conference room, once again with the Wall Street Journal when Susanna arrived at the office. *At least she keeps informed,* Susanna thought to herself as she walked past to her desk where she assembled an assortment of invitations, flyers, listing and sign-in sheets.

She dreaded having three broker opens in one day, particularly so soon after Christmas, but Susanna was convinced the promise of a holiday gathering with catered food and a $100 drawing at each property would bring out every Realtor in the city.

Some Realtors only viewed properties where agents served lunch; other agents managed an appearance where there was a drawing or giveaway. Of course, not all Realtors previewed properties to get something for nothing, there were many who wanted to see the property. It helped them recognize market highs and lows, and permitted them to speak authoritatively on the pluses and minuses of the homes and condos.

"It is so much easier to sell a product you have seen," Susanna often said, especially to new agents who took a pass on the opens.

Pippa was about to leave when Susanna walked into the conference room. "Do you have a moment?"

She folded the paper and replied, "Of course."

Susanna explained her system for the broker opens: an indication in the MLS and packets for each property which she asked Pippa to assemble. Additionally, she gave her stacks of printed flyer invitations to copy and deliver to all the offices near each property. "They have to be delivered today."

Pippa sighed then asked, "Do you seriously think anyone will show up three days after Christmas?"

"Yes, as a matter of fact, I do. A lot of agents have dead time right now, so an opportunity to visit with other agents, gossip about properties and get a fix on market conditions is perfect. Most of them will approach it as party time."

"Yes, but does that help you market your properties?" she asked in disbelief.

"When agents have good feelings about a property, they show it much more. And we're going to make certain they have good feelings."

"By the way, are you going home for Christmas?"

"This is my home," Pippa said firmly. "I occasionally visit my stepmother, but not this holiday."

"Are you very close?"

"No."

"I'm sorry," Susanna said genuinely.

"Don't be. Letitia's an acting stepmother, not the kind of woman one gets close to."

"Oh, well," she stammered uncertain what to say, then suddenly in a brighter tone, "I'm having a group in for Christmas Eve, and I'd love you to join us, that is if you'd like," Susanna offered, surprising herself with her invitation.

"There will be a few people from the office, so you won't be totally at sea."

"That's generous of you," Pippa said, also surprised, as she agreed to attend, mostly out of curiosity to meet Susanna's friends and to see her home first hand.

"The festivities begin at seven and dinner at eight. Bring a guest if you like. Here's my address." She wrote on the back of a business card and handed it to Pippa along with the flyers. "I'll see you tomorrow evening."

Pippa watched her leave, then sat down and called a messenger service.

Moments later, Chuwana's cheerless voice echoed over the office paging system. "Kaye Goody, Kaye Goody, you have a call on your extension."

"Stupid bitch," Pippa muttered to herself. "It's Pippa Kaye-Goody, girlfriend!" She dialed her extension and after the double beep announced her name to the caller.

"Pippa, it's me, Letitia."

"How are you?" she asked coldly. "I'm fine. I hadn't heard from you about Christmas, so I thought I'd call."

"I've been busy, Letitia."

"How do you like Storey & Beckman?"

"It's OK. By the way, I'm sorry about your friend Terry."

"It is a pity, isn't it? Despite our differences, I am sorry she had to die the way she did," she said flatly.

"Differences? Your best buddy had a fling with daddy. I thought you hated her guts."

"Oh, that was a lifetime ago, Pippa."

"Oh right, just after you convinced daddy to get married again. That must have really pissed you off."

"Unlike you, Pippa, I do not hold grudges. May we be pleasant for a change," she pleaded. "I didn't call to argue. Since I hadn't heard from you, I've decided to come to Chicago for Terry's memorial on Monday, and I thought we could spend Christmas together."

A slight smile came to Pippa's lips. "That might be perfect. I've been invited to Susanna Ryerson's for Christmas Eve. She's the agent who has taken over Terry's business. I would love you to meet her."

"Wonderful. I'll drive in tonight. Make reservations for me at the Drake for a late arrival, and I'll call when I get in."

CHICAGO
FROBISHER'S BROTHER CALLS

61

The desk sergeant put a call through to Davis.

"Davis here, can I help you?" he answered.

"I think it's the other way around. You called asking me to help you. I'm Millie Frobisher's brother, Nick Frobinsky," the caller responded.

Davis ignored the attitude and first offered his condolences then thanked Frobinsky for returning his call. He explained that a similar crime had occurred and that the police were determining if there was a connection between the victims. He asked when Frobinsky had last seen his sister.

"About 14 or 15 years ago. She was in college when I left home."

"Have you had any contact with her since?"

"We talked when my mother died. She wanted me to pay half of my mom's funeral. Pretty cheeky, considering she got my mother's house and everything in it. The only thing my mother left me was my father's watch," he said bitterly.

"I take it your mom and sister were pretty close?"

"You can say that again. The two of them were alike, and they treated me as if I didn't belong, so I left when I was seventeen. I never liked where we lived anyway."

"Where were you living then?"

"Northwest Detroit."

"What did your father do?"

"Nothing. He was dead. Died when I was five."

"How 'bout your mom?"

"She was a temp, you know, answered phones, typed letters. She got my sister in for the summers, too. They were the Olsen twins! They even changed their names together. Frobinsky wasn't good enough for 'em. Frobisher! That's a joke. Where are all the Frobisher's now?" he asked sarcastically.

Davis wrapped up the conversation with a few more questions about Frobisher's will and the temp service she had worked for, then thanked her brother once again and said goodbye. *Wow,* he thought to himself, *this guy really has a hard-on for his sister, and from the sound of it, she and momma were two of a kind.*

He made a note to check Frobisher's work history to see if he could get some company names for the job placements the temp service scheduled, for mother and daughter. *Peter and Arnstein have the right idea checking histories,* he thought to himself. He knew it was a flyer, but Davis also knew that flyers sometimes turned into jumbo jets.

His next call was to the Northlake PD requesting a conference call for noon.

CHICAGO
SECOND SHOWINGS

62

Susanna decided to walk to her showing with Stark. It was cold, but she was well-scarfed and bundled in fur.

Stark was waiting in the Michigan Avenue lobby with Ana Marie Fazio when Susanna walked into the building a few minutes after 10. "Oh, I'm late! I'm sorry," she apologized.

"Nonsense," the waiting pair responded simultaneously.

"We are early!"

They all laughed and exchanged hellos, then walked to the elevator and made the usual small talk about weather, traffic and last-minute holiday shopping, until they reached their destination.

Ana Marie led the way to the unit, unlocked the door and stood aside to let Stark enter and get the full effect of the cityscape. She had prepped the condo before her showing: Gershwin spilled softly from the sound system; the warm glow of intimate lighting set the stage for the starring attraction—a symphony of building shapes and heights against a backdrop of a blue-gray lake.

Stark stood at the window and watched, as Susanna watched him, knowing what he most probably was feeling. There was a majesty about the skyline from this perspective and especially at this time of day; man-made mountains, dressed in flickers of sun and honeycombed with people unaware of each other.

He stood a few moments, turned, then walked through the unit once again. Ana Marie and Susanna waited in the living room; only the sound of Gershwin interrupted the silence.

Stark was back in a matter of minutes. "OK, I think that does it. Ms. Fazio, I'd like to thank you for meeting with us today. It's an incredible unit. Susanna will get back to you after I've made my decision."

Fazio stayed behind to turn off the lights and lock up as Stark and Susanna left to see the other unit at 1313.

During the short cab ride up Lake Shore Drive, Stark made some notes as Susanna watched, thinking she was foolish to ever have considered this man to be the Realtor ripper. Just as she convinced herself that Stark was exactly what he seemed, she had a sudden realization: since his move was because of a transfer, *why was he not working with a relocation company? No transferee makes direct agent calls.* A cold chill went down her spine as the cab stopped at the building entrance.

Susanna panicked. She asked Stark to wait in the reception area while she went for the key.

Jake, the doorman, was reading the newspaper and glancing at the closed-circuit television at the desk when Susanna walked up. Handing him her card, she asked for the key to 22C, then slipping a five-dollar bill into his palm, whispered a second request. She asked him to get the engineer to escort her and her client to the unit, confiding in him that she felt uncomfortable alone in a vacant apartment with someone she hardly knew.

Having experienced one murder in the building, the doorman was quick to communicate his compliance. He slipped the fin into his pocket and called the night engineer on the intercom. 'Hey Charlie," he said, "got an agent here, needs to see 22C. Now Betty in the office says I can't give anyone a key unless someone from the building goes in with her. It's you, pal. Roger, and out."

A short cracking sound was followed by Charlie's thick accented voice, "OK, OK, I come."

Susanna finished explaining the new rule to Stark just as Charlie appeared ready to accompany them to 22C.

Stark did not take long to walk through the unit. It was dark; the only light available came from the ceiling fixtures in the hall, kitchen, and baths. His real interest was the view, so he opened the doors and walked out onto the balcony. Due east there was no horizon; the gray-blue lake and deeply overcast sky were one. Below, changing stop lights and blinking automobile headlights gave the shoreline an appearance of a moving border. To the south, the drive curved past the Drake Hotel and the tony co-ops and condos; southeast, the Ferris wheel at Navy Pier was lit with slivers of sunlight piercing the clouds.

He walked back inside the condo closing the doors behind him, and quietly said, "We can leave now."

The three of them rode the elevator to the lobby in silence. Susanna could feel a tension in the air. *He knows*, she thought. *He knows I'm afraid to be alone with him.*

Susanna thanked Charlie and asked Stark if he had any questions.

"No, not really. I'd like to make an offer on this unit, but I'm booked till around 6P.M. Are you free for dinner? Perhaps we can discuss the details then, or tomorrow morning, if that works better."

"No, dinner is fine," she said softly, hoping to mask her concerns.

"Good. Let's meet at the Hancock resident's lobby around 7:30."

"7:30, it is."

Stark hailed a cab and asked Susanna if he could drop her off anywhere.

"I'd appreciate that. I'm heading back to my office."

CHICAGO
CONFERENCE CALL

63

Peter arrived at the station around 11:15 AM. The desk sergeant directed him to an office where Arnstein and Davis had organized crime scene photos and charts on a large bulletin board. The grizzly photos offered a rude welcome.

It could have been a movie set, three principals examining the final moment in the death of six women: a brooding Clive Owen playing Arnstein, a complex Kevin Kline as the smart-mouthed Davis, and an older, wiser David Hyde-Pierce admirably coiffed with a shock of white in the role of Peter Dumas.

To anyone entering the room, the men could have been examining vacation photos, such was their absence of emotion. In truth, though, all three harnessed their feelings, both sympathy for the victims and revulsion for the executioner. Peter particularly hated to see the evidence of man's violent nature; the images became collectibles buried in his subconscious, waiting to plague his sleeping moments with the threat of appearing center stage.

Just before noon, the phone rang announcing the impending call with details of the seventh Realtor victim. Arnstein answered, introducing himself, Peter, and Davis to Detective Ron Solow.

Solow began with a rundown of the murder: "Marsha Marshall was doing paperwork, on the afternoon of the 16th. She was alone at the sales office for a new subdivision she was in charge of...we had a decent snowfall the night before she died, so her assistant didn't show up.

"She went up to one of the home lots with whoever killed her. The name entered in the guest book was Nathanial Cutter. No phone, no address, and there were no signs of a struggle. Two knife wounds to the back then one clean smash to the upper back area with an ax."

"Was she dead before the ax hit?" Arnstein asked.

"Nope, but the ME says according to the blood spatter, she was lying face down when he hit her with the ax. The bugger left it in the snow. No prints. It looks as though it came from the equipment box the construction crew had at the main site."

"Is she from the Detroit area?" Peter asked.

"Yep, she lived in another subdivision built by the same developer."

"Who's that?" Davis quizzed.

"Goody Homes, a big outfit in the suburban Detroit area. High-end homes, not your typical cracker boxes."

Arnstein rested his head on his high back swivel chair, let out a stream of air between his teeth, then asked, "Were you able to get anything from the site?"

"Not much. The road up to the sales trailer had been plowed, but we got a fresh tire track; the car he was driving backed up into a low drift alongside the trailer. And the mailman who found her body saw a white Range Rover leaving as he was turning in. We figure that she drove him to the home site. Didn't find anything in her car, but hell, half the construction crew borrowed that car for the past several weeks. One other thing though, there was an area close to the trailer where the snow was a deep pink. It looked like the killer cleaned the blood off himself."

"Did she have any children?" Peter asked.

"Nope. Divorced, and no significant other. She lived alone."

"How was she positioned when she was found?" Arnstein asked.

"That was the sick part. The bastard dragged her to a bobcat a few feet away and sat her in the front loader. Not pretty."

"Any leads?" Davis quizzed.

"There was a number on her cellular. It showed up several times, but it had to be a burner. Someone was checking on her. There also was a former client/boyfriend who wasn't too happy when she broke it off, but he was out of town."

"How about her ex?"

"He recently moved back to the area, and according to him, their divorce was not a walk in the park. He had a lot of anger, claims she was the reason he started drinking and lost his job. He tried to get alimony, but no luck. And this lady made a bundle."

"Did he look good for it?"

"He has a motive, but not much else. And he drives an old Ford coupe."

Peter suddenly asked, "What's the ex-husband's name?"

"Harman. Douglas Harman. She took back her maiden name."

"Find any perfume containers on her desk?"

"Yeah, there was a perfume bottle."

"Do you have the name?" Peter asked.

"I didn't write it down in my notes, but it's in the Murder book. Let me ask my partner."

"Ask him if it was Boucheron," Peter said.

"Hey, Jerry" he called out, "see if Boucheron is the name of that perfume from the Marshall search."

"We found a perfume gift at several scenes with the brand name Boucheron," Arnstein added.

The men spoke a few minutes longer, Arnstein and Davis offering information about the Chicago case and the other murders.

Jerry interrupted the men to say, "The perfume is Boucheron."

"I guess we've got a common killer," Solow sighed.

"Well, that makes it pretty convincing that we are all looking for the same sicko. The LA guys are coming in on Monday. I'll pass on anything else we find, Ron."

"Ditto from Detroit."

Afterward, Peter confided that he was certain her ex-husband did not commit all the murders "First, he may not have liked his ex-wife, but what motive would he have for killing all the others. No David, when we find what connects all these women, we'll find our killer."

Chicago
More Showings

64

When Susanna reached her office, she could not believe her luck--two appointments, one at 12:00 and one at 12:30. Booking two showings two days before Christmas was great, but the fact that the appointments were back to back was indeed a coup. Fantastic, she thought to herself, one trip to romance two buyers. Susanna grabbed a few listing sheets for a townhome she was selling in Lincoln Park.

She confirmed both appointments and decided to grab a cup of coffee before heading home to get her car. One of the prospects was the client of an agent Susanna particularly disliked. If shabby chic could describe anyone, it described Penelope Eveland. She wore expensive clothes with credible labels; unfortunately, they were almost as old as Penelope, and indeed, as worn.

Her affected voice raised discomfort to a new level for anyone within 5 feet of her. A heavy dose of Botox most likely contributed to her mouth's lack of muscle movement. Susanna could not understand how the woman managed to secure a client base; appearance aside, the voice was enough to send you running.

The second prospect was a real opportunity for Susanna; the buyer had no agent and did not want representation. How foolish some buyers can be, she thought to herself.

Surprisingly many buyers believe they have a financial advantage working with the listing broker. Susanna always explained that the seller paid an agreed commission only to the listing office, and if a buyer had no agent, the listing agency kept the entire commission upon a sale. "The seller does not get a discount," she would tell them.

When an agent represents a buyer, the listing office pays a shared commission to that agent. The listing broker, not the seller, determines the amount of the shared commission.

Regardless, some buyers still believed they were saving the seller a part of the commission, and as a result would offer less for the property. *You can give advice,* Susanna thought, *but you can't make them take it.* She had absolutely no problem receiving both sides of the commission. Of course, some agents gave the seller a reduced percentage if no other agent was involved, but that was discussed up front, not after the fact.

Susanna gave herself plenty of time to drive to the tony townhome in the heart of Lincoln Park, arriving a full 10 minutes before her first appointment. She unlocked the door, punched in the alarm code, and quickly ran through the posh property turning on lights and opening closet doors.

Her sellers were so considerate, always leaving their home in show condition: the kitchen, spotless; the bathrooms, gleaming with toilet seats down; fresh flowers thoughtfully placed on all 4 levels.

Not all sellers were quite so considerate, in fact, an agent who was a close friend of Susanna's was expected to pick up and dispose of dog droppings conveniently deposited on newspapers during the seller's absence.

Susanna went ballistic. She knew some agents made the beds, washed dishes, dusted and walked dogs for their clients... but dog droppings, never! Of course, Susanna would drop any seller who expected her to be a maid or a personal assistant.

The doorbell rang just as Susanna turned on the gas fireplace.

"Hi Susanna," the nasal-voiced Penelope whined. "Thank you for showing your condo on such short notice. This is my client, Robert."

Robert was the epitome of a neutered man; his thinning hair, plastered down severely across his head with an abundance of gel, one emitting a smell that matched the strength of its holding power. Under a nondescript parka that served as both topcoat and weather beater, he wore a 3-button suit, all buttons buttoned. A floral tie completed his ensemble.

Susanna graciously invited Penelope and Robert into the unit cautioning them of the seller's request that anyone entering must remove their winter boots. Penelope grimaced but obeyed, removing tall zippered boots with unbelievably high heels, only to reveal a single large toe with a red painted nail protruding from one of her black hosed feet.

Robert, meanwhile, struggled with the kind of galoshes that one refused to wear in the late 50s after the second grade in elementary school.

The two of them were a trip; Susanna turned to keep from laughing aloud.

The showing took about 15 minutes with Susanna rattling off the town home's features and improvements. She talked about the condo association's healthy reserves and the absence of special assessments, explaining that the gated townhome community believed in progressive maintenance, anticipating repairs and improvements rather than having to react to emergencies.

Robert nodded from the moment he entered the unit until he left; his blandness made him a difficult read. Susanna handed him a listing sheet and a brochure from a stack on the hall table. Penelope thanked her then joined Robert in a struggle to replace the boots they each had so gallantly removed.

The doorbell announced the arrival of Susanna's second appointment just as Penelope pulled up the zipper on her stovepipe boots.

A middle-aged man stamped his feet free of snow as Robert left with Penelope. Susanna was a bit taken aback. He could have been a slimmer version of the man she met with Terry, but this man had hair. Of course, Peter told her the killer most likely wore a disguise, but perhaps this is how he actually looks, she thought. And don't forget, she said to herself, it definitely was a woman who made this appointment. Realizing that he was staring at her, she shook her head clear of her thoughts and introduced herself, then asked, "Is your wife parking the car, Mr. Gallub?"

"Oh no, I drove here myself. My wife had a last-minute appointment, so I'll be looking alone."

The hair on Susanna's arms stood at attention. "Oh, why didn't I ask Pippa to come with me?" she asked herself. Her mind raced trying to decide what to do, and then she calmly reached for the phone in her briefcase and said to the man, "Would you excuse me for a moment? My partner is late, and I just want to make certain he didn't go to my other listing a few blocks away. And while I'm calling, would you please remove your shoes. It's my sellers' request."

"Be happy to take off my shoes, wouldn't want to track up that nice carpet," he said glancing admiringly toward the formal living room.

Susanna knew she was most likely overreacting, *the man didn't look dangerous, but 'Jimbo' seemed harmless and look what he did to Terry,* she thought. The more she argued with herself, the more secure she felt, but she dialed her office anyway and when Chuwana answered, Susanna began talking to an imaginary partner. The receptionist was naturally confused at first, then got the message and asked if Susanna wanted her to call the police. Susanna told her no but repeated the address and the buyer's name, then ended the conversation with "Then I'll see you here in a few minutes."

"I was right. My partner's just a few minutes away," she said to the prospective buyer. "Now let me take you through the unit."

She was careful to let him precede her into every room, never once allowing him to get behind her as she gave her pitch, noting each feature, upgrade and advantage of the building and the complex. He seemed duly impressed, and when they returned to the living room, he said, "I'd like my wife to see this. I think it's perfect for us. Could we do it later today? About 4 o'clock?"

Susanna checked her date planner and said yes.

He slipped on his shoes and bent down to tie the laces. "I really appreciate that you were able to show me this place today. We sold our house in the suburbs, and we have to buy something fast."

He reached his hand out to Susanna's, grasped it firmly and said he and his wife would be back at 4 PM. Then he left.

A deep sigh and Susanna recalled the man for exactly what he was: a middle-aged suburbanite looking for a city home. She was amazed at her sudden fear and reaction to him and knew that her thought process would not have reacted that way before Terry's death. *Is this my future?* she thought.

CHICAGO
A LITTLE DIVERSION

65

Peter headed to Oak and Michigan after the phone meeting with Detective Solow and deciding to walk to the Art Institute. The crisp, cold air was like a breath of spring to him, fresh and restorative; he inhaled deeply then escaped into the anonymity of the city streets.

Bundled bodies passed him in a cloud of steam surging from folds of scarves protecting rosy-cheeked faces. Children, barely able to move their little legs wrapped in colorful snowsuits, held on tight to their mother's hands. No meandering here. Everyone had a destination.

He passed the crowds at American Girl Place anxious to spend hundreds of dollars on fashion-conscious dolls with accessories, and clothes that surpassed even the 'Sunday best' chosen by many of Middle America's children.

Peter headed south on Michigan Avenue passing the new Park Hyatt, a beehive of expensive nests with balconies everyone envied, yet no one enjoyed. The balconies, dotted with quaint suburban barbecues chained to stone walls, appeared more confident than their owners, that they were secure. The lake winds were definitely capable of whipping anything to the streets below, if not battened down.

At Chicago Avenue, he continued south, away from the crowds at the high-rise Water Tower mall and began his trip past a shopper's mecca starting with Ralph Lauren where the windows were filled with the colors of Christmas sparked with honey yellows, bittersweet pinks, and apple greens.

Across the street, Nieman Marcus invited the masses to a better, more fashionable life. At the corner window, a street vendor touted "Streetwise', a publication created to develop job opportunities for the homeless offering them an invitation for a better life with each magazine they sold.

Crowds of shoppers packed specialty chain stores along his path offering everything from exquisite containers to casual clothes. As he passed Tiffany's, he reminded himself to stop there on the way back as he had not yet bought a Christmas something for Susanna.

He pulled up the collar of his shearling jacket and trudged down Michigan past Saks 5th Avenue and those famous footwear palaces, Nike Town and Ferragamo.

The Terra Museum of American Art stood quietly on the west side of the street. Peter loved it because it was an intimate home for a personal and treasured art collection. When Terra, a wealthy industrialist, opted to open the museum and establish a not-for-profit art foundation built around a 450 million dollar collection. Relatively ignored, he opened the doors in 1980 to his museum in Evanston, Illinois so that he could share his love of American Art. He moved his museum to the Michigan Avenue property he owned in 1987, and his foundation began to thrive until an attempt to move it to Washington, DC, after his sudden death in 1996.

The ongoing tug of war between an aggressive board of directors' eager to have the Terra Collection remain in Chicago, and Terra's widow, hopeful of moving the collection to Washington would soon be decided. Peter hoped it would not be lost to the city.

He smiled to himself thinking if only one had control over one's property after death, but those left alive have so many advantages. Wills contested, and heirs unrecognized could turn someone who had been viable and productive in life, into an emotionally disturbed shell after death, one described as incapable of making lucid decisions. No matter how finite the will, when large amounts of money are present, someone or some group will attempt define a way to reinterpret the wishes of the deceased or disqualify their legitimacy. Peter hated that love for money.

Across the street, his eyes focused on the Apple store with products from Mr. Gate's nemesis, Mr. Jobs. The sleek, clean store invited the masses to engage in a little Apple talk, applauded by Peter who happened to be a fan of the Macintosh computer.

Further up the avenue, he passed the sparkling terra cotta clad Wrigley Bulding inspired by the dazzle of the 1893 White City, and to some,

Chicago's answer to the Eiffel Tower and Big Ben.

On the east side of the avenue, stood a favorite of Peter's: the Tribune Tower, a Gothic monument in limestone with a 3 story arched entryway carved in detail with characters depicted from Aesop's fables.

Peter loved Chicago architecture and its history and admired the man who set the stones for the city's lakefront plan and its traditional dignity: Daniel Burnham. What's more, he reveled in the clash of architectural cultures: Art Deco, neo-Egyptian, French-influenced, Classic, Miesian, and on and on, comfortably existing as next-door neighbors, a profundity of thought and expression.

By the time he reached Millennium Park and Gehry's magnificent flying band shell, not yet officially opened, he was filled with awe at the depth of creative genius on the city's stage. The present, indeed, is the child of the past, and he believed, the father of the future.

At the Art Institute, the two official guardians flanking the entrance welcomed Peter, the proud bronze lions, collared in their traditional red-bowed wreaths. He nodded politely and walked up the stairs through the marbled foyer into the home of his eclectic friends: Seurat, Manet, Pollack, and Degas, among others.

CHICAGO
DAVIS LOOKS FOR A LEAD

66

After Arnstein and Peter had gone their respective ways, Davis went back to his office to follow-up on the Frobisher file. His first call was to the temp agency that placed Millie Frobisher's mother into a variety of jobs on a limited time basis.

According to *Temps on Time* Joann Frobisher was one of their best temps--dependable, conscientious, professional, and often requested.

The report for the daughter was not so glowing. She seemed to have a chip on her shoulder and was singled out as someone who expected VIP treatment from the mail guy, up to the man in charge.

Complaints about little Millie Frobisher ranged from talking down to clients on the phone to improper dress for a business environment. Some of the other full-time secretaries went so far as to accuse Millie of sleeping with the enemy, that being one of the supervisors, and of course, who knows whom else.

The manager of *Temps on Time* was quite the fountain of knowledge, and even if most of it were pure gossip, Davis knew where there was smoke, there often would be fire.

When he asked about the companies where Millie or her mother had temped, the manager said she would put him on hold and check the archives for the list.

While he waited for the manager's pleasant voice to return, he wondered what she looked like. *Probably a real dog,* he thought to himself, learning a long time ago that a great voice does not always equate to a great face and body. Hell, he remembered the time some chick, taking a survey on the phone, got him going with a voice that could melt butter. It so happened she worked in Chicago, so he took the bait and asked her out.

"Guess what folks," he said to his pals, embarrassed that he had been duped by a sexy voice. "This woman, most likely, spent a good part of her life standing in front of the fridge. She must have enjoyed opening and closing the door, inhaling most of what she deposited there, without waiting for it to get cold."

The Manager's deep voice interrupted his reverie, "I'm so sorry, but our system is down, and I can't get into the archives. I'll be happy to call or fax you a report of all the companies where both women were placed."

Davis thanked her, gave the office fax number and said goodbye. Next on his list was a trip to see Terry Playmore's attorney to get a peek at Playmore's will.

Meanwhile, Arnstein worked diligently charting all the murders and emailing national real estate groups and associations to determine if the crimes so far uncovered were the tip of an iceberg or an anomaly.

LOS ANGELES
HARRY HEARS FROM J.S. KENNICOTT

67

Harry's call to J.S. Kennicott went unanswered. Evidently, the local real estate company closed early for the holiday weekend. All Harry heard was a friendly 'Merry Christmas' and a recitation of office hours beginning the day after Christmas. Callers were invited to leave a message on the general voice mail or to spell the last four letters of the name of the agent to whom they wished to speak. Harry left a general voice mail with his name, his association with the LAPD and a phone number.

He sat down at a typewriter to write out his notes before he forgot his shorthand. Harry would have gone to one of the computers, but the last time he spent two hours organizing his notes, he lost all of the data. When he remembered how to highlight the pages, there was a tragic error. With a single keystroke, everything he wrote was gone. If someone had told him all he had do was go to the edit tag at the top of the screen and click undo, he would have kissed them right there at the station. But, no one told him anything, and he started again, not at the computer, but at the typewriter.

Harry still hit the computer keys but only for Internet surfing, and he was slowly becoming an actual surfer on the Net.

He finished his notes in under an hour and was ready to leave when the phone rang. It was the managing broker at J.S. Kennicott, curious why the LAPD would be calling his brokerage. Harry crossed his size 12's on the desk and leaned back in his chair, then said he was following up on some information from Ruann Beidermeister's children. The broker suddenly changed gears and began extolling the attributes of *that wonderful woman, Ruann*. He explained further that Ruann preceded him at Kennicott's, so he was not privy to her early days there, but he would be happy to help in any way possible with any information from her file.

When Harry asked about Ruann's initial letter of reference, the broker confided that he could answer with absolute accuracy. "She came highly recommended by one of the principals at Goody Homes in Austin, Texas."

"And, that is good?" Harry asked.

"Better than good. Goody developments are successful in every city they set up shop. Hiring one of their referrals meant the possibility of getting a development to market."

The two men spoke for several minutes, the broker giving Harry a sale-by-sale description of Ruann's phenomenal career at the brokerage. According to the manager, Ruann made more money than he did, and it did not bother him at all because she single-handedly was responsible for bringing in the biggest share of the business.

He was not ashamed to say that J.S. Kennicott needed her more than she needed the brokerage. "Now that she is gone, it's going to be a long cold winter." In fact, he was looking at the prospect that he would be forced to sell real estate once again. "It's a dog eat dog world out there, and I don't know if I'm up to it, being in the trenches, I mean."

CHICAGO
SUSANNA MAKES A DEAL

68

Susanna parked her car in her building garage deciding to work at home until her 4 PM second showing. After checking her voice mail, she found it filled with several calls, surprisingly most of them were requests for appointments. Two of the calls were for Terry's listings, so she forwarded them to Pippa.

It looked as though the few days after Christmas would be busy ones. It's what she hated about real estate, her 24/7 schedule, even during the holidays. She did not have the luxury of a 40-hour week. Saturdays and Sundays ceased belonging to her, evening hours were often interrupted with a solitary showing; clients continually called for feedback as if she wouldn't call if she had good news. And if one more person argued that she was earning a king's ransom, she would scream. A king's ransom, she thought, applies to government employees, not most real estate brokers.

After returning showing confirmations, Susanna pulled together two sales packets, one for Stark and one for the Gallubs, in case they decided to make an offer: disclosures, contract, W-9, dual agency form, address forms, everything her office required to protect the brokerage and her own person. In a litigious society like the current one, paper protection for Realtors was just an important as a condom for hookers and Johns.

She had a few things to buy for the party, and if she finished with the Gallubs quickly enough, she planned to hit Costco after her showing.

En route, she made a stop at Trader Joe's for their spectacular frozen brown rice, according to Susanna, and then a quick stop at Target and her shopping was complete, except for Costco. Not bad, she thought, with twenty minutes to spare before she met her prospect at the townhouse.

She headed north to Clybourn, not particularly thrilled to drive through the new yuppie-puppy shopping mecca. Traffic was unreal from

North Avenue to Cortland; she still could not believe the number of retail chains that invaded the former warehouse ridden avenue.

Perhaps she was just getting old, impatient and intolerant, but a trip that once took 10 minutes was now taking upwards to 30 and 40 minutes. According to Susanna, the blame rested on the scores of SUVs piloted by Botox blasted women doing their aggressive thing on the two-lane roadway.

When she arrived in the complex, all the streets were ablaze with miniature lights dressing every tree, bush and stair railing. It was quite a sight to Susanna as she parked her car on the parking pad in front of the garage door.

She unlocked the townhouse and began her ritual of turning on lights and the stereo to fill the room with an undercurrent of holiday spirit.

Door chimes announcing visitors soon accompanied the sound of Silver Bells tinkling on the stereo.

Mrs. Gallub was a pleasant woman who looked to be 50 going on 70, her cherub face finely lined, her hair peppered with gray, a sturdy wool coat buttoned tightly around a figure as wide as it was tall. She would never attract an admiring glance, never that is until she smiled and her energy awakened. Her lines disappeared, her eyes exploded with pinpoints of reflected light, and her bright pink lips plumped to frame perfect, white teeth. Her smile was one of the most engaging smiles Susanna could remember seeing, and she responded enthusiastically.

"I want to thank you so much for meeting us this afternoon. We really appreciate your being so sweet," Mrs. Gallub said genuinely, as she began to cough into a large white handkerchief.

Susanna thanked her, wished her a speedy recovery, and went on to explain her role as a listing agent and the complexities of being a dual agent—that is, representing both the seller and the buyer. She went on in detail, so there would be no confusion, and offered to refer them to another agent who could represent them as buyers if they preferred.

"Nonsense!" Mrs. Gallub smiled. "You seem like a nice enough lady. Now, let's see if this townhome is as lovely as my husband says."

For the next 15 minutes, Susanna did a dog and pony show, extolling the attributes of her listing, the complex, the area, the potential for transportation options, the proximity of major thoroughfares, and the city proper. She was polished, professional and most believable.

"Sold!"

"I beg your pardon," Susanna said with surprise.

"We'll buy it," Mr. Gallub chirped. "Do you have a contract with you, or should we go to your office?"

"No, I have a contract with me, plus all the disclosures," Susanna said quickly, still in disbelief that she had heard correctly, yet not disbelieving enough to question.

"Do you think the sellers would mind if we sat down at their dining room table and signed the contract?" Mrs. Gallub asked with some hesitation.

"Oh goodness, no," Susanna replied. "In fact, they may be walking through the door in a matter of minutes, so we may be able to negotiate this immediately."

"Oh, there's no negotiation. I don't believe in it," the mild-mannered Gallub responded with a sudden show of strength. "We've been looking for awhile, and we know what we are prepared to spend. We'd like to offer six thousand less than your asking price. Not a penny more. It's cash offer, and we'll close as fast as your sellers want."

Susanna swallowed hard, not at all prepared for his response, so she ignored the attempt to say anything except, "Well, why don't we sit down and put everything in writing."

By the time the Gallubs signed on the dotted line, Susanna had given then all the properties comparable to the building and explained in detail the fairest way to estimate the real estate taxes. She said she could ask for a percentage over 100% or that the amount could be determined by the attorneys. Since taxes in Illinois were paid in arrears, the attorneys with whom she had been working recommended holding back two percent of the purchase price in escrow; it allowed for any tax increases, reassessments or change in the Illinois multiplier. After the taxes were paid, the sellers would receive the balance. Mr. Gallub agreed that it was most fair.

Susanna once again explained her role in a Dual Agent capacity, but the Gallubs were insistent that they were more than happy to have her act for both parties unless of course, her seller objected.

At exactly 5 PM, the sellers opened the front door. They were greeted with introductions and explanations. Susanna then asked to speak with them privately in the kitchen.

The Crowley's were thrilled with the contract and signed on the spot. Susanna had experienced quick sales before, but none matched this one on the eve of Christmas Eve, with the buyer in the living room and the seller in the kitchen. It was the kind of deal one bragged about: a first and second showing within hours of each other, a double bubble, a contract written minutes before the sellers arrive at home. It was the stuff that real estate legends were made of.

CHICAGO
DAVIS MEETS PLAYMORE'S ATTORNEY

69

Davis did not get much from Terry Playmore's attorney other than the fact she had amassed surprisingly extensive real estate holdings. They included several multi-unit properties in Lakeview and Bucktown, some half-dozen condos in the Gold Coast and Streeterville areas, and two west loop loft buildings, all in a trust naming a twenty-one-year-old niece trustee.

According to the attorney, he questioned the niece designation convinced that the young woman was, in fact, the result of a dalliance between Playmore and a lover.

Terry had me set up a trust fund for the girl. Told me that her sister died and left implicit directions for her kid's education, so Terry decided to do the same thing for her niece. But anyone I ever spoke with never mentioned Terry as having a sister."

He took a long drag on a big cigar and continued, thrilled in the knowledge that he was intimate with a murder victim and what's more, that he had an audience who recognized his importance in the relationship. "She was pretty tight-lipped about the girl, so I never asked. I don't know where Playmore got her money, but she never earned enough as an agent to own what she owned. Someone else filled her coffers and if you ask me this kid had something to do with it."

"Where is she now?" Davis asked watching the blowhard attorney play his scene like an actor on Broadway.

"In transition. Phillipa just graduated from the University of Michigan, and she's about to move to Cambridge. Must be a smart little thing—she was actually accepted to Harvard's business school.

"Will she be here for Playmore's memorial?"

"I'm assuming so. She asked me to let her know as soon as the date was set. By the way, any news on when Terry's body will be released?"

"Not yet. Does the niece know the extent of Playmore's holdings?" Davis asked.

"To the penny!"

"Is that criticism?"

"Not really. But she would not take any financial advice from me. She and Terry were thick as thieves. Any call I received from Terry was prefaced with 'Phillipa and I', or 'Phillipa suggested'. This little cookie knew where her bread was buttered, besides being smart as a whip."

Davis nodded, hoping in his heart that the 'little cookie' had enough smarts to get herself a real attorney, not just a mouthpiece in a thousand-dollar pinstripe suit.

With a thank you and a handshake, he gave the attorney his card and asked to be called when Playmore's niece arrived.

Chicago
The Deal Is Done

70

Susanna finished getting all the signatures for the townhouse disclosures and left both of her clients in an exceedingly happy frame of mind. The Gallubs agreed to have an inspection a few days after Christmas, so the timing was perfect as the sellers were leaving in the morning for a week in Aspen. If all went well, the closing would be the second week of January.

What an amazing start to a new year, Susanna thought, a 700,000 sale acting for both buyer and seller. With her commission split, it meant just under $28,000 in her checking account. If only every transaction were so easy, but they were not. Susanna was always amazed how much everyone resented an agent earning a commission. They never took into consideration the cost of doing business, the fact that agents were independent contractors who paid for everything. No company perks, no insurance, no car allowance. Nothing. And most important, there was usually a long time between sales.

According to some of Susanna's agent friends, some sellers expected returns on their home investments of 10 and 15 percent a year, and woe to the agent who did not deliver the bacon. Calls demanding to know why there were no showings were a constant reminder. In the event an offer did come in, pity the listing agent if it was lower than her seller's expectations. The 'insulting' offer would unleash a torrent of abuse on her.

Still, other agents claimed that some sellers expected to be wined and dined, and only at the best restaurants. One of Susanna's developer clients actually said, she owed it to him since he had given her so much business. Owed it to him! What a joke, she would say, as if she didn't earn it.

He called her incessantly for information and appointments, even to learn enough to make a substantial offer on a For-Sale-by-Owner property, thus eliminating any possibility for compensation to Susanna for her time and help. Oh, of course, he would say she would get the listing after he rehabbed the property if she did comparatives and priced it for him, but only if he could not sell it by himself.

In other words, her information, her time, her cost of doing business, her negotiating skills, her market interpretations and her resources and expertise had absolutely no value, except to allow him to make a profit.

One time when she took him and his girlfriend out to dinner, he actually ordered a $300 bottle of champagne.

She dumped him as a client.

The more and more she thought about the business, the more she disliked some of the participants. Forget the condescending buyers and sellers, she would say, how about the attorneys. No one ever questions them, their skills, or their worth.

The same held true in her mind for inspectors who only needed to 'find' something to substantiate their fees. Moreover, according to their contract invoice, they are only liable up to the amount charged for the inspection.

Susanna estimated that if she charged the hourly rate that either attorneys or inspectors did, her former developer client would have paid her five times what she earned.

The time was near. Susanna did not expect to be selling real estate when she turned fifty. She had an incredible feeling that something momentous was on the horizon, and she hoped with all her heart that it would be positive.

Meanwhile, she had an hour and a half to hit Costco and get home to get ready and meet Matthew Stark.

Susanna was amazed at how few cars were parked in the Costco lot. She ran to the entrance, list clutched in hand. Inside, she maneuvered the aisles Andretti-style, having absolutely no intention of pausing at any display that did not correspond to the items on that list.

Ordinarily, Susanna would wander the cavernous warehouse plucking items of interest until she filled her cart with books she had to read, enough paper towels to last a lifetime and frozen tidbits that would serve an army of acquaintances. *If memory serves right*, she thought, *I still have two quarts of olive oil in the hall closet behind those four packages of bathroom cleaner I bought last summer.*

She continued to live in a time warp, buying enough cleaning supplies for a 10-room home she no longer owned, and enough food for a growing family that now numbered one.

In a little over twenty-five minutes, record time for Susanna, she managed to accomplish her task with only one extra purchase: a superbly priced lightweight weekender, on wheels no less, and certainly an improvement over the weighty one she often used. *Besides,* she thought to herself, *I can stuff everything I bought into it.* She rarely remembered to bring bags to the discount giant to carry her purchases home from the car.

LOS ANGELES
MURDER IN MICHIGAN NEWS

71

"Mac, I'm telling ya, all these women were heavy hitters. This could be a simple case of a hired hit-man eliminating agents ready to skip."

"Harry, this case is getting to you. You really think there's a hit man out there pitching real estate offices the advantages of removing agents who bitch or plan on leaving. Come on, nobody kills a golden goose."

"Yeah, I guess you're right. I'm getting pissed that I can't find a real connection between these women, and my gut says there is one. So far all I've got is that 3 of them worked in the Midwest at one point."

"Maybe that's the connection."

"The Midwest?"

"Yeah, I got a call from Chicago. Davis said there was another murder. This time in Michigan. Happened about a week ago."
Harry sat down slowly. "That's five we know this month."

"Yeah, and we got another week left." Mac took a long drink from the cup alongside his computer monitor and then proceeded to bring Harry up to speed on the Michigan stats as well as learn what Harry had discovered.

CHICAGO
GETTING TO KNOW YOU

72

Susanna's luck continued. The trip home was traffic-free, unbelievable for a Friday at 6 o'clock, but she did not complain. She had a glorious hour and a half before meeting Stark, and she took advantage of it, preparing her final list for Saturday, as well as checking her email and voice messages.

When she arrived at the Hancock, Matthew Stark was waiting. Susanna suggested they walk south to a local restaurant on Chestnut, aware that without a reservation their chances of getting a table anywhere else were slim to none.

It was a good call. The bar was packed, but a few tables were still available, and the hostess directed them to one in the corner where they nestled their coats and briefcases on a vacant chair.

A waiter appeared and took their drink order, Stark opting for a martini, while Susanna chose a Cabernet.

"Well, have you decided which unit you want."

"Knowing what you want is easy, getting what you want is sometimes another story," he said quietly.

She felt his eyes peeling away every mask she wore, baring her very soul. She was fascinated and frightened, certain there was more to this man than what appeared.

"I've decided on 22C at 1313."

"I think you'll be quite happy with the building," she said, filling the conversation with babble from her Realtor tour bag.

"I can be happy pretty much anywhere. Are you happy where you are?" Stark responded.

Susanna took a deep breath; she was intimidated by him. *You are acting like a schoolgirl,* she said to herself, *not a mature adult. Attack, don't back off!* "That depends if you are referring to where I live, or where I am in life.

I think most people can be happy pretty much anywhere they live."

Then she said more confidently, "As to life, it's simply a question of priorities; when they change, it's time to move on."

Before Stark could respond, the waiter served their drinks and presented the evening specials.

After they had ordered, Susanna removed a contract from her brief-case and began going over the offer. It was pretty cut and dry, no mortgage contingency, a flexible closing date, the standard attorney review and inspection period. The only issue was the price. Stark went over the comparable properties that Susanna had given him, and then he named his figure. She inked it onto the contract, and he signed.

"Well, that's probably the shortest time I've ever taken to spend just under a million dollars," he laughed.

"Let's wait till we have a deal," she smiled. "I'll call the listing agent right now and give her the specifics." She left the table and went to the entrance hopeful that the noise would be less invasive. It was. After two rings, the agent answered. *I must be living right,* she thought,

In a matter of minutes, she was sitting across from Stark once again assuring him he most probably would have an answer before they finished dinner.

Now that business was out of the way, Susanna was not quite certain what to say, and Stark did not help. He sipped his martini and watched her struggle.

Attack, she thought once again, forcing herself to return his stare. *No pain, no gain.* "So how did you make the triangle from Alabama to LA to New York?"

"It was a hop, skip and a jump," he drawled.

"You don't like to talk about yourself, do you?"

"No."

"Ahhh, a man of my dreams. Just the facts. Yes, No, Perhaps. Care to elaborate on the no?"

"Do you want me to, or are you just making polite conversation?"

"I'm curious."

"OK, I'll tell you why I moved if you tell me why you asked for protection at 1313?"

She almost dropped her wine glass, never dreaming he really knew and would confront her, but she caught herself and took a long sip of the ruby liquid in her glass while she locked eyes with this most challenging man. The cover-up maneuver was provocative, but even Stark could not deny that it successfully diffused a potentially awkward explanation.

"I didn't think you noticed," she said almost playfully after the long pause.

"Let's say I'm observant," he responded with his relentless stare.

Susanna could not read him. No matter what he said, she sensed a double meaning. Prepared to play a teasing game, she began to speak, but her mobile rang, and the spell was broken.

The offer was accepted. It indeed was her day; the sellers did not counter. The conversation turned once again to elements of the contract and purchasing steps, leaving her wishing the phone had not rung.

CHICAGO
PETER & ARNSTEIN RECAP AT DINNER

73

Arnstein was already seated and halfway through a Jack Daniels on the rocks when Peter arrived at the trendy River North restaurant.

The maitre'd, an old friend from his attorney days had given Arnstein a primo spot in the packed room and Peter was dutifully impressed.

"A man who warrants such a privileged location on a busy holiday weekend night must be a friend of the owner, or he may be exercising surreptitious means. Which is it, David?" Peter quizzed with a mysterious air.

"I'm just a lucky S.O.B.," he laughed. "Nah, Louie's a good friend," he said indicating the robust man at the reservation desk.

"I hope you like sushi, Peter."

"I'm a moderate fan. But I'm certain there will be other choices on the menu."

Peter opted for a glass of champagne. "I feel festive tonight. Unlike you, my friend, I took the day off and spent it at the Art Institute reconnecting with creative genius and beauty."

"Well, that certainly was a departure from our morning meeting."

"Yes, but it helps me to balance my thoughts. Too much blood and gore weigh one down, and thoughts become reactive rather than objective. I need to hold on tight to my objectivity to see beyond the physical."

David ordered another Jack Daniels when the waiter appeared with Peter's champagne, then proceeded to give Peter an update. He told him about the Midwest connection uncovered by Harry and the news about Playmore's niece.

"What surprises me, Peter, is that the Realtor associations don't often communicate among themselves so national info on agent kills can get lost. Perhaps the great number of associations makes it difficult. I contacted several local groups and they didn't have any data at their fingertips; they were helpful and provided some links, but as far as I was able to glean, they don't publish specifics, just warnings for agents to be careful."

For the next few hours, Arnstein and Peter were deep in conversation, discussing everything from Harry in LA to Davis's recent findings. Peter listened intently, mentally filing bits of facts, descriptions, and assumptions, knowing in his mind that the killer was here in Chicago, and prepared to kill once again. He could feel it. The connection between the victims was starting to crystallize. When it did, the why would be revealed.

Peter repeated Susanna's information about Julia Deveroux, a Chicago agent who confirmed working with Amanda Brewster in Michigan before Brewster left for Los Angeles. "The Midwest again. Perhaps Texas is another link. Ruann Beidermeister worked there as well as Terry Playmore."

CHICAGO
STARK'S INVITATION

74

Stark signed the credit card receipt, leaving a generous tip for the attentive waiter. He helped Susanna with her coat then followed her from the dining room. "Are you for walking," he asked.

"Always," she answered.

They walked out into the cold and turned east toward the lake, the crunch of their footsteps on the packed snow resonating in the silent street. They passed doormen huddled inside glass towers and vintage mid-rises, waiting to open doors to greet residents. It was a perfect night: cold, clear and crisp.

"Do you have plans for Christmas Eve," Susanna asked.

"I'm flying to New York tomorrow morning to spend the holiday with some friends."

"I'm disappointed," she said.

He looked at her for a moment, smiled then offered, "Let me see, you sought protection from me at 1313, and now you're disappointed that I'm leaving town?"

"I'm not disappointed that you're leaving, I mean, I am, but I'm not... what I really mean..."

"Yes Susanna, what do you really mean?" he said with a chuckle.

"I mean, if you didn't have any plans, I was going to invite you to a Christmas Eve party at my apartment. And I was disappointed that you had plans... oh, never mind." The color rising in her cheeks, she could not believe how ridiculous she sounded. *He had better not be the ripper,* she thought, *or he'll kill me just because I'm behaving like an idiot.*

"Well, if I did not have plans, I would have been most happy to attend your soirée, Susanna. In fact, I'm flattered that you would have invited me, even if it was only based on the condition that I did not have plans."

"I'm sorry, I should have asked you, and you could have said 'sorry, I won't be here', then this whole silly conversation would have never taken place."

"I'm glad you didn't just ask. I wouldn't have seen such a flattering shade of pink in your cheeks," Stark laughed as they entered Susanna's co-op building.

"Oh, it's just the cold," she said as her cheeks turned a shade deeper pink, but she kept her composure, and said very businesslike, "Call me when you return, and we'll set up the inspection."

"Oh, I will, Susanna. I will. Have a wonderful party," he smiled then slowly bowing his head, he kissed her lightly on the cheek saying, "and a very Merry Christmas." He turned and left the building.

"Merry Christmas," she sighed, watching him walk into the night.

SATURDAY
DECEMBER 24TH

CHICAGO
DAVIS MEETS PHILLIPA

75

Davis had not planned on a run to the station, but his sister needed cream for the dessert she was making for Christmas Eve dinner, so after a quick trip to the supermarket, he stopped to see if Arnstein had returned to the office.

A fax was waiting for him at his desk. It was from *Temps on Time*.

According to the manager, Joann Frobisher was a very popular temp, but her major assignment time was divided between two real estate clients, a company that owned Goody Homes and Property Plus, a commercial enterprise. Millie Frobisher, not in demand as much as her mother, temped with the same two companies, plus over two dozen others during the three summers she worked for the firm.

Davis copied the fax for Arnstein and left it on his desk with a note. 'Interesting, isn't it?' he wrote. As he was about to leave, he was paged for a call. It was Playmore's attorney; her niece had arrived and was sitting in his office. Davis told him he would be right over, but first, he delivered the cream to his sister, Emma.

Phillipa Kaye Baggor was almost 6 feet tall with long auburn hair and a redhead's skin. She wore hip-hugging jeans, a cropped t-shirt, and hot pink running shoes. Everything about her radiated 'party girl' including a smile that lit up the room.

No one would mistake her for a Phi Beta Kappa about to enter graduate school and at Harvard, no less.

After introductions had been made, Davis learned the Baggor name and 'niece' title was a convenience Playmore conveyed to protect her.

According to Baggor, when she discovered that Terry was her mother, she asked why she was living with the Baggors.

"Terry told me it was so my father and his wife wouldn't learn about me."

When asked if she would be attending Terry's memorial service, she explained to Davis, "No, I'm going back to Texas to plan my mother's burial. She grew up there, and that's my home as well."

After signing some papers, she turned and left saying goodbye. Attorney Paul Castle was not surprised at her decision, "Everything about Terry and her daughter was far from the norm. Shielding her from a bastard label was understandable, but I am amazed at Terry's efforts to protect her child's father. Nowhere in any of Terry's papers is there a mention of her lover's identity."

"The only other thing I learned from Phillipa was that Terry, in fact, did have a sister, Jane Kaye; she was killed after falling down a flight of stairs onto a concrete patio. No other relatives."

"What about Playmore's husband?"

"Oh, she divorced him, about a year before Pippa was born. I think he lives in New York, not really certain where."

"Thanks, I'll be in touch, in case we have more questions. Merry Christmas."

"Likewise."

LOS ANGELES
HARRY MAPS OUT THE MURDERS

76

Harry sat at his desk re-reading notations he had made in his casebook. *Could they all have worked together at one point,* he asked himself. *Is it the place, the office, the managing broker?*

Valli: Michigan, Texas, California
Texas: Developer (Goodson?) (Per daughter)
LA (current): U.S. Real Estate Properties

Beidermeister: Wisconsin/Texas: Goody Realty provided
a reference (Per Managing Broker); are they affiliated
with Goodson? Wisconsin (current): J.S.Kennicott

Brewster: California/Michigan; Michigan (per Peter & Sec. Candace)
No info. Current: Independent Broker.

Terry Playmore: Michigan/Texas, Goody Homes;
Illinois, Storey and Beckman

Marsha Marshall: Michigan Developer, Goody Homes

Millie Frobisher: Indiana, (Davis checking)

Maggie Palmieri: Santa Fe/Albuquerque, New Mexico

Maybe this Goody company was the tie-in. He was happy that he and Mac were heading to Chicago, convinced they would find their killer with the marriage of detective work between LA and the city on the lake.

While Davis was getting subpoenas to check individual associations to learn if any of the victims worked together, Harry contacted the National Association of Realtors. He prepared a fax requesting information on any other local associations that may have held victim licenses in the past, and what he needed to do, officially to get the information.

Additionally, he asked if it were possible to get the dates and names of the companies who held the licenses of the victims, as well as the names of their managing brokers. He knew it was a stretch, but anything gained would give him a roadmap to collect as much info as possible.

The station was relatively quiet, but Harry knew the action would begin tonight as the holiday got into full swing. He had planned to see who was on that night to determine if a card game would take place, but something told him it was time for a change. Although a creature of habit, Harry was beginning to think outside the box, more and more.

"Why shouldn't I have more than a great apartment and high definition television," he asked himself countless times in the past few weeks. He was tired of restaurant waitresses, bartenders, hookers and other cops for all of his connections and conversation. He had not been in a real relationship with a woman in a long time, and his 50s were coming on loud and fast.

"What the hell", he said to himself as he picked up the phone and dialed the number.

"Good morning, U.S. Real Estate Properties, may I help you," the distinctive voice announced.

"Hey Stella, it's me, Krachewsky."

"Well, well, what a pleasant surprise," she said, a definite smile in her voice.

"I just learned I'm not on today, so thought I'd take a chance and see if you were free tonight. I know it's Christmas Eve, but..."

"Well it just so happens, I can be free," she interrupted. "I've been invited to a friend's home, but I can just pop by for a few minutes, in fact, you could go with me."

"I don't know if... "

"Let's decide when you pick me up," she said quickly not wanting to discourage him, then gave him her address and home phone number. Harry told her he would be there at seven sharp, then put the phone in its cradle. He did it! He could not believe he actually did it. *Maybe my life is ready for change,* he thought.

CHICAGO
SUSANNA'S CHRISTMAS EVE PARTY

77

Susanna had been working all afternoon for the party with Marie and Jana, a mother and daughter team Susanna hired for gatherings. The apartment was ready: the tree, trimmed several days earlier; the buffet table resplendent with a centerpiece of antique brass candlesticks atop a sea of wintergreen, and bright red velvet ribbons. On one side of the table paper-thin crystal, ornate silver flatware and gray and white china waited for guests. Despite the work, she loved preparing for holiday parties, enjoying the formality and the opportunity to unpack the treasures she had collected.

The menu was simple, yet elegant. For appetizers, Susanna chose fresh shrimp; baked portabella mushrooms stuffed with sun-dried tomatoes and topped with feta, blue cheese and Camembert; miniature quiche cups,and an assortment of fresh vegetables with her artichoke dip. When it came to the salad, only one reigned supreme at Susanna's dinner parties, the classic Caesar. For the entree, she decided to offer a choice: traditional turkey festive with a cranberry, champagne and orange glaze, or pork tenderloin medallions with poached peach dressing. An assortment of vegetables completed the offerings.

While Marie and Jana managed the last-minute details, Susanna showered and dressed, choosing a hand-painted sheer silk duster, not quite floor length atop a long, slim silk knit, in bright red, keeping with the season.

Satisfied after a quick look in the mirror, she entered the living room and took a chilled glass of champagne from the evening's bartender. It was almost 7 o'clock. If history repeats itself, she thought, the doorman should announce the first guest around 7:15.

She walked to the window to watch the traffic below, sipped her champagne, and began her wait. The ring of the phone startled her; it was the doorman announcing a guest was on the elevator. She reached the door just as someone rang the bell.

Matthew Stark greeted her when she opened the door. "Last minute change of plans, so I thought I'd run by before meeting my friends who decided Chicago was the place to celebrate the holidays."

He placed a brightly wrapped package under the tree among the other gifts describing it as a token of appreciation for her help. She thanked him and offered a glass of champagne that he graciously accepted. They spoke a few moments then he left leaving her happy, excited, and utterly confused, but the arrival of guests broke the spell.

Julia was first to arrive, Howard in tow. Ty came next with several agents from the office. Chris followed, kissed his mother and made straight for the shrimp. Peter and Arnstein arrived after 7:30 to find a roomful of guests and a tuxedoed musician who filled the room with familiar holiday music at the baby grand.

Peter commandeered a glass of champagne and sought out Julia.

The party was in full swing when Pippa entered with Letitia. Ty's mouth dropped when he saw them together, a Kodak moment caught by Peter's watchful eye. Susanna saw the two women about the same time as Ty did, only she walked toward them, smiling.

"Susanna Ryerson, I'd like to introduce my stepmother, Letitia Goody," a friendlier Pippa announced.

"I'm so glad you were able to come," she said warmly extending her hand to Pippa's stepmother. "We've met before, Letitia, but it was a long time ago."

"I ordinarily don't forget a face," she replied.

"I interviewed Parker Goody for an article I was writing about developers. It was in Texas. You arranged for the photo shoot."

"Oh, that was long before Parker and I married. As I recall it was just before we returned to the corporate office after setting up the Austin location. Didn't you meet Terry there?"

"No, I didn't meet Terry until I started working at Beckman & Storey." Turning to Pippa, Susanna smiled and said, "Pippa, I'm surprised you never mentioned your father was Parker Goody."

"I wanted to make a career without our company's influence. That's why I hyphenated my mother's maiden name and my family name," she said in response.

"That's very admirable," Susanna replied, "but enough about business, it's Christmas Eve, and there are some delightful people I'd like you to meet." She ushered them first to the bar for libation, then toward Peter and Julia.

After depositing them, Susanna went around the room, chatting with her guests, slipping in and out of the small groups with ease until she felt someone staring at her. She turned and locked eyes with David Arnstein. Smiling, she walked toward him. "The purpose of a party is to mingle," she laughed.

"Sometimes it's more fun to observe."

"I agree," she said reaching for a new flute of champagne to offer Arnstein as the bartender passed with his tray.

"Only if you'll join me."

"Of course, but only if you decide the topic of conversation. I'm fairly fluent in most career discussions, but I'm not entirely certain what one asks a detective."

"Oh, you could ask about my hobbies, where I live, if I like the city, how Peter and I are getting along," he said, smiling.

"Mea culpa, mea culpa... I wasn't thinking." She smiled genuinely, "Let's start over. What does a detective do in his non-detective time?"

He laughed. "He reads, he collects wine, he sails, and he studies architecture, among other things. Now, what does a real estate broker do for a hobby?"

"Let's see. He reads, she writes. He collects wine, she collects cookbooks. He sails, she takes cruises. He studies architecture, she sells it."

"I think we're meant for each other," he laughed effortlessly. Arnstein had not spoken to a woman with such ease in a long time. *Peter was right; Susanna Ryerson is a woman worth knowing.*

I understand why Peter likes David so much, she thought to herself. *He is utterly charming.* She would have enjoyed talking more, but Chris came up to say Jana was ready to serve dinner. Susanna introduced her son to

Arnstein and then excused herself to gather the guests for dinner.

Once again, she played hostess stopping to chat with friends and colleagues as they sauntered to the buffet. She noticed that Peter was deep in conversation with Letitia and that Pippa had begun talking with Chris and Arnstein. Meanwhile, Julia had assembled an audience, no doubt entertaining them with one of her many real estate stories, or a profile of the 'perfect' seller and the 'perfect' agent.

As she walked toward the group, Julia was indeed describing the perfect client, "I simply cannot believe anyone selling a million-plus condo surrounds themselves with ticky-tacky art. And they wonder why their condo isn't selling. Everyone is laughing so hard at the Wal-Mart prints; they don't see the frigging place."

Oh dear, Susanna thought, *Julia is feeling no pain.* She took a step back and collided with Ty who had just put the phone receiver back into its cradle. "I'm so sorry, Ty, I didn't think anyone was behind me."

"No damage done. Ahh, Susanna..." he stuttered. "I hate to leave, but something's come up. Everything was sensational, as always." He pecked her on the cheek, said he would call on Christmas and left.

She watched him rush out the door, confident that something was not right. Ordinarily, Ty was the last to leave any party. She promised herself she would call him on Sunday. Then she turned to join her party and find Arnstein to continue their conversation.

LOS ANGELES
HARRY AT MIDNIGHT MASS

78

Krachewsky had not been to midnight mass in years, yet Stella convinced him to join her at services in the California Modern Church. It was a packed house filled with a host of 'Harrys' who had not been inside a place of worship in a year or more.

The church was different from the one he had attended, yet the familiar rites triggered memories buried deep in Harry's heart. He would never forget his parish cathedral with its stained-glass windows, or the magnificent crèche with carved angels surrounding life-size figures, all beautifully crafted by loving hands of parishioners.

Incense permeating the small church flooded his mind with thoughts of his high school chums, his elderly neighbors, and extended family, which had gathered on snowy Christmas Eves, so long ago. He realized how much he had missed the ritual; the prayers, memorized in childhood though not spoken for years rolled from his lips without hesitation.

After the long traditional service, Harry and Stella walked into the night's crisp air.

"The only thing missing is the snow," she said. "I still can't get used to miniature lights on a palm tree."

Surprised, Harry asked, "Aren't you from LA?"

"Heck no," she answered in her deep husky voice. "I'm from Minneapolis. I left because of the snow, and now I miss it."

Harry laughed. "I guess half of LA is here because of snow. I'm originally from Chicago."

He had no trouble talking with Stella. They shared memories of their homes as well as their likes and dislikes of the city they now shared at the shores of the Pacific.

For the first time in a long time, Harry felt really comfortable with a woman.

It was after 4 AM when he dropped Stella off at her apartment. With a sudden burst of bravado, he invited her to join him at Mac's for Christmas dinner. She accepted, of course.

Harry drove off with a smile on his face and lightness in his demeanor, quite proud of his enterprise that evening. It had been a wonderful Christmas Eve, the first in a long, long time without the scent of murder and mayhem around him.

CHICAGO
A GIFT FROM THE KILLER

79

The last guests strayed into the path of the telescope as they said their goodbye's and thank you's to Susanna. When the door closed, the voyeur watched Susanna remove her shoes and snuggle in on the sofa, across from her white-haired friend, Peter, and the dark-haired man with a scar, the infamous Mr. Arnstein.

The voyeur focused on the intimate trio. They were talking and laughing when Peter offered Susanna two small, boxes from under the tree. They were, elegantly wrapped, one white, one blue. She took the blue one, eagerly tearing off the ribbon. Nestled inside was a perfume bottle. It was Boucheron.

The voyeur smiled quietly, "How appropriate. I am glad I decided to give you the Boucheron, Susanna. But, I know you will appreciate my other gift so much more. It's not everyone who gives you the gift of life."

The voyeur snapped the cap onto the telescope and sighed, "Pity. It looks like the party is over!"

Arnstein reached suddenly for the gift box, "Let me have that, Susanna. Do you have a large envelope I could use?" he asked placing the box on the table while retrieving his phone.

She looked at him and then at Peter, surprise written on her face.

Susanna's friend took her hand, his smiling face turning somber. "It's OK, Susanna," Peter assured her. "Please find an envelope for David."

"Have all the china and glassware been cleaned?" Arnstein asked as she rummaged through her desk for a large envelope.

"Most of it. Last I checked, the china was put away, and Janna and Marie were finishing the silver."

"I'll tell them to hold off on the crystal, David," Peter offered.

"What's wrong?"

"I'll let Peter explain, Susanna," he said, turning to finish his call.

Peter came back to the living room and sat beside Susanna. "Do you remember who gave you the gift box? Was it there before the party?"

"Frankly Peter, everyone who came brought some sort of hostess gift. I never actually paid attention to who left what. But the Boucheron just reminded me of something. You kept asking me if I recalled anything unusual about Terry. Well, it's the Boucheron. That is what I couldn't remember about Terry. The last time I saw her I thought something was different. It was her perfume," she said excitedly. "She always wore Opium, but not that day. Does it mean anything?"

He paused a moment then told her that Boucheron had become a link in David's investigation.

"What is it, Susanna?" he asked noting the sudden concern on her face.

"Someone left me a bottle. You think I'm next, don't you?"

"No Susanna, I don't. Your aura is peaceful, serene. I will not deny that evil was present in this room, but it is gone now. I firmly believe you are not at risk." The doorbell interrupted Peter. The techs had arrived.

SUNDAY
DECEMBER 25TH

CHICAGO
CHRISTMAS DAY

80

Arnstein grabbed a quick shower and headed to the station. It was a helluva way to celebrate Christmas, but in some respects, it gave him a release from mood-altering thoughts of what could have been. He still strained to see her face, but it was becoming more difficult to keep it in focus; it was as though a veil masked it, a veil that became more and more opaque as the years passed.

He had three messages waiting for him: one was from Mac with flight information for the following day, another from Davis about Playmore's 'niece', and one from the crime unit. He returned their call.

"Today's your lucky day, Arnstein. We not only have a match, but we also have a grand slam! The LA shower curtain and L.A perfume box, and our print from the contact lens: 9 pointers!"

Arnstein thanked the tech acknowledging his efforts, more so because he pushed to get results on a holiday. *Peter was right, there had to be a connection between the victims and not just real estate,* he thought to himself.

He sat down at his desk and once again made notations on the chart in his red notebook.

CHICAGO
PETER ARRIVES

81

It was after 10 when Peter arrived, carrying several brightly wrapped packages. Jana greeted him at the door explaining that the people from the police had not left until after 4 AM and that Ms. Ryerson convinced her to stay and get some rest.

Susanna was curled up on the sofa reading the newspaper. Frank Sinatra was serenading her with a warning: Baby, it's cold outside. "Is that Peter, Jana?" she called when she heard voices in the foyer.

An ebullient Peter marched into the room, "Yes, yes, it is me, and what's more I am filled with the spirit of the season, ready to take my good friend to brunch."

"Oh Peter, I'm still in my night clothes. Let me throw something together, and we can watch 'Christmas in Connecticut'. It's on at 10:30."

"Is that the old Barbara Stanwyck movie?"

"Yes, where she plays a columnist who writes about her nonexistent home and the perfect Connecticut Christmas."

"I remember. Didn't her paper or magazine insist she invite a naval officer to the house for the holiday?"

"That's right. It's such a precious love story... a woman who can't cook and has no idea how to change a diaper!"

Peter laughed. "Why don't I scramble some eggs for us. You may not be aware of my prowess in the kitchen, Susanna."

She smiled. "No, I'm not. Impress me and don't forget that I like my English muffin barely brown."

He disappeared into the kitchen and with Jana's help prepared a credible breakfast complete with sausage, eggs, and fruit. Jana helped him serve and then announced to Susanna that she had finished the crystal and would be leaving. Susanna rewarded Jana with a hug, a Merry Christmas and a substantial check, all delivered with genuine caring.

After she left, Susanna joined Peter at the dining room table where he plied her with compliments for the party, before cautiously broaching the subject of her Boucheron gift once again. Did she recall the giver? Was the gift there before the party?

"I told you, Peter, everyone who came to the party brought some sort of hostess gift. I never really paid any attention."

He paused a moment then decided to tell her the importance of Boucheron and the reason why the techs dusted her crystal.

"Susanna, I never said what happened in LA"

"You've told me bits and pieces."

"Yes, but not everything. David Arnstein was with me in California."

"I thought you were with the LAPD on a special assignment."

"I was. David came there because of similarities between Terry's murder and the two unsolved crimes that involved my consultation."

"Similarities? What kind of similarities?"

"Susanna, the police are not absolutely certain, but the evidence is beginning to substantiate the purposeful killing of seven real estate agents."

"What!" she exclaimed in disbelief. "Seven Real Estate agents? You mean someone killed Terry because she was an agent. That can't be. A madman killed Terry. Some sicko. People may hate real estate agents, but they don't go on a mission to kill them, especially the way they killed her."

"Someone is definitely on a killing mission. The crime scenes, the method of the attack, the victims, and the gift of Boucheron all speak of the same killer."

She sat still for several moments then whispered haltingly, "Do you think Terry was killed in my place? And the Boucheron, the gift I received, does that mean the killer is coming back for me?"

"No Susanna, I don't believe that."

"But when you did my reading, you expressly told me to be careful."

Peter exhaled slowly thinking of the evil he had sensed at the party, but with no sense of time or source. It had been a little like being inside a computer game, attacks coming from all sides, unable to step back and comprehend the source of the assaults.

"Susanna, I didn't know you were an intended victim. I may have just sensed your propinquity to the danger surrounding Terry. I feel no evil around you now. Your aura is peaceful, almost serene, yet I will not deny that evil was present in this room on Christmas Eve. The gift of Boucheron says that Terry's murderer was here, the same murderer who has killed at least six other real estate agents, and whom I firmly believe, is not finished."

"Why Peter? Why? And why are you so certain that I'm not in danger?"

"Because there is a connection among the victims, and I fail to sense that interconnection with you. But I still want you to be cautious, Susanna; the Boucheron was left here for a reason."

"It was challenging to believe that Terry was murdered, now you want me to believe yet another agent will be killed...and the deaths are not random, but selectively intended," she said, her voice rising. "Chris is right. I must get out of this business. I don't hate it. Sure, some buyers and sellers are tough to deal with, and yes, there are agents who would kill for a...oh forget I said that." She began tearing the napkin into little pieces, stacking them in a neat pile as she spoke in a voice rising with alarm. "Now I must consider I may be risking my life when going out with a buyer, or making a listing presentation to a seller."

"Susanna, don't overreact. I know you have been unhappy, but if you make a change, make it for the right reason. For now, take precautions. First, meet buyers at the office, and check every one of them if you feel the slightest concern. Remember, I believe the connection to the killings is more than a career choice. It's something in their past, something they have in common."

"What is it?"

"That remains elusive. It could be that each victim knows the same secret about another. It could be that they worked together at some point, and each knew something seemingly unimportant, but the sum total of what they knew could be devastating to someone else."

"Did you talk to Julia? Is her friend one of the agents killed in LA?"

"Yes, on both counts. Amanda Brewster also worked in Michigan where another agent has been killed."

"Terry worked in Texas before we met at Storey & Beckman. Remember? Letitia said so, last night."

"David and his partner are trying to learn about each victim's past association membership. So is the LAPD."

"Perhaps Letitia Goody can help. She is Pippa-Kaye Goody's stepmother, and I know her company has offices in several states."

"Good suggestion, Susanna. I'll pass it along to David."

"You know, Peter, I never thought about it, but the very business I am in makes me vulnerable."

"Susanna, living in the very heart of a city like Chicago makes you vulnerable."

"I know. I guess I just don't want to accept it. I don't want to give up my freedom for some nut job, whom I'm sure has far more protection under the law than any victim."

"Susanna, don't. Terry's death has had more of an impact than you realize. Your emotions are on a roller coaster."

"I think we should forget the movies tonight, Peter."

"No, I insist we celebrate the day with Chris. A ritual holiday movie and Chinese take-out should not be abandoned. We need to dwell on the positive, Susanna," he said thoughtfully as he rose from his chair to begin clearing their breakfast dishes.

Susanna stopped him, "You cooked, I clean."

Peter's eyes suddenly turned that familiar blue-black color that Susanna recognized; his mind was in a different time and a different place. "I must go. I will return at 6 after I take care of some personal things. Meanwhile, do not open the door for anyone except Chris or me."

"I won't. I promise, Peter."

CHICAGO
TEA AT THE DRAKE

82

Ms. Chaney was waiting when Peter arrived at the Palm Court. "I'm sorry I'm late," he said.

"Nonsense! I was early, I just love to see all the smiling faces and of course, that incredibly beautiful Christmas tree."

"It is grand, isn't it?"

Ms. Chaney smiled her agreement then began an animated conversation with her friend, pausing when the waitress took their order.

Abigail Chaney was a tall, attractive, white-haired woman with still beautiful bright blue eyes in an oval face gently lined and filled with character. Despite a long, tough career with the Chicago Tribune, she was a gentle soul with eyes that telegraphed a life of pain, oh not to everyone, but certainly to a man with extraordinary gifts of observation.

Peter encouraged her to talk about her son and her grandchildren aware that the topic was a wellspring of unbelievable love and soul-stirring pain. Her pride only let her speak to the love, the talent, the success, yet he knew that sorrow and pain together were the foundation of her feelings.

"How many grandchildren do you have, Abigail, may I call you Abigail?"

"I'm pleased for you to use my Christian name. And I have three grandchildren and one great-granddaughter. My one regret is that I see them so infrequently. I've often thought they won't remember me after I die, we have so few photographs together."

"Amazingly, Abigail, grandchildren and great-grandchildren often search for the grandparents they rarely saw. I have seen it happen, countless times. The curiosity, the unquenchable thirst for answers to learn why someone has been absent from their lives, someone who should have been present."

She smiled, "I hope so. It is difficult to compete with a daughter-in-law's family, especially a daughter-in-law who is intimidated and responds with exclusion rather than involvement. I tried, but the hurt is substantial when one is not welcome."

"Ah, I fear your daughter-in-law has missed an exciting relationship for there is nothing pedestrian about you, Abigail Chaney. I have read your essays and your articles with admiration. You indeed are a gifted woman."

"You are kind, Peter Dumas."

"No, just honest."

"Then thank you. Unfortunately, bylines and printed pages are sorry substitutes for a family."

"But Abigail, you have an incredible family of devoted readers whose lives have been affected by your words. A family that idolizes you and your work."

"I've never thought of it quite that way."

"Few people will remember your daughter-in-law but you, on the other hand, will never be forgotten."

Abigail's eyes smiled a thank you from her heart.

They continued to talk over tea, sharing stories and memories, two acquaintances, now friends.

Peter watched her with eyes that hid his thoughts. He knew that Abigail Chaney would not greet the New Year; in fact, today would be the last day of her 85th year. The hurt and pain would disappear, but her destiny would remain the same. He wished with all his heart that he could change her future. Knowing death was coming for someone who deserved so much more was when Peter most hated his gift.

CHICAGO
DINNER...BUSINESS OR PLEASURE?

83

Susanna was finishing the paper when the phone rang. Expecting the caller to be Chris, she answered with a loving familiarity, "Hi sweetheart."

"If only I were," Stark responded with a voice deep and extraordinarily sexy.

"Oh, I'm sorry," she stumbled. "I thought you were my son Chris. The caller ID said 'Private' and my son, well...never mind."

"Please, don't apologize. It has been awhile since anyone called me sweetheart and I rather enjoyed it. But more importantly, do you know who I am?"

"I'm not sure; your voice is a little deceptive."

"Oh, I didn't want it to be. You have twenty questions," he said, laughter in his voice.

"A recent client?" she asked.

"That deserves a 'yes.'"

"In that case, Merry Christmas Mr. Stark."

"Susanna, are we back to that formality again?"

"I'm a creature of habit," she answered teasingly.

"I think I'd like to help you develop some new habits," he said slowly. "I'm certain you have plans for tonight, but perhaps you are free tomorrow evening. Dinner?"

"Hmmm, I think I'd like that. Who knows, it just could become a habit," she said tongue in cheek.

They both laughed. Susanna asked about his Christmas Eve celebration with friends; he asked about her elegant dinner party. They spoke for several minutes, discussing times and places for their dinner date.

While Susanna and Stark teased and flirted, Abigail Chaney began to walk a few blocks south to a drug store on Michigan Avenue. She did not see the car running the red light as she started to cross the street. He was driving too fast to stop from hitting her head-on. She died instantly.

Three blocks away, a gasp escaped the lips of Peter Dumas, tears flooding his eyes, as he felt the car's impact in his mind.

MONDAY
DECEMBER 26TH

CHICAGO
TERRY'S MEMORIAL SERVICE

84

Terry's memorial service was scheduled for 10 A.M. at Graceland Cemetery on Chicago's North Side, in a resplendent memorial stone chapel that looked as though it belonged on a lane in England. It was filled with English Ivy and dozens of white roses, while an outstanding spray of lilies sat atop a catafalque.

Ty Collins, the managing broker at Storey & Beckman, outdid himself. Standing at the front of the chapel between the catafalque and a large easel with a headshot of Terry Playmore, he was deep in conversation with a Wagnerian figure robed in a white flowing gown belted in gold mesh, hair long and curled around a full face and even fuller breast.

They began arriving around 9:45; the Cadillacs, the Beamers, the Lexus', the SUVs; black, silver, and dark blue, the colors of choice, parking one behind the other with doors opening in pairs and trios.

The Chicago real estate community was paying homage, emerging from leather interiors wearing cloth coats in vibrant colors among pelts of mink, fox, and beaver. Heads of blonde, brown, gray, white and red bobbed above collars pulled tightly to ward off the cold. It was Show Time.

One after another the agents entered the chapel chatting briefly with peers they hadn't seen recently and making certain they were seen by Collins who had sauntered to the back to welcome his girls. They jockeyed for seating positions much the way they jockeyed for special favors in the office.

The whispers created a low-level buzz within the cold, gray chapel. Prayer was not among the whispers.

"God, that is the worst dye job I have ever seen."

"If that's a designer fur, I'm a virgin."

"I hear she's sleeping with anything she can pick up on Rush."

"Oh, oh here comes the dragon queen. I have never seen her with anyone straight."

"She's a joke. She has had so much Botox, she can barely move her lips when she talks. Have you heard her on the phone?"

"I wish he weren't gay... he's gorgeous. What a waste."

"I don't care what you say, Collins is feeding her listings. She's two sandwiches shy of a picnic."

"I did a deal with her... never saw her after she brought her client in the door... had to chase her for the escrow, the application, you name it, but oh, she remembered to show up at the closing for her check."

Ty watched them, mentally recording attendees to his event but when Letitia arrived, his jaw dropped. She turned to see him as he began to walk toward her.

"Well, well, speak of the devil. I was just wondering if you'd make an appearance," he hissed.

Letitia smiled, looked him full in the eye after appraising the scene and said, "The flowers are so you, Ty. It is so nice to see you have not lost your touch. I've never been able to find anyone who could prop a property the way you do."

"Didn't get an opportunity to chat with you at Susanna's. How is everything at the Goody 'ranch' Letitia? Destroyed any more careers recently?"

"I make careers, doll face. You just didn't measure up. But it is good to see that you've found a niche."

Ignoring her jabs, Ty smiled and said, "Letitia, I apologize for not sending condolences on the death of your partner, but I didn't think it was appropriate to offer sympathy for a husband who chased anyone wearing a skirt, and who was planning to divorce you."

Her eyes narrowed. The stab hit home. "At least they were skirts," she said slow and deliberately.

The Wagnerian woman interrupted their tete a tete and saved him a retort. He thankfully excused himself acknowledging that the chapel was almost filled, and the service was about to begin.

Susanna Ryerson was standing in the back row next to Peter Dumas, staring at Letitia and Ty. *There had to be more to her visit than just seeing Pippa*, she thought. *What is her relationship with Ty? They don't look very friendly. And why is she at Terry's memorial? Were they old friends?*

She was about to ask Peter his thoughts, but the white-robed figure at the front of the chapel was approaching the baby grand piano, also resplendent with bounties of white roses and baby's breath. After acknowledging her accompanist, she began a soulful rendition of "On Eagle's Wings" with a voice of an angel. When she finished, the silence was deafening.

Ty quietly broke the stillness when he began his eulogy, surprisingly brief, but especially memorable.

"I've known Terry for almost twenty-five years. She was a testament to the contradictions of womanhood. Strong, yet vulnerable. Aggressive, yet gracious. Practical, yet generous. Loving, yet willing to let go. Honest, yet never harsh. She had many friends you will probably never meet. She lived lives you will never be privy to, but to anyone who knew her, she was full of the life we all would love to live. She was a wonderful woman who gave what she got, but always with kindness. I had tremendous respect for Terry, and I will genuinely miss her."

His words struck the audience, first for their compassion and love, yes, even love, and secondly because they came from Ty Collins lips. Susanna was almost in shock. She had no idea that 'slippery Ty' and Terry went back over twenty years. *Indeed, Terry lived lives we'll never be privy to*, she thought to herself.

Arnstein entered the chapel just as several agents rose to follow Ty Collins with their own form of eulogy, remembering stories and happenings they shared in Terry's life.

Joann Boranic remembered when Terry found her husband in bed with her Polish cleaning lady, Stella. The discombobulated woman ran from the room covering herself as best as she could with her monogrammed apron, but returned according to Terry, to pick up her dust mop and remind Terry, "I clean Tuesday."

To which Terry replied, "I'll clean your clock if you ever walk in this apartment again."

"Of course, Terry's husband got more than his clock cleaned. He got taken to the cleaners." Smiles and titters of laughter ignited the room.

The next agent to speak was someone Susanna had never seen before.

"Since most of you don't know me, let me introduce myself. I'm Bethany May Baggor, and I grew up with Terry in Waco, Texas," she said with a soft drawl. "She was my best friend. I never visited Terry here in Chicago, but she often came to see me. You see, I was raising her daughter." Gasps of disbelief rolled through the chapel.

"I figured you all didn't know Terry had a daughter. She is a wonderful young woman, but Terry wanted her to grow up as she did, with roots, in a family environment, and in a town where most people know each other. When she was a teenager, Phillipa learned that Terry was her mom, not her aunt. Her first words to me? "I've always loved you with my whole heart, but I've always loved Terry with my soul."

"I guess deep down, she always knew.

"I wanted to tell you about Terry's daughter because I didn't want you to feel sorry for Terry and think she died alone. She had family who were her friends, and friends who were her family. Thank you for being her family here in the city."

Tears rolled down her face as she finished speaking. She paused at Terry's photograph and then walked to the back of the chapel. Arnstein followed her.

Pippa watched Bethany May Baggor with interest, but she did not reach out to her or to Letitia. There would be time to talk. Very soon she would meet Phillipa Baggor, alias Playmore.

Susanna opted not to speak. She knew she would break down. She spoke her thoughts silently, her eyes flooding with tears.

After other agents spoke, Ty signaled the Wagnerian soprano, and once again, she filled the air with dulcet sounds, this time vocally caressing Amazing Grace.

CHICAGO
MORE SECRETS REVEALED AT THE MEMORIAL

85

Peter and Susanna waited at the back of the chapel for Ty Collins, Susanna, anxious to speak with him.

Several agents stopped Collins on his way to the exit, complimenting him on his eulogy, as he stood tall and puffed with confidence knowing he had done an excellent job. For once, he had spoken from his heart and not, from his wallet.

As he approached Peter and Susanna, he extended his hand and they each took it warmly, acknowledging his efforts and success in making Terry's tribute so poignant, and uplifting.

They had spoken a few moments before Susanna noticed Letitia Goody walking to a black limousine. "Ty," she asked. "How well did Letitia Goody know Terry, and why is she here?"

He turned, and his jaw tightened when he saw a driver opening the limo door for Letitia. "Terry worked with Letitia in Parker Goody's corporate office after her divorce. He was Terry's brother-in-law. When his wife Jane died, Terry helped him and Letitia set up the new development office in Texas," he answered flatly, as Peter watched his eyes turn cold.

"Was Terry around when her sister died?",

"Yes, she left about three months after her death, a short time before Letitia married Parker."

"Then I met Letitia not too long before she tied the knot."

"You'll have to excuse me. I have a meeting at corporate, and I am late," Ty acknowledged. He turned and strode away, his abrupt departure leaving Susanna surprised.

"Well that was a little unusual," she commented to Peter. "He certainly didn't want to talk about her. And he didn't say how he came to know so much."

"I believe Ty knows a great deal more than he is willing to say."

"I have copies of my old columns; I'm going to see what, if anything, Goody said about Letitia."

"I'll be interested in what you find, Susanna," he said as they walked to her car.

"It certainly has been a revealing memorial service. I am still in shock hearing that Terry was married, and even more, that she had a daughter. Peter, why on earth do you think she kept her a secret?"

Before Peter could attempt an answer, Arnstein approached the car and greeted the pair.

"David, good to see you. Anything on the Boucheron box or the crystal?"

"Not yet, but we have a match on the box from LA and the lens we found," he said smiling a hello to Susanna.

She smiled back. *Funny,* she thought, *he had been so remote and dark when he gave his news about Terry, and now there was lightness in his demeanor and pleasantness in his smile. He was less the brooding police detective,* she observed, *and more someone she would enjoy knowing a little better.*

"I'd like to thank you again, Susanna, for Christmas Eve. It was very kind of you to include me," he said softly.

"Nonsense, it was a pleasure to have you join us."

"Regardless, I promise to take you and Peter out to dinner after this case is solved."

"Hopefully that will be soon, David," Peter interjected. Then, he turned and hugged Susanna with genuine affection, telling her he would be driving back with Arnstein and stopping by later that afternoon.

CHICAGO
TY COLLINS GETS A SURPRISE VISITOR

86

After the memorial, Ty did a few errands and returned to Storey & Beckman. Only a few agents were at their desks. He walked into his office and locked the door, then opened a safe hidden behind a wooden carving of an eagle hoisting a banner that read, 'Don't give up the ship." He removed two manila envelopes, one identified as Goody Tapes and the other Goody Photos.

For the next several hours, Ty Collins compiled a list of topics for the tapes and identification of the photos. When he was finished, he replaced the contents of both envelopes along with the lists. He returned the photo envelope to the safe and put the other in his briefcase.

Before he left, Ty called Tommy Helburg. When Ty had heard about Terry's daughter at the memorial, his head began to swim. He asked himself could it be possible, and when he answered 'yes' he knew he had to talk to his attorney.

Tommy Helburg was on his way to a holiday party in a north shore suburb when he answered Ty's call. Helburg did not understand what the big deal was and why it was so important for him to come downtown, but he promised he would when the party broke up.

"It could be late," he said.

"I don't care what time it is, I'll wait up. I need some legal advice, and I need to give you something."

When Collins entered the Hancock lobby at 7:30, he was surprised to see Pippa and Letitia joining a tall, distinguished white-haired man at the elevator who seemed to know Letitia.

"What is she doing here," he said to himself

The doorman saluted Ty as he walked to the elevator. "Happy Holidays, Mr. Collins, and thank you for your gift."

"You're welcome, Buddy. I'm expecting a Mr. Helburg later. Please send him right up OK."

"Yes sir!"

Letitia stopped her conversation with the white-haired man as Ty approached, "That was a lovely tribute today, Ty."

He smiled slightly. "What do we owe the pleasure of your presence at the Hancock?" he asked as he entered the crowded elevator.

"Pippa wanted me to get a quick peek at her new condo before I returned to Michigan."

"Have a pleasant trip home. I hope the snow doesn't create problems for your drive," he answered sarcastically.

"I've never had difficulties solving problems."

The elevator doors opened, and Ty walked away without responding.

For the next half hour, a steady stream of residents entered or left the building. Upstairs, Ty Collins paced in his condo.

It was after 8 PM when he heard the knock at the door. He put his drink down and unlocked the chain expecting Tommy Helburg on the other side. But Tommy wasn't there. Instead, Ty was face to face with his killer. He stepped back, but before he could overcome his surprise, the knife was thrust upward to his heart.

He fell backward, grabbing at his chest, gasping for air as blood and life left his body. The visitor removed the knife and finalized Ty's life with a quick slit in his throat.

The killer walked past Ty's body, nodded approval at his choice of art and his Louis 14th desk, stopping suddenly upon seeing the envelope with 'Goody Tapes' written across the top. The killer placed the tapes into a duffle bag and removed a slightly oversized raincoat, wig, and hat. After a short powder room visit to adjust the wig, Ty's unwelcome guest sprayed something in the air above Ty's body, then left, closing the door quietly.

Aloud, the killer whispered, "And another Realtor bites the dust."

❖ ❖ ❖

About an hour and a half later, Tommy Helburg arrived at the Hancock. After identifying himself as Ty's attorney, he was sent right up to the unit.

The hallway was deserted when he approached the door. No one answered the knocks or bell chimes, so he returned to the lobby and insisted someone get him into his client's condo.

"Something is wrong. Ty insisted I meet him tonight."

After several attempts to ring Ty Collins one of the engineers brought a key, and with Helburg, entered the unit.

That's when Tommy Helburg dialed 911.

CHICAGO
IT'S DEFINITELY PLEASURE

87

The doorman announced Matthew Stark's arrival at 8:30. Susanna said she would be right down.

Thinking that she was attracted to Matthew Stark was a far cry from actually meeting him for dinner. She carried on a conversation with herself, unsure of what to do. *"How should I act,"* she questioned herself. *Should I get it over with and ask him if he gave me the Boucheron on Christmas Eve? No, he can't be the killer. He didn't know Terry, at least I don't think he did. Maybe, I should just talk about his purchase. Maybe at lunch, not at dinner. I am an attractive woman. Yes, but what if he just wants to talk real estate. Is this a business dinner, or a date? He has been flirting with me; at least I think so. Should I flirt with him? No that's too obvious. And I've never been a good flirt. I know. I'll talk about his family. Oh, that's stupid. If he is interested in me, he certainly won't want to dredge up memories of his dead wife. Oh, why did I agree to go to dinner with him? I'm out of practice.*

When the elevator doors opened, Susanna looked up into the eyes of Matthew Stark and could not think of anything to say, so she smiled. Stark smiled back and said, "Hope you like Sushi? I thought we'd go to Japanne."

"Great choice. I haven't been there for a while. Are you a Sushi lover?"

"Let's say, I'm a lover, period."

Susanna gulped and said to herself, *this is definitely not a business dinner.*

CHICAGO
TY COLLINS' MURDER SCENE

88

It was shortly after 11 PM when Arnstein called to give Peter the news. The little man dressed immediately and hurried downstairs where Arnstein waited.

Outside, the streets were unbelievably busy, due, no doubt, to the holiday revelers still celebrating.

The two men walked the two blocks to the north entrance of Ty Collins' building where an unmanned patrol car parked with lights no longer flashing. Arnstein identified himself to the police officer who gave him a quick rundown of events. He repeated the rough details of Ty Collins' murder as they walked into the building.

"Ty's behavior at the memorial service was most disconcerting, David. Something or someone disturbed him, and the killer knew it, most likely expecting some action on Ty's part."

"Yeah, but did it have to do with our killer?"

"I believe so, but let us see."

The doormen sat behind the desk watching as Arnstein and Peter headed through the doors to the elevators. It was a somber scene in the lobby, not the usual banter and joking. Even the residents arriving home sensed the change, acknowledging the presence of a police officer. But, they chose to wish the men at the desk a Happy Holiday instead of asking why the police were in the lobby. The residents quickly disappeared into the elevator area not wanting to spoil their joyous evening.

Upstairs, Tommy Helburg was pacing the hall outside Collins' condo when Peter and David arrived. The Crime Scene Unit was inside. Arnstein introduced himself to Helburg, said he would speak to him in a few minutes, then walked in to view the body. Ty was lying in the foyer of the dimly lit apartment, a pool of blood circling his body, a wound to his chest, a blackened gash at his throat.

The man who had surprised everyone at the memorial had been himself surprised, but in far more dramatic fashion.

Arnstein left Peter to contemplate Ty's corpse, choosing instead to question the assistant ME.

"What did you know that made your life so expendable," Peter asked with compassion as he slowly walked around Ty's lifeless body, the scent of Boucheron floating above it like a shroud.

"The ME says around three hours, give or take," Arnstein announced as he walked back to join Peter.

"He was expecting someone, but certainly not his killer," Peter responded.

"Why do you say that?"

"He was wearing a silk lounging robe... he opened the door without hesitation...he has a viewer. If he weren't expecting anyone he would have looked through it," Peter replied almost shortly.

"Maybe he did, and it was someone he knew."

"He did know his killer, but he wasn't expecting him to be on the other side of the door. If he saw him through the viewer, Ty would be alive."

"OK, OK, Peter. Let's check it out. At least we know one thing, no one sent Ty Collins a bottle of Boucheron."

"No, but Boucheron is here. It's our killer, without a doubt."

When they walked out into the hall, Helburg was still pacing. He had never seen a dead body and certainly not one that had been murdered. He looked at the two men, his eyes pleading for help, his skin a ghostly hue and his nervousness, even more exaggerated.

David approached Helburg cautiously, questioning the reason and time of his visit, as softly as he could, not wanting the man to lose what control he had on himself.

"Is he really dead?" Helburg asked. "I would have come earlier, but I was at a party. Hell, I'm an attorney, not some frigging brain surgeon on call. I told him I'd get here as soon as I could."

Arnstein let him ramble knowing more questions and answers could come later.

"He called me between 6:30 and 7, asked me to come downtown...
said he needed legal advice. I told him I was going to a party. What the hell is
so important that couldn't wait until Tuesday,' he said rapidly, his voice rising.

"I mean, I coulda been here when the killer was here if traffic wasn't
so bad. Maybe he would have killed me," he cried, tears springing from his
eyes. "He said he didn't care what time I got here. I'm sorry, I'm sorry; I didn't
know it was that important. I would have left earlier."

Jerry Helburg was in shock, sobbing desperately as Peter approached
and quietly sought to soothe, "It was advantageous you did not arrive sooner,
Jerry, as your life would have been in jeopardy. Now you must be strong
because we need your help." Helburg nodded yes as if he were a little child
agreeing with his parent. Peter motioned to David that he would take the
man down to the lobby and get him some coffee.

Another body, Arnstein thought to himself as the techs finished their
work. He walked into the living room and marveled at the calm of the city
outside and the violence and death in the warmth of a luxurious city home.

The sudden ring of his phone startled him. "Arnstein,' he
answered.

Downstairs, Peter learned that the doormen had a coffee stash in
a utility room, for those nights when their eyes needed extra help to keep
open. They generously offered to get some for Peter and Helburg who was
beginning to lose some of the hysteria he exhibited.

By the time Arnstein arrived in the lobby, Helburg was breathing
normally again, and giving Peter his breakdown of the events. David decided
to question the doormen who explained that their shift began at 8 PM.

Sammy, the taller of the two men, confirmed what Peter had
surmised,

"Buddy, he's on the day shift from noon to 8 PM, well he tol' us Mr.
Collins was expecting a visitor and that we should send him right up."

"Yes sir, thas' right," his shift partner agreed.

"So, when the man came and axed for Mr. Collins, we sent him
straight up."

Arnstein made some notes in his red notebook, "Now what time did Mr. Helburg arrive, Zeke?"

"I was at the door, so I didn't check my watch. Sammy was at the desk, so he wrote it down."

"I didn't write it down cuz I didn't call Mr. Collins. I only log calls and the unit numbers."

"Then what happened?"

"The man, Mr. Helberg, came back down and said Mr. Collins wasn't answering, so he asked me to call. "So, I did. I rang Mr. Collins at 9:57," he said reading from his logbook. "When Mr. Collins didn't answer, Mr. Helburg wanted us to get the engineer to check Mr. Collins' unit. He said Mr. Collins had called him and he drove from the suburbs for a meeting."

Zeke, nodding his head in agreement conferred, "Yes sir, he said he was Mr. Collins lawyer, so Sammy sent me to get the engineer."

"A few minutes after they went up, the engineer called me on his walkie-talkie and said the police were coming and to send 'em straight up to Mr. Collins' floor."

"Were there a lot of people in and out tonight?"

"Pretty much," Sammy said confidently.

"Who were the people you recognized who might have known Mr. Collins?" Arnstein asked.

"I didn't see anyone Mr. Collins knew. You gotta check with Buddy. He knows everyone and who they know. He'll be here at noon."

Thanks for your help," Arnstein responded, turning his attention once again to Peter and Helburg.

"Jerry is ready to give you a statement, David, but you may prefer to have him stop at the station," Peter suggested.

Arnstein opted to get a preliminary interview before Helburg could think about events and extract only what he believed to be relevant. Before they walked to a sitting area in the lobby to begin talking, Arnstein briefed Peter on his phone call in Collins' unit.

Peter listened thoughtfully then left the detective to question Helburg; meanwhile, he approached the doormen to initiate his own queries.

He asked about other residents who had returned that evening. The doormen rattled off several names of owners they recognized and of guests who identified themselves as visiting friends who came in after their shift started, but the men assured Peter that Collins came in earlier during Buddy's shift.

TUESDAY
DECEMBER 27TH

CHICAGO
MAC & HARRY ARRIVE

89

The trip to the city was a lively one, what with Davis attempting to do his Indy 500 performance in a traffic jam, Harry pointing out city landmarks and Mac wishing for anything that would cure his heartburn.

When Davis passed a drug store just off the 94 exit, he stopped while Mac ran inside to raid the antacid shelves. "I don't understand you guys having heartburn. Doesn't everyone in California eat rabbit food?" he asked.

Harry looked at Davis with a modicum of envy at his lean and trim runner's body then politely said, "Not me, but Mac sure does. I always told him that rabbit food was meant for rabbits. Is that what you eat?"

Davis laughed a hearty guffaw as Mac returned with a sack of assorted antacid tablets and liquids, and said, "I eat anything the good Lord puts before me, including the rabbit."

This time Harry laughed, "I'm convinced it's all in the genes."

Mac agreed, "It has to be, if I ate what you ate Harry, my arteries would be rock solid. You know Davis, my partner's cholesterol is lower than mine!"

The three were bosom buddies by the time they walked into Arnstein's office shortly after 10 A.M. "The cavalry has arrived!" he said getting up to shake hands with his LAPD pals.

"I didn't give Mac and Harry the latest, Arnstein. Thought you might want to bring 'em up to speed," Davis said.

"You've got news?" Mac asked as he and Harry sat down.

"Good news! Our killer is definitely here in Chicago. We've got a new print, and it matches yours, and the one on our contact lens." Arnstein proceeded to give them the rundown on the prints from the party and on the Michigan victim.

"We've put together a list of everyone present at the party," Davis added, "and we're in the process of getting their prints. Who knows, we may have a live body that belongs to those prints."

"We also made a chart with all the vics. It's time we connect the dots and fill in any missing info," Arnstein continued.

Harry nodded and said, "If you have a new print and are sure the killer is here, I think we found the connection."

The phone ring interrupted Harry. Arnstein answered, "Send him back." To the group, he said, "It's Peter, let's hold off till he gets here."

Harry rolled his eyes, Davis smiled, and Mac rose to greet his friend. Peter acknowledged the men, shaking their hands and offering a thank you for being included.

"Are you kidding, Peter. If it weren't for you, we wouldn't have some of the evidence we have," Arnstein said emphatically, joined by Davis and Mac, and even Harry, albeit begrudgingly.

"Why don't we go through the victim list. Harry and Mac, you can impress us with the connection you've discovered."

"Is this true?" Peter asked.

"Harry and I think so."

"OK, let's get started. I'll lay out the cards, and Harry you play the trump since you think you've got the connection."

He walked to a portable corkboard in the corner of the office then flipped it to reveal a chalkboard with a table of agent deaths.

"Peter believes that the poses also may have a meaning. We broke the list into the basics: victim, perfume source, kill date, Killer alias, and agent history.

"Let's begin with column two, validation for Boucheron gift. According to Harry, Brewster's secretary said she had received a gift of Boucheron two days before she died. Palmieri, the Albuquerque victim, also received the gift according to Detective Gonzales.

"Peter sensed Boucheron at the Beidermeister scene, and it has been confirmed by Detective Wallins in Michigan."

"And one of the Beidermeister kids verified it," Harry chimed in. "She said her mother told her she got a perfume gift with an unsigned card."

Victim	Perfume	Location	Method	Killer	Agt Past
Palmieri	Det. Gonzales	Nov 9 New Mexico	Hammered; Hot Water, pool	Hammer	Hairdresser; Began R.E. career in TEXAS
Brewster	Candace	Nov 14 California	Stabbed, slit Throat, crown, blind-fold	Scalparelli	Chicago Agent Worked in Michigan Goody Homes per Julia
Marshall	Det. Solov	Dec 16 Michigan	Stabbed, axed; Placed in bobcat	Cutter	Current Agent with Goody Homes In Michigan
Valli	Harry	Dec 2 California	Print on Shower curtain		Midwest, Texas,
Playmore	Ryerson	Dec 17 Illinois'	Stabbed & decapitated	Jimbo	Storey/ Beckman; worked for Goody Dev Texas
Beidermeister	Det. Wallins	Dec 18 Wisconsin	Stabbed, slit throat, arms off, hay bales	Colin Axman	JS Kennicott; previous agt in Texas; ref by Goody Homes
Frobisher	Det. Politis	Dec 19 Indiana	Stabbed, slit throat; posed w/money, lamp shade	Mr. Daggert	Dog Groomer, Temp at Goody Homes per Davis
Collins	Peter	Dec 26	Stabbed, slit throat		Mgr. Storey/ Beckman

"OK," Arnstein continued. "Frobisher got the perfume at the office on the day she died, according to the lead investigator in Indiana. Valli got hers at the office too, and thanks to Harry, we got the box and a print. And there was a Boucheron box at the Michigan kill according to Detective Solow. No fingerprints.

"Peter caught the scent at the Playmore and Collins scenes. Susanna Ryerson confirmed the perfume for Terry—she noticed it because it was new. That's makes it 8 for 8, and for the first time we've got a male victim."

This time Mac interrupted, "Which takes this out of the run-of-the-mill serial killer category. This guy has a real agenda, boys."

"We've been going after the work history as you have as well Harry, and so far we've got Marshall and Frobisher working for the same developer, Goody Homes, but in different states and in different roles, so no contact with each other, " Davis interjected.

"But that's the connection, Goody Homes. It's a friggin home building company," Harry almost exploded. "They all had something to do with Goody Homes. Brewster was the only one I couldn't tie in, I contacted the Detroit Association but haven't heard back yet."

"Harry, Susanna's friend Julia Devereux was Brewster's mentor when she worked for a developer in Michigan. She was kind enough to give me a name. It was Goody Homes." Peter whispered to Harry making certain not to take the spotlight away from him.

"That's great news, Peter. Another nail in our killer coffin. Now Beidermeister, she worked for the Goody Homes Development Group, years back, in Texas. They're the ones who gave JS Kennicott in Wisconsin the referral that got her hired.

"Valli's kids' ID'd the Goody Brokerage Company in Texas as the place she worked when she started in the Real Estate business. The Goody developers set it up to market their homes."

Arnstein added, "Yesterday, Peter learned that Playmore worked for the Goody Group as well, in Texas and Michigan, according to Ty Collins at Playmore's memorial service. And, she was related by marriage to Parker Goody, the company founder."

Mac applauded Harry's determination, "Harry was like a dog with a bone." Then, teasingly toward Peter, "I think he was really trying to prove you were wrong, Peter, I mean about a connection other than just a real estate license."

"Nonsense Mac, Harry is a very accomplished investigator. He searched for the connection, and he found it. Our task is to discover the reason why the connection is the key. Then we'll have our who."

"Maybe the Palmieri victim set the ball in motion," Davis said. "At Peter's suggestion, I've been checking why she was forced out of Real Estate in Santa Fe. I didn't think a 20-year-old sexual encounter with a client's husband, would tell us much, but at this point, who knows."

"Perhaps we'll have our who before we have our reason why," Arnstein added.

Whereas Peter responded, "They are intimately related."

"They may well be, and we have two Goody's who were at the party, and I'm not being funny," Davis said. "They could be the answer to why and who."

"Let's bring them in, I'd say they are a good place to start."

"I'm on it," Davis said leaving the office.

The four men continued to hash over the aspects of all the crime scenes.

"I'm still trying to come up with a reason why Boucheron was a signature? Why would the killer use it?"

Peter answered, "Mac, I think it was one method that directly tied the murders together. These killings were like scenes in a film, each one contributing to the climax. And our killer was either putting the blame on someone who wore Boucheron, or he was revenge-killing for someone who wore it, and suffered at the hands of these women."

"I think you are right Peter," Arnstein interjected. "And that someone was integral to the Goody Homes. All of the victims were top sellers for the company or its brokerage. Someone was either hurt by these agents or was the instigator using the women to harm someone else."

"I buy that, David. But what I don't get are the set-ups, you know, the lampshade, the money, the haystack chopping block, why?" Mac continued, "Why was he sloppy with isolated prints, yet unbelievably controlled in other scenes?"

This time Harry took the lead, "I think that's simple, Mac. Those poses set us up for a serial killer, not for someone with an ax to grind."

"I too believe the posing was a diversionary tactic, Harry, but they were personal judgments of the victims as well," Peter said thoughtfully. "The killer knew these women intimately and bared their secrets when he could, fully intent on exposing them, embarrassing them. At one point, our killer suffered in some way at their expense.

"The poses bespeak a payback. And as for the prints, I believe they were not sloppy. They had to be planned. How does one leave only one print on a box or one print on a shower curtain?"

"That was worrisome to me, as well, Peter, but I don't think they were planted. If so, why did he dispose of the shower curtain?"

"Perhaps our killer was just playing with us, David."

"Interesting, Peter," Arnstein replied. "And the vulnerability of real estate agents and property environments gave him the ultimate opportunity."

CHICAGO
PARTY GUEST PRINTS

90

When Matthew Stark had been called to make an appearance at the station, he wasn't prepared for an inquisition. In fact, he had no idea why he was summoned, but Arnstein made him acutely aware that cooperation was of the utmost importance from anyone who appeared at Susanna Ryerson's condo on Christmas Eve. So, he complied.

Arnstein offered Stark a cup of coffee and gave him a list of names to review, then asked if any were familiar to him.

"Yes," he answered. "I know Letitia Goody, Terry Playmore, and Amanda Brewster. My wife had worked with all three of the women."

"Did you know that Terry and Amanda were murdered?"

"Yes."

"Have you been in Los Angeles, recently?"

"No, I've had no occasion to visit since I lived there several years ago."

"Did you deliver a small gift box to Susanna Ryerson on Christmas Eve?"

"Yes."

"Did you enclose a card?"

"No."

"Where were you on Monday evening between 7 and 10 PM?"

"Until 8:15, at the Hancock in a friend's condo. I'm staying there. At 8:30 I joined Susanna Ryerson for dinner. "

"Were you alone at the Hancock?"

"Yes."

"Detective Davis will be in contact with you to verify some dates. Until we can eliminate you from our investigation, I'll have to ask you not to leave the city."

"Are you accusing me of something?"

"No, Mr. Stark. Everyone who attended the Ryerson party is being questioned, same as you. Thank you." They shook hands, and Stark left the room.

Peter, who had been watching Stark's departure, walked into the interrogation room. "You don't like him, do you, David?"

"I don't know. There is something about him. Maybe I'm just jealous," he answered gingerly picking up Stark's cup and placing it in an evidence bag.

"Maybe you are."

Davis, who announced that Pippa Kaye-Goody had arrived, interrupted their conversation.

Arnstein gave Stark's cup to one of the detectives, while Peter walked into the hall careful to avoid being seen by Pippa.

"Offer her coffee or water and get her prints, then bring her back Davis. And when Letitia Goody gets here, make sure the guys give her some water and get her prints as well. You, Harry and I will question her. Peter and Mac can observe." He turned to Peter saying, "If there's anything we are missing, say it out loud. I'll hear it in my earbuds."

After offering Pippa Kaye-Goody a glass of water, Davis chatted for a few moments, and when she put her cup on the table, Davis quickly told her they were ready and escorted her into the interrogation room. Harry followed, while another detective picked up Pippa's cup and put it into an evidence bag.

Pippa was dressed smartly in a pinstriped tailored suit, a mink coat tossed casually over her shoulders, her slim legs wrapped in tall, hug-fitting boots with heels that gave her a majestic presence. Harry was a big man, yet Pippa came close to matching his 6'4" height.

Arnstein introduced his fellow detectives then he and Pippa exchanged pleasantries about their meeting at Susanna's. Finally, she said, "I suppose you've asked me to come because of Ty's death?"

"That and a few other reasons," Arnstein responded.

She laughed, "My goodness, that sounds ominous. Do I need an attorney?"

"I don't believe so, unless of course, you feel that you need one."

"No, not at all."

"Ms. Goody," Arnstein began.

"Pippa! Please," she interrupted.

"How did you know Terry Playmore?"

"She was my mother's sister as well as my step-mother's friend."

"Did she contact you?"

"No. I contacted her."

"Why?"

"I decided to seriously consider a career in real estate, and she worked for one of the top brokerages in the city."

"But you and Letitia Goody became sole owners of your father's company, after his death. Why would you need Playmore?"

"I'm a very detailed individual and wanted to gain experience in a first-tier market. I've been considering the possibility of opening a Goody office here."

"Are you equal partners with your stepmother?" Davis interjected. She uncrossed her legs, then crossed them again before looking directly at Davis and slowly answering, "No. She owns 51% of the company."

Peter and Mac watched intently through the two-way mirror.

"She's a cool cookie, Peter."

"She's surprisingly calm. No emotion. No sense of fear. No anxiety."

They listened as Pippa recalled meeting Millie Frobisher and Ruann Beidermeister as well as knowing Marsha Marshall. They heard her describe Frobisher and Beidermeister as women who slept their way to listings and referrals. And when asked how she could make that statement, she credited her stepmother.

"My stepmother keeps tabs on everyone who has worked for Goody Homes. Besides, she ought to know about sleeping around, that's how she ended up with my father."

"How did they meet?" Harry asked.

"She had a supporting role in a film shoot in Texas. Ty Collins introduced her to my father who happened to like actors. And she went to school with my Aunt Terry. My dad thought Letitia would be an asset to the company and eventually hired her. Shortly after my mother died, he married Letitia," she said wide-eyed. "Unfortunately, he played around after their marriage as well. His affair with Aunt Terry was the reason she left the company."

"Did Letitia tell you that?"

"Initially it was Ty, but eventually she confessed as well. She enjoyed telling me about my father's exploits."

"Yet your father left 51% of his company to her, why do you think he did that?"

"Probably to keep her from punishing him for playing around. His will left her 51%, but in the event he produced another child, he or she would own 49% of the company, same as myself. Letitia's share would be reduced to two percent. Alas, he died before he could father any offspring."

"Your stepmother didn't mind his roaming?" Arnstein asked.

"The only thing my stepmother ever minds is losing…anything," she said almost caustically. "However, I fail to see what my family secrets have to do with Ty Collins death?"

"Probably nothing, but it is curious that she and Ty Collins had a connection years ago, and she suddenly appears at Playmore's memorial, a woman she also knew from several years ago. Two old acquaintances, both murdered."

"Do you think my stepmother is in danger?" she asked with genuine surprise.

"No, we don't believe so. By the way, what kind of perfume does your stepmother wear?"

"Boucheron, same as I do. She's worn it as long as I can remember. In fact, it was the one thing I loved about her. Boucheron is one of my favorites, as well."

Peter watched quietly, knowing finally without question, who had taken the lives of seven women and one man.

"Thank you, Ms. Goody. Now if you will go with Detective Davis, we'd like you to confirm your schedule for the past several weeks. It's just a formality."

"No problem," she responded, smiling her Cheshire smile. She rose slowly, and then followed Davis to Arnstein's office.

CHICAGO
THE KILLER IS REVEALED

91

Hours later, the men waited for the print reports, and hopefully substantiation of the killer's identity. Davis and Mac had their money on Stark, a man in the right place and the right time, at least for 3 of the crimes that corresponded with his timeline.

Harry? He was convinced it was one of the Realtors who had known all the others; those attending the Ryerson party narrowed his probe. He left the room to call the airlines again to see if they were able to find any matching passengers who'd arrived a few days before both the Valli and Brewster murders; and perhaps to add one more link to the chain.

Arnstein was about to announce his choice when suddenly his mobile phone began to ring. The crime lab was calling.

"I'm telling you, Arnstein, you oughta buy a lottery ticket. Another winner. We got a match."

"Who is it?" he asked the tech. "Yes!" Arnstein responded when he heard the name.

Suddenly the pieces of the puzzle began to fall into place for him: The perfume, the changing appearance of the killer, the relationship to the victims, the mysterious jogger, the poses, the reason why. It all made sense. He turned to Mac and Harry and announced, "We've got our killer!"

Peter walked into the room just as Arnstein disclosed the print match. The high fives were flying. Before Peter could utter a word, an officer entered the room and said: "Letitia Goody's still waiting."

"Davis, why don't you get her," Arnstein smiled, expelling a breath of relief.

Davis took a long, hard look st Letitia Goody. *She is one beautiful lady,* he thought.

Close in height to her stepdaughter and equally as confident, it was easy to understand her success in business. Ageless with a deadly combination of inherent class and practiced bravura.

She seated herself across from Davis, Her posture, rigid. Her answers in response to Davis' questions: short, indignant.

"How long have you been in the city?"

"What time did you leave the Ryerson party?"

"Where are you staying?"

"Why are you visiting?"

"How long did you know Terry Playmore? Ty Collins? Ruann Beidermeister? Janna Valli?"

"Was Terry Playmore a friend, or an enemy."

"Did she ever sleep with your husband?"

"Did you ever hire anyone from *Temps On Time*?"

"Did you remember ever meeting Maggie Palmieri?"

"When did you learn that Ty Collins had been murdered?"

"Why were you at the Hancock the night Ty Collins was murdered."

"Were you and Collins, enemies?"

After twenty minutes or so, she began to cease being polite. "Just what the hell are you doing? I agreed to help, but I don't see where your line of questioning is going."

The door opened as she was about to rise, and Arnstein entered. He apologized for any inconvenience then suddenly asked the brand of perfume she was wearing. Taking the question as a compliment, she uttered, "Boucheron" in a husky voice.

He tried to imagine her in men's clothing, hunched over or tall and statuesque, with wisps of gray or dark curling hair, bold and cruel. The actor? An impersonator? She looked at him coldly not at all anticipating his next words.

"Letitia Goody, I'm arresting you for the murder of Terry Playmore." *Mac and Harry's turn will come,* Arnstein thought to himself, *so too will it for Wallins in Wisconsin, Politis in Indiana, Gonzales in New Mexico, and Solow in Michigan. And hopefully, justice will be served for Ty Collins as well.*

She stared at him, her jaw slack, "Are you insane?"

He read her rights, fully expecting an expression of outrage and demand for her attorney. However, no outrage came, only shock, spilling from her eyes as Davis handcuffed and ushered her out. Peter who had watched the men with their prey, stopped Arnstein when he left the interview room.

"Letitia Goody is an unpleasant woman, David, but she did not murder the agents."

"Peter, as much as I respect you, I have to disagree. We've got too much on her. Harry got a confirmation that Goody arrived in LA two days before the Brewster and Valli kills. We've got prints. Politis is checking local hotels in Central Indiana against a picture we just sent him. It's just a matter of time before we lock her into all the other murders."

"She's not the one, David."

"Peter, trust me. She's the one. Her prints are on the Valli shower curtain and the Boucheron box in LA, the partial print in Chicago, and it's her print on the contact lens."

Harry and Mac joined the two men as Peter continued, "Anyone can plant a print, what is her motive?"

Mac answered, "Revenge? Most of these women had something to do with her husband, maybe she decided to get back at 'em."

Arnstein started, "I'm convinced it's revenge and money. Playmore had a child after fooling around with Goody's husband. I'm betting she's his daughter and if Playmore let it drop to Letitia, she signed her own death notice. You heard Pippa Goody about her father's will."

Harry finished, "She planned these murders to hide her real victim, Terry Playmore before she spilled her secret."

"Why now? Maybe Peter's got a point," Mac interjected.

"I don't know. Playmore could have told Letitia about her daughter after Goody died, but Letitia didn't want to lose control of Goody Homes,"

"Good point, Arnstein. Maybe the old man was paying Playmore off to keep the kid a secret. Even her attorney admitted she had an outside income," Davis added. "Let's get a subpoena for Goody's bank records to check for consistent and substantial withdrawals that match Playmore's deposits."

"I'm sorry, Peter, everything we pick up leads us right back to Letitia Goody."

"David, Terry Playmore didn't need to keep her daughter's birth a secret. She chose to. She could prove her daughter was in line for the Goody fortune, anytime she wanted with the girl's DNA. Parker Goody may have been paying support for their daughter, on Playmore's terms. Don't forget she wanted her child to have a normal life in Texas."

Arnstein thought for a moment, then responded, "If, and I repeat if, Parker Goody was supporting her daughter, Terry most likely knew about Goody's will, and she may have been afraid of what Letitia would do. And don't forget Collins' reaction at the memorial, Peter. He was not the same after he heard about the announcement of Terry's daughter. Then suddenly, he's dead. He knew something. And whatever he knew, it concerned Letitia Goody. You saw the tension between them at the Memorial."

"What about the death poses? They could have been an attempt to connect the killings to each other, so they eventually would lead to Letitia Goody. Punctuation, if you will, to the Boucheron," Peter added.

"I'm sorry, Peter. The titles we gave the poses are strictly our guesses. I could come up with a dozen titles and so could you. And the pendant that says 'mother' could have been dropped by a buyer, or the owner. The real evidence is going to nail Letitia Goody, not make-believe titles for the death poses."

Peter nodded slowly. There would be no convincing his friends. His hands were tied; the killer had indeed been cunning.

CHICAGO
EVIDENCE IN COLLINS' SAFE

92

Rather than call her attorney after she was booked, Letitia Goody called her stepdaughter to explain the situation and to ask her to call the company's law firm for the name of a criminal defense attorney. Pippa agreed and said she would also call the corporate office and put Letitia's assistant in charge until everything was settled.

Meanwhile, the detectives took to the phones.

Davis called Baggor to verify Terry's wishes regarding her daughter. She was questioned about Parker Goody's involvement, but told Davis that she did not know the identity of the father, nor did Terry ever mention Parker Goody. She did say that according to Terry's attorney in Chicago, Terry left an envelope with papers for her daughter in a safe deposit box. She and Phillipa were scheduled to return to the city for a meeting to settle any legal requirements and to check the box.

Arnstein called Letitia Goody's assistant to provide Letitia's complete schedule since Parker Goody's death. He also asked if Terry Playmore had attended the funeral; she answered 'yes' and said she would fax a copy of the schedule.

Harry repeated his calls to the Realtor Associations for confirmation of each agent's membership. He told them a subpoena would be forwarded for written confirmation of the information.

Mac called all the lead detectives in Michigan, Indiana, and Wisconsin for any hotel backup they could provide regarding Letitia Goody in the two-day period before the agent deaths. He also checked LA hotels within a two-mile area surrounding the Brewster and Valli scenes.

Bugs Kramer checked Goody's credit card receipts for any charges related to the crime cities—gasoline, hotel, restaurants, car rentals. Terry Calahan, with subpoena in hand, went to meet Attorney Jerry Helberg to investigate Ty's office at Storey and Beckman.

Nothing but real estate related papers filled the files in Collins' desk, but it was a different story in his safe. A slew of photographs in a manila envelope revealed Letitia Goody's relationship with every one of the murdered agents. A particularly revealing photo caught Parker Goody kissing Terry Playmore at a Christmas party with Letitia in the background, staring venomously at the couple's more than just friendly embrace.

Each of the photos was identified by date, going back some twenty years. There were pictures of Collins and Letitia cutting the ribbon at a new development in Texas.

There was a folded poster, that was particularly interesting. It featured the star of a community production: Letitia Powell, in full makeup and dress as a man. She was unrecognizable.

One other discovery was a copy of an article announcing the death of Jane Kaye, wife of Parker Goody. The word 'accident' was circled in red and the words, 'no way' written across the page.

Chicago
A Question

93

Little by little, the detectives amassed an avalanche of evidence against Letitia Goody, more than enough to convict her.

Arnstein took everyone to dinner before Mac and Harry left for Los Angeles. Harry was disappointed at Peter's absence. He genuinely wanted to thank him for all his help. "We couldn't have done this without Peter," he said to the others.

"No, we couldn't. He made the critical difference. I'm sorry he thinks we've identified the wrong killer," Arnstein replied.

"You're all gonna disagree with me, but Peter may have a point. The motive could just as well belong to her stepdaughter. And that article in Collins' safe, it bothers me. Was it a murder? If it was, did Parker or Letitia do it? Is it the real reason for all these deaths?"

"Come on Mac. The kid was what, seven, eight? I know you are a personal fan of Peter's, but evidence is evidence. The fingerprints, the schedules, those pictures in Collins safe. We got the right person," Harry said.

"Well, there will be a trial, and justice will prevail. But Mac, don't worry, we'll uncover everything we can," Arnstein said as he paid the bill.

CHICAGO
WHAT STARK KNOWS

94

Susanna was just finishing her makeup when the doorman called to say her guest had arrived. "Send him up," she said.

Peter was not whom she expected to see when she opened the door. "Peter!" she exclaimed.

"I won't stay long, Susanna, I just needed to talk for a moment."

"Peter, what's wrong?"

"They've arrested the wrong person."

"Whom did they arrest?"

"Letitia Goody," he said, his voice devoid of emotion.

"Letitia Goody? For Ty's murder?"

"Terry's murder. But Ty and the others will no doubt be added to the list."

Susanna sunk slowly into the down pillows of the oversized sofa. "She killed Terry? Why?"

"Letitia didn't kill Terry, but she has been arrested for the murder."

"But Peter, I met Terry's killer. He wasn't Letitia. Not at all."

"I told you, Susanna, the killer was a master of disguise and because Letitia had a theatrical background she fits the mold, according to the police."

"But Peter, they wouldn't arrest her without more proof than that."

"Oh, they have mountains of evidence, circumstantial and planted, including much for which I am responsible. But she is innocent, and I can't do anything about it."

Susanna looked at her dear friend, convinced that perhaps Peter had been too involved and had lost his objectivity. She had never seen him so distraught, so agitated.

The phone's ring interrupted her thoughts. Her dinner date was on his way up. She poured a drink for Peter then walked to the foyer to open the door.

Matthew Stark greeted Susanna warmly as he walked into her home, but stopped suddenly when he saw Peter. After introductions, Susanna explained that Peter brought news, "One of my party guests, Letitia Goody has been arrested for my friend Terry's death and possibly my broker manager's death as well."

Stark directed his question to Peter, "Are they certain?"

"Yes," Peter answered.

"It doesn't surprise me," he said. "She is a thoroughly nasty woman."

Susanna was taken aback, "I didn't realize you knew Letitia Goody." Suddenly Matthew Stark was not the man she thought she knew.

"My wife worked with her when Parker Goody was married to Terry's sister."

"I still can't believe Terry had a sister."

"They were close. Terry took it very hard when she died. It was the result of a fall in one of Parker's developments. Happened when their daughter was around 7 years old. Highly suspicious, but even though the accident was questioned, a homicide was never confirmed. Parker eventually married Letitia, and the talk at the time was that he bedded Terry Playmore not soon after his first wife's death."

"It's like a soap opera!" Susanna exclaimed.

"Yes, somewhat, but justice will not prevail in our drama, Susanna."

"You don't believe Letitia's guilty, Peter?" Stark asked.

"No. I don't believe she's guilty of the agent killings.

"Peter, you've been wrong before," Susanna chided.

"Not wrong, Susanna. Unable to read the signs? Yes, but not wrong."

Susanna understood Peter's reaction. Although he was recognized as one of the most accurate clairvoyants, when hard evidence seemed to disagree with him, his opponents suddenly christened him a ranting 'fortune teller', 'a mumbo-jumbo psychic'.

She recalled his words only a few weeks earlier about three men in her life and a dark-eyed woman who was not what she appeared. *Letitia had dark eyes,* she thought to herself.

Then she thought about Stark and David Arnstein, two fascinating men who had entered her life. Had the third been the killer in disguise?

"The twins Peter. You said a man, possibly a twin, would appear. Could it have been a woman disguised as a man? Two faces?"

"It's irrelevant now, Susanna."

> The voyeur watched them, smiling. It had been
> an exhausting day, but one that delivered a major
> accomplishment: Letitia had been arrested.
> "This time," she said aloud, "stepmother dear,
> you will finally pay for killing my mother."

"Peter, why don't you join us for dinner?" Susanna asked.

"Yes Peter, do," Stark added.

"Thank you, that's very kind, but I would not be enjoyable company. Besides, Mac and Harry are flying back to LA and I want to say goodbye. I was unable to attend the early dinner David arranged."

He grabbed his coat, shook Stark's hand and hugged Susanna. "I'll call you tonight, Susanna."

He turned suddenly, looking up before he reached the door. He could not see Pippa watching him from her Hancock perch, as she raised her hand to send him a small wave. "Till we meet again, Mr. Dumas. But now, I must meet my step-sister."

He nodded, almost in response to her, but he was smiling at Susanna. As the door closed, Susanna turned to Stark, "I'm worried about him."

"I'm certain he'll be fine. From what you've said about Peter, he is a strong, confident man. Don't worry. Let's not spoil our evening."

"Yes, let's not spoil our evening," she said with a hint of sarcasm. *Perhaps,* she thought, *my knight's armor is not quite so shiny.*

CHICAGO
PETER ASKS MAC AND HARRY FOR HELP

95

Peter turned west as he left Susanna's co-op. The air was brisk, and a light snow was falling. He loved Chicago's weather; it stimulated his body, his senses, but mostly his mind. Thoughts and images exploded behind his startling blue eyes.

The Tremont Hotel was a short walk but offered enough time for those thoughts and images to create new ideas for discussion with Mac and Harry, and later, David.

The two men had checked out of the hotel and were waiting for Peter at the bar. When he entered, Harry smiled and gave him an upraised fist in approval. Peter smiled back, but his eyes did not match the smile on his lips.

"I apologize for not joining you at dinner. I had some personal obligations to take care of, but I couldn't let you leave without saying good-bye personally."

"No apologies necessary, Peter. I'm just happy we could meet," said Mac.

"Ditto from me," Harry chimed.

"I wanted to say goodbye, but I also wanted one more opportunity to convince you of Letitia's innocence, at least with these recent murders."

"Ah Peter, we got it right. Without your help, we'd probably be looking at more kills," Harry cried.

"Peter, we'll do anything you suggest to make certain we've got the right one," Mac said as he turned to Harry. "Won't we, Harry?"

"Yeah, yeah. But I still think we got the right one."

"All I'm asking is for a check on two things: I would like you and Harry to check the flights to kill cities to and from Chicago, and flights and car rentals to kill cities from other kill cities. Letitia Goody's flights are verified but what about Pippa Kaye-Goody? Did she fly to those cities?

She is a very clever young woman. Check on her name and the aliases she used, and don't forget security cameras."

"For you, Peter, anything," Mac nodded.

"You got it, Peter." added Harry "Besides, you know how much I love digging for evidence."

"Like a dog after a bone, Harry," laughed Peter.

The men continued to talk until Mac and Harry had to leave for O'Hare to catch the Red Eye.

Once there were two friends, but now there were four—brought together by a chameleon killer.

WEDNESDAY
DECEMBER 28TH

CHICAGO
PETER BIDS SUSANNA FAREWELL

96

The Goody case was now in the hands of the District Attorney. It was a new day.

The clock said 6 AM as Arnstein poured himself a cup of coffee. He sat quietly thinking his past was disappearing. It was becoming more and more difficult to resurrect his wife's face in his mind. The image was becoming less defined, almost transparent. Meeting Peter and even Susanna Ryerson had started him thinking that it was time to start living again, in the present. He thought he might even invite Susanna Ryerson to join him at dinner, but first, he had to call Peter when he got to the station. He did not want to lose a friend who had made such an impact on him and his life.

He grabbed the paper from the front stoop and tossed it on the sofa just as his phone rang. It was Peter.

"No, it's not too early, Peter. I was just about to head out. Got tons of paperwork to catch up on."

"I'm flying to Louisiana at 9:30. Could we meet at your office?"

"Of course. I planned on calling you, but I'd rather see you in person. I'll be there in about 20 minutes."

"Thank you, David. I'll leave after I make a few calls."

Peter was notorious for calling friends at all hours. His next call woke Susanna from a deep sleep. "Hello," she answered groggily.

"Susanna, it's Peter."

"Of course, who else calls in the middle of the night."

"Come now, it's a little after 6. It's a bright new day."

"It's pitch black out there! Why didn't you call me last night?

"Some personal issues I had to take care of."

"Anything serious?" she asked. "No, just some complications with a family member who needs help with a land purchase. I'm on a flight to

Louisiana at 9:30."

"Can I drive you?"

"No, no. I've scheduled a limo. How was your evening with Matthew?"

"Interesting."

"Does he pass muster?"

"I haven't decided."

"A little bird tells me that you should spend a little time with David before you decide."

"I just may do that."

"I'm meeting with him shortly. Perhaps I should tell him what the little bird is telling me."

"Don't be obvious, Peter. Please."

"Fear not, my lady."

"You sound so much better this morning."

"I feel better. Mac and Harry have agreed to do a little more investigative checking for me. And hopefully, David will also agree to my request. I have to run, Susanna. After Louisiana, I'm heading to Detroit for a bit. I'll keep in touch, so don't make any rash decisions while I'm gone. Love you, my sweet."

"Love you, too, Peter. Have a safe trip."

CHICAGO
PETER ASKS ARNSTEIN'S HELP BEFORE LEAVING

97

The station seemed to be moving in slow motion when Peter walked into Arnstein's office. The two men acknowledged each other in a friendly embrace; perfect strangers a little more than a week ago, now integral parts in each other's lives.

"God, Peter, I'm glad you called. I felt bad for you after we arrested Letitia Goody."

"No need, David. Evidence is evidence in the real world. How we feel, how we think is presumptive until proven. We will have many disagreements, disbeliefs in our friendship but because we are friends, we will acknowledge possibilities—that is, until proven wrong.

"Before I leave, I ask but one favor. Investigate one factor not associated with Letitia Goody. Check purchases of Boucheron by Pippa Kaye-Goody, or the names of the aliases. Chicago, LA, and Michigan are the most likely places, at least in my mind. That's all I ask of you. Oh, and on a more personal note, invite Susanna to dinner in my place; I'll be gone for a few weeks."

"Peter, you devil," Arnstein laughed. "Of course, I'll invite her to dinner. And as to the Boucheron, count on it, my friend."

They spoke for a few more minutes than Peter left to meet the limo driver waiting for him.

As he began his trip, Peter said aloud, "I'll call Letitia's attorney when I land."

98

After checking his bags, Peter bought the Chicago Tribune but stopped when he noticed the headline on the first page of the Chicago Sun Times.

Heir to Goody Homes Murdered

Late Tuesday evening, 27-year old Pippa Kaye-Goody, one of the Goody Home heirs, was killed after showing a foreclosure to a prospective buyer. Ms. Goody was struck from behind as she was replacing the home's key in a digital locking system, commonly used by most real estate brokerages.

The former owner, Shayne Clark, angry at the loss of his home, hit Kaye-Goody repeatedly with an ax. When Chicago Police arrived, they found Clark seated next to the body, a bloody ax in his hand. A cousin, Phillipa Baggor-Playmore, survives Ms. Goody.

Peter reached for his phone to call David and Mac. "Perhaps justice has been served, twice," he said aloud.

CHICAGO
PLAYMORE'S CONFESSION

99

When Phillipa and Bethany Mae Baggor met Terry's attorney at the bank to retrieve the documents in the safe deposit box , they were not prepared for the letter Terry left.

My Dearest Phillipa,

If you are reading this, most likely I am dead. So, it is critical that you learn the truth.

As you know, Jane Kaye Goody is my sister, but what you don't know is that her husband Parker Goody is your father.

When my sister Jane died, both Parker and I were devastated. I loved Jane, and I loved Parker for loving her. Both of us doubted that Jane's death was an accident, but there was no proof of foul play.

Pippa took Jane's death extremely hard. She became distant, moody and somewhat self destructive. It was difficult for Parker to live life with Pippa. She was the image of Jane despite the fact that she was adopted. So, he ignored Pippa which isolated her all the more. Nannies and boarding schools took the place of mother and father.

When Parker married Letitia, he expected to have another child. Parker loved Pippa, not like Jane had, but in his own way. He wanted his own child. Unfortunately, Letitia did not want children. She loved business, and she took to Pippa because she could have a child without the inconvenience of birthing or rearing it.

So, Parker asked me to have his child, and I agreed with certain conditions. You were that child.

I knew I would never marry again; I hated married life, but I so much wanted a baby with someone I knew and cared about. And for once I could dictate the conditions:

Parker would have a blood relative, but he could not announce your existence, or see you until you were college age.

You would never want for anything. You would be financially independent, and inherit half of his holdings when he died.

I would send him photos and anything else to let him know your progress—he was aware of your acceptance to Harvard, and so very proud.

Parker prepared a will dated the day you were born. A copy is in this box along with important papers regarding your birth, as well as Pippa's. Because he died so suddenly, I opted not to tell you until you finished your education.

Frankly, I was concerned for your welfare. I did not think Letitia would take too well to your existence And I also worried about Pippa. According to Parker, she had never accepted her mother's accidental death, and she is not aware of her adoption. She may look to you as the usurper.

I am hopeful though that you and Pippa may become friends. Perhaps you will be the family she never had.

So, my dearest Phillipa, now you know why I kept you in hiding, and why I insisted on giving you a normal life. I wanted to keep your balance as well as prepare you for a very different life style when you claim your stake to the Goody Company.

Forgive me for bringing you into this world the way I did but know I'm not sorry—for nothing compares to the joy you've given me. Know that I love you so very much. Always,

Your mother

Phillipa closed her eyes, tears falling down her cheeks She was beginning a new life with the unknown, now known— without her beloved Terry. "I'll make you proud, Mom. Dad, too. I promise."

POSTSCRIPT

A note from Peter to Susanna and Arnstein upon seeing a
copy of Terry's letter to Phillipa.

If only... Terry had revealed Phillipa's blood relationship to
Parker Goody before his death, or even shortly afterward.
If only... she had not waited, the lives of many might have
been spared. *If only...*

Peter

Epilogue

The following is a list of murdered Realtors I discovered when I began to write For Sale MURDER. During my search I found limited information about many of the murder sites, as well as the guilty who committed the crimes. But my book is fiction and only borrows from reality with respect to the potential dangers an Agent can face without taking safety measures.

Yes, Agents have survived rape, burglary and brutalization but as you'll see in this list, the brutality is not make-believe, and not all agents live through it. What's more, if the list could include those who have survived brutalization or rape, the numbers and locations would be memorable.

For Sale MURDER is a mystery, but it's also a wake-up call for Realtors, and for owners who choose to sell their properties themselves.

2017

Zakir Kahn, 44, Throgs Neck, Bronx; Stabbed to death in front of his 12-year-old son.

2016

David Abassi, 32, Atlanta, GA; Fatally shot in an abandoned house he was viewing.

Tom Niblo, commercial agent, Abilene, TX.; Shot in his home. Not random. Not classified as a burglary, or a robbery.

Christina Louise Kessinger, 62, Ashville, NC; Found dead in the trash a screwdriver stabbed in her skull.

2015

Michael Arcega, San Jose, CA; Pronounced dead of one gunshot wound.

Sidney Charles Cranston, Jr., Kingman Az.; Shot to death and buried in the desert; body found, January 2017.

2014

Carey Furlow Griggs, 42, Texarkana, TX; Shot in her mouth.

Beverly Carter, 50, Arkansas; Kidnapped and killed after showing a home to her killer. She was found in a shallow grave wearing a duct tape mask that kept her from breathing.

2013

Mary Beth San Juan, 56, Honolulu, HW; Bound, gagged, stabbed to death
   and wrapped in a rug.

Vern Holbrook, 79, Yakima, WA; Beaten and left to die in a vacant home that
   he planned to sell. He died 8 months after being hospitalized in a
   coma for 6 weeks.

2011

Ashley Okland, 27, Des Moines, IO; Shot in the chest while working a model
   townhome by herself.

2010

Andrew VonStein, 51, Cleveland, OH; Fatally shot at one of his listings by a
   man blaming him for the foreclosure of a home he purchased 7 years
   earlier from VonStein.

Vivian Martin, Youngstown, OH; Found strangled and burned in a flame
   engulfed home she had listed for sale.

Brenda Wilburn, Pulaski, TN; Found in a closet, bound, robbed, and
   murdered.

2009

Ricardo Contreras, 45, Westchester, CA; Found stabbed to death in a foreclosed home.

2008

Lindsay Buziak, 24, British Columbia; Stabbed more than 40 times in a
   home she was showing to a couple.

Troy Vanderstelt, Muskegon, MI; Shot to death in his office by a client whose
   home was no longer worth what he paid for it.

Ann Nelson, 71, Jefferson, WI; Lured, robbed, hit at least 9 times with a fire
   place poker, then strangled at a listed home set ablaze by a supposed
   buyer.

2007

Linda Stein, New York; Clubbed to death with Stein's own 4-pound exercise
   weight by an assistant reportedly having entitlement issues.

2006

Dotti Lanier, a 27-year veteran, Hattiesburg, MS; Shot 4 times when she
   opened the door for a prospective buyer at a home for sale.
   She survived, but the owner who was also shot, died.

Sarah Ann Walker, 40, McKinney, TX; Beaten, bitten and stabbed 27 times
   by a man who was targeting Realtors—at a model home Open House,
   that she was hosting,

2004

Garland Taylor, 74, Albuquerque, NM; Shot to death at a showing of a
   $900,000 listing.

Jannell Hatton, Columbia MO; Shot twice and buried in a shallow grave. One
   of the 8 defendants may have been the agent's former tenant.

2003

Brian Heywood, 50, Calumet City, IL; Shot to death while showing a client
   an apartment.

Cyndi Williams, 33 and Lori Brown, 21, Atlanta GA; Killed at their on-site
   sales office by a man who forced them to undress and give him
   their ATM pins. Ms. Brown was shot in her back and head; Ms.
   Williams was shot in her head.

2001

Mike Emert, 40, Seattle, WA; Stabbed 19 times and left in a bathtub with the
   water running by a man who was seeing the home for the second
   time.

1997

Charlotte Fimiano,40, Decatur, IL. Beaten and strangled in a secluded and
   vacant home listed for sale.

1996

Michelle Lee Anglin, 22, Maricopa County, AZ; Raped, strangled, beaten and
   stuffed under a bed at a showing.

1994

Sherry Lewis, Decatur, IL; Beaten and strangled after an appointment
   with a floor-call Buyer whom she hadn't met.

1993

Patricia Bentley, 59, Denver, CO; Found dead in a townhome she was
   remodeling—the result of a blow to the head by a blunt instrument.

Nancy McManus, 46, Woodridge, NJ; Found after being repeatedly stabbed,
   a knife still in her chest, by a seller whose closing had to be
   rescheduled. The seller died setting the home afire in an attempt to
   hide the murder,

Lynne McCoy, 57, Baltimore, MD; Robbed, raped and bludgeoned to death
   with a heavy antique clothes iron by a potential buyer.

1988

Billie Dean Hamilton, Birmingham, AL; Kidnapped, raped, beaten with a
   wrench and stabbed.

1979

Donna Kuzmak, 26, Portland OR; Beaten, strangled, stabbed and sexually
   assaulted.

STAYING SAFE... SOME TIPS FROM AGENTS

Be Prepared:

1. Set up an office Buddy System: Ask 2-4 agents to be in a group that will buddy with you, and you with them— at Open Houses, call-in showings, night meetings, and listing presentations

2. Invest in a personal alarm system. Here is one that is reasonable and easy to use: Wearsafe.com: The company often offers a free panic tag. It's small and actually sends your voice in real time, and alerts whoever is on your list. Low monthly service fees.

3. Consider buying mace or pepper spray.

4. Always keep your handbag money and personal items in the trunk of your car when showing properties.

5. Consider buying a cheap pre-paid phone as a back up in your pocket, just for showings.

6. Don't wear expensive jewelry, fur coats and branded hand bags with new Clients. Some agents have been targeted be cause of the car they were driving.

7. Keep a file handy on your desk with your picture; a picture of your car and license plate; a note of the car's year, make and model; plus an emergency name and number to contact.

8. Get to showings early: check escape routes, write arrival time and date on a business card and leave it in a kitchen drawer.

9. Consider taking self-protection classes.

10. Use your phone's camera—shoot a picture of a possible client, their car, their license plate.

11. Leave a trail.Take phone movies at showings—share them with a buddy via text, or share them with yourself via email. They will know where you are and with whom.

Be Active:

1. Ask your brokerage to include agent safety discussions and speakers for a 10-minute segment at monthly office sales meetings.

2. Get involved with your local association. Ask them to promote agent safety tips on their website as well as emails, and make safety a monthly feature in the association's magazine.

3. Check out the NAR website, often. There is a wealth of agent safety information to incorporate into your Real Estate activities.

4. Ask your brokerage to set up an emergency alert text for any warnings.

5. Ask NAR to publish murders and personal assaults monthly online and in print. No need to publish names, but locations and type of assault are important for Agents to recognize that it can happen to them.

Be Aware:

1. Investigate the I'm-standing-in-front-of-your-listing shopper; or the floor-call shopper who wants to meet you at a listing; or the surprise would-be buyer or seller who saw your ad, your house sign, or found you online.

2. Get their name, phone, and email. At the least, Google the name. Better yet, check out the National Sex Offender Public Website by name, even address or zip code: https://www.nsopw.gov/

3. Request an Office Meeting if possible, if not, meet at a public place, even the library. Or, ask an agent buddy to go with you.

No buddy available? Ask a husband, boyfriend or family
member to meet you.

4. Pay attention to your gut instinct.

5. Do not advertise verbally or in print that your listing is vacant.

6. Do not discuss an owner's in-town or out-of-town status—
in public places.

BE SAFE!

ACKNOWLEDGMENTS

THANK YOU

Erika, Helen, Ralph, Toni, Doug, Barb, Sharon, Dana and Corey
for your encouragement, your patience, your friendship and
especially the time you generously gave.

Adult Services at the Library in Barrington, Illinois: The department head, Rose, for
her encouragement and friendship; Librarian Eileen who read the manuscript and
offered suggestions, encouragement, and research direction.

Chicago Dan, IT extraordinaire, who kept me sane when my laptop crashed,
and who miraculously recovered my lost files.

Los Angeles Dan, the creative man who designed three exceptional book
covers, and who perfected the chosen one.

My LinkedIn colleagues, along with friends
and associates, who voted for the perfect cover design.

The following media sources that gave me the nudge to acknowledge
the true vulnerability of Real Estate Agents:
WABC; AJC.com; WSBC.com; reportnews.com: housingwire.com; KTXS.com;
Citizentimes.com; KRON4.com; Kingman Daily Miner; ABC15.com;
Crimewatchdaily.com; KFOR.com; staradvisor.com; USA Today; KULR8.com;
Slideshare.com; ABCnew.go.com; Homicide.LATimes.com;
globeandmail.com; Zimbio.com; Murderpedia.org;
Ill. Unsolved Murders—HuffingtonPost.com; DenverPost.com/blogs;
articles.Baltimoresun.com; agentsonline.et, al.com; KPTV.com;
portlandcrime.blogspot.com; Wikipedia.com

Finally, my daughter Erika, an extraordinarily creative young woman who believes in
me; and my son, Jason, a young man who challenges me to always do more.
Plus a host of other friends and acquaintances.

CPSIA information can be obtained
at www.ICGtesting.com
Printed in the USA
FFOW01n2122100418
46228163-47563FF